Praise for the Crime of Fashion Mysteries

"Devilishly funny . . . Lacey is intelligent, insightful, and spunky . . . thoroughly likable." —*The Sun* (Bremerton, WA)

"Laced with wicked wit." —SouthCoastToday.com

"Byerrum spins a mystery out of (very luxurious) whole cloth with the best of them." —Chick Lit Books

"Ellen Byerrum has a hit series on her hands."
—The Best Reviews

"Fun and witty . . . with a great female sleuth."—Fresh Fiction

"[A] very entertaining series."
—The Romance Reader's Connection

Grave Apparel

"A truly intriguing mystery." —Armchair Interviews

"A fine whodunit . . . a humorous cozy." —The Best Reviews

"Fun and enjoyable . . . Lacey's a likable, sassy and savvy heroine, and the Washington, D.C., setting is a plus."
—The Romance Reader's Connection

"Wonderful." —Gumshoe

Raiders of the Lost Corset

"A hilarious crime caper. . . . Readers will find themselves laughing out loud. . . . Ellen Byerrum has a hit series on her hands with her latest tale." —The Best Reviews

"I love this series. Lacey is such a wonderful character . . . . The plot has many twists and turns to keep you turning the pages to discover the truth. I highly recommend this book and series."
—Spinetingler Magazine

continued . . .

S0-AXZ-701

"Wow. A simplistic word, but one that describes this book perfectly. I loved it! I could not put it down! . . . Lacey is a scream, and she's not nearly as wild and funny as some of her friends. The story line twists and turns, sending the reader from Washington, D.C., to France and finally to New Orleans. . . . I loved everything about the book from the characters to the plot to the fast-paced and witty writing."　　　—Roundtable Reviews

"Lacey is back, and in fine form . . . .This is probably the most complex, most serious case that Lacey has taken on, but with her upbeat attitude and fine-tuned fashion sense, there's no one better suited to the task. Traveling with Lacey is both entertaining and dicey, but you'll be glad you made the trip."
　　　—The Romance Reader's Connection

Hostile Makeover

"Byerrum pulls another superlative Crime of Fashion out of her vintage cloche. . . . All these wonderful characters combine with Byerrum's . . . clever plotting and snappy dialogue to fashion a . . . keep-'em-guessing-'til-the-end whodunit."
　　　—Chick Lit Books

"So much fun."　　　—The Romance Reader's Connection

"The read is as smooth as fine-grade cashmere."
　　　—*Publishers Weekly*

"Totally delightful . . . a fun and witty read."　　　—Fresh Fiction

Designer Knockoff

"Byerrum intersperses the book with witty excerpts from Lacey's 'Fashion Bites' columns, such as 'When Bad Clothes Happen to Good People' and 'Thank Heavens It's Not Code Taupe.' . . . Quirky . . . interesting plot twists."
　　　—*The Sun* (Bremerton, WA)

**Other Crime of Fashion Mysteries
by Ellen Byerrum**

*Killer Hair
Designer Knockoff
Hostile Makeover
Raiders of the Lost Corset
Grave Apparel*

Armed and Glamorous

A CRIME OF FASHION MYSTERY

Ellen Byerrum

AN OBSIDIAN MYSTERY

OBSIDIAN
Published by New American Library, a division of
Penguin Group (USA) Inc., 375 Hudson Street,
New York, New York 10014, USA
Penguin Group (Canada), 90 Eglinton Avenue East, Suite 700, Toronto,
Ontario M4P 2Y3, Canada (a division of Pearson Penguin Canada Inc.)
Penguin Books Ltd., 80 Strand, London WC2R 0RL, England
Penguin Ireland, 25 St. Stephen's Green, Dublin 2,
Ireland (a division of Penguin Books Ltd.)
Penguin Group (Australia), 250 Camberwell Road, Camberwell, Victoria 3124,
Australia (a division of Pearson Australia Group Pty. Ltd.)
Penguin Books India Pvt. Ltd., 11 Community Centre, Panchsheel Park,
New Delhi - 110 017, India
Penguin Group (NZ), 67 Apollo Drive, Rosedale, North Shore 0632,
New Zealand (a division of Pearson New Zealand Ltd.)
Penguin Books (South Africa) (Pty.) Ltd., 24 Sturdee Avenue,
Rosebank, Johannesburg 2196, South Africa

Penguin Books Ltd., Registered Offices:
80 Strand, London WC2R 0RL, England

First published by Obsidian, an imprint of New American Library,
a division of Penguin Group (USA) Inc.

First Printing, July 2008
10   9   8   7   6   5   4   3

Copyright © Ellen Byerrum, 2008
All rights reserved

OBSIDIAN and logo are trademarks of Penguin Group (USA) Inc.

Printed in the United States of America

ACKNOWLEDGMENTS

Some years ago, when I was happily laid off from a miserable job, I mentioned to a friend that I had always thought it would be fun to see what being a private investigator was all about. That free-spirited friend and fellow playwright, Barbara McConagha, dared me to do it and promised that if I found a course, she would take it with me. In the Commonwealth of Virginia, successfully completing a state-certified course is the basic requirement for becoming a PI. I located a school in Northern Virginia, and off Barbara and I went to study the art and craft of private investigation. We learned the federal and state laws, failed a vehicle surveillance exercise (and passed on the remedial exam), fired handguns at the range, listened attentively (and otherwise) in class, and, of course, gathered lots of material for later works of fiction. It was a great experience, and I'd like to thank Barbara publicly for making that dare and taking that class with me. A bit of that material might have made it into this book, as part of Lacey's experiences in taking her PI course.

Thanks also go to PI Howard Miller for his patience and information through the years and for letting me return again and again to take those in-service classes. Any errors in the art and craft of being a private investigator are, of course, my own.

Many thanks go to my friend Lloyd Rose for listening to me throughout writing this book and assuring me yet again that I would live through it. Thanks also to my friend Jay

Farrell, for reassuring me that the more arduous the book writing process, the better the book.

I would also like to thank my editor, Anne Bohner, and Liza Schwartz, and my agents Donald Maass and Cameron McClure.

Finally, there are not enough words to describe the love and loyalty that my husband Bob Williams has always shown during the process of writing my books. He is my best friend, my champion, my critic, my supporter. I am eternally grateful.

chapter 1

NO LOADED WEAPONS IN THE CLASSROOM.

The handwritten notice was the first thing that caught her attention as she strolled into class one blustery Saturday morning in January. Lacey Smithsonian, fashion reporter for *The Eye Street Observer*, took a seat at a table in the front row. The warning notice was taped to the classroom door, and it made her wonder. Were loaded weapons an everyday problem here? Was someone likely to draw a loaded pistol in the middle of a lecture and shoot himself in the foot? Or worse, *her* foot? Was taking this class such a good idea after all?

"No loaded weapons? Is that sign really necessary?" Lacey pointed to the door.

The instructor sat at the desk at the front of the room, reading *The Washington Times*, the District of Columbia's only conservative daily newspaper. He took his time before looking up at Lacey. He put down his newspaper and sized her up. A big guy, Bud Hunt was rumpled, crumpled, and cranky, but he was a bona fide private investigator, and he was the class instructor.

"Like this one?" He smoothly drew a large black pistol from the back of his waistband, dropped the clip to unload it, racked the slide and locked it open, and set it down on the desk in front of him.

Lacey nodded. "Like that."

"Nah, y'all can bring your guns to class here." There was general laughter from the other students taking their seats. "I just have to post the notice for liability. Insurance. Just don't shoot anybody in my class, okay? You plan to shoot somebody, take it outside." Hunt slipped the clip into his pocket, reholstered his now unloaded pistol, and stood up.

"Everybody locked and loaded?" More laughter. "If you haven't guessed already, I'm Bud Hunt. You're whoever you are, so let's get this show on the road."

So this is Bud Hunt, Lacey thought. Vic warned her the guy was a character. Hunt passed around an attendance sheet for them to sign. There were nearly a dozen students in this class of wannabe PIs, mostly men, a couple of women, one Lacey Smithsonian.

The room was chilly, but Hunt didn't seem to feel it. He wore a thin blue work shirt with the sleeves rolled up to display his well-muscled arms. On his wrist was a large watch with a round, complicated-looking face. He clipped his cell phone to his belt like a gun. When it buzzed he looked at it, pressed a button, and reholstered it like his pistol. Hunt proceeded to spell out the whys and wherefores of the first session.

"Gumshoe 101," he called it. His welcoming speech seemed designed to discourage them from ever coming back. They had signed up for sixty hours of class—every weekday evening for two weeks—plus all day for two Saturdays and another half day to wrap it all up. Hunt made it sound like boot camp. Someone behind Lacey tried to lighten the mood with another question. Was private investigation just like the movies, he asked, and would they have exotic clients?

"Like the movies? Oh, yeah, it's just like the movies." Hunt laughed. "And your clients? Let me tell you something about the clients in this business. Most of them come to you because they have really screwed up their lives." He looked his students in the eye, enjoying his well-practiced speech. "Give them half a chance and they will screw up your life too. Never trust the client. Some are okay, but some are lunatics, and you never know who's who. And that's the fun part."

Hunt paced the room right past Lacey, but he looked over her head and directed his remarks to the male students in class. That was all right with her. She wasn't there to be the center of attention. Hunt had already had some fun at her expense. She knew that was all right too, for the moment. *Always better to let them start by underestimating you.* Her notebook was open, but the page was still blank. She was waiting for the good stuff.

"I've had clients try to burn me, break my cover, just to see if they could do it," Hunt continued with relish. "Idiots. They try to follow you on surveillance, try to show they can outsmart you, like they could do your job for you." He allowed himself a small smile. "Then they want to be a big shot. They tell people how they 'put a private eye on the case,' people who should not even know there is a case. The butcher, the baker, the candlestick maker. And maybe the drug dealer next door. Your clients share it with the world, somebody blows your cover, and then they say, 'Well, I didn't tell nobody!' " He shook his head. "You warn them if they want this investigation to be a secret, then they damn well better keep it a secret. And then you got other kinds of trouble."

Hunt was just getting warmed up. He rubbed his hands together. "Female trouble. Maybe the client is a woman. She's screwed up her life, usually with a little help from a man or two. Or ten. Maybe she's in a nasty divorce. She's vulnerable to you, because you're helping her. You're vulnerable to her, because you're a *moron.* She's your damsel in distress, you're her knight in shining armor. Instant romantic entanglement. She thinks she's in love. She thinks it's an old movie and she's Lauren Bacall and you're Bogart. But she is not Bacall—she's big trouble. And take it from me, buddy, you're no Bogey."

Lacey suppressed a smile. Bud Hunt was definitely no Bogey. He was an ex-cop and he looked like one. Lacey mused that Hunt might be somewhere between his early forties or early fifties; it was hard to tell. He had muscular arms and broad shoulders—a hard guy gone a little soft around the middle and thinning on top, brown going on gray. He looked like he'd had a rough life, but he'd held his own. A man's man.

But something about him was compelling. His eyes were large and deep brown and seemed to hold some rough wisdom. His eyes, she decided, could make a woman look twice at him.

Lacey Smithsonian was enrolled in private detective school at Hunt Country Security Specialists in Falls Church, Virginia. They offered state-certified training classes in private investigation, their Web site proclaimed, also training in corporate and personal security, personal protection and bodyguard services, civil process serving, and firearms and self-defense. Hunt Country Security seemed to be principally Bud Hunt. The classrooms were in Hunt's offices on Little Falls Street just off West Broad Street, on the ground floor of a faux-colonial building, red brick with white wooden shutters and trim. Five steps down from the back door on the left side of the building, the small tasteful brass plaque read HUNT COUNTRY SECURITY SPECIALISTS, INC. A less tasteful handwritten sign inside the door said PI CLASS DOWN THE HALL, SECOND RIGHT.

The place was small, but not cozy. Lacey glimpsed a reception area, a couple of offices, and a conference room. A tiny kitchenette squeezed in between the reception area and the first office. The décor, complete with dead and dying plants, might be called "gunpowder and testosterone." The oatmeal-colored walls were plastered with the Declaration of Independence, the Constitution, the Second Amendment to the Bill of Rights, well-used paper pistol targets, a large picture of Osama bin Laden drilled full of bullet holes, and class schedules. Lacey caught the faint aroma of gun oil and gunpowder on the air. The oatmeal and beige and brown blended into a bland any-office-anywhere-USA décor. *Any office anywhere*, Lacey thought. *Plus bullets.*

Inside the classroom, battered metal and faux-wood tables made a lazy horseshoe facing Bud Hunt's desk. Looking around, Lacey saw no fresh young, dewy-eyed college grads seeking a career as a private investigator. Instead, there were not quite a dozen tired-eyed midcareer working Joes and Janes, each seemingly looking for something new, a break, a change of pace and place.

"All right, people, let's get started. First let's get to know each other a little. I've been teaching this class for a while, I've been a private investigator for a lot longer, and I've learned a few things." Hunt liked to hook his thumbs through his belt loops while he talked, when he wasn't pointing to something, gesturing, or posing like a tough guy with his hands on his hips. "I've learned something about the kind of people who take these classes. Let me give you a rundown and we'll see if I'm right."

Everyone sat up straight in their seats.

"Who takes a PI class?" Hunt asked. "Mostly you got your ex-cops and your retired military. Do your twenty years, take the money, and run. Time for a change. Or maybe you get injured in the line of duty. Or maybe the system was cramping your style. Maybe you had a problem, a bad shooting, a bad review, a discipline beef, whatever." Lacey heard chairs squeaking. Hunt laughed.

"Yeah, I hear you," he said. "Cops, top sergeants, MPs, right? You think being a PI is a cakewalk? Divorce, embezzling, white-collar crime, no heavy lifting? All your experience, this stuff'll be easy as pie, right? You'll find out it's a little different when you're out there on your own, without the authority of the Man to back you up. Next type: I generally get a bounty hunter or two, wanting to class up his act with a PI ticket. And shackling bail jumpers gets pretty old, right?"

"That would be me, Bud." A ponytailed man with old eyes and a young face raised his hand and grinned at Hunt. Lacey was fascinated by the colorful tattoo of a python writhing up his neck under the ponytail. "Name is Snake, Snake Goldstein. That's me. I'm your bounty hunter here." Snake had a New York accent as thick as his neck.

"Goldstein, huh? You're a tough guy?"

"Tough enough." Snake wore a tight, dark blue sweater over bulging muscles.

"Good luck to you," Hunt said. "Tough is good. But you might want to moderate your skill set somewhat as a PI. We don't generally shackle our clients, or our subjects. Sometimes a bounty hunter needs a lighter touch."

"Duly noted." Snake's voice was a low rasp. He smiled beatifically. "I'm as gentle as a lamb." There was more laughter from the group.

"Okay. That's covered. Let's see, every once in a while I get"— Hunt winked at them—"a *writer*. Mystery writers. Thriller writers. Someone who wants to write a crime novel. The kind of novel where nothing *real* ever happens. But if you do write that best seller, be sure and spell my name right. Only if it's a best seller. If it bombs, leave me out of it."

He looked over his student body judiciously. "Sometimes I get people here with a personal problem. Cheating spouse, abusive boyfriend, kids on drugs. Let me caution you, friend, if you think you're going to solve your own private troubles here, you're not. Don't try to be your own PI. This job is damned hard, even if you're a pro. Ten times worse when it's personal. You'll only get the basics here, enough to get your Virginia PI registration, not a lifetime of professional experience."

Hunt sighed and rubbed his chin. His eyes surveyed the crowd. "Every other class or so, a woman walks into this room with a serious problem. Maybe she's been abused, beaten—a little or a lot—but now she's worked up some courage. She wants to learn how to deal with the bastard herself. That's generally not a good idea. Anyone here got a personal problem, you can talk to me. Later."

The dozen or so students looked around, eyeing Lacey and the other woman, sizing one another up, slotting one another into Bud Hunt's categories. Hunt clapped his hands for their attention. He lifted his coffee mug toward Lacey.

"Okay. You. Smithsonian, isn't it? Lacey Smithsonian?" She heard a smirk in his voice. "Smithsonian ain't a name, it's a museum. You two related?"

Everyone laughed, except Lacey. Someone was bound to make a crack about her name. The truth, Lacey thought, was that many people had silly names. She kept a little list of all the wild and wonderful names she came across in her newspaper, names like Hezekiah Witherwax, Jeremiah Fussfield, Cricket Blicksilver, and Sherry and Jerry Derryberry and their kids, Gary and Mary.

Lacey blamed her grandfather. A Cockney from London named Smith, he brought his Irish wife to America and decided to fancy up the family name. "Smithsonian" sounded pretty grand to him. *If he'd only known the trouble that name would cause me.*

"It's my name," she said through her teeth. "It's a long story."

"It's always a long story. Let's start with you anyway. I'm guessing you're not a bounty hunter like Goldstein here. Why are you here?"

Why? It was January, the air was chilly, and the trees were bare. In northern Virginia, freezing drizzle was falling on dirty snow. The sky, low and the color of pewter, matched her mood. If Lacey was not having a dark night of the soul, she was at least having a dreary gray wintry afternoon of it. Lacey Smithsonian was a news reporter stuck on the accursed fashion beat and going nowhere, in spite of everything she'd accomplished. Some unexpected adventures, some major scoops, all of which had served only to sentence her to the fashion beat.

That's the problem with being good at the wrong thing, she thought. *You get stuck in a box and labeled forever. And no one else will take the job, so why would anyone promote you out of it?*

In Washington, D.C., the fashion beat was something *The Eye Street Observer* couldn't give away with a free toaster. And always hovering around Lacey's consciousness was this: The last fashion editor at *The Eye* actually died on the job, hunched over her keyboard, her death unheeded on the forgotten fashion beat. Mariah "the Pariah" Morgan, Lacey's predecessor, had been dead for hours when the news editor finally realized his writer who had missed her deadline wasn't just taking her usual nap. She had to be wheeled out of the newsroom in her desk chair in full rigor mortis. The chair came back. Mariah didn't.

It's a proven fact. The fashion beat can kill you.

chapter 2

"Don't be shy, Ms. Smithsonian," Bud Hunt said, clearing his throat. "We're all friends. Tell me and Snake here why you're taking this class."

"Curiosity. I'm curious about what it means to be a private investigator."

Looking for a clue how to escape my beat, she thought, but didn't say. The truth was, Lacey needed a change. A big change.

She could come up with lots of reasonable explanations, ones she could write about for her "Crimes of Fashion" column. She even had some possible headlines. Being a reporter, she often thought in terms of newspaper headlines. A PRIVATE LOOK AT PRIVATE EYES: FASHION CLUES IN DIRTY GUMSHOES? Or perhaps: UNCOVERING THE INSIDE STORY ON UNDERCOVER COVER-UPS! No, not that. Maybe: SNEAK A PEAK AT SPY COUTURE: LOOKING TRENCHANT IN A TRENCH COAT.

But Lacey didn't want just another insubstantial fashion story. She wanted a great story in a big way, something that might get her off the accursed fashion beat for good. Her successes inspired envy in some of the more testosterone-deprived guys in the newsroom, the ones who thought of themselves as hard-driving newshounds but were really lazy-day dogs. They couldn't understand how the lousy fashion beat kept getting a scoop on murder.

Yet nothing had broken her free of the fashion beat albatross. Perhaps this PI class, Lacey thought, might lead to something, somehow. At least she'd learn more about what her PI boyfriend, Vic Donovan, did for a living. He was always telling her she should leave the investigating to the professionals. Maybe here she could pick up some professional private investigation skills any news reporter could use and score her PI registration, and then he couldn't say that anymore. Maybe she'd even find an angle for a real non-fashion-related story. *A reporter can dream, can't she?*

Hunt gave her a smug grin. "What it means to be a *particular* private investigator, I'm guessing. I hear you're Vic Donovan's girlfriend. You just want to see what he does when he's not hanging out with you. Or maybe you want to out-gumshoe the gumshoe?"

"You know Vic?" Lacey felt stares from the rest of the class.

"Donovan and I go way back." Hunt bared his teeth in a crocodile smile. "It's a mistake, you know. Never investigate the ones you love. It's bound to disappoint you."

"Thanks for the professional advice." Lacey hated it when people played with her. She raised her eyebrow at him, a professional skill she had perfected over the years.

"That Bogey and Bacall stuff. That bother you?" he asked.

"No. Should it?"

He shrugged his shoulders and smirked. "It shouldn't. You're the closest thing to Lauren Bacall that's ever walked into this classroom."

He's still playing with me. Lacey's personal style, the sass and class of the 1940s lovingly updated into the twenty-first century, prompted Hunt's crack. Her honey brown hair skimmed her shoulders in a long pageboy, the blond highlights, courtesy of her stylist, Stella, accenting the waves that brushed her cheekbones. She was wearing a fitted burgundy vintage jacket from the 1940s, nipped in smartly at the waist and featuring large cuffs with giant buttons. On the right lapel she'd attached an enameled pin—two pink birds with blue stones—just for luck. The rest of her outfit was modern enough, she thought: blue jeans, black turtleneck, black leather boots, Gypsy hoop earrings, red lipstick. She felt ready for anything. Except possibly this grilling. Lacey felt herself blushing. She was about to unleash a smart comeback, as soon as she thought of one, when someone else spoke up.

"She's a femme fatale too, just like Bacall. If she whistles at you, buddy, you're a dead man."

A new student had let himself into the room, looking like a beatnik who'd lost his bongos. His boyish black hair needed a trim, and his severe square, black-framed glasses and scruffy goatee looked like a failed attempt to seem older and hipper. His clothes were all black too, jeans, turtleneck, boots, jacket, as if he'd rolled in on a Harley-Davidson instead of the early 1960s dirty blue and white Volkswagen Bus out in the parking lot, emblazoned with his Web site address and the slogan, DIG THE TRUTH! Lacey's spirits sank. It was Damon Newhouse, smiling and waving at her from a seat near the door.

"Closest thing to Bacall," Newhouse repeated, laughing. "You got that right! Lacey Smithsonian's a dangerous woman. Lethal with implements of female persuasion, the scissors, the hairspray, the quip. I've been there to chronicle it. Check it out on my Web site, DeadFed dot com."

"What the hell are you doing here, Damon?" Lacey tried not to sneer.

"Following your lead, Smithsonian, as always," he replied.

"I get all the funny classes," Hunt grumbled. "Lucky me. As I was saying—"

Newhouse tossed business cards to the guys sitting near to him. "Smithsonian as a femme fatale? Bacall to Vic Donovan's Bogart? I'm using it on the Web. Check my blog later today."

"Use it, Damon," Lacey muttered, "and yours will be the next body to fall dead at my feet."

"Hey, Smithsonian, I'm your biggest fan," Newhouse protested.

"For those of you who are not in the know," Hunt said, commanding their attention again, "our Ms. Smithsonian here is a fashion reporter at *The Eye Street Observer.* That's a little newspaper of some sort over in the District. Generally speaking, private eyes don't much like reporters. Personally, I only read *The Washington Times*, but I don't see any harm in her writing about all that girly fashion stuff. How having a PI ticket will help her do that is beyond me, but welcome to PI school, Ms. Smithsonian."

Girly fashion stuff? Apparently Bud Hunt was unfamiliar with her recent front-page stories. Murdered women, lost corsets full of jewels, homeless children at risk in the District . . . *Serves him right for not reading* The Eye. Hunt turned his attention to Damon Newhouse. Lacey was glad to share the hot seat with him. *May he find it even hotter.*

"Newhouse, right? You volunteered. Who are you, what do you do, why are you here?"

"I'm a journalist too," Damon said proudly. "A reporter. Just like Smithsonian."

"Not even close," Lacey cut in.

"Oh, lucky me again," Hunt snorted. "Two reporters. Reporter for what?"

"Conspiracy Clearinghouse, better known as DeadFed dot com." Damon Newhouse fancied himself the Woodward and Bernstein of cyberspace, a crusading newshound in a parallel universe of fringe phenomena, complete with aliens and Bigfoot and Area 51. But he was a lone ranger, a self-styled journalist without a legitimate news organization. Lacey considered him little more than an out-of-control blogger. He was also her friend Brooke's boyfriend, so she couldn't always avoid him. *But Damon? All the way out here in the burbs? In PI class?* It was a setup.

"DeadFed dot com? God help us," Hunt said. "A cyber-space cowboy."

"I hope this class will polish my investigative reporting skills and help me break the kind of stories the print media won't touch," Newhouse continued grandly.

"Yeah, right," Hunt chuckled. "Remember, everything I say, in or out of class, is confidential. Copyrighted and trade-marked. You got that, kid?"

Obviously Brooke told Damon about Lacey's plan to take a PI class, and here Damon was, copycatting her. *The nerve of him, stealing my class! And my rationale too.* Lacey felt steam rising from her brain. *Oh, yeah, Brooke has a lot of explaining to do.*

A noise from outside the window caught Lacey's attention. She gazed out at the exit of the parking lot and a sliver of wintry sky, the clouds knitted together in a dull gray lament that threatened more rain and snow. Lacey watched at hubcap level as the bottom half of a car rolled past the window.

Probably looking for parking for the Falls Church Farmers' Market across the street, she thought. Farmers and craftspeople sold their wares every Saturday morning under colorful awnings of red and green, yellow and blue, a cheerful suburban oasis on a chilly day. Parking could be tough. The car disappeared.

Hunt turned from Newhouse to the only other woman in class, a well-tended matron who gave her name as Edwina Plimpton. She looked fortysomething, but Lacey guessed her real age at fiftysomething. Her straight white-blond hair fell to her shoulders in a long smooth bob, held in place by a black velvet headband. She wore black slacks and a white oxford shirt beneath her buttoned melon-colored cardigan. *Talbots*, Lacey surmised of her outfit. *Nothing but Talbots.*

The woman's face was long and her chin disappeared into her neck. Her eyebrows arched in a supercilious way. A Rolex adorned her wrist; her manicure was French and expensive. Her voice resonated expensively of private schools and country clubs, polite but with just the faintest tinge of superiority.

"Just call me Edwina," she invited Hunt chummily. "Are you quite sure my car will be all right in your little parking lot? I belong to the big silver BMW," she added with a tinkling laugh.

Lacey confessed silently to wondering the same thing. She "belonged" to a very different BMW parked in the same lot, a green vintage 1974 model 2002tii that Vic had restored himself, his surprise Christmas present for her. Possibly the most amazing present she'd ever received. She was still babying the little car as if it were made of crystal.

"Lady, this is Falls Church, Virginia. It ain't exactly the

District. And the police department is right across the street." Edwina laughed as if she were holding a highball and he had made a witty cocktail-hour remark. Hunt kept a straight face. He sighed deeply and waited to learn why she was honoring his class with her presence.

"Well, if you say so," Edwina said with a flourish of her left hand, which was decorated by a two-carat emerald-cut diamond ring with a diamond-encrusted band set in platinum. "Actually, I'm here because I made a little bet with Mary Lou, my bridge partner, on which one of us could do the most unusual thing this winter. She chose skin diving. In the Bahamas." Edwina snickered as if the Bahamas were *so last year.* "I chose this. I win!"

"You win?" Hunt said. "What about me? What do I win?"

"I've been skin diving for *years*," she confided at large. The big detective closed his eyes for a moment, perhaps to ban the vision of Edwina's body in a wet suit.

"You don't win unless you finish the course, Ms. Edwina Plimpton. Sixty hours. Classwork, fieldwork, and a written test." He stepped away to his next student, then turned back to her. "And by the way, dilettantes never finish this class."

"I am not a dilettante." She gave him a genial I'll-show-you look. "Of course, I was a *debutante* once, but I'm not saying when." The tinkling laugh again.

Hunt rolled his eyes. He focused on a new arrival, a woman who slipped in quietly while Edwina was charming them. "Glad you could join us. What's your story?"

Hunt made a show of checking his fancy watch. Lacey became aware of someone settling into the seat next to her. The latest addition to the class was a young woman who kept her head down and said nothing. In her late twenties or early thirties, she had dirt brown hair and pale eyes. Her hair, slacks, and khaki sweater all blended with the décor as if she were camouflaged in office-drab camo.

Blending into your environment might be an admirable trait for a PI, Lacey mused. *Pretty hard to score a date when you're invisible, though.*

The woman peeked up at Hunt warily through her bangs and mumbled her name: Willow Raynor. She said something else, too softly for Lacey to hear. Willow Raynor looked like she was about to crawl right under her desk.

Hunt sighed and let Ms. Raynor off the hook. He smiled at the guy sitting in front of her. One of those just-between-us-guys-ain't-these-dames-nuts kind of smiles. The man smiled back at Hunt. Perhaps also fortysomething, Lacey guessed, but he seemed somehow older than forty, with tired eyes and deep crow's-feet at the corners. The wrinkles gave him an air of maturity, as did his silver-tipped hair and dark suit. His brown eyes looked steady and somber.

"You." Hunt's face lit up: Here was a solid citizen, someone he could talk to man to man. A guy's guy. "You're a serious guy. What's your story?"

The man looked him in the eyes. "My name is Martin Hadley and my story"—he straightened his shoulders—"my story is this: I'm a victim of government mind control."

"Mind control," Hunt said, blinking. "Okay. That's a new one here. Tell me more."

"We call it psychotropic terror." Hadley's voice was deep and calm. "The cutting edge of insidious governmental harassment and intimidation. So many victims. So few solutions."

Hunt stifled a chuckle. "So you wear tinfoil in your hat to block it out?"

"Some of us believe that's effective." Hadley wore a look of pure martyrdom. "I don't."

"This a setup?" Hunt smirked. "One of the other PIs pay you to come here and yank my chain? Sure, tell me all about this mind control."

Mind control? Newhouse gave Lacey a "thumbs-up" sign. His sardonic expression had turned into a huge Cheshire cat grin. He was a cat with an unexpected saucer of cream, and now he could say Lacey Smithsonian had led him right to it. Damon was sitting right next to Hadley, no doubt pondering how best to exploit the poor guy. Some half-baked "exposé" of the "dark government conspiracy" behind the innocent victims of mind control, Lacey thought—and all citing Lacey as an "informed source." She wanted to roll up a newspaper and smack him over the nose like a bad cat. She shook her head and watched Hunt, who wore his own look of pain. Pained skepticism.

"That's right," Hadley was saying. "Mind control. Your skepticism is understandable, but simply put, agents of the government use a secret technology to broadcast hostile voices into my head and assault me with electromagnetic radiation, causing me pain and anguish. They are ruining my life."

"Ah. Right. So you're here to learn how to bug the buggers?" Hunt asked. "Or how to contact the mother ship so they can beam you aboard?"

Edwina laughed again. Damon was writing down every word. Hadley suddenly groaned and grabbed his head. He doubled over in pain. The classroom went silent.

chapter 3

"Are you all right?" Lacey jumped to her feet. Hadley was sweating profusely. He mopped his forehead with his handkerchief, took a deep breath, and straightened. He looked very pale.

"I'm fine," Hadley said. "This happens rather often."

"I'm not buying this act." Hunt folded his arms.

"Mind control!" Newhouse piped up hopefully. "Would that by any chance happen to be a conspiracy perpetrated by the United States government?"

Lacey wondered what Newhouse was up to. If anybody would swallow a cockamamie story like that, she thought, it would be Damon Newhouse of DeadFed dot com. Maybe he'd planted this guy in the class? No, she thought his look of happy wonderment at stumbling upon this potential story seemed genuine.

"That's right," Hadley sighed. "Our own government. And by the way, I don't particularly care if any of you believe me."

Hunt made an elaborate display of eyeball rolling.

Hadley might or might not be crazy, but Lacey felt for the guy. It was tough to open yourself up to the scorn of strangers and their callous gibes about tinfoil hats. At least he wasn't a crime of fashion, accessorized with Reynolds Wrap like a meat loaf ready for the oven.

"I've read about mind control," Damon said. "But so far, no one's been able to prove anything conclusively. I'd be very interested in talking to a real TI, a 'Targeted Individual.' Isn't that your terminology?"

"Yes," Hadley said. "I'm a TI. There are many of us."

"You don't say." Their instructor looked nonplussed. He pressed his lips together and glanced at the clock on the wall. His expression said, *I get all the nutcases.*

"It's not a comedy routine. There are thousands of us," Hadley said in a near monotone.

"Then what do you expect to get out of this class?"

"Maybe nothing." Hadley's gaze was level. "Or maybe some ideas about how to investigate this mess I'm in. Find the bastards behind this. Ask them why, why me, what they want from me. That's all." He sounded calm and lucid. He wasn't twitching or drooling. And he didn't appear to be listening to disembodied voices. *Or was he?*

Lacey wanted to laugh, but the man's dignified carriage and serious expression stopped her. She noticed Damon slipping his card to the man. Hadley looked at it blankly and then at Newhouse.

"I'm not laughing, man," Newhouse said. "I'd like to talk to you. Maybe we could put your story on the Web. Let people decide for themselves." Hadley nodded.

A new conspiracy for Damon! A victim willing to talk! Go Hadley! This might be a promising development, Lacey thought. Maybe Hadley would keep Damon Newhouse busy and she could get through this PI course without having him Velcroed to her side.

"What's it like?" Newhouse asked Hadley.

"There are voices. They come and go."

"Are they talking to you now? What are they saying?"

"That you all think I'm nuts. Particularly Mr. Hunt." The glare Hadley sent Hunt's way sent a chill up Lacey's spine. She made a mental note not to cross him. "That I'm a fool to be here."

"It's okay." Newhouse clapped the man on the shoulder. "I hear that all the time too. Anyway, we're all fools sometimes."

"No one believes me." Hadley rubbed his temples in circular motions with his middle fingers. "That's his mantra today." Lacey was inclined to agree with the mysterious unheard voices. Hadley shut his eyes and grimaced. "He's laughing. I hate it when they laugh at me." Everyone stared at the man.

"No one here is laughing," Damon said. The others, however, were rolling eyes at each other and making faces.

Hunt glanced at the clock and looked relieved. He clapped his hands. "Fun is fun, boys and girls, but it's break time. Take ten. Make it twenty. Be ready to work when we come back." He shook his head, trudged down the hall to his office, and slammed the door.

Lacey slipped off to the ladies' room. The stalls were painted a depressing shade of brown, and she looked green under the room's fluorescent light. She needed a splash of makeup to combat the gray day and the beige classroom and Martin Hadley's scary but strangely flat story. She pulled her blush compact from her purse.

"Good God! Who decorated this hovel?" Edwina strode through the door, inspecting her manicure. She fished in her bag for lipstick. She opened her mouth wide and traced a girlish pink stain on her lips, smeared some on each cheek, and rubbed. "That's better." She flashed her perfect nails. "Isn't this exciting? I'm so glad I picked this class! Everyone is so weird." She paused and their eyes met in the mirror. "Make that interesting, not weird, and not *you*, of course, Ms. Smithsonian. But isn't this fun?"

"It has its moments." Lacey dragged a comb through her hair. She didn't want to indulge in girl talk in the cramped ladies' room. She wasn't quite sure how much she liked Edwina Plimpton, the dilettante on sabbatical from her bridge club. It was never a good idea to be too chummy too soon.

Edwina kept chattering away. Lacey looked for a chance to escape. Willow Raynor, the invisible beige-clad woman, barged through the door and headed for the sink, nearly slamming into them. "Sorry. I just want to wash my hands." She glanced up at the others and then returned her gaze to the floor. "Sorry."

"I was just saying how exciting this whole class is!" Edwina was determined to be chatty, still the Head Girl after all these years. "It's Willow, isn't it? Willow's a pretty name. Don't you think this is all just so fascinating? And such exotic characters! Like that insane Martin Hadley. And Snake Goldstein with the tattooed neck! My bridge club is going to love this." Her eyes glowed with pleasure. "Mary Louise will be so jealous. Scuba diving! Ha!"

"I suppose so." Willow didn't seem to want to chat. She washed her hands and face thoroughly and grabbed a handful of paper towels. She pushed her hair off her face, but it fell back into her eyes like a dirty dust mop.

"This will make fabulous cocktail conversation." Edwina smiled at herself in the mirror and powdered her nose. "At least it will once I improve it a little, right girls?"

"Maybe there's more coffee in the kitchen," Lacey said, slipping through the door to make her escape. But she wasn't fast enough.

"Coffee! Good idea, Lacey," Edwina chirped. "We'll all go."

What am I, the scout troop leader? Lacey led the other women down the hall into the small makeshift kitchen, which must have once been a closet. It now had a miniature stove, a small under-the-counter refrigerator, a tiny sink, and a window on the parking lot at kneecap level. Happily, there was a fresh pot of coffee. And, utter bliss, on the gold-speckled Formica countertop sat a box of fresh Krispy Kreme doughnuts.

Lacey silently thanked Bud Hunt. She assumed the doughnuts were his idea, being an ex-cop. Her growling stomach thanked him too. Edwina and Willow crowded into the kitchen behind her. There was barely room to breathe, let alone pour coffee. Grabbing a chocolate-iced Krispy Kreme doughnut, Lacey scooted into the reception area to have a few moments alone with her doughnut and coffee. She was just congratulating herself on having avoided any fashion chat when Edwina and Willow caught up with her. Edwina zeroed in on Lacey's vintage burgundy jacket.

"That's so nice! And classically tailored! Is it one of the new vintage looks?"

"No, it's one of the old vintage looks," Lacey said. "Late Forties."

"Pretty color," the beige-on-beige Willow mumbled. "I

love red." Lacey nearly choked on her doughnut. "Well, not on me, but—"

"Lacey, speaking as a fashion expert," Edwina continued, "what do you think of the spring collections? Are dresses really back for spring? Because I'm a separates kind of gal." She proudly indicated her own preppy outfit.

As if I even get to cover the spring collections. It would be a kick to cover the various Fashion Weeks in New York, if the paper would pay her travel expenses. But *The Eye* was too cheap to send her to New York to cover *fashion*, an unfamiliar concept in Washington, D.C., the City Fashion Forgot. Besides, the spring collections had been shown the previous fall. Who could remember that far back in Lacey's crazy fashion world, littered not just with waistlines and hemlines but with bodies? Death and fashion intersected oddly in Lacey's life.

"I don't write much about the big fashion collections, Edwina. I rarely get to leave D.C. Besides, I write for the common woman, which is not to say she's an unimportant woman. The average Washington woman just needs a little help, a little color, a little confidence." Lacey took a bite of her doughnut.

"The common woman? Really?" Edwina's expression made it clear she didn't know any "common women." Edwina was obviously not a reader of Lacey's "Crimes of Fashion" column in *The Eye,* Washington's youngest and least respectable newspaper. Edwina no doubt read *The Washington Post*, the dowager paper.

"It sounds very interesting, what you do," Willow said, carefully stirring her coffee.

"Not really. Well, sometimes," Lacey admitted. "By accident."

"I could use that kind of help," Willow whispered shyly. "A little confidence. I never know what to wear. Maybe sometime you wouldn't mind talking to me, giving me some fashion hints?"

Lacey groaned inwardly. She didn't want to talk fashion, but she also didn't want to squash this shy woman with rudeness, at least on the first day of class. Lacey wondered what help she could really offer. Beige-on-beige people generally resisted change. Clearly Willow needed some help. Hair, makeup, clothes, style, and judging from her demeanor, perhaps a spine transplant. But Lacey couldn't give the woman a whole-life makeover.

"What did you have in mind?" she asked.

"Your hair looks really pretty." Willow fingered her own limp and dull locks.

"Thanks, I owe it all to Stella," Lacey said. "My stylist."

Willow hesitated before lifting her eyes. "Stella. Do you think she might see me?"

"Why not?" Stella had been known to work miracles. Perhaps Willow had good bones under the pale skin and lips and colorless hair. "I'll give you her number. She works at Stylettos at Dupont Circle."

Lacey found few things as life affirming as a great makeover. She wrote Stella's information on the back of her business card. Willow took it gratefully, her eyes fixed on the floor.

Lacey made a break for the classroom with her coffee and the rest of her doughnut. She needed to hear some guy talk after all this girl talk. Snake Goldstein wouldn't be talking fashion, she was sure of that. The guys would be talking crime or cops or sports. Or cars, or mind control. Guy stuff, anything but fashion. As she entered, Damon Newhouse bumped into her, spilling her coffee on his pants and shoes.

"Sorry, Lacey. I didn't get you too, did I? I'm such a klutz. Helps to wear black." He knew she was irritated by his appearance in her class, but Damon refused to be anything but good-natured, even wet and scalded.

"Wear your coffee a lot, do you?"

"Often enough," he replied, wiping his shoes.

Lacey checked her clothes for coffee stains. She had escaped without a spot, but now her coffee cup was half empty. Her doughnut was safe, however, which made her feel much better. She sat down in the back of the room. Newhouse followed her. A bit of the men's conversation drifted past her. Lacey caught something about touchdowns, Hail Mary, the Redskins, and the Super Bowl. She hadn't missed much.

"Totally cool class, huh?" Newhouse said. "I can't believe we're here together."

"Yeah, me neither. How did that happen?" Lacey let her sarcasm drip like spilled coffee.

"Coincidence?" he offered.

"What are the odds? You believe in fate, Newhouse?"

"Absolutely." Damon ignored her dig. "And what about Martin Hadley, our very own mind control TI? Pretty radical. Crazy stuff, mind control. What a break. And I'm going to get to the bottom of it."

"Be my guest." She swirled the last of her coffee in her cup.

"Golden opportunity, Smithsonian. First day of class too."

"You can't possibly believe him. It's ridiculous."

"I don't believe or disbelieve," Newhouse said. "Not my job. But you can't ignore the thousands of people in this country who claim to be victims."

"Sure I can." *I just wish I could ignore you.*

"It's a massive conspiracy. If the U.S. government isn't behind it, who could it be?"

From the vantage point of an experienced journalist in the Nation's Capital, Lacey firmly believed the government was too incompetent and too inefficient to run a massive conspiracy. A sophisticated secret program to torture Joe and Jane Average Citizen? What was the purpose? Where was the funding? Where were the headquarters? Where was the U.S. Bureau of Mind Control subway stop on the D.C. Metro? *Show me the line item in the budget and I'll believe.*

"You gotta have an open mind, Smithsonian."

"No, I don't. I'm a journalist. I just gotta have the facts."

chapter 4

Bud Hunt pushed through the knot of PI students with the last cup of coffee in his hand. He left the classroom door open.

"Break's over, guys and gals. Take your seats. We've got a guest speaker today. It's a little early in the course to be talking about surveillance, but our guest expert was, um, unexpectedly available today. He's here and you're here, so here we are."

Hunt waited, sipping his coffee. The class waited. No one entered. Hunt poked his head out the door. "We're in here! Just leave your stuff in my office. Anytime you're ready." He turned back to his students.

"Surveillance is the art and craft of waiting and watching," Hunt said, filling time. "There are many kinds of surveillance: walk-around, vehicle, long-term, short-term, fixed, mobile, overt, covert. Watching someone often means following someone. Sometimes you do it while you're undercover. It's like acting—you become part of your subject's universe. Sometimes you just sit in a car and wait and watch and pee in a cup." He glanced over his shoulder as his guest strode into the classroom. "And this guy can tell you all about it. He's an expert, and an old pal. They're all yours, Greg." Hunt and the new guy grinned at each other and shook hands; then Hunt left and closed the door behind him.

One glance at Hunt's so-called surveillance expert and Lacey sat bolt upright. The black ten-gallon Stetson, the bushy mustache, the close-cropped thin blond hair, the sheer

size of the man, it all gave him the air of a bronco-busting
cowboy from a Western movie, but Lacey knew that was just
a cover. The man's sharp features in his round face were an
arresting combination, and his pale blue eyes were unread-
able. He threw his big hat on a hook and perched on the desk
facing the group for a moment, smiling, not speaking. His
gaze crossed Lacey's face without a flicker of recognition.

The blue eyes belonged to a man Lacey knew as Gregor
Kepelov, an ex-KGB spy and a jewel thief. Or a "jewel recovery specialist." He was a Russian with an American
dream, or so he once told her, and a cosmopolitan love of
money. Danger he was not so fond of, but he could be dangerous himself. Gregor Kepelov might not even be his real
name. But "Greg"?

Lacey had met Kepelov in Paris the previous fall, under
less than civil circumstances. He was a bitter burr under her
saddle on a story that turned out pretty well, no thanks to
him. *What on earth is going on here?* She felt disoriented.
What was Gregor Kepelov doing here, teaching surveillance
to a private investigation class? In Falls Church, Virginia, of
all places?

"Hello. I am happy to be here today for my friend Bud,
to talk with you about surveillance. It is one of my favorite
topics, and one of my top skills. My name? I have many
names. You may call me Greg."

Kepelov may have gone Wild Wild West, Lacey thought,
but he still hadn't lost his slight Russian accent. Maybe it
wasn't so surprising that Gregor "Call-me-Greg" Kepelov
was still hanging around here under an alias. According to
the Spy Museum, there were more spies in Washington,
D.C., than anywhere else on earth. Lots of job opportunities
for a spy, and he'd been chasing something that had ended
up in Washington. She told herself not to be paranoid, that
he wasn't after her. *Not again.*

"For many years," Kepelov said, "I work for KGB." The
class was silent. "You have heard of it?" He laughed. "No?
We were famous at one time." Lacey heard laughter around
her. "My job description? If I tell you, I have to kill you. As
everyone should know, Washington, D.C., is full of spies.

They tell me every sixth person I see is a spy." He counted the class. "Ah, must be two spies here! After class we must meet at Spy Club. Drinks on you." There was more laughter. Kepelov's stand-up routine was a hit so far.

"Where is this Spy Club, Greg?" Damon Newhouse squinted, trying to place him.

"Spy Club? Is a secret. If you were a spy, you would know," the ex-spy said. More laughter. *A KGB comedian*, Lacey thought. *Who knew?* "To begin. You may think you would know me anywhere. My look, my face, my walk. My hat. I have very distinctive look, do I not? But you would be wrong. My profession requires me to be a chameleon. Another time, another place: You will see me, but you will not know me. But I will know you."

Hunt poked his head through the doorway. "This guy cracks me up. Have fun, y'all. I got paperwork to do. They're all yours till lunch, Greg." He disappeared, leaving Kepelov in charge.

"You are wondering perhaps why I am here. Am I not rich like other espionage agents? Do I not live life of James Bond on the Riviera? Sadly, not all spies are James Bond. I have no Aston Martin or double-oh-seven lifestyle. KGB pension plan? Not so good." Kepelov shrugged extravagantly at the laughter, then smiled. "You have heard of course that every spy is a ladies' man, irresistible to women. That part? Is all true." Every man in class laughed. Edwina too was enjoying his performance. Poor Willow just looked dazed.

Lacey did not laugh. A loud rumbling sound caught her attention. She was seated right by the back window, and a large blue garbage truck rolled noisily past, drowning out Kepelov's comedy for a moment. She turned her attention back to the ex-spy and jotted some notes in her notebook. *Why is he here?*

As if to answer her question, Kepelov said, "Today I am here for the money. Never do anything except for the money. Is first lesson of being a private investigator: Don't do anything except for the money. My friend Bud Hunt will tell you also. It is capitalism, yes? Good business. I do this for a little of your money. *Spasibo*. Means *thank you* in Russian. Now I have a question for you. What is a spy?" He looked straight at Lacey and nodded ever so slightly to her in recognition. No one answered him.

"A spy," Kepelov went on, "is someone who watches. To spy is to watch, to watch in secret. To observe and be unobserved. A spy sneaks into your life, your business, learns all about you, stays invisible. Every little thing, where you work, where you play, what you read, what you buy at grocery store, what you do when you think no one is watching. But the spy is watching."

Edwina giggled, drew something in her notebook, and showed Lacey a stick-figure PI in a trench coat. Perhaps Edwina dreamed of a more exciting life than being a country club wife.

Kepelov's smile suddenly warmed his sharp features. "Why does the spy or the PI watch? For money! Other reasons too. For governments. For private business. For clients. Maybe for love, maybe for patriotism. For a purpose. But not for *your* purpose, if you are the spied-on. For the spy's own purpose. That purpose will tell us best way of watching. One kind of watching is to conduct surveillance. I teach you a little surveillance today," Kepelov said. "Today we learn some basics, later we will do actual surveillance exercise. But let me warn you, takes a long time to perfect these skills. Do not be discouraged. No KGB final exam for you today."

"Did you train for a long time in the KGB to do surveillance?" Damon had his pen poised to write.

"Oh no. One week only. KGB final exam? Very final. You must be fast study in KGB or they shoot you." Kepelov mimed a gun to his head. "Bang bang." There was silence. "Is a joke!" He laughed and the class laughed with him, except Lacey. He leaned against the desk and folded his arms. "I have even conducted surveillance on someone sitting in this classroom today. Strange but true." He had the audacity to wink at Lacey. "All over Paris, Normandy, France, back into this country. New Orleans."

"You chased a fashion writer?" Goldstein cracked. "Must have been important."

Kepelov turned to him with his chilly blue glare. "Mr. Snake, with that attitude you would have missed out on the jewel recovery of the century. More for me." He grinned at Lacey. "Good times. Is that not right, Lacey Smithsonian?"

Lacey smiled. "It didn't get you what you wanted though, did it, Kepelov?"

Damon Newhouse's eyes went wide as saucers. He'd played a tiny part in that adventure, dogging Lacey's heels there as well, and he'd heard tales of the elusive Kepelov, but he'd never seen him in the flesh. Damon started furiously taking notes. Lacey wondered how soon he would plaster this story all over Conspiracy Clearinghouse.

"You would be surprised, Smithsonian. My wants are . . . adaptable. We must talk about American dream again, sometime." He gestured toward Lacey. "My friend Lacey Smithsonian is not laughing yet, but one day we will laugh over how we met. Very amusing."

"Yeah, that was hilarious." Lacey still wasn't laughing. "Care to tell me what secret Russian knockout chemical you used on me?"

"Professional secret."

"I probably have residual brain damage from it," Lacey said, much to the amusement of the group. "That's probably what I'm doing here."

"No no. Lots more brains left in you, I think." His blue eyes focused on the rest of the class. "This Lacey Smithsonian, she found the fabled corset of a long-ago Romanov princess," he told the class. "Full of diamonds! And do you know how she found it? With her woman's intuition. This technique I cannot teach you. She calls this technique her 'fashion clues.' Something KGB did not teach."

"And who got to the corset first?" Lacey said.

Kepelov bowed gallantly. "You win, Smithsonian. At least I was spying on the right woman, yes? A lesson, class: Looking for something? Follow someone smarter than you. Try to follow around a woman who has such talents. Yet she wastes this amazing talent as a fashion reporter."

Lacey finally laughed. "Tell me something I don't know." There they were in agreement.

"Maybe in this class my friend Lacey Smithsonian will learn to be the spy she was born to be."

"You mean to tell me," Edwina blurted out, "I missed all this because I wasn't reading that scandal sheet, *The Eye Street Observer*?" Lacey rubbed her face and sighed. "Why, I'm subscribing today!" The class burst out laughing. Again at Lacey's expense.

Lacey didn't know what to make of the new, improved Gregor Kepelov. She'd never known what to make of the old Kepelov, for that matter. He came on like a big bully, a comic strip version of a Cold War spy. Then he'd turn into a big sentimental teddy bear. He'd once confided to her his dream of owning a ranch in Texas. He called it his American Dream. So far, at least he had the ten-gallon hat. *Why are you mad at me, Lacey Smithsonian?* he had once asked her. *I did not kill you!* Maybe in Kepelov's warped universe, she reflected, either he killed you or he was your buddy, with nothing in between.

"Smithsonian and me, we are good friends now," he told the class. "Bygones."

Lacey's eyebrow expressed her skepticism. He ignored the eyebrow and continued his lecture/comedy routine. He got a big laugh with his impression of KGB agents trying to follow people stealthily around Moscow and East Berlin in their ancient, rattling, smoke-spewing Eastern European cars. The mysterious Kepelov that struck such fear into Smithsonian last year in France and New Orleans seemed to have turned into a fine Russian ham.

Lacey didn't know what to take seriously and what was a joke. Maybe the comedy act was simply another cover. Maybe he owed Hunt a favor. At the rate former Soviet spies were being poisoned by polonium, he was lucky to be alive, but a lucky ex-spy might still be doing business in the U.S. for Russian interests. Perhaps Vic could help her sort it all out later. He might be very interested that Kepelov was still hanging around town. By the time noon rolled around and the class broke for lunch, Lacey was contemplating writing an article on Kepelov and his new comedy act: THE SPY WHO BUGGED ME.

Damon Newhouse headed her way, waving at her, with Martin Hadley in tow. Lacey grabbed her white all-weather trench coat and tote bag to make a fast exit. She wanted to avoid going to lunch with anyone. She hoped to take a quiet break at the Farmers' Market and the vintage clothing store down the street. She wasn't fast enough.

"Hey, Smithsonian, what do you make of Kepelov here? Wasn't he the one Nigel Griffin thought was so deadly? The one who tried to kill you?"

She shrugged. He moved in closer and hushed his voice: Big Conspiracy Time. "You know the Russkies were deep into mind control, right?" He arched one eyebrow melodramatically. "Kepelov's here? Hadley's here? Do the math."

"Not a math major, Damon. I'll wait for the big print edition."

"Lunch?" he asked. "We can talk about it."

"Sorry, I have plans. You guys go ahead. Ask Kepelov. He likes math, I bet."

She just reached the classroom door when a scream cut through the air. Everyone froze. Silence. The first long scream was followed by sharp shrieks, as if from a frightened animal. Everyone unfroze and rushed toward the sound.

Newhouse and Hadley followed Lacey up the stairs and out into the parking lot in the chill January drizzle. Hunt and the others were already outside, running toward the back of the lot where a woman was screaming. It was Willow Raynor, the PI student who was too shy to say her name above a whisper. She stood there shaking, her arms at her sides, her fists tightly balled up. Flanked by a stunned Edwina, who was gagging and trying not to cry, and a stoic Snake Goldstein, Willow was still shrieking, short jagged shrieks, a scream in hiccups. She seemed unable to stop. Bud Hunt stepped up to her and slapped her across the face and then put his arm around her. She stopped.

It took Lacey a moment to realize that Willow wasn't actually injured in any way. Willow finally pointed to a silver-blue S-Type Jaguar that was partly blocked from the building by a stand of trees and a large Dumpster.

Lacey followed Kepelov to the car. The windows of the Jaguar were wet with rain and lightly fogged inside, but slicing through the condensation were long thin streaks of bright red blood. They traced a grim but delicate design on the inside of the glass, reminding Lacey somehow of an Asian painting. She took a step toward the driver's door of the Jaguar. Then she stopped.

Through the windshield Lacey saw a woman sitting very still behind the wheel, deadly still. There was a bullet hole in her head and a lot of blood. Through the misted car windows and their tracery of blood Lacey realized she saw something else, something worse.

She knew the woman.

chapter 5

What on earth is Cecily Ashton doing here? And what the hell happened? Hot and cold chills ran up and down Lacey's spine. She took a big gulp of the icy air and issued a silent command to get ahold of herself. There was nothing she could do to help. Nobody could help the woman now.

Lacey felt awful, disoriented, sick to her stomach. When she daydreamed about finding the big story that would help her leave the hemlines and high heels beat far behind, it didn't involve another death. Still, she took another look through the delicate sprays of blood on the windshield.

The dead woman had a small hole on the right side of her head, blood congealing where a bullet had entered. Cecily's large brown eyes were open and there was a surprised look on her face.

Why the expression? Lacey had no idea. Did Cecily kill herself? Maybe dying hurt more than she expected, maybe death was different than she thought, maybe she changed her mind at the last minute. Or maybe someone else had surprised her.

The dead woman was Cecily Ashton, one of the more notorious Washingtonian socialites, the former trophy wife of an aging billionaire who once owned a baseball team in the District of Columbia and a football team in a state further south. Cecily was a Washington gossip column staple for her many misadventures, romantic and otherwise.

Decades younger than her billionaire husband, Cecily was a free spirit who conducted her personal affairs rather publicly. She tended to get the wrong kind of press coverage for her husband's taste, so the split was inevitable. Washington society had once embraced her as the wife of Philip Clark Ashton, but cut her dead, so to speak, as soon as the ink dried on the divorce decree. Cecily joined the growing ranks of the cast-off Mrs. Ashtons. After more than a year of a bitter courtroom battle, Cecily had recently received a hefty financial settlement.

Lacey was current on the details of the scandal because she had interviewed Cecily Ashton the previous week for *The Eye*. She had focused on Cecily's couture collection and style; the scandal was just background. The socialite was said to possess the most fabulous wardrobe in all of Washington. Lacey could confirm that she had marvelous closets. Closets full of beautiful clothes—and secrets.

In a frank moment, Cecily told Lacey she didn't know how she could ever regain her place in the rarefied ether of old-money Washington society, and that she would give anything to find her way back into that world. She still had, however, her amazing collection of designer clothes and accessories, more than two thousand outfits, a portion of which were to be featured in an upcoming exhibit next month at the Bentley Museum of American Fashion in Washington.

Smithsonian's article on Cecily was to appear in *The Eye*'s Sunday magazine section, the very next day. The thought crossed Lacey's mind that she should call the news desk and tell them about the woman's death, but she didn't reach for her cell phone. Not yet. News was transitory, but death was permanent. It felt wrong to her somehow to celebrate the demise of someone she knew for the news value. And she had rather liked Cecily, maybe because she had punched D.C. society right in the snoot. Perhaps if Lacey waited to make the call, Cecily wouldn't have to be officially dead quite yet, meat for the press buzzards to gather round.

What brought Cecily all the way out to Falls Church? Lacey wondered again. The PI students huddled in the chill in the parking lot, talking and eyeing the car. Bud Hunt was on his cell phone with the police. As he'd pointed out in class, the police station was across the street. It wouldn't take them long to get there.

Lacey found it hard to look at the woman, and hard to look away. Cecily's official age was thirty-nine, but Lacey suspected that number was off by at least a few years. It didn't matter, the notorious divorcée was still beautiful, even though her skin was a bit too taut over her bones, thanks to a recent facelift. In death, Cecily looked like a wax mannequin splashed with blood, a clever approximation of the real thing, but not the woman Lacey had known.

What business did Cecily have on a suburban Saturday in Falls Church, Virginia, when she lived high above Georgetown in one of the most expensive enclaves of Washington, D.C.? Lacey didn't think she was visiting the Farmers' Market. Could Cecily have had something important to tell her and tracked her down somehow? But that was crazy. Cecily Ashton had no way of knowing Lacey would be here, this very day, at this very building in Falls Church. She didn't even know Lacey's home phone, or where she lived. At least Lacey didn't think so.

Willow was still crying quietly, but she tried to speak. "We were just heading for Edwina's car to go to lunch, and there she was and she was. . . . And I—" Willow sobbed again and started to collapse. Snake held her up and handed her off to Kepelov, who helped walk her back to Bud Hunt's offices. Behind his sunglasses, Damon Newhouse was green around the gills. Hadley looked as blank and somber as he had in class, giving no hint what he was thinking. Or what the voices in his head might be saying.

"Oh my God! It's Cecily Ashton!" Edwina swallowed hard and stepped closer to peer into the parked Jaguar. She whirled on Bud Hunt. "You told me this parking lot was safe! That could have been me in that car! How could this happen to somebody like Cecily?"

"You know Cecily Ashton?" Hunt stared at the body, then at Edwina. He was sweating in spite of the cold. Something about the way he looked at the dead woman made Lacey think he knew her too.

"Everyone knows Cecily Ashton!" Edwina met quizzical

glances from the others. "Well, I used to know her. Socially. The opera, the club, the charity galas and things. I haven't seen her much since, well, the divorce." Edwina kept rubbing her hands together in the cold. "Good God, do you think she killed herself? *Here?*"

Cecily's left hand was still hooked over the steering wheel. The other rested on the seat next to her. Lacey could see the woman's French manicure. It looked perfect, with immaculately squared white tips. She didn't see a gun. On the passenger seat was a cherry red Hermés Birkin bag in some ludicrously expensive species of crocodile.

Lacey wondered why she hadn't seen the silver blue Jaguar pull up. She'd seen other cars cruise past the window, and the noisy garbage truck. The Jag wasn't there before class, when she parked her little green BMW in the corner by the back door. Then she realized the building had a driveway on each side, one marked ENTRANCE, the other marked EXIT. The PI school windows faced the exit driveway. Lacey would have seen Cecily Ashton's car only when it left the parking lot. But Cecily had never left.

Hunt cleared his throat and Lacey looked up. The police were there.

The Falls Church detective sat behind Bud Hunt's desk. Seated opposite him, Lacey realized his chair was at least six inches higher than hers. He towered over her. She felt like a first grader in the principal's office. Lacey smiled: *Interrogation 101.* The difference in chair height is a subtle way to establish dominance, over a client or a job applicant. Or an interrogation subject. Lacey knew the trick, so she wasn't about to let it work on her.

Detective Tom Jance was tall and thin, but muscular, with sandy blond hair, sable brown eyes, and fuzzy eyelashes. In his early thirties, she guessed, about her own age. The boy next door who just happens to be a cop. Jance had an open face, but the circles under his eyes made him look tired. He wore khaki slacks, a yellow knit shirt, and a brown jacket. Lacey noticed his bare ring finger, but only as a practiced reflex. She wasn't looking for a man.

He'd been watching the game at home, Jance said. Lacey had no idea what game he was talking about. Football, perhaps. He certainly seemed sorry to have left it. She murmured something sympathetic.

"I have just a few questions, Ms. Smithsonian."

"Shoot," she said. *Oops. That was insensitive.* "Sorry."

He smiled. "No problem. I understand you're a reporter?" His nostrils flared. "I'd appreciate it if I don't see this conversation played out in tomorrow's paper." Detective Jance was obviously not familiar with her byline, or her previous brushes with crime.

"I'm a fashion reporter," she said, and he relaxed. Lacey didn't exactly promise not to write anything. She remembered again that she hadn't alerted her own newsroom yet. *There goes my scoop. So much for me getting off the fashion beat at* The Eye.

Lacey confirmed to the detective that she and the others, except for Hunt and Kepelov, had been in class all morning, that she hadn't been outside since she arrived, that the Jaguar hadn't been there when she parked, and that she knew nothing about the shooting. He wrote it all down. *This is going well,* she thought.

"Did you know Cecily Ashton?" he asked, poised to tick one more item off his list. "Other than by her reputation, I mean."

"Actually, yes. I interviewed her last week."

Detective Jance sat up a little straighter in his high chair. He was suddenly a little more interested. His eyes narrowed and he looked a whole lot less friendly.

Well, it was *going well.* She braced herself.

"You interviewed her? What for?"

"For my newspaper. *The Eye Street Observer.*"

"What did you interview her about?" The detective scowled at her. He picked up a small blue stress ball from Hunt's desk and tossed it from hand to hand.

"Her clothes," Lacey said. "You know, *fashion* reporter? Part of the job description."

"Her clothes?" He seemed dumbfounded. He glanced at his shirt and jacket and back to her. "Why?"

There is no hope for the clothing clueless, she decided.

"Cecily Ashton was famous for her wardrobe," Lacey explained patiently. "Among other things. She has an incredible collection of haute couture from famous designers all over the world, and some amazing vintage pieces that are quite valuable. Museum quality stuff." He still looked skeptical. "My interview will be in tomorrow's paper. With photos. The big Sunday edition, you know." *You can read all about it in* The Eye Street Observer.

"Well, then, Ms. Smithsonian, can you tell me about her state of mind? From your fashion reporter's point of view, of course."

Her state of mind? "You think it was suicide? Did you find the gun?"

"Can't say, ma'am. The crime scene guys are going over her car right now. But can you tell me if she was depressed? Despondent?"

"Depressed?" Lacey shrugged. "She was unhappy about her divorce, but that was a while ago, and she just won a huge settlement. It was in all the papers. She was making plans to exhibit her collection, she was pretty excited about that."

"Did you hear the gunshot?"

She shook her head. "No. The classroom doesn't face the parking lot. The only thing I heard was the garbage truck. Very screechy."

"Could have masked the sound of gunshots." He nodded. "Shooter uses the truck as noise cover, could have tossed the gun in it. Very neat." He was taking notes. "Rich lady—motive could be robbery."

"It was murder?" Lacey pressed.

"That hasn't been determined. She's just dead. I'm just thinking."

"Whoever it was left a fifty-thousand-dollar purse on the seat."

"Excuse me?" His expression left no doubt that he thought Lacey was crazy. He didn't believe for a minute that a handbag could cost as much as a car. "Anything else?"

"Cecily was still a little upset about the break-in."

"The break-in? What break-in?" This guy really wasn't up to speed, Washington crime-wise. Detective Jance put the stress ball away and jotted down a note, but for all Lacey could tell he was writing a grocery list. *More beer for the big game.* "Please continue."

At least he said "please." "There was a burglary at her house a few weeks ago. It was in the papers too." To be fair, it was a three-paragraph brief and it failed to mention football. "But that wasn't what my story was about. I'm not the police reporter. I was there to see her clothes and house and closets and get her personal take on owning such a fabulous collection. The break-in was just a footnote."

The break-in was odd, however. Cecily told her there were only a few things stolen, the most unusual being a one-of-a-kind makeup case, a piece designed by Louis Vuitton for Rita Hayworth in the 1940s. It also featured a hidden compartment for a fabulously expensive pearl necklace that belonged to the movie star. The thief knew exactly what he was looking for. Why only those things, Lacey wondered, when one of Cecily's couture ball gowns alone could cost $100,000 and a couture blouse $10,000, not to mention the array of Hermés bags? Yet none of her clothes had been taken.

The detective jotted down a few more notes. Lacey thought about her meeting with Cecily Ashton. She tried to remember everything Cecily said to her, suitably filtered for this detective. She didn't tell him Cecily wanted to join the class of big-moneyed, tough-minded, pearl-wearing women who directed the society agenda in Washington, D.C., women like *Eye Street Observer* publisher Claudia Darnell. Cecily planned to reenter Washington society, now that she had her big financial settlement. But Lacey thought there was something about Cecily that was too wounded and hesitant to allow her to really become one of them.

Lacey also failed to mention to Detective Jance that she'd taped the interview. The tape was in her desk at the newsroom. Why bother this clueless detective with extraneous details? He obviously had no interest in fashion matters. Or fashion clues. Her stomach growled, and she wondered if she'd ever get to go to lunch. *Are we through now?*

Detective Jance put down his notes. His boy-next-door face was assuming that hardened, skeptical-cop look she knew so well.

"So you knew the deceased. What a coincidence. Why don't you start from the beginning, Ms. Smithsonian?"

Oh, who needs lunch anyway.

chapter 6

It was Claudia's idea. The feature story on Cecily Ashton's wardrobe had been suggested to Lacey by *Eye Street* publisher Claudia Darnell. When Claudia *suggested* a topic, it was a suggestion in the same way Moses brought the "Ten Suggestions" down from the mountain carved in stone. Claudia's suggestions were orders from on high, pleasantly issued and charmingly phrased, but orders nonetheless.

Lacey didn't need any persuading to interview Cecily Ashton. A scandal-plagued socialite with a fabulous house and legendary closets? Plus, it was a great excuse to get out of the office on a winter's day.

Although Lacey was sick and tired of the fashion beat, she would never pass up a chance to view sartorial bounty of such mythic proportions. With some two thousand outfits in Cecily Ashton's capacious closets, the woman could get dressed for nearly two years, averaging three outfits per day, without repeating a look. It was a rarefied art collection, with unique pieces from all over the world, and to view them Lacey had only to travel to the lovely Foxhall Road in extreme Northwest Washington, D.C.

Part of the appeal of the collection was its diversity. Cecily Ashton didn't have a clearly defined style, like Jacqueline Kennedy's, the clean simple lines and geometric shapes of the early 1960s, or Grace Kelly, whose elegant wardrobe, two parts glamour, one part fantasy, one hundred percent class, was fashioned by the best Hollywood designers. Cecily wasn't quite a star, she was more like an ambitious

Hollywood starlet—but with a big star's budget. She wore
whatever her stylist of the moment suggested, and like any
starlet, she had made some fabulous missteps. Like the Versace minidress with far too much cleavage she barely wore
to a formal dinner at the White House. Gossip columnists
quipped that her dress was smaller than her dinner napkin.

In addition to her vast array of tarty modern clothes, Cecily had a knockout collection of vintage Chanel, Christian
Dior, and even, it was rumored, some items by Madame
Grès, "The Sphinx," the famed French designer of the Forties who made magic by draping and pleating her folds of
material. There were Diors and Balmains, ball gowns by Ba-
lenciaga, dresses by Oscar de la Renta, Armani, and Marc
Jacobs.

Hoping to make up some lost ground in Washington society, Cecily was lending a portion of this collection to
Washington's new Bentley Museum of American Fashion.
Some three hundred designer outfits and their accessories
would be on exhibit for six months, beginning the first of
February. After all her public faux pas, Cecily was notoriously skittish with the press, but she and Claudia Darnell
were neighbors and ran in some of the same social circles.
Claudia suggested doing a feature on her collection over
cocktails at some gala or another, and Cecily eagerly agreed.
Ms. Darnell, a master of post-scandal PR, promised to time
the feature to publicize the museum exhibit.

Lacey surmised that in some ways the two women, Darnell and Ashton, were kindred spirits. Claudia Darnell had
once been a spurned Other Woman, the notorious blonde in
a forgotten politician's Capitol Hill sex scandal. She was
publicly shamed and shunned, but she vowed she would be
back. Claudia was smart and tenacious and burning with
ambition, and she wrote a bestselling tell-all book. With
some smart investments she made a lot of money, and she returned to the Capital City in triumph and bought herself a
newspaper. *The media: If you can't beat 'em, buy 'em.* Now
everyone took her calls.

Lacey's interview fit neatly into Cecily's new public rela-
tions strategy. Exhibiting her collection was a coup for the

Fashion Museum, and the interview was a coup for *The Eye.*
Not even the *Washington Post* had snagged a one-on-one in-
terview with the now-elusive Cecily Ashton. But then *The
Post* had made far too much of that notorious Versace
miniskirt fiasco. That was before Lacey had even started at
The Eye, or she might have made the same mistake.

The feature article should be a piece of cake, a guided
tour of the legendary closets, a peek at Ashton Hall, one of
the most fabulous Foxhall mansions, which Cecily had won
in her nasty divorce. Lacey hoped Cecily would dish: About
her famous ex-husband, for example, or her notorious "bottom dance" on the hood of that Washington, D.C., police
cruiser, and possibly her revolving-door, Euro-trash
boyfriends. *Girl talk.*

As Lacey peered into her own tiny dark closet that morning, all she could think about was the incredible luxury of
having a closet the size of her entire apartment. She finally
pulled out her best black wool slacks, her vintage Bentley
jacket, the one with the jeweled button covers, and her black
Ferragamo heels. Nobody expected a reporter to dress well
for an interview, but Lacey liked to show respect for herself
as well as her source. If you can't dress up to see the best
closets in Washington, you might as well stay in bed in your
silk nightgown. It was time to dress up.

But not for "Long-Lens" Hansen, her favorite staff photographer. Hansen wore his usual faded blue jeans and
shabby navy sweater, countless press ID cards on a metal
chain, and at least twenty pounds of cameras and lenses. No
one made Hansen dress up.

At Ashton Hall, the housekeeper swung open the carved
wooden front doors to the immense French country-style
house. She ushered them into a library off the main hall decorated in creamy yellow and pale blue. Lacey was admiring
the Monet over the mantel when Cecily popped in to greet
them warmly.

She was deliberately casual in expensive blue jeans, bare
feet, and an oversized gray cashmere sweater. She wore
minimal makeup, and her luxurious dark hair was left long
and loose. Around her neck she wore a spectacular choker of

freshwater pearls. She was rarely photographed without pearls. In the right light she could pass for years younger than her official thirty-nine. While Lacey and Cecily chatted, tea and tiny sandwiches arrived on a tray. Lacey declined the sandwiches, but took the tea. Hansen wolfed down half a dozen sandwiches and asked for a Coke.

"Only my closest friends have ever seen my closets," Cecily was saying. She turned her dazzling smile on Hansen. "So let's all be friends, shall we?" Hansen glanced at Lacey, eyes wide, as if to say, *Don't leave me alone with her, dude!* Cecily struck her as a woman who instinctively seduced the nearest camera and whoever was behind it, but then most women responded to Hansen's shaggy blond hair and easygoing surfer-boy charm. If Cecily opened up to *The Eye*'s long, tall photographer, Lacey was fine with that—as long as she was around to catch it on tape. Whoever charmed whom, Hansen's photos from that day were unusually warm and intimate.

Lacey and Hansen followed Cecily up the wide central stairway to the second floor's master suite and the connected boudoir. They paused on the landing to admire the view of the wide wooden staircase, the colorful oriental runner, and the grand entry hall to the house.

Cecily stopped for a moment in the hall at a double door with crystal doorknobs. The wood gleamed and the knobs twinkled. She explained that her closets could be entered through either the master bedroom or the long hallway. She had worked with the contractors and architects to achieve the proper look, "elegant, but comfortable, and definitely not stuffy." She turned to smile at them slyly, and then she threw the doors open wide with a flourish. They entered a wonderland, an adult woman's dress-up playground.

Just like my closet, Lacey thought. *Times a million.* Cecily's closets were a luxurious labyrinth, full of couture dresses and designer skirts and pants and hats and bags and shoes and thousands of vintage accessories. The so-called closets were as large as bedrooms, which they were before the renovation. *Closet* was not even the right word, Lacey decided. They were fully furnished dressing rooms that happened to be lined wall to wall and floor to ceiling with fabulous clothes and full-length mirrors.

The first dressing room was casual. Cashmere and silk sweaters neatly folded on shelves took up one entire wall, enough to stock a boutique. It led to another connected room and then another, each dedicated to a season or time of day, each with its own color scheme and theme. Several were reserved for evening wear, sorted by period, by designer, and by the occasion on which the dress or outfit had been worn. Usually only once.

"I don't want people to think I'm crazy," Cecily was saying. "Really, this is an art collection. My personal wearable art collection, with so many wonderful one-of-a-kind pieces. I feel sometimes as if I'm just their curator, not their owner." Lacey was enthralled. Judging from the expression on Hansen's face, he'd stopped listening at the word *crazy*.

The largest dressing room was nearly as large as Lacey's living room. It smelled sweetly of lavender and linen. Cream-colored walls with peach accents behind the mirrors created a flattering backdrop for the clothes. Cecily proudly demonstrated the special lighting system. With a flip of a switch, she could see her chosen outfit in an approximation of bright or cloudy daylight, or various indoor lighting schemes for evening. A floor-to-ceiling three-way mirror filled one corner.

It was exactly the closet Lacey would have herself, she thought, if she were Queen of the Universe. Sadly, when last she checked, she was not. Aside from the many racks of clothes, custom-fitted cabinets, and specialized shelves and drawers to accommodate every manner of accessory, Lacey was dazzled by an enormous crystal chandelier that hung from the ceiling. She had seen one very similar to it in the Russell Senate Office Building, in a hearing presided over by Senator Ted Kennedy. The hearing had been so dull she'd spent part of the afternoon admiring the chandelier, and this could have been its little sister. Light from the Swarovski crystals was reflected in the gold-framed mirrors on every wall. *Angels might change their robes in such a room,* Lacey thought.

In the center of the room, beneath the chandelier, was a soft blue velvet sofa with generous padded seats. It invited you to sit down and breathe in the pure scent of unadulterated luxury. A deep pile cream-colored Chinese rug covered much of the floor, with a border of flowers that picked up the accent colors. Lacey imagined herself luxuriating there to ponder life's most vexing problem: *What will I wear tomorrow?*

An armchair in a white silk striped fabric was angled near it, obviously for one's best friend or stylist to offer expert advice. Lacey found it almost impossible to imagine a man, at least any straight man of her acquaintance, in this setting. Hansen was gaping open-mouthed like a fish out of water.

Cecily perched perfectly at ease on the edge of the sofa and demonstrated the sound system. Speakers were mounted invisibly in the walls behind the clothes racks, and the electronics were hidden behind double-door cabinets. She pressed a button on a remote and Vivaldi's *Four Seasons* began to play softly. She pressed another and a closet within a closet clicked open like a safe. It held Cecily's priceless jewelry collection and her most valuable accessories.

"That's where Rita's makeup case was stored," Cecily said wistfully. Apparently she was on a first-name basis with the late movie star, Ms. Hayworth. Cecily pointed to a recessed shelf inside the inner closet. It had been built to display the famous makeup case Louis Vuitton had made especially for Rita.

"Philip gave me the Vuitton makeup case when we were first married," Cecily said. "I don't know where he found it. He said my smile was like Rita Hayworth's. He was so sweet to me back then. And because Philip thought he looked like the younger Orson Welles and had more money than Prince Aly Khan—those were two of Rita's husbands, you know—he said I deserved something just as special as Rita Hayworth did. It was charming and romantic and silly of him, but it was very sweet. It was such a beautiful thing. Of course, I never thought he looked like Orson Welles."

Hansen whistled. "Must have cost him a bundle."

"I don't know what it cost," Cecily smiled. "A small fortune. Whatever it was, the pearls cost even more."

"The pearls?" Lacey said.

"The pearls Rita Hayworth wore in that famous photograph, you know. The Vuitton case included a hidden compartment made for the pearls. Round natural pearls. Very rare." Cecily fingered the pearls around her throat. "Did you know that Rita's real name was Margarita, which is from the Greek word for pearl? And once she modeled a dress made entirely from pearls. Can you imagine?"

I imagine she couldn't sit down in it. Rita Hayworth was one of Lacey's personal style icons as well. She tried not to let her voice squeak with excitement.

"And where is the makeup case now? Will it be in the Fashion Museum exhibit?"

"Where is it? I wish I knew." Cecily shrugged sadly. "That maniac must've gotten it." Lacey looked confused. "The burglary. I thought you knew. I thought reporters knew *everything.*"

"Sorry," Lacey said. "I'm one of those reporters who doesn't know everything."

"Well, that's a relief!" Cecily described the burglary. Only a few weeks earlier someone had stolen the case and the pearls, and a few other pieces with sentimental value. The security system hadn't stopped the thief. There were no leads and no arrests.

"I know they're only things," she said sadly. "They're insured, but still, I felt violated. I still do. I'm particularly sorry about losing Rita's things. They always reminded me of happier times. Philip was so different then." Cecily picked up an unframed photograph, all that was left on the shelf where the makeup case had lived: an autographed picture of Rita Hayworth, wearing a gold satin dress and a million-dollar smile. And the pearl necklace. Cecily sighed. "This picture is all I have left of his wedding gifts to me."

"The thief took the frame and left the picture?" Lacey asked.

Cecily nodded and handed the photograph to Lacey. It reminded her of the movie star photos her Aunt Mimi had collected. This one was signed boldly across the front, "With Love, Rita Hayworth." Lacey turned the photo over to see if it was dated. It was, in ink: 1942. There was also a small picture scrawled in pencil, almost a doodle. Some kind of exotic creature, perhaps a bird of some kind, with something like bars holding it captive in a cage.

"What an odd little drawing on the back," Lacey said. "A bird in a cage? Do you know if Rita drew this herself?" In 1942, she recalled, the movie star was either still married to her first husband Edward Judson or freshly divorced and about to marry Orson Welles. Lacey knew Rita Hayworth's life story pretty well, but she had too many husbands to keep track of.

"What drawing?" Cecily looked where Lacey pointed. "A bird in a cage? It does look like that. A little." A caged animal might also be an apt metaphor for the wealthy but obviously not very happy Cecily Ashton, Lacey thought. "I never noticed the drawing before. The photo's never been out of the frame. That was a pretty thing too. Antique silver filigree, set with gemstones."

"So whoever broke in thought the frame was valuable enough to steal, but not the photograph?" Lacey asked. "Maybe there are still fingerprints on it. The thief must have handled it when they took it out." *Of course, now my prints are on it too,* Lacey thought. *Brilliant move.* "Don't you think you should show this to the police?"

Cecily took the picture back and held it gently. "The police have already been here and made an ungodly mess of things," she said, gazing at Rita in her pearl necklace. "No, I've lost the other sentimental things, I'll keep this for myself. Just as it is."

Hansen had been working unobtrusively, photographing the rooms and the clothes. Now he snapped Cecily in profile holding the photograph. "Oh, another one, please," she requested. "That one was too sad. With my Rita Hayworth smile this time." Hansen complied and Cecily smiled winningly for the camera.

"Of all the rooms in this house, I'm really most comfortable in here," Cecily told them, lounging on the sofa. "It's a very secure room. I used to sleep in here sometimes, when I was feeling a little—you know, down. After my divorce. Not since the burglary though." She touched a button and steel panels slid silently down in front of the doors. They slid up again at another touch. "No one can get in here. Or so I thought." She smiled sadly. It gave Lacey the creeps.

Hansen took more photographs, but Cecily asked them not to take pictures of the security system or the not-so-impenetrable panels. Lacey looked for another way in or out, but she didn't see one.

"And yet there was a break-in. How was that possible?"

"Supposedly somebody forgot to reset the alarm system codes properly after a power failure or something. But that's ridiculous. I know exactly who did it."

"Who was it?"

"That bastard, Philip. My ex-husband. He knew all the codes. He knew what he wanted. Things he couldn't win in court. Things he knew it would hurt me to lose." Cecily leaned back against the velvet cushions and closed her eyes. "He's the only one who knows about the important things, the sentimental things. Philip."

"Why would he do that?" Hansen said.

"Why does Philip do anything?" She opened her eyes. "Power. Control. Or just to hurt me. He casts evil on everything he touches, including the grass, the trees, the air."

Lacey felt the hair prickle on the back of her neck. "You're accusing Philip Clark Ashton of a burglary." A man who was worth a billion dollars and had very powerful friends.

"Of course. Not him personally, oh no, he doesn't slip in like a cat burglar, not Philip. He hires people. He owns people. Breaking into a security system designed by his own architect? Not a problem. He's behind all of it. All of it." Cecily held her head and sat very still, as if listening to her thoughts.

Lacey never found out what Cecily meant by "all of it." She didn't mention any of that in her feature on Cecily and her lonely labyrinth full of beautiful things. It was the kind of thing people say after a bitter divorce, and Lacey had no corroborating sources, no evidence, just hearsay. She knew her editor Mac would have a stroke if she took on Philip Clark Ashton without a lot more than an ex-wife's accusations.

After a moment's silence, Cecily popped up brightly from the blue velvet sofa and led Lacey and Hansen down the hall into the next room. There were many rooms still to be seen in the guided tour of the closets of Ashton Hall.

"Now here! Oh this is a wonderful room! I love this room, and you must let me show you my Chanels and my Madame Grès . . . ."

Lacey Smithsonian's

FASHION BITES

Pistols at Twenty Paces—or Pearls?

As everyone surely knows by now, diamonds are a girl's best friend. And pearls are her perfect companion, whether you're arguing a case in court, chasing a witness, running a corporation or a country, or dueling at twenty paces.

All across this Capital City of ours, there are Powerful Women In Pearls (PWIPs), past, present, and future, and they're often the ones really running things behind the scenes in this town. How can you spot the PWIP? Look for the pearls, girls. Diamonds may dazzle the eye, but pearls are what really puts your polish on, whether cultured, natural, or even really good fakes (RGF). Even Jackie Kennedy wore RGF, and she was unmistakably a PWIP. Barbara Bush was never seen around Washington without her large signature pearls, and Speaker of the House Nancy Pelosi owns a set of very impressive Tahitian pearls. As you may glimpse from these few examples, pearls are attractive, appropriate, bipartisan—and powerful.

That is the lesson learned by many a savvy style maven in Washington, D.C. (or as stylish as one can be in this town). The PWIP is strong, resourceful, stylish, well groomed, and in charge. She is a publisher, a congressman, a lawyer, an Indian chief. She might be your boss. Someday she might even be president. Do presidents wear pearls? Just wait and see.

The PWIP looks soft and feminine, she wears heels and

hose and classic couture with her strands of pearls, but never doubt that there is an iron fist in that velvet glove. You don't cross these women, because they will thrash you soundly with those ropes of pearls and then sue you for damages.

Her classic clothing is a kind of calling card, as well as a camouflage. It says she is familiar and approachable, even if she isn't. She knows who's in charge here, and it's her. Her heart is not hard, but she has a will of iron. How can you identify the PWIPs around you? Here are a few subtle fashion clues. Feel free to beg, borrow, or steal these tips for your own poised and polished and pearled look. The Powerful Woman in Pearls:

- Does not fool around with fads. Or fishnet. Or sequins.
- Does not dye her hair blue, but she does hide the gray.
- Does not pierce anything but her ears. And your self-confidence.
- Does not tattoo, except the heel of her Manolo on your backside. If she does tattoo herself, you and I will never see it. And it will not say PROPERTY OF SNAKE.
- Does not accept your challenge to duel with pistols at twenty paces—unless she knows she's the better shot. And she is.

So take a fashion cue from Washington's own Powerful Women In Pearls. When you pack your personal arsenal of style, remember this rule: Diamonds are for girls who dazzle, but pearls are for the ladies with the *power*.

chapter 7

Lacey looked up. Detective Jance was staring at her.

"She accused her husband of the burglary?" He whistled and put his pen down. "Philip Clark Ashton? The old football team billionaire?" Detective Jance didn't look pleased.

"Ex-husband." She stared back at him.

An ambulance crawled slowly past the window, gravel crunching under its tires, a sadly appropriate accompaniment to this gray day. Lacey felt a weight settle on her shoulders. "Cecily?"

"Yes, they're taking the body away." He had one last question for her. "And your story, when exactly does it appear in print?"

"In tomorrow's *Eye Street Observer*," she said. "But it won't help you much, it's all about fashion."

Jance swore under his breath.

By the time Lacey exited her interview with the detective, she was starving. She felt as if she'd been trapped in that room for hours. She checked her watch: half an hour. *Impossible*.

Most of the PI students were still there, milling around. Lacey's interview had taken the longest; most had been over in five minutes or less. They were free to go, but no one seemed to know if their instructor would hold the afternoon class session or not. Willow Raynor and Snake Goldstein were gone. Kepelov was nowhere to be seen. Bud Hunt had made another pot of coffee and was parceling out the remaining doughnuts in lieu of lunch.

Detective Jance called Hunt back into the office and left

the remaining students to their own devices. The caffeine and sugar kept everyone chattering. The ex-cops and ex-military guys all seemed to be buddies now, arguing about sports, women, cars. Edwina Plimpton poured herself another cup of coffee and brought one for Lacey.

"I can't believe this is happening." Edwina's eye makeup was starting to run. When she made her bridge club bet she hadn't bargained for a brush with death. But she'd have something new to talk about over cocktails.

"You knew her pretty well?" Lacey asked.

"Yes, but we'd lost touch."

"Why is that?" Lacey asked, although she suspected she knew the answer.

"Lacey, no one wants to be on the bad side of Philip. Socially. Business. Politics and all that. But no one deserves to die like this, in some dirty little parking lot. She must have been miserable."

Lacey sipped her coffee and wondered if Cecily could really have killed herself.

"This is all so horrible." Edwina warmed her hands on her coffee cup. "I called my husband. He's meeting me for lunch, if we ever get out of here. Or cocktails. And is that young detective cute or what? He certainly kept *you* in there for a long time!"

Lacey had no doubt Edwina's bridge club would get an earful. Her adventures in private eye school would certainly beat her scuba-diving bridge buddy. Her rival would need a close encounter with Moby Dick and the ghost of Jacques Cousteau to top Edwina now.

"Smithsonian, we need to debrief." Damon Newhouse butted right in, as usual.

"No, we don't."

"We have to get our stories straight." Newhouse pulled his BlackBerry from his black leather jacket.

"My story is straight." Lacey gave him The Eyebrow. "Why, are you a suspect? Call your lawyer. Say hi for me."

"We could all be suspects. You, me, all of us." He seemed excited about this, no doubt planning a first-person exposé on his brutal interrogation as a murder suspect.

"Damon, when she died we were all sitting in class watching Kepelov do his spy shtick. We make lousy suspects. Do you really think you need a lawyer?"

"Hadley makes it a seventy-thirty probability the government did it," Damon said. "I call it ninety-ten. So to make the investigation look good, the government will be hauling in innocent people and calling them suspects. Like us."

"She was murdered, you know." Martin Hadley was suddenly next to them. His lips were a tight line. "She was one of us."

"One of you?" Lacey put her coffee down. "One of who?"

"One of the tortured," Hadley said. "One of the damned."

"Cecily Ashton was a victim of mind control? Your 'psychotic terror'?"

"Psycho*tropic*. They got to her." Hadley stared off into the gray January sky. "They killed her. Whether they pulled the trigger, or made her do it herself, they killed her."

Cecily Ashton heard voices in her head that told her to kill herself? Lacey tried to make this image fit the Cecily she'd met. It seemed ridiculous. What kind of game was Hadley playing? Was he trying to use Damon Newhouse to spread this wild conspiracy theory? Damon was certainly willing to be used.

People like Cecily Ashton didn't fit Lacey's image of people involved in crazy fringe groups. Cecily's group was the Washington high society she craved. It was like saying the ritziest neighborhoods in Georgetown had been invaded by big-eyed aliens beamed down from the mother ship. But then, people like Cecily didn't fit the image of a woman dying by a gunshot in her own Jaguar in some random parking lot.

"You're saying the government did this?" Edwina said. "What on earth are you talking about?" Edwina was not the type to browse Conspiracy Clearinghouse at DeadFed dot com. *Poor deprived woman.* Lacey envied her innocence. "Do you mean Congress? Because we have a neighbor who's a congressman and he's the most harmless little—"

"A secret rogue agency within the government with far-reaching powers to invade our privacy and infringe our rights," Damon said blithely. "Like MK-Ultra, Majestic-Twelve, Area Fifty-One, men in black. You know."

Edwina clearly did not know, but she said nothing. Kepelov had reappeared among them, wearing a faux fur–lined jean jacket and his big black cowboy hat. He seemed very calm. He slipped silently to Lacey's side.

"The dead body, the suspicious circumstances. This is always where Lacey Smithsonian comes in, isn't it?"

"Suspicious circumstances?" She glared at the big smug Russian. "Isn't that your specialty, Kepelov? You're the most suspicious character here. Where were you when Cecily Ashton was shot? And what *are* you calling yourself these days?"

"Call me Greg." He smiled. "Interesting, this mind control. Don't you think?"

"Interesting, but impossible." Lacey crossed her arms and hugged her shawl tighter. "I presume you do have an alibi. So, what is it?"

"Excellent alibi, Smithsonian." Kepelov's blue eyes twinkled. "Visiting old friends at the police station across the street before class. They let me park there. Go ask for yourself. Tell them Greg sent you."

"If you were really KGB," Hadley said, "then you know mind control is possible, don't you?"

"Many things are possible," the ex-spy said cagily. "Smithsonian, you do not believe in mind control? Ha! You never see *Manchurian Candidate*? Soviet Union was heavily involved in mind control experiments. Drugs, sensory deprivation, electromagnetic, psychics, many different tactics. KGB, full-service spy shop. Successful?" He shrugged. "Depends who you ask. Still going on? Depends who you ask."

Hadley smiled. "That's more than I could get the U.S. government to admit to."

"But did the Soviets figure out how to do it?" Lacey smirked at Kepelov. "And if you did, why didn't you save the Soviet Union with your mind control rays? Tell me that!"

"Who knows? Maybe budget problems. Lack of rubles. Not my department. Another time and place. Evil Empire is history now, right?" He had the nerve to find her amusing. "But I am not so evil, Smithsonian."

"Jury's still out on that. And I still think mind control is science fiction."

"Let's continue this debate at lunch," Damon suggested.

Hadley recommended a nearby Mexican restaurant, where he said he found the voices harder to hear. "Let's go."

Lacey thought of the one thing that could distract Newhouse. "What does Brooke think of it?"

"Brooke?" His eyes widened. "Oh my God, I haven't had a chance to talk with her. She should be back from her run by now." He tapped on his BlackBerry to call his girlfriend and brief her, or "debrief" her, whatever he might mean by that. "Thanks for reminding me, Lacey. You might need a lawyer too, you know. I'm serious."

Lacey reached for her own phone and moved out of earshot. She had her own much-delayed call to make to her newspaper. The weekend editor, Shirley, hadn't heard a thing about the violent demise of Cecily Ashton. But she found the news "energizing" and promised to call Mac Jones at home for her. It would be too late to change Lacey's feature story to reflect Cecily's death. The Sunday supplement was already in print. But she assured Lacey a link directing readers to her article would be boxed on the front page of tomorrow's edition.

To Lacey's dismay, Shirley assigned the story to Kelly Kavanaugh, the newest addition to the police beat, who had drawn newsroom duty that weekend. Kavanaugh was equal parts freckles and enthusiasm, but light on experience. Kavanaugh called Lacey back immediately.

"Are you sure you can't tell me whether it's suicide or murder? Come on, you saw the body, right?"

"Kelly, I'm not a medical examiner. I saw her through a car window."

"Can you at least take a guess? Please?"

"Don't beg," Lacey said. "Reporters never beg. Borrow and steal, yes, but never beg."

"What was Ashton doing in that parking lot all the way out there? Does this have anything to do with your story? It must, right? And what were *you* doing in that parking lot? Are you working on another story? You can tell me, I'm the police reporter on this, so we could double-team whatever you're—"

"Give me a break, Kavanaugh," Lacey said. "I'm on personal business here."

"Do you at least think it's one of those crazy Crime of Fashion things you keep getting mixed up in? And by the way, do you need any help on the style beat? Your stories tend to be pretty freaky, except for all the fashion stuff, that would be boring, but wow, some of the stories you've landed, I'd do anything to—"

"See you around, Kelly." Kavanaugh in her collegiate khakis and cross-trainers and contagious perkiness would be a definite *don't* on Lacey's fashion beat. Lacey hung up and turned off her cell phone.

Hunt returned from his second interview with the police, ashen-faced and sweating. He summoned up some scraps of bravado. "Go home, everybody, or go to lunch. No more class today. If y'all paid attention out there, you got a lesson in what a crime scene investigation looks like up close. Next class is Monday night at seven sharp. If you're not up for it, you can drop the course right now. Full refund due to unusual circumstances." He looked around the room, from face to face. "Any takers?"

Did he want them all to drop out and let him off the hook, so he could cancel the course? Lacey wondered. *No such luck.* No hands went up. The ex-cops and ex-military guys all grunted or nodded. They would be there. Edwina Plimpton took his words as a personal challenge. She too gave Hunt a brave thumbs-up.

"Well, great." Hunt mopped his forehead with a red handkerchief. "That's just swell. I'll see y'all Monday night. What about you, Ms. Fashion Clue?"

"I wouldn't miss it for the world," Lacey said.

He looked at Damon Newhouse with a hopeful expression.

"Are you kidding? Me too. Unless we're all in jail," Damon said, BlackBerry in hand. He was keying in a text message as he spoke.

Hunt turned to Martin Hadley, the only student who, so far, had said nothing.

"I'll be here," Hadley said. "Unless I'm the next victim on their damn list."

chapter 8

The Farmers' Market was closed by the time Lacey eased her car out of the parking lot and onto Little Falls Street. Not a trace was left of the colorful tents and tables. Lacey was happy to be away from the yellow crime-scene tape and the noise of her fellow students, but her plan to shop for lunch at the Farmers' Market evaporated.

At least she felt safe and secure in her little green BMW, the car Vic had restored and given her for Christmas. It was a joy to drive, and she was beginning to like it even more than her beloved (but sadly stolen) Nissan 280ZX. Vic had thoughtfully updated the 1974 vintage model 2002tii with an excellent CD player and a GPS navigation unit. Lacey slipped in an Aimee Mann CD and turned up the volume on one of Aimee's quirky laments.

Sean Victor Donovan was giving a paper on "Managing the Business of Corporate Intelligence" at a PI conference in Santa Barbara, California. It sounded like a pretty cushy gig to her. He and his dad were partners in a private security company with government contracts and high profile clients, including the Department of Homeland Security. Vic said giving his paper would raise his profile in certain circles. And it would bore him to tears to be there without her, he told her. She was glad she had the PI class to keep her busy and not pining for her handsome six-foot man with his devastating green eyes. Of course, that was before she saw Cecily's body in the Jaguar. She wondered what Vic would make of this mess.

Lacey drove him to the airport the previous evening in the BMW. She kissed him hard before she let him get out of the car. He rewarded her with that smile that had such power over her. She wanted to lasso him and convince him not to go, to stay home with her. *He must never know that,* she told herself. Besides, she had things to accomplish.

"Tomorrow is the first day of school, sweetheart," Vic said when he kissed her good-bye. He had warned her it wouldn't be what she expected. He said it would be *boring.* "You really think you're going to learn all my secrets taking this class?"

"One way or another." She smiled at him. "I'll learn them all eventually."

"I was afraid of that." He laughed and stroked her cheek. "You might find out how crazy I am for you. Have a good time, sweetheart, and don't go looking for trouble."

"I never go looking for trouble, Vic. You know that."

"I know. It comes looking for you." He put his plane ticket in his jacket pocket.

"You think you know everything."

"I know this class will bore you senseless. It's not all cops and robbers, it's procedures and laws and regulations and knowing the Constitution backward and forward, and how Virginia, like every other state, tinkers with the law every year to make our job a little more difficult. It's a litany of everything you *can't* do as a PI. Doesn't that sound like fun?"

"Fun enough."

So far her PI class definitely wasn't boring, Lacey thought. But *fun* wasn't exactly the right word either.

The midafternoon sky was a dispiriting shade of gray. It made the world seem flat and shadowless, neither night nor day. Her stomach, however, told her it was well past time to eat. She spotted a little Thai restaurant a few blocks down Broad Street.

The restaurant was nearly empty and the waitress seemed happy to greet her. Lacey ordered the tom yum something-or-other, a spring roll, and a pot of tea, and leaned back in her quiet booth to admire the shelves lined with colored crystal vases. Her cell phone rang: Vic. *Let's see how far I*

*can get without telling him about the dead woman in the
Jaguar.*

"Hey, sweetheart, I thought I'd catch you on a break."
Lacey closed her eyes to shut out everything but the sound
of his voice. It was like hot buttered rum for her tattered
soul. Better than hot buttered rum. "So how's your PI class
going?" Vic asked. "Are you at lunch? Is it as boring as I
promised you it would be?"

The shooting in the parking lot seemed to Lacey like the
wrong place to start.

"Well, it's a little difficult to say," she said. "But it hasn't
been boring. The very opposite of boring."

"Bud Hunt's a character, isn't he? That sign still on the
door, the 'no loaded weapons in class' thing?"

"Sign's still there," she said.

Vic sensed something in her hesitation. "Hey, what's
wrong, sweetheart? Did you drop out already?" He chuckled. "Did somebody get shot?"

"Well, I didn't drop out."

"Lacey, are you saying—" He sucked in some air. "You
aren't telling me—someone *did* get shot?"

"'Fraid so." It was Lacey's turn to take a deep breath.
"Cecily Ashton. The woman I interviewed last week. Shot.
Dead. In her Jaguar. Not my fault, Vic, I swear."

"Shot dead? The crazy woman with the closets who was
married to that old sports guy, what's his name, Philip Clark
Ashton?"

"Yes." She waited.

"I hate to ask this, Lacey." She could hear exasperation in
his voice. "I'm three thousand miles away, darling, and you
know I trust your instincts. I do. But I'm confused. How
does this have anything to do with you, or your PI class?
You're supposed to be learning the deadly dull rules and regulations of private investigation, not getting involved in
some random shooting—"

"Cecily Ashton was found dead in the parking lot behind
Hunt's office today, just as we broke for lunch. With a bullet hole in her head. Some other people found her. I came in
later, after all the screaming."

Vic paused. "I'm so sorry you had to see that. Awful. Falls Church?"

Lacey suspected she knew exactly what Vic was thinking. Something like, *Oh my God, what is it with my girlfriend and dead bodies?* She also knew Vic was now wise enough not to say this, at least not to her face.

"Gunshot? Inside her car? What do they think? Suicide or murder?"

The waitress arrived with Lacey's pot of tea and her platter of chicken and noodles and scooted away. The tom yum whatever-it-was smelled delicious.

"The cops didn't say," she told Vic, "but we didn't see a gun."

"Cops. You were questioned then? You gave a statement?"

"Darling, it's that fine insight you have into police procedure that makes me so hot for you." She heard Vic chuckle over the miles between them. "Yeah, I got the second or third degree. A Detective Jance, Tom Jance."

"Don't know him. Lacey—" Vic fell silent.

"What is it?" Lacey asked. "What are you thinking?"

"I'm thinking this will be pretty rough on Bud Hunt. How long did they question him?"

"I don't know. They talked to him a couple of times. He sent us all home early. Offered us refunds. He seemed rattled, but anybody would be. And why would Hunt be taking this so hard, other than it looks bad, having a shooting right in your parking lot? Bad for business?"

"No, because they had a thing, a few months back. A fling. The Ashton woman and Hunt. Big mistake."

Lacey's mouth dropped open. "Cecily Ashton and Bud Hunt? No way! You can't be serious!" Lacey was getting a headache and her lunch was getting cold. "I don't believe it. No way, he's not fling material. Not for *her.* Vic Donovan, tell me everything! What, where, when, why. Even how. I want everything you know."

"Gee, you sound like a reporter."

"Off the record, for now."

He thought for a moment. "I'm not breaking any confidences here, it wasn't much of a secret. Everyone noticed

Bud started going to a lot of football games. Box seats. People saw them together. Also she was a client of his, something to do with her divorce settlement. Probably she needed someone to dig for the ex-husband's hidden assets. And maybe she needed to dig up some dirt on the ex, to tilt the settlement in her direction. Divorce can be nasty work."

"But a fling? With Bud Hunt?"

"It happens," Vic said. "A mystery of the universe."

Lacey snorted. Hunt was just a beefy ex-cop with war stories to tell. Cecily Ashton was rich and beautiful, if a little damaged.

"I don't get it, Vic. He's a frog and she's a princess. Princesses don't kiss frogs. Not unless they're incredibly rich frogs. Like Philip Clark Ashton."

"Lacey darling, no man ever believes he's a frog."

"I suppose not." There was a kind of desperation about Cecily, Lacey remembered. If she were very afraid of something or someone, maybe it made sense for her to latch on to the big ex-cop, a tough-talking guy who could handle a gun. And who would feel pretty damn lucky to be with her.

"Hunt was a cop, he knows this game," Vic said. "The police will be all over him. He'll lawyer up. Standard operating procedure."

"But maybe it really was suicide. Why would he kill her? And he'd be crazy to kill her behind his own building, right?" Lacey dug into her chicken. Not bad, but it needed soy sauce. She waved to the waitress.

"I wouldn't figure Hunt for a killer, but people do strange things when love and sex and money are involved. They had a personal connection. Suicide or murder, either way she's dead. On her ex-lover's doorstep? Looks bad. Looks bad for Hunt."

Lacey wondered how many PI students would really go back to class on Monday. "You don't think he'll cancel the course, do you?"

"He might have to, if the cops lean on him hard. Might be the best thing," Vic said. "I hope he doesn't cowboy it out alone and try to solve it."

"Ah, because private investigation is even tougher when it's personal?" she asked.

"Yeah, you must have been listening in class."

"I listen a lot." Lacey sipped some tea. "You're not gonna quote that 'murder magnet' thing again, are you?"

"You? A magnet for murder? No, I think you're more like duct tape for trouble, Lacey. It just sticks to you. Like I do. I wish I were stuck to your sweet side right now, so I could keep you out of trouble."

Lacey wished that too, a lot. Trouble seemed to follow her now and then, and the question of self-defense sometimes arose. She used whatever was at hand, hairspray, scissors, shampoo, or her mother with a golf club. But what if she really needed a gun?

"Maybe I should get a concealed carry permit," she said. She wasn't quite sure if she was testing Vic or not. She was conflicted about the idea, but this seemed like the right time to bring it up. "Since I seem to be 'duct tape for trouble,' as you say, and you never seem to be around when I need you, I better learn how to defend myself."

"You seem to do pretty good for yourself. But—"

"And a concealed carry permit would look nice next to my PI registration, wouldn't it?"

"And a shoulder holster under your vintage Bentley suit?" Vic laughed. He'd taken her shooting at the pistol range once, months ago. She'd surprised them both by being a pretty good shot. "Wait till I get home, darling. We'll go back to the range, you'll get qualified, do the paperwork. Go to class and stay out of trouble, and I'll be back in a few days, okay?"

Vic had to say something soothing to calm his own nerves, she realized. He needed to have a plan. He wanted to take care of her. *Silly, adorable man.*

"It's sweet of you to care," she said, knowing she was trying to say much more than that. Vic just laughed. He had to go. They signed off with *I love you.*

Lacey smiled and closed her eyes again, the better to visualize Vic in all of his muscular, masculine, curly-haired, green-eyed glory. She realized she'd forgotten to tell him so many things. And she had neglected to tell Vic she had a date to go shooting at the pistol range that very night. Without him.

chapter 9

"What is *she* doing here?" Brooke Barton hissed at Lacey while pulling her nine millimeter Glock pistol from her black leather range bag and racking the slide. An irate Brooke nailed Lacey with her best inquisitorial attorney's glare, while managing at the same time to look wounded.

It was a nice trick, but Lacey wasn't buying it. She had her own bone to pick with Brooke, a not-so-funny bone named Damon Newhouse. They'd met at the range as planned, but they hadn't had a chance yet to "discuss" why Brooke had let her boyfriend Damon trail Lacey to her PI class like a bad puppy. They hadn't mentioned the Cecily Ashton shooting either. Lacey assumed Brooke knew everything Damon knew. However, she wasn't eager to open up that subject, and Brooke would hardly talk about it in front of the third member of their party.

"Well?" Brooke inquired testily. "I thought this was *our* night at the range! But no, *she* has to tag along—"

The "she" in question was Lacey's friend and stylist, Stella Lake. Stella had breezed in swathed in a huge hat and coat, waved hello, and immediately disappeared to the ladies' room, to "freshen her makeup," she said. Just one more thing for Brooke to be annoyed at Stella about: Wasting range time fixing her face *before* they started shooting.

"I *might* have mentioned we were going to the range, just in passing," Lacey replied. "And Stella just *might* have invited herself. You know Stella." She decided to let Brooke's little snit blow over before she tackled the Damon issue. She accepted the stainless steel .357 Magnum revolver Brooke offered her.

"I do know Stella. And pistol shooting at the range comes up all the time in your everyday hair salon conversation, right?" Brooke fumed. "You just said one day, Hi Stella, I need a shampoo, cut, blow-dry, and a box of those cute little nine-millimeter hollow points! You know, the ones that look like little lipstick tubes? Say, you wanna come shooting with us and drive Brooke nuts?"

"It was exactly like that," Lacey agreed. They were waiting in the locker room for Stella to reemerge. They heard the muted pops of gunfire from behind the indoor range's soundproof doors. Lacey also heard Vic's voice in her head, repeating Rule Number One of gun safety: "Assume all guns are always loaded." She opened the cylinder of her borrowed Smith & Wesson to check the chambers: clean and empty.

"Exactly the same way you apparently said to Damon, Private eye school won't be hard enough for Lacey, just being the Girl Reporter stuck in that testosterone shark tank! So Damon honey, why don't you tag along and make fun of her, bug the hell out of her, just for kicks?"

"I know Damon gets very—enthusiastic. I shouldn't have let it slip. I think taking the PI class is a terrific idea for you, Lacey. He does too. He's just so awestruck by you."

"Sure he is. Just be nice to Stella," Lacey said. "Please? This is silly. You two are my best friends. I don't know what that says about me, but you are. The way you needle each other, it's like we're all still in seventh grade or something." Brooke sighed. The weapon felt heavy in Lacey's hand.

The Pine Ridge Arsenal shooting range was tucked into a warehouse complex off Route 50 in Fairfax County. In the front of the building they sold guns, ammo, and shooting supplies. Behind the gun shop, soundproof doors led to the range. The pungent smell of gunpowder drifted out every time someone opened the doors, and it whetted their appetites for shooting.

Visiting the range seemed like a great idea when Lacey and Brooke made their plans days ago. Even Stella climbing aboard sounded like fun, a high-adrenaline girls' night out without their guys. But after seeing Cecily Ashton in the parking lot with the gunshot wound, Lacey wasn't so sure.

Brooke pulled out a third gun, one for Stella. It was Brooke's favorite .22 caliber target revolver, a Smith & Wesson K-22 Masterpiece.

"I'm sorry you're upset about Damon," she said. "I'll talk to him."

"And this is just one night with Stella. Please give her a break. She really is excited to be here with us."

"Right. I've seen what she can do with hair. I can only imagine what havoc she can wreak with a deadly weapon."

"Hey, I'll have sixty-some hours of Damon snarking at me in class. Not to mention the conspiracy of the month— mind control."

"I'm jealous." Brooke flicked open the cylinder of the .22. "You'll see more of Damon than I will for the next two weeks."

You can have him, Lacey thought. "You appreciate him more." She bit her tongue.

"You don't understand how much he looks up to you. Damon thinks you're the best reporter in Washington." She looked down the hall. "What on earth is Stella *doing* in there, taking a bath?"

Lacey laughed. She had opted for comfort with a little style in her most comfortable faded blue jeans, old cowboy boots, and a black turtleneck sweater. She'd pulled her hair off her face into a chignon so it wouldn't get in her way.

Dressed for the range with her blond hair flying out of her long braid, Brooke looked more like a one-woman shooting safari than an up-and-coming young Washington lawyer. She wore khakis tucked into her boots, and the many-pocketed khaki shooting vest over her black cotton shirt was stuffed full of ammo and essentials: BlackBerry, iPod, Leatherman multitool, Ray-Ban shooting glasses. Her hearing protectors were looped casually around her neck, and she had earmuffs for Lacey and Stella too.

"I'm serious, Lace. I don't know if Stella's up to this. Tonight is serious business. Tonight is about self-defense and self-empowerment. And guns."

The ladies' room door flung open and Stella pranced into the room as if she were leading a conga line. The last time Lacey got a good look at her stylist was the previous week. Something had come over her since then. Stella twirled and struck a pose.

"Stella! What have you done with yourself?"

Brooke stared, the corners of her mouth twitching. "That's not what just anyone would wear to go shooting, Stella. More like what *no one* would wear. But I always expect the unexpected from you."

Stella grinned. Lacey had watched Stella's hair careen through a moody rainbow of dark dramatic colors, red, magenta, chestnut, purple, black. It had been gelled into spikes, glued into faux-hawks, pushed this way and that, and recently dyed jet black and sleeked back like a Roaring Twenties screen siren. Stella had grown her hair out several inches from the near-buzz cut Lacey had first seen her wearing, but there had always been some stylistic consistency to her look: the punky spikes, the colors du jour, the eye-popping satin bustiers and leather corsets, the dragon-lady red fingernails with attitude to match. "Punk Goddess with a Heart of Gold," Stella had once captioned her own look, and Lacey could only add, "On acid." But none of that prepared Lacey and Brooke for "Gidget Goes to the Gun Range."

Stella was now a blonde. Not just any blonde, she was a bubbly blonde with a retro-space-age 1950s vibe, a perky short Doris Day bob and a pink headband. Gidget would have died for Stella's pistachio green capri pants, bubblegum pink sky-high stilettos, and matching pink nails. Her shocking pink cardigan sweater was tight and curvy and revealed Stella's trademark cleavage. Without that peek, or more than a peek, of the photogenic assets she called "The Girls," no one would have believed it was Stella. Lacey wasn't sure she believed it anyway.

"So, what do you think?" The vision in pink and green did a spin and shook her blond bob. "Totally hot, right?"

"Don't ask me, Stella." Brooke shot Lacey a pleading look. "Please don't. I mean it. Besides, I'm not the fashion expert here."

My friend the attorney, Lacey thought, *leaving no buck unpassed.*

Stella adjusted her pink headband over her new blond locks and fluffed her bangs, brushing them out of her long black lashes. "I like your outfit too, Brooke. You're like Safari Girl, right, out hunting wildebeests or something?"

"Or something."

"Well, don't keep me waiting, girls," Stella prompted. "We have wildebeests to shoot! So what do you think, Lace? You like it?"

"I don't know what to say, Stella." Lacey wondered if it was a good idea to mix this fashion show with gunpowder. "It's . . . different."

"Isn't it? It's a whole different Stella. You're speechless, right? That's okay, I'll fill you in." Stella spun around again. "I am totally channeling that Swinging Sixties thing, like Twiggy or Jackie O. Way before our time, I know, but a totally timeless look. Only, you know"—she indicated her bountiful chest—"with boobs."

"Like Sandra Dee without the surfboard," Lacey offered. "Or Judy Jetson without the—" She stopped. *Without what? Without the good taste of a cartoon character?*

"Yeah, Sandra Dee! Gidget Gone Wild! That's good, I like that, 'cause Sandra Dee was really stacked in that Sixties beach blanket bimbo kind of way, wasn't she? And I'm thinking now I need another new outfit too, one of those classic dresses you always write about, Lace."

"A little black dress?"

"Yeah, totally, for cocktails. A little black dress, like Audrey Hepburn, only with boobs. Simple, elegant, classic. That's me."

"The little black dress," Lacey said, "is a simple concept, but it's not so simple to find the right one. Especially with your . . . you know."

"Boobs. We'll go shopping then, the three of us. It'll be fun! You know, sometimes I look in a mirror in this outfit and I don't know who the heck that chick is. But she rocks, and I gotta tell ya, Nigel thinks I'm totally hot in this look."

"Nigel? Nigel who?" Lacey handed her revolver back to Brooke and stared at Stella, the born-again bubbly blonde. Brooke checked the guns and slipped them back in her range bag. "Not Nigel Griffin! Not that Brit twit nitwit again, Stella. Please tell me this is some other Nigel."

"There is only one Nigel Griffin, Lacey. My Nigel. We are an item again! Didn't you know?" Stella scooted in between Lacey and Brooke and took their arms. "Me and Nigel, sittin' in a tree, K-I-S-S—"

"Stop that rhyming!" Brooke commanded. "It's bad luck."

"Hold on, Stella," Lacey said. "That was over last fall. After New Orleans."

"It was. But that was totally a misunderstanding. We are together forever."

"How long is forever on your planet?" Brooke asked. Stella stuck her tongue out.

"Oh, Stella. Not Nigel!" *Stella, once again under the influence of that toxic English import known as Nigel Griffin?* Women considered Griffin handsome, Lacey knew, in his pale English way, and he could exude a certain pale English charm, but she thought there was absolutely no character to the man. "He's a thief. And a liar."

"He used to be a thief, and I wouldn't say 'liar' exactly. He might exaggerate a little, but don't we all? Even me, and I am an open book."

"I hope you're not changing your look just for that weasel Griffin," Lacey said. "I mean, not that I don't like the new look, Stel, but really, for Nigel?"

"I have to agree with Lacey," Brooke said. "I met him before you ever did. When the going got tough, Nigel got himself gone. Very gone."

"He's changed," Stella protested. "Nigel is sensitive. He's a lover, not a fighter. I been with fighters, Brooke, and believe me, lovers are way better. I think he's very hot, and he's got that cool English accent going on. Besides, I would never change who I am inside for some guy, you know that, Lace. The Girls and I are still the same. I just wanna know: Do blondes really have more fun?" She gave Brooke's blond braid a yank.

"Ow! Only if you're a real blonde," the real blonde replied huffily. "Are we going to shoot, or are we going to stand around talking about clothes and boys all night like a bunch of teenagers?"

A couple of guys in blue jeans and tight blue T-shirts entered the locker room from the range. With their precision buzz cuts and combat-ready gear, Lacey pegged them as serious shooters, probably cops or military. They stopped at the soda machine. One dug in his pocket for change while his eyes took in Stella's curves. Stella grinned.

"Gee, it's getting a little hot in here, isn't it, girls?"

"Really?" Lacey said. "My nose is cold."

"I don't mean *you* girls!" Stella wiggled her pink cardigan open to reveal an eye-popping pink and green bustier and a shiny jeweled skeleton key dangling provocatively in her décolletage. The boys in blue grinned at Stella and tipped their caps as they left.

"And here I was afraid you'd changed, Stel," Lacey deadpanned.

"If only. Let's go shoot." Brooke was not amused. She shouldered the range bag with the guns and ammo and targets. Stella nestled her dangling gold key back in between The Girls.

"Pretty key, Stella," Lacey said. "Story there?"

"This old thing? Just an antique pendant. Nigel gave it to me."

"Move." Brooke ordered them down the short hallway to the range.

"We started off last fall pretty hot and heavy, you know, me and Nigel, in New Orleans. Then we kind of fell apart. But he came back, bearing gifts." Stella showed Lacey the rubies that decorated the ornate fluted bow of the key. "He is an ace purloined jewel retriever, as you know."

"He's an ace con man," Lacey replied. Nigel Griffin worked as an investigator for big insurance companies. The title "jewel retriever" was his attempt to give himself an aura of respectability.

"Are we gonna shoot or chat, ladies?" Brooke was running out of patience.

Stella paid no attention. "Nigel calls it the key to his heart, Lace. Is that romantic or what?"

"A key isn't a ring, and Nigel is not known for his fidelity," Lacey said. "And what do you really know about him anyway? Vic says he's a complete and total—"

"I know I'm crazy about him!" Stella grabbed Lacey's arm. "Nigel found this key in a little antique shop somewhere. He says it symbolizes how he's never given his heart to anyone but me. It's solid gold, you know."

"Gold plated," Brooke sniffed. She handed out eye and hearing protection at the heavy soundproof door to the shooting range. "Do you two even remember what we're doing here?"

"Course we do, we're going shooting!" Stella hugged Brooke and pointed her finger at Lacey. "Bang bang! Look at me, Annie Freakin' Oakley!" Brooke and Lacey exchanged a look. "I am so excited about tonight! I cannot believe the three of us haven't done this before. Girls' night out, with guns and ammo. And just look at us, ladies: armed and glamorous!"

chapter 10

"Armed and glamorous," Brooke said sarcastically. "That's us, all right. Stella, we are here to learn gun safety and some basic shooting skills. And maybe blow off a little steam. You've never fired a gun before, correct?"

"Oh, like, how hard can it possibly be?" Stella shrugged. "Point and squirt, right?"

"Why don't we go find out?" Brooke challenged her.

"Hey, you guys, lighten up," Lacey said. "This is supposed to be a fun evening."

"I can't wait to get my hands on a gun—any gun!" Stella declared. "The bigger the better, Brookie. Like a forty-five, or a fifty-five, or something." *"Gidget Goes Gun Crazy."* Lacey sent her a warning look. "What? Come on, let's go shoot something!"

Brooke and Lacey both donned their protective gear. Brooke handed Stella a pair of safety glasses and earplugs and earmuffs to go over her ears.

"You're kidding me, right?" Stella gasped. "We gotta look like dorks? They don't wear this stuff on TV!"

"Safety dorks get to pull the trigger and keep their hearing," Brooke said, clamping earmuffs on Stella's blond bob and sliding a pair of clear shatterproof plastic safety glasses on her face. Lacey pointed to a sign: NO ADMISSION TO RANGE WITHOUT EYE AND EAR PROTECTION.

"All right, all right, we'll be safety dorks together." Brooke helped Stella lift the earmuffs and stuff the soft plugs in her ears. Stella grimaced. "I bet I look like Adam

Ant." She realized they were all wearing their earmuffs now. "I SAID I MUST LOOK LIKE—"

"I can hear you!" Lacey adjusted her own safety glasses. "You're just muffled."

Brooke opened the door and led them to their lane in the middle of the busy range. She plopped her range bag on the floor at their shooting station. The narrow firing lanes were separated by carpeted partitions, and each station was a small open booth with a counter and a motorized line overhead to carry the target downrange. The staccato rhythm of target shooting filled the charcoal gray room. It was loud, even through the earmuffs, but not painful. The air was rich with the smell of gunpowder, and the floor was carpeted with brass cartridge cases.

The lane was cozy for two, snug for three. Lacey watched over Brooke's shoulder. Brooke pulled out the Smith & Wesson .22 revolver and showed Stella how to open the cylinder and check to see whether it was loaded. Stella reached for the gun. Brooke pulled it back.

"Okay, okay, I get it," Stella yelled, earmuff to earmuff with Brooke. "Let's shoot. But I want a bigger gun than a twenty-two. Like a real Dirty Harry gun."

"Your first shooting lesson is crucial," Brooke said over the sound of muffled gunfire. "Safety rules first, then shooting skills. We start with this gun, or we go home." She held it out of Stella's reach. "Safety first. You with me?"

They sized each other up. Stella nodded. "Absolutely."

"First rule: Assume all guns are always loaded. So always check, every time you pick up every gun, even a gun you unloaded yourself two seconds ago. Second rule: Never point a gun at anything you don't intend to destroy. Never."

"Duh! Even I know that." Stella's pink fingernails were itching for the trigger.

"This is a twenty-two-caliber revolver," Brooke said sternly. "You can kill someone with this. I would be handing you a cap gun if I could."

"You think I'm an idiot, don't you?"

"No. Honestly, I don't, Stella. You're a beginner. Are you ready to listen and learn?"

"That's why I'm here. My dad had guns, on account of he was a cop," Stella explained. "But my mom used to hide them from him, on account of he was a drunken bastard. So I've been around guns, but I never actually had my hands on a gun. I'm just—you know. Excited, I guess. I'll be good, I promise. Can we go on? Please?"

Brooke relented and ran through the rest of her gun safety lecture. She watched as Stella opened the gun, checked the chambers, and loaded and unloaded the weapon until she had it down. Brooke was a good teacher, and Stella proved to be a quick study. Lacey was impressed.

Brooke clipped a head-and-shoulders human silhouette target to a hanger on the target line, flipped a switch, and sent the target down the lane about five yards. Stella el-bowed Lacey and pointed to another lane. Those shooters were taking aim at a full-size photo of Osama bin Laden.

Brooke showed Stella how to control her breathing and align the front and rear sights and the target, and to let every-thing intersect before squeezing the trigger. Brooke loaded the .22 and quickly fired six rounds, double-action, as a demonstration. She reeled in the target: six little holes in the silhouette's center X-ring. She handed the gun to Stella to reload while a fresh target went downrange.

"It's harder than it looks." Brooke stepped aside for Stella. "Take your time. And rule number three: Get your finger off that trigger till you're ready to shoot!"

Stella concentrated and slowly squeezed off a shot. "Whoa!" She stared at the .22 in her hand. "It jumped!"

"That was recoil," Lacey informed her.

"Wow! That was so cool! Did I hit anything? Lemme do it again!"

Lacey and Brooke watched Stella empty the gun down-range. Bullet holes were sprayed all over the target, but at least they were all *on* the target. Stella squealed for joy.

Lacey's turn. She chose the .357 and another target and a box of .38 target loads for the shiny stainless revolver. She suddenly had to fight a sharp wave of nausea. Her pulse raced. She flashed back to that afternoon. Instead of the black silhouette on the target, she saw Cecily's lovely face, her slightly surprised look, the bullet hole in her head, the blood spurting from the wound, the blood spattering the car windows. She closed her eyes and lowered the gun, shaking.

"Lacey, are you all right?" Brooke was right behind her. She put her hands on Lacey's shoulders to steady her. "Take a deep breath. You can do it."

Lacey pushed the image of the dead woman out of her mind and steadied her hands. She lifted the gun back into position, aligned the sights, controlled her breathing. The target was just a target. She squeezed the trigger and felt the gun jump and twist in her hands, making a much bigger boom than the .22. A warm blast of gunpowder blew past her face. She lowered the gun again.

Brooke reeled the target in and whistled. "Bull's-eye," she said. Lacey squared her shoulders.

Now let's see if I can do that again.

chapter 11

"I rocked it, I totally rocked it!" Stella blew imaginary gun smoke from her trigger fingers, a pair of imaginary pistols. "Guys, I am so grateful you let me crash your party."

Lacey, Stella, and Brooke clinked their margarita glasses in a toast to themselves. "That's true, Stella, you totally rocked the range," Lacey said. "And you still have all your fingers and toes, and so do I."

"And so do I," Brooke chimed in. "We all rocked the range tonight."

Anita's Mexican Restaurant, a few blocks from the range, was cozy and unpretentious, with red and gold glass lamp-shades glowing over the booths and some of the best Mexican food in Northern Virginia. The sound of sizzling fajitas and the spicy Tex-Mex aromas were making Lacey hungry. The margarita was making her feel warm and lazy. Target shooting had pounded the stress out of her. She leaned back against the booth and closed her eyes to let go of the awful sight she'd seen that afternoon. This moment was her reward for getting through this long strange day.

Stella and Brooke chattered happily about how *rockingly* they had all conquered the pistol range that night. Not surprisingly, Stella thought maybe she still had a spent cartridge stuck in her cleavage somewhere.

Brooke and Stella, bonding over gunpowder and margaritas! Who would have thought?

"You'll get better with practice," Brooke was saying.

"The better you get, the more fun it is. Next time we'll set the target a little farther downrange."

"Next time?" The evening had turned out great, no blood was spilled, but Lacey hadn't planned on making girls' night out at the gun range a regular event.

"Of course we'll have a next time. This was badass fun." Stella grabbed a tortilla chip and loaded it with salsa. "Know what? They have Ladies' Night twice a month, I saw a poster. Half-price lane rental! Lots of hunky guys with big guns too, I bet," Stella purred. "Course it would be nice if the place wasn't practically in West Virginia."

"Fairfax County!" Lacey protested. "The burbs. Hardly West Virginia."

"Ha! Practically beyond the known universe," Stella insisted. To Stella, Washington, D.C., was the known universe, and Dupont Circle was its center.

Lacey waited for Brooke to make some snarky comment about how the District wasn't even part of the United States proper, or that Stella should spend more time in the red-blooded red state of Virginia, where men were men and women were dead-eye shots and everyone still believed in the Second Amendment. It didn't happen. Brooke sipped her margarita and gazed fondly at Stella like they were old pals.

This is weird.

"What about trick shooting? You ever do that stuff?" Stella asked. "You know, like shooting backwards over your shoulder with a mirror on horseback?"

Lacey visualized Stella blazing away backward on horseback and choked on her margarita. Brooke thumped on her back until Lacey put up her hands in surrender.

"I'm okay," she squeaked. "Just something I tried to swallow."

"I saw it in a movie!" Stella protested. "Could you really do that?"

"If you're Annie Freakin' Oakley," Lacey managed to say.

"I am! She's my new role model."

"You did hit the target, Stella," Brooke said. She lifted her margarita glass. "Here's to Annie Freakin' Oakley."

The waitress arrived with red chili enchiladas for Brooke,

tacos for Stella, and steak fajitas for Lacey. "Good night at the range, I see?" She smiled. "Enjoy."

After the adrenaline rush and emotional release of shooting together, they ate as if they were starving. But even great Mexican food couldn't quiet Stella for long.

"Guess what! I discovered the most awesome romantic place way out here in Virginia! Well, Nigel took me there. Great Falls, way up the river? Can you believe it?" Stella grinned. "Me, crossing the Potomac? Except to go to Lacey's place, of course. Nigel knows all sorts of out of the way places. I never even knew it was there. It was gorgeous. We must be pretty close to it way out here."

"Great Falls? Of course," Lacey said. "It's beautiful."

There were Great Falls parks on both sides of the Potomac where the river ran through a narrow rocky canyon upstream from Washington. In the spring the Virginia bluebells grew wild there, carpeting the green woods and the winding riverside trail with brilliant azure. The Virginia side was the more dramatic, with craggy cliffs high above a very different Potomac from the wide, slow-moving river that flowed past Washington and Lacey's Alexandria balcony. Kayakers paddled the treacherous whitewater below the Falls while hawks and eagles soared overhead. It was the most dangerous section of the river. Nearly every year someone fell from the rocks into the swirling foam and drowned.

The cherry trees around the Tidal Basin and their blizzard of pink blossoms were the springtime tourists' favorite, but Lacey preferred Great Falls when the bluebells were in bloom. Maybe she would plan a picnic there with Vic in the spring; at the moment spring seemed very far away. So did Vic.

"We did it there, you know. At Great Falls. Nigel and me." Stella giggled. "It was awesome—totally, rockingly awesome. Trust me."

"You did it at Great Falls?" Brooke blinked. "You had sex there? In the park? Where? In a car, or out in the woods?"

"It was out of this world, though we didn't exactly bring the satin sheets. We were out on one of those observation decks over the river, like the highest one, I think. It was just getting dark and there was no one around but us. It was so romantic. And so dramatic! What with the falls right down there and everything. Who knew water could be so loud! Nigel may be very English and kind of tweedy, but he is also like, very adventurous, if you know what I mean, when he wants to be."

Lacey wondered what was in her margarita. She was seeing strange visions. Stella on horseback, guns blazing. Stella having sex among Lacey's personal bluebells. *No more for me, please.*

"Aside from giving me a mental image I'll never forget, Stella, it's January!" she said. "Did you both freeze your buns off giving the whole park a free show? Or did Nigel just let you freeze *your* buns?" Stella laughed so hard she spilled her pink margarita.

"That was adventurous of you," Brooke said. "Not to mention illegal."

"Oh, come on, honey. You mean to tell me you've never done something fun that was maybe just a little bit over the line?"

"I'm invoking the Fifth Amendment." Brooke sipped her margarita demurely. Lacey knew Brooke wasn't a prude; she simply thought sex on anything less than 640 thread-count sheets was roughing it.

"Different strokes, I always say." Stella pointed her fork at Lacey. "Lacey never does anything adventurous and illegal either. She just stumbles over dead bodies and murderers and stuff."

"Let's leave me and dead bodies out of this, Stella."

"Hey, if you don't want to hear about me and Nigel making love on the rocks at Great Falls with the river roaring in our ears," Stella said, "you can read the whole thing on my blog. So there."

"You have a blog?" Brooke's interest was piqued. "I love blogs." And the more bizarre the better. She started each day with her favorite blogs, along with a latte and way too much sugar. And Damon's DeadFed dot com.

"Like, *duh*. My new *nom de blog* is TotallyStellariffic! I'll send you the link."

Lacey thought "Radio Free Stella" had already broadcast far too many secrets of Stella's clients, hers included. Gossiping at the salon seemed so natural, under the influence of warm shampoo suds, Stella's excellent scalp massage, and the cozy just-us-girls atmosphere. *But a blog? Stella? On the Web for all to see? Oh, dear Lord!* Stella would soon be in league with the likes of Damon Newhouse.

"What do you write about?" Lacey had a queasy feeling in her stomach. It was fighting with her fajitas.

"Only my totally true most innermost thoughts," Stella said. "What I do all day at the salon, who I see, what I hear, what I'm thinking. Me and Nigel. Oh and some poetry too. Cool stuff. You know. You've read it."

"No I haven't." Lacey didn't recall Stella dropping this particular conversational tidbit. "I never knew you had a blog."

"You did too! I keep telling you about it! I can't believe you haven't read it!"

"I've never even seen it!"

"Come on, Lacey, I mean I blog about you all the time." Stella mock pouted. "Well, once or twice anyway. Every time you trip over a dead body."

"I'll have to check this out." Brooke was laughing. "Just to keep tabs on Lacey."

"If you write about me on your blog," Lacey warned, "it better be accurate. No embroidering the truth. Or I'll have Brooke here sue you."

"Wait a minute," Brooke said, "I might have a conflict."

"Not to worry," Stella pledged. "One hundred percent accurate."

"Couldn't you just leave me out of it completely?"

"Are you crazy, Lace? People read my blog for the real deal, the Stellariffic scoop! Things you can't print in your paper. But you know, if I gave you a different name, only people in the know would know. You know? That would be cool, huh?"

"Getting warmer," Lacey said cautiously.

"Like a code name?" Brooke suggested.

"Yeah, a code. I've been thinking—" Stella slurped her strawberry margarita, which coordinated nicely with her

Sandra Dee outfit. "We're like a club, the three of us, like in that movie, you know with the English guy? Not Nigel, but he looks kind of like Nigel? The one who says, 'We happy few, we band of brothers'?"

"You saw Branagh's *Henry the Fifth*?" Brooke asked, surprised. Stella nodded.

"Cool battle scenes, but super talky. Like it was Shakespeare or something."

"So our club should be, 'We happy few, we band of *sisters*'?" Brooke suggested.

"Exactly." Stella raised her glass. "And we need more than just a name for Lacey; we need names for all of us. Ladies, we need a code. A secret code."

"You already speak in code," Lacey said. "I never know what you're talking about."

"Yeah, like that, that's what I'm talking about, but even more so!" Stella was building up steam now. "*Nobody'll* know what we're talking about. We'll invent this code. For us, so only we understand it."

"A secret code. For just the three of us?" Stella had said the magic word. The word that tickled Brooke's appetite for intrigue: *secret.* "I like it."

"You like it?" Stella looked surprised. "Wow, that's awesome. Terrific!"

"Please don't encourage her, Brooke," Lacey pleaded.

"Go ahead, encourage me!"

"What kind of code?" Brooke asked.

"The kind of code only a woman would understand." Stella took a sip of her rosy pink margarita. "A *pink* code."

"Aha. A pink *collar* code." The attorney pulled a legal pad from her bag. "Pink collar, for the women in society who get no respect. Women need the advantage of a secret code. Men have their own code. The Old Boy Code."

"Yeah, just for us girls," Stella said. "No boys allowed in this clubhouse. So like the first thing we need to do—"

Lacey rolled her eyes and communed with the rest of her steak fajitas. She heard the chatter, but she stopped paying much attention. Stella liked to talk, Brooke liked to talk, neither one liked to listen, and they were actually getting along.

It was some kind of bonding miracle, gossip, guns, and margaritas, so who cared what they were talking about?

" 'Permanent solution,' like we use in the salon?" Stella was saying. "That could mean *death*." She made a throat-slitting gesture.

"I like it," Brooke said. "So 'giving somebody a perm' could mean killing them, right, like murder?"

This conversation was sounding to Lacey a bit like "Salon of Death," the game Stella's hairstylists played sometimes at Stylettos when they were bored, dreaming up creative ways to knock off annoying customers and management with improvised weapons found in the salon.

"Salon phrases could all have double meanings," Stella continued. "So if you say, 'My curls are too tight,' it means, 'The bad guys are closing in, I'm in big trouble!' "

Brooke's margarita poised in midair. "Of course. The terminology of women's work is perfect for a code, because men trivialize female employment and don't understand its true significance. Code Pink Collar." She put her drink down and started writing.

"Using the 'perm rods' means 'guns,' get it?" Stella continued. "And Wednesday means Washington, Monday means Maryland, and, um, Valentine's Day could mean Virginia, because 'Virginia is for lovers,' right? I can testify to that one." Stella gave Lacey a wink. "Any kind of permanent means 'This is like deadly serious,' and 'buzz cut' means 'You better get over here quick.' "

What a good game, Lacey decided as she dug into her fajitas. The "Pink Collar Code" was keeping the two of them laughing and distracted and off Lacey's case. Maybe she wouldn't have to discuss the body in the parking lot with her best friends while trying to eat her dinner. *Here's hoping.*

"And by the way, Lacey, I think your PI course is totally radical." Stella pointed a pink-tipped nail at her. "I'd have loved to go with you to keep you company, but *you know*. Pretty busy right now with my Mr. Wonderful. So what's it like? All cops and robbers?" She twirled the gold key that hung from her throat. "You expecting somebody to drop dead in class? You are such a murder magnet, you know."

Lacey dropped her fork. It clattered off her plate.

"Yes, Lacey." Brooke's lips broke into a wicked grin. "Tell us all about today's murder." Brooke had been biding her time, one of her lawyerly skills. "You remember, the woman who died today in the parking lot outside your class? Damon might have mentioned something about it in passing."

"Murder! Never joke about murder with Lacey, Brooke. She'll murder us both—" Stella stopped laughing when she saw Lacey's face. "Murder? No way! Way? Lacey's got another murder going on? Oh my God!" Stella dropped her fork too.

Lacey eyed them both coolly. "The last I heard, it was still being called a suspicious death. It might have been a suicide." She smothered her last sliver of steak in guacamole and rolled it up in a warm tortilla. "It was not necessarily a murder. Just a coincidence that I happened to be there. And I am not saying another word about it."

"Oh my God." Stella slapped her forehead. "I should have known. Marie told me I was stepping toward something momentous tonight. The beginning of something big, she said. She was talking about a murder! I just thought she meant I should wear my hot new outfit to go shooting. Oh my God."

Marie Largesse was Lacey's friendly neighborhood psychic. She owned a tiny store in Old Town Alexandria called The Little Shop of Horus, where she purveyed candles, metaphysical books, tarot cards, and psychic advice. Lacey hadn't seen her for a while, but Stella obviously had. *It's probably all over her blog.*

"Suspicious death, Stella," Lacey said. "We don't even know if it was a murder."

"Just for the record," Brooke said, "I do believe there may be true psychics in the world, but your friend Marie? Call me crazy, but any so-called psychic who faints at crime scenes because she is, quote, 'overloaded by psychic vibes'? Please."

"I've seen it happen, she faints dead away. Pretty spooky," Lacey said. "Probably a blood sugar thing, if you ask me."

"So she's a happy psychic," Stella said cheerfully. "Marie

can foretell mildly bad stuff, like, you know, the weather, but she can't handle really tragic stuff. Which is okay, I think. Who wants to find out the really tragic stuff anyway, at least before you have to? Course, if she ever fainted on me, I'd totally freak."

"One thing about Marie though, she is dead on about the weather," Lacey added between bites. "The woman is a human barometer. What else did she tell you? Storm front coming in?"

"Oh yeah." Stella closed her eyes to recall Marie's predictions. "Be prepared, she said, we're gonna have a 'thunder snow.' And it's gonna change things big time."

"Did she say when?" Lacey asked.

"No, but soon, maybe. Sooner or later. And Marie said she saw 'multiple snow dogs' last night before sunset, and that's like an omen or something. What's a snow dog?"

"I think she must've meant a sun dog," Lacey offered.

"Sun dog? Like a dog laying out in the sun? But it's the middle of winter! Okay already, so what's a sun dog?"

"It's kind of like a rainbow around the sun, like smaller suns in a halo around the sun. It's a refraction of sunlight through ice crystals in the air," Lacey said. "I saw them with Vic once. Looks like multiple suns in the sky. Pretty amazing sight."

Brooke looked up from her notes. "Multiple suns? Pretty ominous. Like something out of Revelations. It's the End Times. We should order more margaritas!"

"I hope it doesn't mean multiple murders!" Stella looked around the restaurant.

"It probably means," Lacey said, "we'll have a tremendous snowstorm, maybe with thunder and lightning, a 'thunder snow.' Sooner or later. Someday. Big deal. That's my prediction, and I'm no psychic."

"Start talking, Lacey." Stella's eyes shone with excitement. "Tell us about this murder! You think you're in danger? Can we help? Annie Freakin' Oakley at your service!"

"Hold your horses. And your guns." Lacey had been having such a nice time until Brooke let the cat out of the bag. "Isn't there anything else we can talk about but that poor dead woman in the parking lot?"

Lacey knew, despite all her denials, she was going to be involved in the awful mess of Cecily Ashton's suspicious death. She happened to interview Cecily. She happened to be at PI class when the woman happened to die a few yards away. The PI who taught the class happened to have had a relationship with Cecily. Even Hadley, the "crazy kid" in class, knew Cecily! Lacey couldn't avoid this story.

Vic was always telling her cops didn't believe in coincidence. She didn't either. Maybe this was the "big story" she'd been waiting for. Maybe the big story had come looking for her.

chapter 12

"No, Mac, I don't know anything else about the woman. You probably know more than I do at this point."

Lacey rubbed her eyes and looked at her alarm clock. Seven a.m. She moaned and threw on a favorite warm black silk robe embroidered with roses. It was way too early on a Sunday morning to be fielding a call from her editor.

"You working on a follow-up?" Mac asked. Her story on Cecily Ashton and news of the woman's death had just hit their subscribers' front porches.

"I'm working on getting my eyes open. And maybe a cup of coffee." She padded barefoot into her small 1950s-era apartment kitchen with the phone to her ear and opened the fridge with her free hand. It didn't look promising. She pulled out a half cup of cold coffee from the day before, popped it in the microwave, and pressed the button. Mmmm, half a cup of nuked leftover day-old coffee! *Could be worse,* she decided. *Could be a whole pot of fresh-made newsroom coffee.*

"What are you doing up this early anyway?" she asked Mac. "It's seven o'clock in the morning. Sunday morning."

"We're taking the girls to church."

"Why, Douglas MacArthur Jones, you're a churchgoing man! I never knew."

"Gotta set an example," he snorted. "Those are good little girls, have you heard?" The Joneses seemed unlikely foster parents. They were older, in their forties, and they had never had children. At least Mac seemed an unlikely dad. He'd struck Lacey as the type to eat kids for breakfast. She'd been wrong about Mac. Kim, on the other hand, was clearly a natural foster mother. The moment she saw Jasmine and Lily Rose, two orphaned and homeless little girls, just before Christmas, Kim wrapped them up in her love like a warm cashmere blanket and they were her little lost chicks.

The girls didn't believe Lacey at first, when she told them she knew parents who wanted them and would be perfect for them. But they all fit together even better than Lacey had dared hope. The little girls' resilience amazed them all, and being a father seemed to have a calming effect on Mac. Jasmine and Lily Rose were an ethnic blend of black and white and Asian. Mac was African-American (and half white), and Kim was Japanese-American. They blended well, not because of color, but because of love.

The girls learned their mother was never coming home again just before Christmas. Lacey had to tell them the bad news, and it was the hardest thing she'd ever had to say. Sometimes the girls had nightmares, Mac told her, but the bad dreams were fading. They adored Kim, and gruff old Mac too, and they were learning little pleasures they'd never known before, like baking Christmas cookies and riding bikes. Mac showed off their latest pictures at the newsroom the previous Friday.

"Those two little girls have turned you into a big sentimental softie," Lacey laughed.

"Why not, they're not reporters." She heard him rustling newspapers in the background. "You seen your story yet?"

"Not yet." Lacey opened her apartment door. *The Eye Street Observer* was hanging on her doorknob in a plastic bag. She tossed it on the table and pulled out the Sunday LifeStyles section: Her story was the front page feature. There was Hansen's best shot of Cecily Ashton, leaning back glamorously on the blue velvet sofa in her fabulous dressing room, flashing her Rita Hayworth smile. She looked like a woman whose every wish had been granted.

"It's kind of a fluffy story," Mac said. "For a dead woman."

"It's a feature on the woman's closets and clothes, Mac,

what do you expect? And she was very alive at the time. Was I supposed to know this would happen?"

"That's why we do follow-ups. Especially for high-profile murder victims. Maybe you could start thinking a little deeper. Once you've had your morning coffee."

"What if it's suicide? Last I heard—" A part of Lacey still hoped that perhaps Cecily had turned the gun on herself. That would be just as tragic a story, but perhaps not such a complicated one. Lacey didn't need any more complications in her life.

"It's not suicide. Just confirmed." Even over the phone Mac could sound smug. "No weapon in the car, wound wasn't self-inflicted, so it's murder. Trujillo left the message on my voice mail. He's already out of bed and working the story."

"You put Tony on this story? What happened to Kavanaugh?"

"Tony doesn't want you to skunk him on his own beat. You know how he hates it when you scoop him. You gonna let him scoop you back?"

Lacey wasn't about to let Mac goad her. "Nobody in D.C. could care less about what happens out in Falls Church, Virginia."

"Not unless someone like Cecily Ashton meets her maker there," Mac said. "What was she doing there? Do you remember anything else she said? Did she mention anyone making threats? And by the way, what were you doing there?"

She ignored his last question. "Not threats exactly. She'd said her ex, the one and only Philip Clark Ashton, was responsible for 'all of it.' Whatever 'all of it' meant." But men like Ashton did not kill their ex-wives, Lacey thought. Not personally. If they really wanted them to disappear permanently, they hired specialists to do it for them, quietly and efficiently. But why was Cecily in Bud Hunt's parking lot? And why would someone kill her there? To pin it on Bud Hunt? Or because the killer *was* Bud Hunt?

"You still there, Smithsonian? I need a follow-up. Tomorrow."

"What kind of follow-up?"

"Surprise me," he replied. "Fashion stuff. Your readers expect it."

"You realize there is no fashion angle. You always want a fashion angle."

"You always say there isn't one." Mac chuckled. "And yet isn't it amazing that you always find one. She was wearing some kind of clothes when she was killed, wasn't she? And if she wasn't, that's a fashion angle too. Hang on a second." Lacey could hear a happy commotion in the background, consisting mostly of high-pitched giggles. Mac came back on the line. "Jasmine wants to talk to you."

The next voice she heard was a happy "totally almost" thirteen-year-old girl.

"Hi, Lacey! It's me, Jasmine! When are you coming over?"

"Hi, Jasmine. I'm not sure, but soon. How's life with Mac and Kim?"

"Good," the girl said. "Really good. We're going to church and then we get doughnuts! And later me and Lily Rose get to ride our bikes down the trail. Mac promised, and he's riding his bike with us too." She giggled again and Lacey heard Lily Rose laughing in the background. "But we're lots better bike riders than Mac! We go like the wind!"

Mac on a bike chasing two little girls. There's a front-page picture, Lacey thought. Maybe she could get Hansen to take some incriminating candids. For Christmas, Mac had assembled (with a little help from Vic Donovan) pink and blue bikes for Jasmine and her little sister Lily Rose. They'd never had bikes before.

"Isn't it too cold to go out riding today?"

"No, no, no!" Jasmine giggled. "We have the warm coats you gave us and besides you stay really warm when you ride like we do. And guess what, we have our matching helmets now, Lily Rose and me, did you know that? Mine is blue and hers is pink of course and they're perfect! You have to see them. Mac has a helmet too. His is red and I make sure he wears it so he doesn't hurt himself."

"Good for you!" *I'm a fan of any woman who can make Mac behave.*

"We think he looks funny in it," Jasmine added softly, "but we make him wear it anyway." Lacey was also a fan of anyone who could make her boss look funny. "When are we gonna see you, Lacey?"

"Soon. Maybe when you go see Stella to have your hair trimmed." A visit to the salon at Dupont Circle was going to be a big treat for the girls. "She told me you're coming this week. I'll stop by."

"Cool! You have to be there, it'll be fun! I gotta go now, we're going to church. Bye Lacey! Say good-bye to Miss Lacey, Lily Rose."

Lacey heard Lily Rose giggling her good-bye. Then the phone changed hands and in the distance she heard Jasmine say, "Hey, Lily Rose, we're gonna see Lacey this week when we go see Miss Stella!"

Mac came back on the line. "Time for church. Tomorrow we'll talk about your follow-up story. And you'll have some ideas for me, right?"

"Right. I can hardly wait." Another sip of the warmed-over coffee convinced Lacey to get dressed and get a clue and get some real java.

"Mac!" Lacey heard Jasmine in the background, giving her new dad his marching orders. "Kim says we are *late* and you have to say good-bye to Miss Lacey now!" Lacey heard Lily Rose's voice too, then a loud chorus of good-byes from the girls, followed by more giggling. She heard Mac laughing, and then the call clicked off.

Lacey glanced at the clock. If she hurried, she could just make it to church too. She'd get to see what early Mass at her neighborhood Catholic church in Old Town looked like. She was usually a slip-in-the-back-late kind of Catholic, at the late morning or the occasional late-afternoon Mass. But a Catholic, nonetheless. Even if the sermons often lacked passion and the soloist tortured the hymns with her off-key vibrato. Lacey headed for her closet.

She had candles to light.

chapter 13

"Stella tells me you think I'm a— What was the phrase? A 'man slut'?" Nigel Griffin had some nerve asking Lacey what she thought of him. As if he didn't know. Much to Lacey's dismay, the "man slut" himself was sitting at her dining room table, up close and personal. Way too personal.

Nigel Griffin was good-looking in that pale smarmy way of his, Lacey thought, and his teeth were good. *For an Englishman.* He was wearing what appeared to be his overage preppy schoolboy uniform, a navy blazer over a light blue oxford shirt, khaki slacks, and cordovan tassel loafers.

"Man slut? I've called you so many things, Griffin, it's hard to remember them all." Lacey glared at the little blond tattletale sitting next to him. *Leave it to Stella.*

"You know you always say that about poor Nigel, Lace." Stella looked deceptively innocent. "Maybe not those exact words, but the sentiment, you know?"

Stella looked like a sexy sugarplum in today's pastel outfit, a baby blue angora sweater with a low-cut neckline and puff sleeves, matching slacks, and white high-heeled boots. Her perky blond bob was set off with a matching blue headband. She sat next to her man slut and gazed at him with undisguised ardor. Where, oh where, was the punky little smart-mouth bad girl Lacey knew and loved?

"Well, man slut will do." Lacey looked Griffin square in the eye. "I have heard allegations to that effect, Griffin. Some of them directly from you."

When they first met, Nigel Griffin told Lacey he didn't

like his women to be "too refined." He preferred his females a little trashy, he said, he was a "cheap one-night-stand kind of guy." Then he started seeing Stella. Lacey hadn't seen any evolution in Griffin, so she assumed he included her friend in the "cheap one-night stand" category too. Lacey was still holding that against him. Among other things.

"Stella's my friend, you know. I don't want to see her get hurt."

"And that's so sweet of you, Lacey!" Stella piped up. "But what we want to tell you is that, you know, Nigel is now a *reformed* man slut. He has totally changed his ways. And he quit smoking too, did you notice?"

"Now that you mention it, thanks for not polluting my air. Not that I would have let you."

"The new me," he said. "It's all because of Stella."

"You kept me in line when I was quitting, Lace, and if I can do it, Nigel can do it, and he did it for me." Griffin smiled sheepishly. Stella jumped up from the table and hefted the coffeepot. "And as you know, speaking of man sluts, I used to be kind of—*you know*—myself."

Lacey wisely kept her mouth shut.

"Let me just say, Smithsonian, your bad impression of me was partly my own fault. I truly am sorry. But everything is different now. Water under the bridge. As you can see. I am not smoking, as you can see, and it is killing me. But anything for Stella."

"Yeah, you're still thinkin' of the old Nigel," Stella said. "The BS Nigel. Before Stella. More coffee, anybody?"

And here I thought BS was Nigel Griffin's middle *name.* Lacey sighed and nodded for more coffee. She'd returned from Mass feeling uncharacteristically filled with peace and love for her fellow man and woman, only to find these two waiting for her in front of her apartment building. Lacey was looking forward to making herself a cozy breakfast and settling in with the Sunday *New York Times.* Wrong. It was amazing how fast her peace and love vibe could dissipate around Nigel Griffin. She didn't even have a chance to change out of her church outfit of the day, an emerald-green short-waisted jacket over a long black wool skirt and black high-heeled boots.

"Lacey! Wow, you're up and dressed already," Stella had said, hugging Lacey in the chilly sunshine. "Cute outfit. Retro retro! Sort of *Wuthering Heights* meets *His Girl Friday*, right? Can we come up and talk?"

Just when I was feeling all calm and generous of spirit.

Stella had assumed, correctly, that Lacey's pantry would be "as bare as Mother Hubbard's cupboard." Knowing Lacey would be more welcoming after "a little something," the newly domesticated Stella took over Lacey's kitchen and made coffee from a bag of freshly ground beans she had thoughtfully brought along. The same Balducci's bag also carried fresh bread. Stella sliced the bread, toasted it in the broiler, slathered it with butter, cinnamon, and sugar, and then slid it back into the broiler until it bubbled. The apartment filled with a sweet savory aroma Lacey hadn't smelled since she was a little girl. Her mother used to make cinnamon toast for her as a special treat. She almost forgave Stella for bringing Nigel along. *Almost, but not quite.*

"There you have it, Smithsonian. I am a reformed man slut. The AS Nigel, *Anno Stella.* Behold, a new man. *Ecco homo nuovo,* or however you Catholics would put it." Griffin spouted his fractured prep school Latin easily, and he had the nerve to smile engagingly. It gave his face that boyish English movie star charm some women found so attractive. "Now that's out of the way, I'd like us to be friends."

"The three of us," Stella clarified.

"Am I supposed to believe this big change in you, Griffin?" Lacey sipped her coffee. "You'd sell your grandmother if you got a good price for her."

"Quite true. Never cared for the old bat. No market for grandmothers anyway, so she's safe enough. But really, Smithsonian, we need to talk. Send Granny to her room."

"Talk about what?" Lacey inquired. "To what do I owe the pleasure of your company?"

"We have certain mutual interests. Cecily Ashton, for starters." Griffin tapped a soundless tune on the table with his fingers. "I'd very much like to know what you know about her recent sad demise. Tell you why in a minute."

A chill ran down her spine. A fever, or maybe a warning

from her intuition. From their brief acquaintance last fall, Lacey's opinion of Griffin was that he couldn't be trusted to tell the truth until the bitter end. Maybe not even then. He'd dole out bits and pieces of half-truths, like an annoying news source, and keep the real information to himself. It was transparently obvious to her why he'd be interested in Cecily Ashton. Her missing pearls. *When there's blood in the water, watch out for sharks.*

"Let's start with you," Lacey replied. "What do you know?"

"I know this." He reached inside his jacket pocket and pulled out a folded copy of her feature story in *The Eye Street Observer.* "Cecily Ashton spoke to you about the burglary before she died. Therefore, you must know something useful."

"Useful to you?"

"Among other people. Yet this article of yours doesn't illuminate a thing."

"Well golly, Nigel. I'm so flattered you even read it." Lacey bit into a piece of cinnamon toast. *Delicious.*

"Smithsonian, I'm your biggest fan!" Lacey almost choked on her toast.

"Next to me, Lacey," Stella offered helpfully. "And you interviewed Cecily Ashton! I would kill for that woman's closet space. Um. Figure of speech. I didn't even know people lived like that. Except in the movies, maybe, not around here." She topped off their coffee cups.

"Smithsonian," Nigel implored, "what are we to make of these oh-so-telling fashion details? The clothes, the closets, the chandeliers! And the grand metaphorical significance of a doodle of some exotic bird in a cage on the back of a photograph of Rita bloody Hayworth, possibly drawn by the one and only star herself? Who bloody well cares? What inquiring minds really want to know, Smithsonian, is who did the late lamented Cecily finger for the bloody burglary?"

He really wants those pearls. Lacey's article, and perhaps the drawing as well, was a miniature portrait of a woman trapped in the ruins of her dreams, nothing more.

"But Nigel," Stella spoke up, "don't you see, babycakes, it's like that doodle says it all. Even if you're rich you can still be unhappy and trapped, like a bird in a cage. Whether you're a famous movie star or a rich bimbo, you can still feel lost and lonely."

"Lonely my arse, sweetheart," Griffin said. "Stella, my dear, the tragically wealthy Mrs. Ashton boffed anything in pants. Or out of pants. Her bed was about as lonely as Charing Cross Station." He caught Lacey's scowl. "Of course that doesn't detract from her being an absolutely lovely and tragic person, now does it?"

Lacey picked up the clipping and took another look at what she had written.

CRIMES OF FASHION
SPECIAL FEATURE

The Social Lioness, the Rich, and the Wardrobe

By Lacey Smithsonian

"I never meant to be scandalous," Cecily Ashton says, a half smile playing on her lips. "I was young and I didn't know how to act around Philip's friends. I've learned a lot since then." Her smile dims for a moment, but then it returns, a little brighter.

The familiar media images of the madcap socialite, scandalizing a formal White House dinner in a micro-miniskirt, hitching a drunken ride through Georgetown on the hood of a Metropolitan police car? Those images are not really her, claims Cecily Ashton.

They were snapshots of a naive young woman who didn't know the ropes in this unforgiving city. "Washington is such a tough town," she told *The Eye* in an exclusive interview. "But people change. I just hope people will take another look at me and see who I've become."

The former wife of billionaire sports team owner Philip Clark Ashton, Cecily Ashton made her triumphs and her mistakes in public, and her public image has paid the price. Her well-publicized divorce from Ashton is now final, and Cecily Ashton is eager to begin the next chapter of her life.

The Capital City will see a different side of Cecily Ashton in February, when the Bentley Museum of American Fashion unveils a major exhibit on loan from her fabled collection. The collection includes one-of-a-kind haute couture pieces and unusual vintage clothing from many of the world's leading designers, many of the pieces with remarkable histories.

"My collection is not frivolous," she said. "It's really world-class art, wearable art, and I see myself as its curator as much as its owner." Cecily Ashton's collection of clothing and accessories fill a fascinating complex of custom-designed closets and dressing rooms in her Northwest Washington home. With this exhibit she hopes to give the public a glimpse of her private life, the life behind the public image.

"I want to leave something beautiful behind after I am gone," Cecily Ashton said as she opened her home to *The Eye Street Observer* . . . .

Chapter 14

It sounds different now that she's dead, Lacey thought. She stopped reading and tossed the newspaper clipping on the table.

"It's not exactly hard-hitting journalism," Nigel Griffin said. "And not even a trace of that snippy snarkiness Smithsonian is famous for."

"It's a fashion feature. What do you expect? How would I know she would be murdered? And just how did you find out I was anywhere near the crime scene?" Lacey looked at Stella, who had heard about it last night at dinner after the gun range. What Stella knew, Stella told. So much for the Sisterhood of the Code. "Oh, Stella. Do you have to tell everybody *everything*?"

"I had to tell him, Lacey. There are no secrets between us. We're a couple now. A *couple* couple, if you know what I mean."

"Then we're done here, Griffin. You already know everything I know."

"Not at all. Perhaps we'll get to why you want to be a private detective later, which, believe me, is fascinating. But first, what about the unusual coincidence of Mrs. Ashton shot dead surprisingly near you, just a week after speaking with you? She must have had juicier stories to share than this fluff. Did she come all the way out there to divulge them to you?" He rose from his chair and leaned over her. "Did you talk to her again before she died?"

Lacey stood up and looked him in the eye. "For your

information, Griffin, my story was written a week ago. A week before she died. I never spoke to her again."

"You're quite sure? No e-mails, text messages, late night phone calls?"

Lacey snorted. "To get something, you have to give something, Nigel. So give. Your visit is related to her stolen jewels, am I right?"

"It's rather more complicated than that." Griffin rubbed his jaw.

"You knew the late Mrs. Ashton too?"

"Yeah, he did, Lacey, he told me all about it," Stella blurted out. "Nigel knew her, but not in the, you know, biblical sense."

"Not in the 'biblical sense'? Meaning there was no Bible in the motel room?"

Nigel rushed to smooth the waters. "Smithsonian, whatever you think of me, we do need to know what happened. Cecily Ashton's body was found in a parking lot where you were taking a PI class. You're in a position to know. Why was she there?"

"That's the million-dollar question, isn't it?" Lacey wondered what his angle was. Stella looked anxiously from Griffin to Lacey, nibbling on the last piece of cinnamon toast.

"I'll make some more," Stella squeaked. She scurried back into the kitchen and started clattering pots and pans.

Lacey picked up her article and studied the picture of Cecily. "I don't know why she was there. She never got in touch after the interview. She was already dead when I saw her." She smiled knowingly. "Why don't you ask your old buddy Kepelov?"

"Kepelov? Kepelov was there?" Nigel's eyes widened in surprise. He sat down with a plop. Lacey wondered if the surprise was genuine. Griffin was such a liar, it was hard to tell.

"Didn't you know? But you two are thick as thieves, right? Underscore *thieves*."

"No, no, not thieves," Nigel insisted weakly. Lacey had knocked him completely off balance. "Far as I know, he's a retriever like me. A freelance finder of lost objects of value.

What with the KGB out of business and all. He was there? I had no idea." Griffin picked up his coffee cup. It was empty. He laughed nervously. "Kepelov is always in the thick of things. Funny old Bolshevik, isn't he? That's brilliant, just brilliant. So is he a suspect?"

"Says he has an alibi," Lacey said. "And he's quite the capitalist these days. He'll be happy to see you, Griffin. Maybe we should have let him shoot you that time in Paris."

"It was New Orleans." Griffin's coffee cup rattled on his saucer. "And he wasn't serious about that."

"Don't tease him, Lacey, he's sensitive about being shot at. Now Nigel, you have to be completely honest with Lacey." Stella poured him a fresh cup of coffee.

"I am the soul of honesty, my dearest Stella." He took the coffee, his hands shaking. "It's true, I'm surprised Kepelov is still a man about town here. We are *not* thick as thieves, as you put it. Our partnership never really bore fruit. Well, you were there, weren't you?"

Nigel had never been straight with Lacey about his relationship with Kepelov. The equation kept shifting: partners, mortal enemies, both. First Nigel didn't know the notorious ex-KGB spy, except by reputation. Then they were deadly competitors. Then, surprise, suddenly they're partners, working together all along. Then they weren't. They had been after a fabulous fictitious Fabergé egg. They thought Smithsonian knew where it was hidden.

"I was there, and I was way ahead of you," Lacey said, though she knew it was partly just luck. And the blessing of good intentions.

"You were indeed, and that's why I come, hat in hand, begging for stray scraps of information from the intrepid Lacey Smithsonian." Griffin was back in his charming mode. *Must be Stella's coffee.* "And so Gregor Kepelov was on the crime scene too. We must get in touch. Well, here's to the old bolshie. Never burn the bridge all the way to the ground, I say." He topped off his coffee with milk and added three teaspoons of sugar. "Kepelov has always been in search of rare antiquities, interesting artifacts, or the rare Russian jewel, as you may recall. Sometimes he finds them first, sometimes I do. And every so often we've thrown in our lot together. All is fair in love and jewels."

"So collaborating with jewel thieves is part of your job description as an insurance investigator?"

"Jewel *retriever*. Please!" Griffin looked unperturbed. "And the job is my own, uniquely tailored to my unique skills. Besides, my clients are happy with my work."

"Because you just make it up as you go along." Lacey sipped Stella's coffee. It was quite good. Coffee was always better, Lacey thought, when someone else made it.

"Children, children," Stella chided them. "Stop squabbling, the both of you, or there'll be no more cinnamon toast for you."

"But that is not the matter at hand," Griffin said. "Sorry, Stella, for being peevish. I'm a man in pain. This no-ciggies-with-my-coffee thing is agony."

"And what is the matter at hand?" Lacey wondered how much of her precious Sunday this would use up.

"You have something unusual, Smithsonian, even unique. Something I admire."

Stella opened the broiler and checked her second batch of cinnamon toast. "Fashion clues, Lacey. I've been telling him how you got that EFP thing going on for you. You know, your *extra-fashionary perception*."

Lacey studied the coffee in her cup, trying not to laugh.

"Whatever you call it," Nigel said, "what does it tell you about her death?"

"Nothing. Yet. Tell me why you're so interested in Cecily Ashton."

"It's pure business, Lacey." Stella brought her freshly toasted cinnamon concoctions to the table. "His company insured Cecily Ashton."

Aha! Here's the angle. "But so little was taken," Lacey pointed out. "Relative to the size of her fortune. So is it really such a big deal?"

"My firm has a reputation to uphold," Griffin sniffed. "Cecily Ashton is very high profile, or she was. The objects stolen were unique. Historically significant. And of course, it would be a coup for me to recover the stolen goods. Never underestimate personal gain as a motivation, you know."

"There's more, or you wouldn't be here. Look, Nigel, I can't share if you won't share." Not that she had anything to share with him anyway.

"Nigel's job is on the line," Stella cut in. "His reputation is at stake." Lacey raised an eyebrow at that.

"You might as well know. God knows you might suss it out with a fashion clue. The way I button my shirt might scream *unemployed*. Ashton's demanding I be sacked."

"Because he hasn't found the jewels. You see, Lacey, Nigel's reputation is a double-edged sword thing, he's that good," Stella added.

"Old Ashton thinks I should have wrapped it up by now. Of all the lunatic things, he thinks I might have staged the burglary, or be an accomplice."

"Is there more?" Losing his job? Now she understood Griffin humbling himself before her. He looked miserable. Even Lacey could see he needed a cigarette.

"Um, yes. Certain people may be under the impression that we had a sort of intimate relationship. Cecily and I."

"Tell me again how you're a reformed man slut?"

"Like I said, Lacey," Stella intervened. "He's not a man slut anymore, and he didn't sleep with her. I'd know. I'm like a bloodhound on the scent of lost relationships. Hey, maybe I should blog that." Her pink-tipped fingers waved a piece of toast, spilling cinnamon and sugar all over the table. "This is the real deal. She threatened to get another insurance company if he didn't do the deed with her. Honest. Swear to God."

"But you didn't have an affair with her? Why not? And let's skip over the 'I'm a new man' stuff."

"Cecily, lovely though she was, could be unpredictable. Unstable. Unattractively unstable." Nigel reddened. He looked very embarrassed. "A little scary, let us say. As well as a bit of an emotional blackmailer."

Lacey paradoxically felt a sudden rush of sympathy for poor Cecily. Her looks were her main lure for men's attention, and when that didn't work, Cecily dangled money and power in front of them. How desperate she must have been, for so many things she couldn't buy. *But good grief,* she thought, *what bad taste in men she had!*

"What was the most valuable thing taken?" Lacey asked.

"Rita Hayworth's makeup case, no question," Nigel said. "A one-of-a-kind case made by Louis Vuitton for a star of the silver screen? Difficult to even put a price on it, it might go for any amount at auction. Commissioned by Orson Welles before he married Hayworth. Her second husband, I believe. The case has secret compartments, specially made perfume bottles, all sorts of expensive little details. A unique history. A very exciting piece." The jewel retriever in him was very excited. "And that perfect strand of natural round pearls tucked into the hidden compartment makes it really quite priceless."

"I've only seen it in photographs," Lacey said.

"I saw it in Philadelphia. I vetted the security arrangements for the company when it was exhibited there. It's exquisite. What a find it would be."

Lacey was familiar with other types of antique cases, but the Vuitton Rita Hayworth case clearly was the most exotic and ingenious. Lacey's Aunt Mimi had left her Lacey's great-grandmother's vanity set from the 1920s. It was a black leather case with all the necessities a lady would require while traveling, fitted combs and brushes and mirrors, jars for hand and face creams, a compact for rouge, drawers for her jewelry. Each piece was accented with silver and mother-of-pearl and set against the blue satin lining.

Lacey loved to play with the set as a child, fitting the pieces together like a puzzle, lovingly memorizing every piece. The vanity set now decorated her dresser. She treasured it, with all its bottles and brushes and pretty compacts. The Rita Hayworth makeup case with its tooled red leather and brass fittings would be something to see.

"What do you want from me, Griffin? I don't have it. I know who Cecily said took it, but I don't have any evidence."

"Philip Clark Ashton?" Nigel shook his head. "I know he's everyone's obvious suspect, but use your imagination, Smithsonian."

"Your EFP, Lacey," Stella added helpfully.

Lacey wanted to smack them both. Then it dawned on her. "You don't think Cecily burglarized her own home? Why? To blame it on her ex-husband? Out of spite?"

"First prize! To keep Philip from taking the things back from her somehow. And to entangle me with her. Or both."

"Oh please, Griffin! All the world revolves around you!"

"Scoff if you want, Smithsonian. That very curious and priceless assortment of very sentimental items went missing, and Cecily came calling on me."

"So? You're the big jewel retriever, right? For her insurance company?"

"In my opinion, the makeup case is not really missing at all. The phony burglary was just a lure to get me involved." Nigel stood up. Stella stood by him and took his hand.

"You see, Lacey, Nigel thinks she's hidden the loot somewhere. But now the insurance company might have to cut a very large check. Like I said, Nigel's job and reputation are on the line. And his freedom. He's a suspect!"

"You're a suspect in the burglary? Or in her death?" Lacey thought this was getting clearer and muddier at the same time.

"Take your pick. I've had a little chat with the police." He pressed his lips together. "I have an alibi, but they don't like it and there are things they're not telling me. Cops are like that, I know, but—"

"Why would you be a suspect, Nigel?" Lacey half held her breath. "Did you kill Cecily Ashton?"

"Of course not! Don't be absurd. You don't think I'd come to you if I did it! I didn't kill Cecily. Or burglarize her. I didn't kill anyone."

"Come on, Lacey," Stella said. "You know Nigel can't even defend himself in a fistfight."

"Thank you, Stella darling," Nigel replied. "Not quite the rousing defense of my character I was hoping for."

"Cecily wasn't in a fistfight, Nigel, she was shot." Lacey put her index finger to the side of her head. "Right here."

"Smithsonian," he pleaded. "Lacey. I had no earthly reason to kill her."

"Then why are the police looking at you?"

"Ah." Griffin paused and took a deep breath. "My own fault. My old reputation as a 'man slut.' My word is considered slightly less reliable than a gentleman might hope. And my alibi for the day of the murder is considered a bit weak."

"So you did have an affair with her."

"I did not, swear to God, but she hung on me, she made a fuss over me, she led people to believe we were together. And we'd had a rather loud confrontation over the burglary. I made the mistake of suggesting it was a very inside job. She threw a Jimmy Choo shoe at me. A stiletto. She could have put my eye out. Unfortunately, this unpleasantness was witnessed by the housekeeper."

"When did this happen?"

"Two days before she was killed."

"And your alibi?"

"I was driving to Richmond yesterday, all by myself, to take in the museum down there. And to see about some possible professional connections, should I need them. The museum has a lovely little collection of Fabergé items from the Romanovs. I have a professional interest."

"Honest, he was, Lacey," Stella said. "That's why we could all go to the range together last night for girls' night out, 'cause I didn't have a hot date with Nigel."

Stella's expression held far too much naive faith. Lacey felt her own doubts must be written all over her face. She'd have to cut that out, it would make wrinkles.

"Just what do you expect me to do?"

"I don't know how you suss these things out, Smithsonian, but you do, so I need to know if you come up with something. I don't even care if it's one of those famous-yet-ludicrous fashion clues, or your EFP, I just want to know what it is. And in my fondest dreams, I dream that you might bring this fashion clue to me before you show it to anyone else. For the sake of all the good times we've shared."

"For the sake of the jewels?"

"For the sake of truth and justice, let's say."

"Keep dreaming, Griffin." *This scoop is mine.*

Griffin reached for the toast plate. "Oh, and while you're

at it, why not find the killer too and get us all off the hook?"
He had the audacity to smirk at her while munching the last
piece of cinnamon toast.

The sunshine was so bright Lacey reached for her sunglasses. But the air was frosty, so she buttoned up and
picked up the pace. After the dynamic duo finally left her
apartment she walked down to King Street in Old Town
Alexandria to clear her head, telling herself if only she could
think about something else, she would feel better. She
needed to get her mind off the late Cecily Ashton.

It was fashion, as usual, that diverted her. It was the middle of winter and yet the little dress shop in Old Town was
featuring sleeveless dresses. On behalf of women everywhere, Lacey cursed the sleeveless state of style. When was
the last time, she wondered, there were actual sleeves for
women? Somewhere around 1987?

Talk about a conspiracy, Lacey thought. *This is a conspiracy worth considering.* And the designers were in on it. When
would this mania for exposing every shapeless arm on the
planet end? She thought about her own arms; they could be
better. Perhaps she could wrangle a "Fashion Bite" out of it for
tomorrow and get Mac off her case for one more day. She
opened her purse and dug around for her notebook and pen.

Her cell phone rang. *Leave me alone,* she begged the universe. But she recognized the number and answered it
anyway.

"Hello, Brooke. What's up?"

"Where are you?" The voice was petulant. "I'm at your
place. And you're not."

"How dare I? You're in Old Town?"

"Evidently. I have something for you. Top secret."

Oh, no. That could mean anything. Lacey looked around
to see who might be listening to her phone call. "It's not a
gun, is it?"

"Don't be silly, but it is important." The lawyerly voice was
insistent. "Meet you at the funny place. You know the one."

Brooke caught up with her in their favorite trendy furniture and interior furnishings store near the river. It featured

housewares, glasses, candlesticks, dishes, and an eclectic and eccentric mix of overpriced, overstuffed, and over-whelming furniture. There was barely enough room inside to turn around. It set Lacey's headache in motion.

"You want to look around in here?" Brooke asked.

Lacey fingered a lovely blue and gold plate, wondering where people had room to put all these things, unless they had closets like Cecily.

"No. It's pretty, but it makes me claustrophobic. I feel antsy, Brooke, I need to walk. Think. You can stay here if you want."

"Don't be ridiculous." Brooke ducked under a funky chandelier with multicolored crystals, unlike anything in her own sleek, chic, ultramodern town house. She handed Lacey a manila envelope. "Don't open it here. Put it in your purse."

"Top secret?"

"Do not mock me. And yes, something like that."

"Do I need a security clearance?" Lacey tucked the envelope securely in her bag. Brooke grabbed her arm and led Lacey out to the sidewalk. They started walking toward the Potomac River.

They cut left through the diagonal passage to the water-front past the Torpedo Factory. Once an actual World War Two–era factory that built torpedoes for the Navy, the building had long since been converted into artists' studios and galleries. The docks behind it were filled with plush power-boats, a few sailboats, and the usual flotilla of sightseeing and dinner cruise vessels, the *Admiral Tilp*, the *Miss Christin*, the *Miss Mallory*, swaying to the rhythm of the water and the wind. But Brooke didn't let them stop until they reached the very end of the dock near the riverboat, the *Cherry Blossom*.

"Okay, you can open it now."

Lacey ripped open the manila envelope. "What is this? A legal brief? Do I need a lawyer?"

"It's the Code."

"The Code?"

"*Our* Code."

Lacey Smithsonian's

FASHION BITES

A Call to Arms!
Reprieve the Sleeve!

Once again we women are the victims of a cruel impractical joke. It is the middle of winter, the Washington windchill makes exposed skin frostbite bait, and yet in dress stores all around The Nation's Capital we see nothing but sleeveless dresses. *Sleeveless dresses in January?* Are you feeling a bit chilled by this news, or are you steamed from the sheer aggravation of it? Ah, now I'm getting warmer!

What can we say of confronting the dreaded wintry mix of a Washington winter's ice and sleet and snow in nothing but the ubiquitous sleeveless dress? It makes no sense, you say. And you are right! Designers would never do that to a *man*. Do guys walk into Men's Wearhouse in January and see nothing but racks of Bermuda shorts and Speedos? No! Nor would menswear designers give men pointy-toed stilettos or clothes without pockets. Men would arm themselves with pitchforks and torches.

The fad of sleeveless dresses in winter is in a class with other dopey designer trends, such as collars on bathing suits, strapless dresses in gray flannel pinstripe, business suits with ruffles, and the idiocy of baby doll dresses that make even a department store mannequin look fat.

And if it makes the mannequins look fat, believe me, it ain't gonna make you and me look thin.

Then there is one of my personal favorites, the sleeveless turtleneck. *The sleeveless turtleneck!* For those times of year when your throat is too cold and your arms are too hot? Which season is that exactly? And on which planet does it occur? Are sleeveless dressmakers in league with the cardigan sweater coalition, with a plan to hang a button-down sweater on the back of every office chair in America to compensate for the preposterous sleeveless turtleneck's shortcomings?

Just when are designers going to remember the poor forgotten *sleeve*? Yes, that low-tech invention of infinitely variable length and size and cut that cleverly employs a variety of fabrics to cover and protect the *arm*. Women have arms too—why don't we have sleeves to cover them? Despite the time-honored utility of the sleeve, unflattering skimpy sleeveless dresses in unforgiving fabrics continue to run rampant through the fashion world. In January! But how can we laugh up our sleeves at the folly of fashion—if we have no sleeves? You may think I'm wearing my heart on my sleeve here. I assure you I am not. *I have no sleeve to wear it on.*

It's one thing to design a sleeveless dress for fabulously toned women with fabulously toned arms to wear in the fabulous Washington summer when the humidity is beastly. But what of the rest of us, those women whose arms are not toned and not ready for prime time and are covered with goose bumps in the freezing Washington winter?

Save the endangered sleeve! Please, designers, have mercy on those of us with imperfect arms and who live on planets with intermittently cold climates. Please put a sleeve in it, in our dresses and in our shirts. Give us a choice. Give us back our sleeves! They can be short sleeves, long sleeves, three-quarter sleeves, full sleeves, tight sleeves, or even mutton chop sleeves, for heaven's sake. Just please give us a sleeve. *Free the sleeves!*

I alone cannot effect this vital change, but you, women of America, or just the women of the Washington, D.C., metropolitan area, you can do something about this. Demand some sartorial sanity. Boycott the sleeveless scourge. Draw up petitions and solicit signatures for our cause. Write them on your sleeves, if you have them. Call your congressman and demand hearings, call the designers to testify and demand their heads—and a sleeve.

Remember our battle cry: *Put a sleeve in it!*

chapter 15

"Our code, the Pink Collar Code. Or if you prefer, the PCC."
Brooke thought about it. "Wait, that sounds like some sort of
commerce commission. Or an illegal drug."

Lacey pulled out the document, but before she got a good
look, Brooke grabbed it away from her. She opened the
black leatherette binder and traced her fingers on the document lovingly.

"I expect you to read this and learn it, Lacey," Brooke ad-
vised. "And hide the code in a secure place, please."

"In a lockbox?" Lacey deadpanned. "Or a vault? Should
I get an armed guard?"

"Funny. Very funny. The point is, you don't want people
to think it's valuable. Stick it under the bed between a stack
of dusty women's magazines and last summer's bathing
suits or something. Or just memorize it and destroy it."

"Come on, Brooke, why all the precautions? How many
spies do we know?"

"Gregor Kepelov, for one."

"He's a lunatic. Really Ms. Barton, I think you're labor-
ing under an intense Nancy Drew fantasy and it's getting
worse."

"Ha! We may know lots of spies, Lacey. That's the thing
about spies, they don't tell you they're spying on you." Brooke
warmed her nose with her gloved hands. "It's really getting
cold out here. And just for the record, I want to state that Ms.
Nancy Drew had a lot going for her. A keen intellect."

"A rich daddy," Lacey countered.

"A blue roadster."

"Poor little rich girl always solves the mystery and gets the cute guy."

"Even rich girls need love." Brooke handed the folder back. "The code might be important, Lacey, especially at the rate you collect dead bodies. Can we go inside now and warm up?" Brooke was wearing a light navy jacket over a gray turtleneck. The deceptively sunny weather looked warmer than it was.

"To set the record straight, counselor, I am not now and never have been a collector of dead bodies. You've seen my apartment. Where would I put them?" Lacey returned the Code to the envelope and stuffed it in her bag.

"Good grief, Lacey, I was being metaphorical or something. Objection sustained."

"I need a walk." Lacey strode toward the dock master's office to admire the *Cherry Blossom*, a handsome yellow and white double-decker paddleboat with fancy iron railings, popular for wedding cruises and graduation parties. "You can go on home if you want. My head is too full of thoughts, all of them colliding. I must evaporate them with physical exertion. Or else food, and exertion is more slimming."

"Jumbled thoughts. I love that sort of thing. We'll organize them. Let's walk," Brooke said. "But pick up the pace so I can get warm! And start talking."

Lacey marched them up the Alexandria waterfront, past the Torpedo Factory and the Chart House restaurant toward Founders' Park.

"Good choice, Smithsonian," Brooke commented. "No one to hear us out here, and the lapping waves will muffle our conversation on recording devices."

Lacey hoped her friend was kidding. "Life is more interesting on your planet, isn't it?"

"It's more suspenseful at any rate," Brooke returned. "You're really too trustful of people, Lacey. Despite your sunny optimism, there are monsters and evildoers out there. And close at hand. Don't forget Kepelov. Funny he should pop up now."

"I'm not Little Mary Sunshine, Brooke, I hardly trust a

soul. I simply can't believe you actually wrote down all that stuff you two came up with over margaritas. I know I said to be nice to Stella, but this is above and beyond the call of duty."

"*Stuff?* You mean the Code? And I have produced, written, organized, and now distributed the Code. I'll update it, too, as it evolves. Now, I gave you an extra copy for Stella when you see her next. She's waiting for it. I'd e-mail it, but unencrypted e-mail is *so* not secure."

"Right. Stella." They stopped near the empty volleyball court. "That reminds me, Brooke. We have to do something about Stella. We have to save her."

"From Nigel Griffin, you mean? Of course we will. Now pay close attention to the Code, when you read it. I think you'll be impressed with its simplicity and elegance."

Lacey opened the leatherette folder. "And I'm impressed with the complexity of your thought processes." Brooke looked very pleased. "In fact, I'm dazzled."

"Not to be immodest, but I think there is some genius in its simplicity," Brooke said. "I credit Stella too. This is our own little secret code, a simple word substitution in the context of hair salon language. Easy to learn, and we can use it to create innocent-sounding conversations that will have a deeper meaning."

Lacey closed her eyes for a moment and tried not to laugh. "I know what a code is, Brooke. So many of your conversations have a deeper, not to mention *wackier*, meaning."

Brooke ignored her dig. "We could have used a much more complicated cipher, but complex codes *sound* like codes. Ours doesn't have to be complicated because it doesn't sound like a code, and men won't understand it anyway. And men are generally the people women want to keep secrets from, right?"

"You sure you haven't shared this with Damon, your alleged soul mate?"

"It killed me not to, Lacey, because he *is* my soul mate and I want to share everything with him, but I must honor the Sisterhood of the Code. You don't plan to share this with Vic Donovan, do you?"

"Are you kidding? Vic would find it far too hilarious. Believe me, I would never tell a guy about this." She leafed through the pages. "Do we have code names?"

"Do we have code names! What do you take me for?" Brooke grinned. "You're *Girl Friday*, you Rosalind Russell, you. Stella is *Shagalicious.*"

"Oh, brother. Why not *Stellariffic?*"

"Too many people read her blog."

"Of course they do." Lacey was afraid to read Stella's blog. "And you?"

"*Blonde Ammunition.* Pretty good, huh?"

Lacey was grateful they hadn't called her something awful, like *Helmet Head.* "Now if we had our Secret Pink Decoder rings, life would be rosy."

"I'm beginning to think you aren't taking this seriously." Brooke cocked one eyebrow over her blue eyes.

"Don't be silly! By the way, your lips are turning blue to match your eyes. How about something hot to drink? Race you to Starbucks! Winner gets the fireplace!"

The coffee shop was on the ground floor of an eighteenth-century building on Union Street. It had evolved from a George Washington–era shipping warehouse into a seafood restaurant and now a cozy coffee shop with exposed stone walls. They ordered peppermint hot chocolates with whipped cream and took the table near the gas fireplace.

Lacey licked whipped cream off the top. Her pounding headache had disappeared somewhere along the river and she sipped her hot chocolate gratefully. Brooke checked her messages and reported that Damon had a rendezvous with someone from the PI class.

"Martin Hadley, no doubt," Lacey said.

"Shhh, I'm not through." She listened and then tucked her BlackBerry away.

"What else are you up to?" Lacey savored the rich chocolate and its healing qualities. "Aside from authoring top-secret code documents?"

"What do you think?" Brooke slid her sunglasses up like a headband.

"Don't know, could be anything. You're wearing your Grand Inquisitor look that I've come to dread."

"Good, I'm perfecting it. We need to debrief on Cecily Ashton." Brooke sipped her hot chocolate. "According to our Mr. Hadley—"

"*Our* Mr. Hadley?"

"Yes, the man who hears voices. And yes, he is quite sane. Well, reasonably sane. What he's going through would drive anyone crazy. Damon and I had brunch with him, before I came to see you."

"So you and Damon are interviewing possible witnesses? I should have known. Planning on solving this murder?" Lacey had to stop herself from laughing out loud. "Sorry. Be my guest, you and your Mr. Hadley and his chorus of voices. I'll check DeadFed for updates."

"We're not trying to take this case away from you and play detective, Lacey, we just want to *help* you."

"You don't have to help me, because I'm not a detective."

"Skip the 'I'm only a fashion reporter' riff. I've heard it." Brooke's smug look went so well with her navy and gray attorney's wardrobe. "In fact, I've memorized it."

"You don't believe Hadley's voices-shouting-in-my-head story, do you?" Brooke and Damon were clones in so many ways, Lacey thought. Maybe *they* were the real mind control conspiracy.

"I don't know if there are external forces involved." Brooke paused. "He says he hears voices, but he does not present the usual symptoms of, well, you know, nuttiness. You saw him. The point is that the fix is in, he says. He's convinced he will be arrested for the murder of Cecily Ashton."

"Martin Hadley?" Why were people like Hadley and Griffin insisting on being suspects? "You expect to defend him?"

"You know I'm not a criminal attorney, oxymoron as it is, but I'd be willing to consult with one. He didn't kill her, if that's what you're thinking. But he's a suspect."

"Everyone's a suspect at this point, except me. I don't know if the police have fixed the time of death yet, but we were in class together all morning."

"But you all took a break at some point," Brooke

prompted. Lacey nodded. "Cecily's Jaguar was not in the parking lot when you arrived around eight-thirty. So someone killed her while class was in session? Or drove the car there with the body in it? Hadley knew Cecily, so that's one place for the police to start. Her known associates."

Like Bud Hunt. And Edwina Plimpton. Did everyone in class know Cecily Ashton? *I'll ask Snake Goldstein if he knew her too,* Lacey decided. The heat from the fireplace felt delicious. Brooke pulled a notebook from her purse.

"Aren't you going to take any notes?"

"I am," Lacey said. "Mental notes."

She didn't want to argue with Brooke about the correct way to take notes. They had once gotten into a serious tiff over it. Brooke's notes were *organized.* They were neatly printed in proper outline form, with Roman and Arabic numerals and small block letters, capital and lowercase.

Lacey's written notes were dashed off quickly, as they struck her, the way her mind organized them, not the way a lawyer (or a sixth-grade teacher) would organize them. Her ear was always listening for the good quote, the illuminating turn of phrase, and she wrote fast, trying to catch it all. Lacey dotted asterisks over the parts she thought would be good material for the lede in a story. She wrote in between the lines, and up and down the margins, and she sincerely hoped her scribblings would never be subpoenaed. She couldn't possibly decipher them for the judge, and she would go to jail for contempt of court. But mental notes couldn't be subpoenaed, and so far, her notes on the Cecily Ashton affair had no asterisks, merely question marks.

"As I was saying," Brooke said, "Hadley knew her."

"Lots of people did. Not a reason to be arrested for murder. What's his rationale about 'the fix' being in?"

"The voices are telling him he's being set up. Government agents are going to frame him as the killer. The knock on the door is just a matter of time."

"Why him?"

"Hadley believes Cecily was there at the school looking for him, to apologize."

"She knew he would be there? And apologize for what?"

"They had some sort of spat in front of his mind control support group. But he also thinks there's a chance she was already dead. Maybe the Feds put the body in the car in the lot? Maybe they concocted the whole crime scene specifically to frame him? They might even have gotten his fingerprints somehow and transferred them to the car."

"Oh, please, Brooke! Impossible."

Always unwise to tell Brooke something was impossible. "Not if they kidnapped him, knocked him out, and transferred his prints to latex gloves so someone wearing them would leave Hadley's prints," she said. "They probably implanted a chip in him while they were at it, GPS or something similar."

"If his prints are on the car, maybe there's a simpler explanation," Lacey protested. "Like maybe he killed her?" Hadley didn't seem the type, Lacey thought, but then, who did? "He could be laying the groundwork for his defense by speaking with you. An insanity defense."

"Maybe." Brooke scowled. "I don't like that idea."

"No, it's much better to have an enormous government conspiracy that Damon can crack wide open and save the free world." Lacey rubbed her forehead. The headache started pinging around inside her cranium again. Maybe that was part of the conspiracy too. *If they can put voices in your head, what else can they put in there? Ball bearings?*

"Don't be snide. And remember, Hadley had a public fight with her."

"Public how? You said it was just among their little group," Lacey pointed out.

"Public is public," Brooke insisted. She looked around cautiously. "And if they really are victims of what they say they are, they're under constant surveillance."

"Hadley said she was 'one of us.' Meaning one of *them*, people like him?"

"She didn't quite join the group, which has been lobbying Congress to legislate against mind control. As I understand it, she wanted to meet more people with the same problem, hearing voices. She met Hadley there. But when Hadley pushed her to go public, she freaked out. She didn't want to be openly associated with a bunch of, quote, lunatics, because she was already trying to live down her crazy reputation. There was a scene. Was this woman difficult, or what?"

Dim sunlight filtered through the windows, giving the coffee shop a soft glow. Lacey watched shadows of people on the street, passing by in sweet anonymity. Or were they part of Hadley's conspiracy, always watching themselves, always listening to voices no one else could hear?

"When you hear voices, what's worse?" Lacey asked. "Thinking you're simply crazy? Or thinking the government is after you? No one wants to believe you're losing your mind all alone. Better to be a victim of someone else. And then you might find other victims to share it with." Lacey could understand Cecily grasping at straws, reaching out to other people with the same problem, then running headlong into a bigger problem. "But what if the other victims suddenly want you to be their poster girl?"

"Right. She thought he was after her money and connections." Brooke jotted down another Roman numeral on her notebook full of neatly printed notes. They were becoming complex. She underlined a note and added a footnote. *A footnote.* Lacey couldn't help but be impressed.

"She didn't need her voices to tell her that."

"That's the gist of it." Brooke put the notebook down, but she dotted her point in the air with her pen. "And then there was the question of the fabric."

"What fabric?" Lacey hadn't heard anything about fabric. It caught her by surprise, and she noted Brooke's look of satisfaction. "Okay, spill it, Brooke. I'm clueless. You don't have to smirk."

"Do too! Gotcha!" Brooke laughed, and Lacey laughed too, in spite of herself. "There's some sort of project to develop a mysterious fabric. Something unlike anything else available anywhere. Supposedly it can deflect the electromagnetic rays the government—or whoever it is—was broadcasting into her brain. To block the voices."

"Thank goodness! This is where the tinfoil in the hat comes in!"

Lacey imagined a feature article, or maybe a "Crimes of Fashion" column, with artists' renderings of the latest styles in tinfoil hats. Aluminum dunce hats with shiny cones, chic chapeaus with shimmering veils of aluminum, and of course snappy silver fedoras with gleaming antennas stuck in the band like feathers. All of it a symphony in crinkled cooking wrap, a love song to American industry and ingenuity.

"Sorry. No tinfoil. The foil-lined hat as a radiation shield is falling out of fashion among mind-control victims," Brooke said. *There goes my feature article,* Lacey thought. *Not that Mac would buy it anyway.* "Apparently it's being developed by someone who worked for some research institution. I don't know the whole story, so don't quote me."

"We're not in quotable territory here, Brooke," Lacey said. "Believe me. We're off the map."

"The goal was a lightweight, wearable material to protect the wearer from electromagnetic radiation. Lots of applications there. Medicine, research, nuclear power, the military. And of course the ozone layer is disappearing, so we may all need this stuff soon to keep from getting fried by the sun's UV rays."

"This research scientist, is he legitimate?"

"Who knows?" Brooke said. "A mad scientist with a pet project? My favorite kind."

"Would someone kill for this fabric?" Lacey asked. Brooke shrugged and put down her pen.

A brand-new fabric would be a very interesting story, a new kind of fashion angle. Lacey tried to remember the last time a truly new fabric had been introduced. Rayon was invented in the 1920s. Nylon was introduced in 1938, a year after its inventor killed himself. Kevlar, invented by a woman, was patented in the 1960s, Gore-Tex for rainwear in the 1970s. Polypropylene fleece made from recycled pop bottles in the 1990s: warm, but not particularly stylish.

A new cloth, whatever its original purpose, whether for the military or for mind-control victims, might have a fashion application. Lacey wondered what this stuff might feel like. Could it even be attractive? Designers would make clothes out of anything for shock value: gold coins, liquid latex, credit cards. Was it workable, was it light or heavy, scratchy or smooth, did it drape and fold, was it woven from some kind of natural fiber or something concocted out of chemicals in a test tube? What would it take to develop such a fabric, and where might it lead?

"Maybe this conversation has possibilities, Brooke."

"Maybe this researcher had a serious project, went looking for money, and found Cecily Ashton," Brooke said. "Or maybe she found him. Hadley doesn't know."

"And then she found Hadley's tinfoil-hat people."

"I thought lining your hat with aluminum foil was some sort of urban myth, but Hadley says some victims really do it," Brooke said. "They'll try anything, the voices can be so overwhelming. An ex-FBI agent I know tells me people call the Bureau regularly to complain about aliens or the government bombarding their brains with secret rays. He used to tell them to line their hats with Reynolds Wrap, just to get them off the phone. But Hadley says a recent study shows aluminum foil can actually increase the transmission of electromagnetic radiation to your brain. Makes a better antenna than a shield."

"So much for fashion advice from the FBI," Lacey noted.

"The real question," Brooke went on, "is why would the government target *these* people? They aren't politicians or scientists, most of them aren't even very interesting, and the voices don't say much of anything meaningful. It seems like pure harassment."

Lacey sighed and swirled the last of the chocolate in her cup. "The problem with any conspiracy theory, Brooke, is that no one, especially in the government, can keep that kind of secret. Secrets get out. People talk, they brag, they talk to reporters, they write blogs. For heaven's sake, they put it on YouTube."

A strong breeze signaled the door opening. The coffee shop was filling up with hearty bicyclists, no doubt fresh from a trip down the bike path to Mount Vernon, in search of hot fuel laced with caffeine.

"And yet every single day, a new secret is born."

"Okay, Brooke, so where is this alleged magical mystery fabric?"

"You didn't know about that either?" Brooke's face lit up again. She loved knowing something Lacey didn't. "Cecily Ashton had the only known sample. It was taken in her odd little burglary. The magical mystery fabric is missing."

chapter 16

"Of course it's missing!" Lacey felt deflated. The artist's sketches of hats in her head crumbled into tinfoil dust. "Highly secret stuff is always mysteriously missing, Brooke. It's missing because it never existed in the first place. Besides, Cecily discussed the burglary with me, but she never mentioned any secret fabric. You know what, Brooke? Not only is it missing, it's a myth."

Sources often left out the most important or the most intriguing part of the story, even with a sympathetic reporter. Lacey knew that. They did it to her all the time. Did Cecily not think the fabric was important enough to mention? Or was she focused that day in her dressing room only on the sentimental items she'd lost, and the mystery fabric didn't qualify? Or was it all Hadley's fantasy, destined soon to become an urban myth, courtesy of DeadFed dot com?

"It exists all right. Hadley may be troubled, but he is very concrete." Brooke tapped her pen on the table. "And I assume the inventor has the patent information."

"How does Hadley know all this?"

Brooke pointed the pen at Lacey and grinned. "Guess."

"Voices in his head? Great. Will they testify for him in court?"

"No, no, no. Cecily. She told him about it when she was considering hooking up with the victims' support group. Apparently the mysterious stuff was secured in a special case of hers."

Lacey slammed her empty cup down in exasperation. "It

was in the Louis Vuitton case? The Rita Hayworth makeup case?" No mystery fabric could possibly compare in her mind with the Rita Hayworth case. "Of course it was! How convenient."

"Louis Vuitton? Really?" Brooke dashed off another note in her notebook.

"Oh, now you're interested in the old makeup case too?"

"I have a Vuitton bag or two," Brooke said. "Or three. I have to dress to impress, as you very well know, and my clients are very impressed with status symbols."

"Impressed that they're getting their money's worth in a lawyer?"

"That's why you're the fashion expert," Brooke agreed. "Vuitton is very impressive."

One of the cyclists brushed close to Lacey. She noticed his lean and tightly muscled legs encased in bright blue tights, definitely too tight in certain areas. He wore a neon yellow jersey and his aerodynamic bike helmet made him look like an extra in a Flash Gordon movie. He caught her eye and winked. Lacey wondered if that was the sort of protective gear envisioned by the inventor of this mythical fabric, a sleek, skintight, radiation-proof suit. Hollywood always seemed to be saying that in the future everyone would dress like bike messengers. Or else like postapocalyptic zombies. *Set my time machine to 1939, please.*

"I read your article," Brooke said. "On Cecily."

"I know." Lacey put up her hands in surrender. "I've already heard it's a lousy article. It doesn't even hint that Cecily Ashton would be found dead a week later, suspiciously near where the fashion reporter was taking a private investigator class. How could I have left that part out?" Lacey snorted in disgust. "Good grief, Brooke, do people think I arrange these things?"

"Getting some feedback, huh?"

"All I have to say is that I am not a freaking psychic and it was just a fashion article." Lacey caught people at the table near the window staring at her. She raised an eyebrow at them.

"I don't agree with your critics. I thought it was a wonderful look at a troubled woman in pain." Brooke pulled the article from her purse and unfolded it. "There are lovely details in here, Lacey, telling details. For instance, she says her divorce was difficult and she was no longer in contact with Philip Ashton. But you noted that there is a picture of them together from happier days, that she hasn't put that picture away or smashed it into pieces. Instead, her fingers stroked the glass, and she seemed to forget you were there. And the moment in her dressing room when she mentioned the burglary? Beautiful."

Lacey smiled, relieved. Brooke hadn't made a dig about the scrawled sketch on the back of the Rita Hayworth photo.

"I'm not being nice, Lacey. You really captured her regrets, her mixed feelings, the darkness in her life. You even mention, and so delicately I might add, the particular clothes she wore at pivotal moments in her life. Different dresses, different men, different versions of herself. The highs and lows. The older she got, the more daring the décolletage, right up to that shocking little black dress she was wearing when she rode the hood of that police car careening through Georgetown. Each outfit reflected a different state of mind, a different stage in her evolution. You saw her lose herself, dress by dress."

"You really got it." Lacey felt her cheeks flushing pink.

"You did the impossible—you made the too-rich out-of-control party girl sympathetic. Moving. Even tragic." Brooke folded the article back precisely into thirds. "And I must say, I'm green with envy over those closets. They sound like a spa and a private club and a magic labyrinth all wrapped up in one."

"I left out the part about the safe room. It was supposed to be invincible and impregnable. But it didn't save her. Or her Louis Vuitton case."

"A safe room?!" Brooke's eyes opened so wide Lacey laughed. "You left out the most important part! Tell me everything."

Lacey described the "secret" security features of Cecily's innermost dressing room, the secret buttons and sliding steel panels, the secure phones to the outside world. Brooke made detailed notes and sketches. Lacey filled Brooke in on her morning too, her editor's call and the irritating visit from Nigel and Stella.

"Griffin thinks he's a suspect. Hunt's afraid he's a suspect. Hadley *wants* to be a suspect," Brooke said, summing it up. "What fun. Maybe in this case, the more you think you're a suspect, the more you're not."

"It's a theory. And don't forget Edwina Plimpton, she knew her socially. And Kepelov, who knows everyone."

"Sleep on it, and Damon and I will do the same. I'll call you tomorrow."

Lacey slipped on her coat. "And remember, Brooke, Cecily blamed all her troubles on her husband, or ex-husband. And when a woman is murdered, isn't it always the man?" She stood up to go. "So Ashton is the real suspect."

"Spoilsport. You want a lift home?"

"I'll walk, thanks. It's a lovely afternoon."

"It's freezing and I gotta run." Brooke gulped the last of her chocolate. "Damon and I are meeting to compare notes."

"Rock on, Blonde Ammunition. But don't mention my name."

"See you around, Girl Friday. Read the Code." Brooke tucked her notes into her bag and headed up King Street to her car.

The afternoon light was softening into deep violet shadows. The colonial town homes looked inviting, with the electric candles glowing softly in their windows, illuminating handsome rooms painted in deep shades of green and red. A few beribboned wreaths from Christmas remained on some of the doors. The aroma of wood smoke perfumed the air. Lacey's cheeks were pink and she felt energized, but her thoughts were troubled.

A violent death happens and people want to make sense of it, she realized, and in the process they may see patterns that aren't there. After mentally sorting through all of Cecily's other troubles and all the students in her PI class and all the self-announced suspects, one obvious fact remained. Cecily had been involved in a bitter divorce with a rich and powerful man. Lacey's own words rang in her ears. *When a woman is murdered, isn't it always the man?*

But which *man?*

chapter 17

"I miss you like crazy."

"I miss you crazier," Vic said.

Lacey leaned back against the headboard of her bed. The phone against her ear was a poor substitute for Vic's presence. She flicked the bedside light off so she could see the moon spill over the river.

"I wish you were here, Sean Victor Donovan."

She felt sorry for herself. It had been an exhausting and unfruitful day. She wasn't ready for Monday morning and her meeting with her editor.

"I'll be there soon, tiger," he said. "Now tell me what's been going on. Tell me you're safe and warm and the police have it under control. Tell me that, even if you've gone off half-cocked and you're skulking through the dark alleys of Washington, D.C., in your one-woman crime crusade to find the killer of the billionaire's wife. Tell me, Lacey, so I won't think you've grabbed the sword from the stone without me."

"You know, if I didn't know you better, Sean Victor Donovan, I'd say you were making fun of me. I don't skulk through dark alleys," she protested, "I strut!" There was a chuckle on the other end of the line. "Okay, I don't often strut through dark alleys either. Very seldom, in fact. Not that fond of alleys."

"Just tell me you're safe."

"Of course I'm safe, cowboy. By the way, how was your presentation?"

"It went great, but it would have been better if you were there."

"That's sweet of you to say."

"You really should be here. No one died. Boring convention, business as usual, I made some new contacts, I have some new clients to see, and I miss you. Okay, now you can tell me what's going on," Vic said. "But remember my heart condition."

His only heart condition was Lacey, and she knew it. She sank in among the pillows and tallied up today's annoyances and the rapidly multiplying list of potential murder suspects. Vic didn't like it, as usual, but he offered a tidbit of information.

"I understand the boys in blue are pressing Bud Hunt pretty hard." Vic heard it through the grapevine, all the way out at his convention in California. Hunt wasn't the kind of private investigator to go to PI conventions, but many people there knew him, or knew of him, and bad news travels fast. It made a good cautionary tale about getting involved with your clients.

Hunt was one of the few quarters in the Ashton murder that hadn't been heard from. Lacey pulled the covers up. "So is he really a serious suspect, or do they just want to lean on him? He was a little busy with our class yesterday morning. Although I don't know exactly when the murder happened, and Hunt left the room for quite a while, so maybe he had an opportunity."

"Shooting a woman you've been involved with and leaving her sitting in your own parking lot? Hardly the work of a smart or seasoned killer, or a PI with half a brain. My guess: Either Hunt's alibi is weak and the cops are pounding on it just because that's what cops do for lack of a better suspect, or they're misleading whoever might have framed Hunt for the hit. That's pretty subtle for cops. I know 'cause I was one, but it's possible."

"So maybe they're looking at the ex-husband, but they want him to think Hunt's the main suspect for now?"

"Could be."

Lacey paused. "I forgot to tell you about the comic relief.

Gregor Kepelov and Nigel Griffin. It just keeps getting better, sweetheart."

"Those knuckleheads? The Two Stooges?" His voice shifted subtly. "They're involved in this thing?"

"Kepelov is teaching surveillance for Hunt. Seems to have an alibi."

"Hunt must be hard up for instructors."

"Oh, and Damon Newhouse followed me to school. I'm his alibi."

"He's the Third Stooge." This time Vic laughed. "Your little shadow."

"More like a big dark cloud. But Brooke loves him, so maybe we're both wrong about him." Lacey and Vic both laughed. Neither one thought they were wrong about Newhouse. "And it turns out Griffin was the insurance investigator for Ashton's insurer, or one of them. He was involved in the burglary investigation. He thinks she stole her own jewelry to lure him into her bed somehow and pin it on her ex. Don't laugh yet, Vic, there's more. Griffin says the burglary was strictly amateur hour, but he can't find a lead on the stolen jewels, so that proves it was obviously Cecily who burgled herself to seduce him, poor Nigel, who is as pure as the driven snow, because he was saving himself for Stella. So it's all about Nigel."

"It's good to see Nigel's ego is intact." Vic was amused. "But Cecily Ashton sounds like a complete mess. Does he have a clue who might have bumped her off?"

"No, but he's very interested. He's sure he's a suspect but swears he didn't do it. His job is also on the line. Ashton wants Griffin fired for possibly colluding with Cecily on the burglary, but mostly for sleeping with Cecily, I think, which as I said, he denies. And it gets better. Or worse. Stella and Nigel are back together."

"She didn't get enough of him the first time?"

"What can I say? She's susceptible to his dubious charms. I'm trying not to freak out about it and drive them closer together. I'm counting on her short attention span when it comes to the opposite sex. And counting on Nigel to do something really stupid."

"What's Nigel doing with himself at the moment?"

"I don't know, but he seems very nervous, underneath the smarmy patter." Their morning visit replayed in her head. The cinnamon toast was by far the best part.

"Wait a minute, you've seen the two of them together? You didn't just get all this from Stella?"

"I've seen the Nigel and Stella show, live and in person. They popped in on me this morning. Wiped out all the charitable feelings I got at church and then some. Made themselves right at home. It was pretty darned domestic."

"Sorry I missed it."

"So am I." She could imagine Vic ejecting his old friend the Brit Twit from the premises. It made her smile. "If you'd been here, Vic, he'd have sent Stella alone, as his emissary. Do you think Nigel is capable of murder?"

"Lacey, honey, everyone is capable of killing, given the right circumstances."

"Yeah, I was afraid you'd say that." Nigel Griffin gave an impression of being so mild and bumbling, charmingly so when he tried. Could that act hide a calculating killer? What did he really want from Lacey? What he said he wanted, inside information on the investigation, as if she had any? Or something else? Or to mislead her? She closed her eyes and thought about asking Mac for a personal day off tomorrow. *No, he wouldn't let me off the hook.*

One of the tourist cruise ships was making its way down the river, festive white lights outlining the vessel. Lacey had never been on one of the Potomac dinner cruises. She wondered if it would be romantic, like the Bateau Mouche she and Vic had ridden up and down the Seine in Paris, or would it be just another Washington tourist trap. She really missed Vic. His voice on the phone was not enough.

"Griffin wants to know everything I know," she said.

"He couldn't know half of what you know, darling."

"Sweet talker. On the positive side, Stella tells me he's now a *reformed* man slut."

" 'Man slut'? The things you women talk about."

"I'd rather be talking with you." Lacey suppressed a giggle. "And maybe *not* talking with you."

Vic laughed, but she could hear the frustration in his voice. "Do you think you can stay one jump ahead of this mess, until I get home? I'll be back in a couple of days, after the conference." His voice was like honey and rum, seeping down her spine and through her veins and over her nerves, so soothing and sexy. She closed her eyes and saw his face, his green eyes under dark brows, his strong jaw.

"I always do take care, don't I?" It was a bit of a lie, but a soothing one. She tried to stay out of these messy stories, but somehow they followed her and grabbed hold of her, like quicksand.

"Stay safe, Lacey. And do me a favor and think carefully about whether you really want a concealed carry permit. If you want to do it, we'll do it together. Anyway, we need some more range time."

"Of course I'll think about it, Vic, honey." *After all, I'm practically Annie Freakin' Oakley after our girls' night out at the range.*

"And Lacey—"

"Yes, Vic?"

"Why don't you take a trip through Aunt Mimi's trunk tonight?"

"Are you making fun of me?"

"Not me," he laughed. "You and that trunk have some kind of magical connection. Anyway, darling, it helps you sleep. When I'm not around to rub your shoulders. And other things."

They said good night. A trip through the trunk was tempting, but Lacey thought she owed Brooke and her Pink Collar Crew a little homework time. She pulled the Code out of her bag and opened its black leatherette cover. Good camouflage, she thought. It looked like a very dull legal document.

The first page was the executive summary, followed by the index. *Trust Brooke to include an executive summary for a secret code! And an index! And a glossary. And illustrative usage examples.* Brooke suggested using the acronym PCC, for "Pink Collar Code," or the phrase "pretty cute curls," as a signal that the conversation should slip unobtrusively into the Code.

Lacey read the summary and started to turn the pages, but she found it was putting her right to sleep. In person, Brooke could be endlessly amusing, but on paper she wrote like a lawyer, even a lawyer writing a wacky secret code. This really *was* a dull legal document. Lacey closed the cover. She would try to wing it if Brooke or Stella ever hit her with a pop quiz. Vic's suggestion was much more to her liking. The siren song of Aunt Mimi's trunk was calling her.

The trunk was a treasure trove of vintage clothing and patterns and fashion memorabilia, most of it from the Thirties and Forties. It was packed with fabrics and half-finished outfits in various stages of completion, all preserved in pristine condition along with their patterns. The trunk stood sentry in her living room, doubling as her coffee table. She cleared away magazines and candles, unbuckled the leather straps with their brass fittings, and gently lifted the lid.

As Vic said, Lacey and Aunt Mimi's trunk had an almost magical connection. She loved to wander through it, touching the fabric, feeling the past come alive in her hands, full of textures and colors and memories. It made her feel almost as if she were visiting with her late great-aunt, her favorite relative, soaking up the wisdom and the worldview of another era. Besides clothes and fabrics, Mimi saved letters and photographs and the occasional old magazine article. Her great-aunt's personal time capsule always calmed her. Lacey found strength and clarity in it, two things she needed at the moment. Sometimes the trunk seemed to let the busy unfinished thoughts of the day tumble into place, like shaking the pieces of a puzzle and seeing a picture start to emerge.

She loved the clothes too. These clothes from the past seemed to be meant for Lacey, as if Mimi had unconsciously collected them in her youth to save for her yet-unborn greatniece. Some of them had come to Lacey's aid when she needed them, like her favorite black Gloria Adams suit with its neatly tailored lines, and the spectacular Gloria Adams dress that Lacey had resurrected from the designer's patterns and sketches and a few key scraps of fabric. The only thing missing, Lacey often thought, was a sack of gold doubloons.

Maybe she'd find them waiting for her, at the bottom of the trunk.

She reached into a corner and pulled out a small white paper sack she had scarcely peeked at before. It held a heather green wool crepe, soft and heavy, a lovely piece of fabric, and the pattern Mimi had selected for it. The sketch on the package featured a smartly tailored jacket with patch pockets and strong but not outlandish shoulders, from the early 1940s, Lacey guessed from the style. Mimi also included a handwritten note, with a faded color photograph clipped from a magazine. The note said this jacket would "look smashing" with wool trousers in cream or light tan and her "new plaid scarf." Lacey agreed. This, she decided, might be her next project. She wondered about Mimi's plaid scarf. Maybe it was in there somewhere too.

Lacey lifted the note to look at the photograph: A smiling movie star, wearing a very similar jacket over a silky white blouse. Mimi often took her fashion inspiration from the movies. She loved the styles of the golden age of Hollywood, the era of her own youth, and Lacey too loved the glamour of that long-ago era.

The flame-haired actress in the tailored jacket was Rita Hayworth, standing in her dressing room at a movie studio. On the table in front of the makeup mirror stood the one-of-a-kind Louis Vuitton case. Around her neck she wore a string of large, round, perfect pearls.

Are you trying to tell me something, Mimi?

chapter 18

"Hey, Lois Lane, what's your angle on the Ashton murder?"

Police reporter Tony Trujillo jumped on the elevator just as the door was closing. He gave a nod to her outfit and gazed at Lacey expectantly. She gave him a look and said nothing.

"Nice outfit, Smithsonian. Take no prisoners. Putting Clark Kent in his place today?"

"Today and every day, Tony."

"I've been warned."

Lacey thought this day might call for aggressive, don't-mess-with-me dressing. She pulled out Mimi's deep red suit and curled her hair to fall in 1940s waves around her shoulders. She finished her outfit with a faux pearl choker, bright red lipstick, and a deadly look in her eye. The only accessories she was missing were Wonder Woman's magic bracelets.

The suit fit Lacey like a dream. The jacket was tailored close to her body for a perfect hour-glass silhouette, and she blessed the designer for that illusion. Deep red velvet cuffs on the sleeves were folded back to reveal large covered buttons, marking the suit as fashioned by a seamstress, not a factory. The wartime clothing restrictions under which Lacey's Aunt Mimi had chafed outlawed such things as French cuffs and excess material. Fabric was needed by the men and women at the front, not meant for such fripperies as covered buttons.

"Have a nice weekend, Tony?"

"Sure. Nice quiet weekend. No one even called me to tip

me off to the murder of the month. Possibly the murder of the year, but then it's only January." He leaned against the elevator door and crossed his arms. "But why tip off the poor hardworking senior police reporter at your own newspaper? Why not just keep the murder of the year for yourself? Must be a fashion angle in it somewhere, right, Lois Lane?"

"You snooze, you lose," she smiled at him. "I did call it in, and Shirley gave it to Kavanaugh. Since when did you want to work weekends, Trujillo?

"Since the craziest rich socialite in Washington got whacked. Any theories?"

"No, I'm done with Cecily Ashton," she lied. "I did my little feature. The fabulous closets, remember? And I haven't been talking to the cops, like you have."

"You're not done, Smithsonian. Mac wants a follow-up."

She shrugged. Elegantly, she hoped. Lacey had only the vaguest idea of where to go with the story, at least on a fashion level. An allegedly unknown fabric in a missing makeup case that once belonged to Rita Hayworth. Volunteer suspects. The upcoming museum exhibit. Bud Hunt. The ex-husband. Mind control. She didn't know where to start.

"You're not sharing a thing, are you?" Trujillo said glumly.

"I haven't even had my coffee yet, Tony."

"Enough said." He backed off. "We'll talk later. Over coffee." The elevator doors opened and Trujillo strutted his cowboy boots toward the corner of the office that belonged to the police reporters. Female heads turned as he walked by. His olive skin and seductive smile worked on nearly everyone, but it didn't work on Lacey.

She turned in the other direction. She was relieved to see her own corner of the newsroom was empty, including the desk across the aisle from hers. It belonged to Felicity Pickles, the food editor. If only she could have a few minutes and a cup of coffee to herself before life—and Mac—came roaring at her like a locomotive.

"Smithsonian!" Too late. "Editorial quality meeting this morning."

"Good morning to you too, Mac."

Her editor's brow was furrowed, his eyebrows undulating.

Mac meant business. His café au lait complexion matched the coffee in his cup. "Upstairs conference room. Now. You're on the list."

"Editorial quality? Me?" She groaned audibly. "What have I done now?"

"You, me, and everybody else in Editorial. Another damned content quality meeting. Don't blame me, I hate the whole thing. Blame our publisher, Claudia."

Lacey reluctantly gathered her notebook and pen. She grabbed a cup of the early morning sludge (not quite fully burnt) that the staff kitchen called coffee and trudged upstairs. Trujillo fell in beside her with his own mug of steaming sludge.

"I thought you were too slick to get caught in one of these roundups," she said.

"Mac used his cattle prod," Tony said. "If you want to make a break for freedom, I'm with you. Wanna light out for the border?"

"The border of where? Maryland? Don't tempt me." Lacey felt a scowl creeping over her face. She tried to erase it, but it was a losing battle. She focused her mind elsewhere. The basics: means, motive, opportunity. Who could have killed Cecily Ashton. Who wanted her dead. Who was there and did the deed.

"Man, I totally forgot about this meeting," Tony said. "I don't have time for this crap, I have a murder to work."

"I never filed it in my brain in the first place."

"There was a massive company-wide edict by e-mail."

"That explains it."

The meeting had already started when they arrived. They signed the attendance sheet with a growl. *The Eye*'s reporters weren't the kind of people who respond to groupthink and team-building exercises. They couldn't deal with hug therapy, trendy business speak, and big egos, and they especially hated being dragged into endless meetings to be indoctrinated with the half-baked management mantra of the month. They just wanted to be left alone to do their work. Lacey and Trujillo looked for seats near the door.

Unfortunately, the only seats left were near the moderator, Jeff Dryden, one of the business reporters. Dryden had bought into all the current upper management-speak. This month's buzz phrase was "editorial quality," which meant management thought there weren't enough readers and it was time, once again, to blame the reporters.

Dryden had big round grayish eyes and a bowl haircut. He wore a crisp white shirt and pressed gray slacks. Lacey suspected his mother dressed him. He was talking about "quality content," whatever that was supposed to mean. It seemed to Lacey management's idea of *improving* content usually meant simply *removing* content.

It isn't "content," Lacey wanted to scream. *It's NEWS, damn it! News! Stories, articles, columns, opinions. People want to get the news. They don't get up in the morning and run out to get the "content."*

Dryden invited the copy editors to get the ball rolling. They were busy complaining about everything the reporters did wrong. Copy editors: the forgotten wallflowers of journalism. They never get out of the office to tango one on one with the ever-changing dance of the news, the way reporters do. Copy editors and reporters at *The Eye Street Observer,* as at most newspapers, were locked in an age-old rivalry. Reporters considered copy editors merely failed reporters. Copy editors considered reporters something far worse: failed *writers.*

Lacey thought their editing at *The Eye* routinely betrayed this jealousy. Some of them vengefully removed context and nuance and added commas and hyphens, all without the responsibility that came with the byline. The copy editor's mantra, per Lacey's observation: A successful story? Thank the copy editor. A failure? Blame the reporter! *I'm in purgatory,* she thought.

Felicity Pickles was furiously writing in a notebook. As a feature reporter and a part-time copy editor, she had a foot in both camps, and Lacey was afraid Felicity looked a little too interested in all this blather about *content quality driving consumer brand loyalty.* She peeked over Felicity's shoulder at her notes. To her relief, she saw the words *avocados, lemons, pickled ginger.*

Next to Felicity sat Harlan Wiedemeyer, her new
boyfriend and the death-and-dismemberment beat reporter.
To amuse Felicity, Wiedemeyer was making little faces behind the moderator's back whenever he turned to write
something on his big pad of paper. That made Lacey feel
better too. Dryden focused his bulbous eyes on Lacey.

"Okay, let's start with something easy. Fashion. You,
Smithsonian. Thanks for joining us. A little late. Big day on
the Style section?" He made a show of looking at the wall
clock and she wanted to pitch her coffee at him. She hoped
it was hot enough. "What can we do to improve the content
quality on your beat? Give me a concrete example."

"Less buttons and bows, more blood and guts," someone
yelled from the back of the room, to much laughter.

"The corpse wore a boa—*constrictor*," another one
hollered, one of the less literate sports reporters. Hilarity en-
sued. Lacey didn't even bother to look around. She was just
about to say, *Take this beat and shove it!* But she didn't have
a chance.

"Who killed Cecily Ashton?" Tony Trujillo's voice
boomed out. Lacey stared at him. He gave her a smug little
smile: Payback for not tipping him off. There was a sudden
hush in the room. Dryden was momentarily struck dumb.
Wiedemeyer and Pickles both turned to stare at her and
Tony. She crossed her arms and lifted her eyebrow. A long
moment passed before the voices started buzzing again.

"It appears some people haven't had enough coffee,"
Dryden said, to weak laughter. Lacey clearly wasn't about to
play along, so he stumbled on to his next victim. Unfortunately for him, but to the delight of the rest of the room, he
picked on Harlan Wiedemeyer.

"Content?" Wiedemeyer asked. "Would you be talking
about how I do my job? Because when you say 'content,'
I'm really not sure what you mean, Dryden. Are you talking
about the news, or about my beat, or about my sources? Or
about what I do all day?" Harlan took a deep breath. Dryden
closed his eyes. Lacey thought, *Good, let's send the inquisi-
tors to purgatory too.*

"I'll tell you what will improve my job," Wiedemeyer

continued, warming to the subject. "Letting me do it, without these preposterous meetings! Right now, some poor bastard out there is dying in some horrible way. Getting sliced in half on some unprotected conveyor belt, getting his arm ripped off by some ungodly unsafe obsolete piece of machinery, getting smothered in a vat of cranberries because his company is too damned cheap to buy him a reliable respirator. I should be reporting the news to let other poor bastards know what they can do to keep from dying like the first poor bastard. But no! I can't do my job because I'm sitting in this ridiculous meeting, listening to people who don't know my job ask me what I can do to 'improve' my 'content.' My content is what it is! My job is to go out and find it. So just what the hell are you talking about?"

Lacey remembered what she liked about Harlan. He loved his beat.

"The comments on content quality from the death and dismemberment beat are duly noted," Dryden said, in visible pain. "Let's move on."

He asked the senior obituary writer the same question. The obit writer, Chester Bardwick, was a grizzled old guy with a neatly trimmed white mustache, and he always wore a vest and a crisp bow tie. Lacey didn't know him well; he was a veteran who didn't mix much with the younger reporters.

"Well, to borrow from Wiedemeyer here, it would help me a lot if the 'poor bastards' would have the consideration to die before my deadline," Bardwick said. Laughter rippled through the room. "Really, Dryden, I try to write a lot of obits ahead of time, the ones for celebrities that you know are coming. But like they say, it ain't over till it's over. And others come at me right out of the blue. Cecily Ashton is a good example. I'll have to really scramble on her obit, and sitting in this meeting isn't helping any. I don't have much control over life and death, much as I would like to. And that's my content: life and death. So take it or leave it."

Mac was sitting conveniently by the door at the very back of the room, ready to make a quick escape should the opportunity present itself. Lacey saw someone open the door a crack and slip him a note. He stood up, looked her way, and said one word: "Smithsonian." She stood up and gathered her things and threw a triumphant grin toward Dryden, now sweating under the lights.

"My content calls," she said. "I think I'll take it—and leave," and she got a laugh. Mac met her in the hallway.

"You're wanted upstairs," he said. He pointed to the elevator. "Claudia has spoken."

chapter 19

"Why?"

"No idea. Tell her the EQ meeting's going just *swell*," he said sourly. Lacey waited at the elevator while Mac walked away. She hoped she wouldn't somehow be blamed for the demise of Claudia's friend Cecily Ashton. There were too many suspects already. She exited on the sixth floor and made her way across the marble floors.

Lacey was waved in by Claudia's receptionist, and she stepped through the dark wood doors into the soft glow of Tiffany lamps. It was the only room at *The Eye* free of the nasty green glow of fluorescent lighting. Their publisher's office was the most elegant at the newspaper, with its cherry wood furniture and deep red oriental carpet on the gleaming hardwood floor. The walls were painted deep green, contrasting with the bright white crown molding. Claudia Darnell's office overlooked Farragut Square, a one-block-square patch of green between Eye Street and K Street, with the proud statue of Admiral David Farragut at its center.

"Lacey, come in." Claudia sat behind her desk and beckoned her in with a wide smile, which gave Lacey pause. It was a little too bright for this early in the morning.

The publisher of *The Eye* was a fabulously well-preserved woman of a certain age, perhaps in her mid-fifties, though in the soft Tiffany light she could pass for late thirties. She had buttery tan skin, most likely from a spray at the spa rather than a tanning bed. Claudia took very good care of herself. Her turquoise eyes were as bright as the two-carat diamonds that decorated her ear lobes. Her pale blond hair was tucked into a bun at the base of her head and her understated makeup looked perfect. Today Claudia wore a winter white pants suit. As usual, she was dazzling.

Lacey was glad she had dressed in the red vintage suit that fit her curves so well. It never felt good to feel like a ragamuffin next to Claudia.

"Lacey, thanks for coming."

"No problem." *Was there a choice?*

"I would like you to meet Philip Clark Ashton, Cecily Ashton's—um—" Claudia struggled for the appropriate term. Lacey turned and noticed the older man sitting on the sofa that angled away from Claudia's desk.

"Ex-husband," the man said. "I saw your article yesterday, and I wanted to ask you a few questions."

Lacey's stomach did a flip. *Fabulous. Just what I don't need.* She was curious to meet the man Cecily had blamed for all her troubles, but she wasn't prepared. A command face-to-face meeting in the publisher's office suggested a factual error of the worst kind. Or maybe a lawsuit? The newspaper's legal staff was absent from the meeting. *Good sign or bad sign,* she wondered.

Ashton did not rise to greet her. Normally that wouldn't bother Lacey. The newsroom was a very informal place. But coming from a man of Philip Ashton's status and background, it was a subtle insult. A gentleman rises to greet a lady; but he does not, for example, rise to greet the hired help. He did, however, consent to offer his hand, forcing her to lean down to take it. Ashton had a firm handshake, and he added a little extra squeeze that hurt her fingers. He had said nothing, but he had already conveyed that he intended to be the boss in this meeting. Lacey glanced at Claudia. Her face was carefully composed and betrayed nothing.

It was common knowledge that Philip Clark Ashton bought and sold people as easily as he bought and sold professional baseball and football teams. Actually, it was probably easier. And cheaper. Ashton was taking his time before he spoke. It gave Lacey a chance to look at this man who was a legend in Washington. She knew nothing about sports or his controversial record as a team owner, so her interest was purely in the man. His style spoke volumes.

Of course his watch was a Rolex. On his wedding ring finger, he wore some kind of insignia ring with a large diamond. It probably had something to do with football, Lacey thought, rather than love. Instead of a suit, he wore slacks and a navy jacket, a casual pale pink shirt without a tie. Obviously expensive, and nothing worn or wrinkled. He was tanned, but not over tanned. His head was mostly bald. What there was left of his hair was gray and cropped close. Although there were wrinkles around his eyes and mouth, his skin was smooth for his age. His hands, covered with age spots and large blue veins, were older than his face. If he'd had plastic surgery, it was good work.

Behind his trademark black square-framed glasses his eyes were steel gray, their expression without warmth. It was no wonder Cecily Ashton looked for heat in younger and less serious men, Lacey thought.

Ashton waved Lacey's article on Cecily and her closets. "This was a frivolous article you wrote about my wife, but I suppose I've seen worse," he grumbled in his famous raspy voice. "There were no obvious factual errors."

How about unobvious ones? "Are we here to discuss my article?" Lacey met his eyes with a direct look. She sat down in a cream-colored brocade wing chair opposite the pale green sofa on which Philip Ashton sat. She refused to stand as if she were the maid.

"I had a visit from the police Saturday night to inform me of Cecily's death. The husband is always the first suspect. I know that." He paused, looking away for a moment. "But now it's up to me to bury her and take care of everything. I don't plan to deal with flatfooted cops who should look elsewhere for her killer. Apparently, those geniuses said she'd told some reporter that I was responsible for all her misery, pointing to me as a suspect. That reporter would be you." He coughed to clear his voice. "That sounds very like Cecily to say that."

"That's what she told me, but as you can see I didn't disclose that in print."

"Good thing too." He looked directly at her. "Or we'd be having a very different kind of meeting. I had to buy a copy of your newspaper Sunday and read it myself." He sounded aggrieved by the effort. "You should know I never willingly read anything but the sports pages."

"Oh, were you in sports? Sorry. Not my beat." Lacey detected the faintest curl of a smile twitching at the corner of Claudia's mouth. Ashton ignored it.

"Ms. Smithsonian, about what Cecily said, you must understand one thing. People say horrible things in a divorce. And Cecily—this isn't easy to say. My wife, Cecily, that is, my ex-wife, was mentally ill. She heard voices."

"She heard voices?" *So Hadley was right—maybe she was one of "them."*

"Oh, yes, Cecily never did anything halfway. She heard voices. She had hallucinations. She was paranoid and depressed and increasingly unstable. And that information is medically verifiable by her doctors, but it is not for attribution."

He didn't say "not for publication," Lacey noted. He didn't mind if the information got out, and he would probably make sure it did. His concern was merely that it should not be attributed to him. He knew how the news game was played. It came with the billion-dollar territory.

"At the time I married her I had no idea about her illness. She hid it very well. At first." Philip Ashton's voice never softened. He spoke of his former wife as if she were simply an imperfect possession, an acquisition that had proved a disappointment. "I believe she committed suicide."

"Interesting theory. I heard the police found no gun in the car," Lacey said. "Of course, my information could be wrong. But I assume that means it was murder."

"Your information is correct. Your assumption is wrong." Ashton looked irritated. He wiped his glasses with an ivory handkerchief.

"By all means illuminate us." Lacey started a slow burn over his cavalier attitude.

"Cecily was a tortured woman."

"Really?" Lacey restrained herself from saying she had an idea who tortured her.

"Yes, really," he snapped. "She often spoke of killing herself, but she said she lacked the courage. I believe it is entirely possible that Cecily arranged for someone with more courage to do the job for her."

Claudia Darnell sat up straight in her seat, but she said nothing. She kept her cool blue-eyed gaze on the billionaire.

"You're saying she hired a hit man to kill her?" Lacey asked.

"I'm not saying anything. I'm merely suggesting the possibility. She was a very sick, unhappy woman. And our financial settlement was not quite as extravagant as it has been reported in the papers. It had a time limit, and certain conditions were attached. Her money would be running out soon, at the rate she was spending it." He flashed a wide cold smile full of expensive porcelains. Ashton seemed pleased that he had engineered a settlement that would end by ruining the lifestyle to which his ex-wife had become accustomed.

"Would she have to give you back the Rita Hayworth case, and all the other sentimental gifts she treasured?"

He took his time considering her. "I'd have to have my lawyers check the settlement papers."

"Did you ever love your wife, Mr. Ashton?"

"Isn't that perfect." The smile twisted into an ugly sneer. "I suppose that is the kind of cockeyed question a fashion writer would ask. Tell me, Claudia, do you have any real reporters at this toy newspaper of yours?"

Claudia slapped both hands on the desk and opened her mouth to answer, but Lacey pressed on.

"Because I think she still loved you. Or the man she once thought you were. It seemed that way to me when I interviewed her. She told me she never understood why you stopped loving her. Did you ever love her, or was she hallucinating about that too?"

"I've wasted enough of my time here," Ashton rasped, his lips pressed together in a tight line. He stood up a bit shakily, his hand clenching the arm of the sofa. "I should have just sent my lawyers. Next time I will. I don't want to read any wild allegations about me that my late wife may or may not have made. I don't want to read any slander from two-bit newspapers. I don't want any more visits from two-bit detectives. Do you hear me, Ms. Smithsonian?"

"Oh I definitely hear you." Lacey folded her arms and glared at the man. She didn't get up. She could smell his cologne as he walked past, it was expensive and sickly sweet, mixed with the aroma of decay. Claudia stood up imperiously behind her desk.

"You can see your own way out, Philip. And don't even think about making threats to me, my reporters, or my newspaper again."

He looked from Lacey to Claudia and smiled the same cold smile. "You may think you're tough, Claudia, but if you tangle with me, you will be sorry." Ashton threw open the door and thundered out. "Good day!"

Lacey lifted herself to her feet, a little light-headed. *Well, at least he did say there were no factual errors.*

Claudia sighed. She perched on the corner of her desk. "He's an ass, Lacey. Don't let him get to you."

"It's not that. I can't believe he would say those things about his own wife. She's dead. It's not like she can hurt him now, can she?"

"Some things never stop hurting, I suppose, and Philip's not one to forgive and forget. But remember, Lacey"—the publisher smiled—"*The Eye* always supports its reporters."

Easy for you to say, she thought. "Next time it'll mean lawyers, you know."

Claudia shrugged. "That's what we pay them for. This newspaper will not be bullied, not even by the likes of Philip Clark Ashton. I didn't get into the newspaper business to be bullied," she said, her blue eyes blazing with indignation. "Cecily brought a lot of her trouble on herself, but she didn't deserve a Neanderthal like that."

"I'm going back to work," Lacey said.

"Are you working on a follow-up to your story?"

"Mac ordered one. I just don't know what it is yet."

Claudia nodded. "I'm sure you'll find something. Follow it wherever it takes you. But be careful around Philip. He could have killed his wife, or had her killed, he's certainly capable of it."

"You're not buying his theory that she hired her own assassin?"

"Philip is an idiot if he thinks he can make that story stick just by saying it."

Lacey wasn't so sure about that. She knew powerful people used and manipulated the media all the time. It was a big game, especially in Washington, D.C., where it was one of the biggest games in town. Politicians, pundits, congressional staff members, bureaucrats, activists, lawyers, lobbyists and more, even some reporters, they all deliberately floated lies, half-truths, and rumors in the press, just to see what would fly. Someone in the media, in the newspapers or on television or on the World Wide Web, would print or broadcast Ashton's allegations, whether they believed them or not. And if you print it, Lacey mused on the way down in the elevator, someone will believe it.

She made a note to herself to tell Brooke to head Damon Newhouse off at the pass and not to let DeadFed dot com be used by this creep or his puppets. She hoped Damon was more interested in Martin Hadley's mind-control angle on the Cecily Ashton murder than in a billionaire who thought he could buy anyone. But you never know.

Lacey decided to forego the pleasure of rejoining the editorial content quality meeting. Instead she headed back to her desk to check her e-mail. There was a press release from the Bentley Museum of American Fashion, reassuring the media that the upcoming Cecily Ashton Collection exhibit would open as planned despite her "tragic and untimely death." It gave Lacey enough information to write a quick follow-up on Cecily, with a fashion angle. That and maybe a "Fashion Bite" might stall Mac while she asked some questions elsewhere.

She put in a call to the Metropolitan Police Department about the burglary at Cecily Ashton's home. She was told exactly what she expected to hear. No arrests, no leads, no recovery of the stolen goods, no further information available. "Do you even care?" she asked the officer.

"Yes, of course, ma'am, crimes against property are a top priority here in the District of Columbia. No ma'am, we haven't put it on the back burner, we wouldn't do that, ma'am. And now Virginia's got a much bigger case to solve, with Ms. Ashton's murder. That's not a quote, ma'am."

While Lacey was on the phone trying to pry a fact or two from the public information officer, her fellow reporters began filing back into the newsroom, stiff and grumpy from the accursed editorial quality meeting. With the phone to her ear she scanned the rest of her boring e-mail, skipping over a local fashion show for charity, a boutique opening in Bethesda, a fashion industry trend forecast for spring, when something unusual caught her eye: A press release from the White House. On the subject of fashion.

Stop the presses!

Fashion Bites

Style Emergency: White House Bans Provocative Displays of Apparel!

Stop the presses! The latest fashion buzz, or anti-fashion buzz, around the Capital City is that the Provocative Display of Apparel, or PDA, will no longer be tolerated at the White House. What is a Provocative Display of Apparel? In D.C., many everyday fashion crimes qualify as a PDA. And no, by PDA we do not mean Public Display of Affection. That kind of PDA was banned in Washington *long ago*.

On the White House PDA hit list, according to an official press release: jeans, sneakers, shorts, miniskirts, T-shirts, tank tops, and flip-flops. (No more flip-flops in the White House? Dream on, Washington!) Their goal: no more flashing of bottom cheeks or décolletage before the dignified portraits of our Founding Fathers.

That's right, the National Apparel Propriety Police have banned America's most popular casual wear from America's House! In addition to gutting the off-duty wardrobes of most government workers and the jeans and T-shirts of many style-impaired journalists, these new anti-PDA rules are aimed straight at the hearts (and suitcases) of *tourists*. Tourists, those indispensable, clueless, shoeless folks who snap photos, smile, wave at the camera, spend money at museum gift shops, wander for hours on the Mall in neon T-shirted hordes, and clog the stairways of the Metro at rush hour. We love them—*and we don't love them.* We want their money. Just don't dress like them and expect to be allowed into the hallowed halls of the White House anymore. No PDAs allowed.

We are all created equal under the White House dress code, tourist and Washingtonian alike. The White House does not want us to arrive dressed to hang out or flip-flop, to dangle, mangle, tumble, or stumble. No admittance if you're dressed to plow the field or mow the lawn, or to go for a swim in the Tidal Basin with the nearest intern. Dress the way you would in your own house? In the White House, that's now a Provocative Display of Apparel.

It's about respect, the White House press release notes. Respect for yourself, and respect for the highest office in the land, the Office of the President. Toe the line—and no toe cleavage—or you won't get past the West Wing gate.

But fear not. From what I've seen recently, Congress is still a fashion-code free zone. And very nearly a fashion-free zone. Tourists welcome! Reporters on the loose! Beaten and battered blue jeans, free-range flip-flops, and rude, crude political-message T-shirts are all alive and well and roaming the halls of Congress.

So attention Washington tourists! If your Provocative Display of Apparel makes you persona non grata in the White House, go hang out in Congress. There you can be casual where your tax dollars are misappropriated and misspent. And where the flip-flop is not just casual footwear, it's a treasured American political art form.

chapter 20

Lacey was tapping diligently away at her follow-up on the Ashton museum exhibit when she became aware of a strange sound nearby. The sound of giggling. It was coming closer. Lacey glanced up in the direction of the sound. Felicity Pickles and Harlan Wiedemeyer were laughing and cooing like hormonal teenagers, bumping their hips together like drunken sailors as they walked. They stopped at Felicity's cubicle right across the aisle from Lacey. There was no ignoring them.

Oh, good. More unlikely lovebirds, Lacey thought. Stella and Nigel. Brooke and Damon. Felicity and Harlan. *Who's next?*

Love in bloom in the newsroom might be distracting, but she had to admit the atmosphere was happier now that she and Felicity were no longer glaring daggers at each other. Lacey helped connect her with Harlan, and while the fashion reporter and the food editor were not quite friends, they were no longer enemies.

Felicity was also looking more attractive these days. Being in love agreed with her. Her chestnut-colored hair was glossy and her milk white skin was clear. The job of food editor was clearly an occupational hazard to her figure, but her well-padded curves had met their soul mate in chubby little Harlan Wiedemeyer. Today Felicity wore a shapeless blue sack dress, which did nothing to flatter her figure, but it matched the color of her eyes.

The man with his arm around Felicity was equally round,

from his round head to his round belly. His brown tweed sports
jacket strained across the chest, but it was too long in the
sleeves. His khaki slacks were standard reporter wear, maybe
a little shorter, a little tighter in the thighs. Under the jacket, he
wore a brown shirt with a loosened tie, liberally sprinkled with
powdered sugar from his last doughnut at Krispy Kreme, his
second office. *One reporter, standard issue, slightly used,*
Lacey thought. *With doughnuts. And in love.*

"Lacey!" Harlan spluttered. "We have big news! Front
page news! Stop-the-presses news!"

"Does it have anything to do with exploding toads?"

He and Felicity both burst out laughing, gazing fondly
into each other's eyes.

"No! But wasn't that a great story I wrote on that? Those
poor bastards!" Known around the newsroom as the death-
and-dismemberment reporter, Wiedemeyer had a nose for
news of the bizarre and the bloody. It wasn't just his off-the-
beaten-path beat that seemed to disquiet the other reporters,
it was the sheer glee he took in it.

"Nope. No exploding toads this time," he said, barely
containing his joy. "No spontaneous human combustion, no
house cats that foretell the angel of death. Something even
more amazing than any of that."

"Oh Harlan, what is it? What could be more shattering
than exploding toads? It isn't exploding goats, is it?" Lacey
braced herself. Harlan gulped and gazed down at the floor,
suddenly shy. He took a deep breath.

"Well, you see, my amazing Ms. Pickles, my sweet Felicity, she has agreed to—" Harlan's voice broke. He wiped his
eyes. Felicity smiled at him encouragingly and squeezed his
hand.

"Go on, Harlan, honey. You wanted to tell Lacey. He
wanted to tell you first, Lacey, because—well, you know."

"Because the woman of my dreams has agreed to accept
my proposal. And you're the one who brought us together!"
Wiedemeyer danced a little two-step with Felicity Pickles,
the woman of his dreams. "We are getting married!"

"Married?" *Aw shucks, no exploding goats?* "You two are
getting married?"

Harlan swept Lacey up into a big unwelcome surprise hug, but it was over soon. *Please! Reporters don't hug!* Felicity thrust out her left hand to display a one-carat diamond solitaire in a platinum band on her ring finger. She wiggled her fingers and her grin was nearly as bright as her diamond.

"Why it's beautiful, Felicity. It's so sparkly!"

Perhaps not as sparkly as Felicity at that very moment. Lacey had noticed the very same style of engagement ring on many fingers in the District recently, but that made the ring no less lovely. It had the seal of approval of betrothed interns, besotted Capitol Hill staffers, and young lawyers in love. No one had asked for Lacey's hand in marriage lately, she thought, but it might happen, someday far in the future.

Lacey murmured more compliments about the ring. It was lovely, tasteful, elegant, and not ostentatious, and she realized it must have set Harlan back a chunk of cash. Anyone on an *Eye Street* reporter's salary would pale at the price of a good quality one-carat diamond ring.

"It's the most beautiful thing I've ever had." Felicity had tears in her azure doll eyes. "I told Harlan that really it's too much and that we should be sensible and save for a nice house but— Oh my, just look at it—" She gazed at the ring with a passionate and possessive fervor. Lacey knew that ring would never leave Felicity's finger.

"Throw sensible out the window," Harlan said. "Love isn't about being sensible, it's about being passionate." His voice was rising. A few reporters looked over, then away again. "I'm such a lucky bastard!"

"Spoken like a true romantic." Lacey was charmed by Harlan's over-the-top declaration of love.

"I was going to wait until Valentine's Day to pop the question," Harlan said, still pumped with energy. "I always thought the little cherub with the arrow was an appropriate expression of my feelings, and I wanted to wait till it was his day. But wouldn't you know it, I just couldn't wait. So here we are. Isn't it amazing?"

A mischievous child with a quiver full of deadly arrows? Certainly that was appropriate to Harlan Wiedemeyer's reputation as the newsroom jinx, Lacey thought. As soon as

Felicity developed a crush on Harlan, her minivan had been blown up. *The Eye*'s Capitol Hill reporter had once tangled with Harlan and saw his car destroyed almost on the spot by a city bus. Lacey herself had barely escaped being flattened by a falling Krispy Kreme doughnut sign, merely for accepting a ride from Harlan. Their editor Mac liked to say there was no such thing as a jinx, but even he conceded that unusually bad luck seemed to follow those who crossed Wiedemeyer's path. Mac tried to keep his distance. Lacey hoped she'd been cured of the jinx by helping connect Harlan with Felicity. *But if there's no such thing as a jinx,* she wondered, *is there really a cure?*

"My feelings just exploded, so to speak," Harlan continued. "Like an exploding toad." He chuckled at his own joke, gazing at Felicity in adoration.

There's a resemblance, Lacey thought. But if she squinted just right, she could see Wiedemeyer as a romantic hero who would battle dragons for his fair Felicity. If the Wiedemeyer Jinx was real, that dragon was in big trouble.

"Congratulations. I'm thrilled for you both. Have you two lovebirds set a date?"

"I don't know, but we're thinking about September," Felicity said. "We could have a harvest theme! Oh, there's so much to do. So much to plan. The menu, the appetizers, the main dishes, the desserts, and of course the most important thing of all, the wedding cake." Felicity's skin glowed, her cheeks were brushed with color, and the look in her eye said this was what she had been waiting for all her life: planning her wedding, and planning the food. "And the main entrée! So many choices. Perhaps Cornish game hens for two hundred?"

"Don't worry about a thing, my sweet little gherkin." Harlan had recently taken to creative terms of endearments of the cucumber kind, a nod to Felicity's last name, Pickles. Felicity thought this was particularly adorable. The rest of the newsroom rolled their eyes and make gagging noises. Lacey tried to keep a straight face.

"If anyone can tackle two hundred Cornish game hens, Felicity, it's you," she said.

"And not just the wedding cake! There's the groom's cake to plan too."

"The groom's cake?" *Good Lord,* Lacey thought. *Nobody told me about a groom's cake.*

"Oh, it's essential! It's such a great old Southern wedding tradition." Felicity nodded sagely. "The groom's cake is supposed to reflect something personal about the groom. Well, I've been thinking: a tower of doughnuts! We could sprinkle it with the same color of seasonal sprinkles they use at Krispy Kreme. Or if we do a fall wedding, it's football season! We could stack those little football-shaped doughnuts they make into a delicious and unique groom's cake. Can't you just see it, Lacey?"

"Of course she can," Harlan said. "I can see it too. We must put our own stamp on this wedding. Make it unique and individual, just like you, my little dilly pickle."

Lacey nodded sympathetically. It seemed the right thing to do. It was either that or roll her eyes and make gagging noises.

"Felicity, you are a dream come true," Harlan said. "Pickles and doughnuts, a match made in heaven."

"Sounds lovely," Lacey said, getting a grip on herself. "So it'll be a small, intimate wedding?" Lacey doubted that she'd be invited, but she secretly longed to witness this spectacle. *Maybe the cake will explode.*

"Good heavens, no," Harlan declared. "We want everyone to know how happy we are. It's going to be big! A real mob scene." Felicity giggled and gazed at her man in adoration.

Lacey tried to imagine this one-of-a-kind wedding. Felicity's all-encompassing love of seasonally themed sweaters was well known in the newsroom; Lacey visualized the bridesmaids wearing matching fall sweaters in autumnal shades, decorated with knitted apples and pumpkins. Or little red schoolhouses and autumn leaves, another staple of Felicity's fall collection, perhaps worn over matching plaid skirts. The groomsmen would all wear matching plaid ties and cummerbunds, the best man would produce the ring from a Krispy Kreme doughnut box. And then they would all dance. Lacey had to pinch herself to keep from laughing. She tried coughing instead.

"We'd better go tell Mac now," Harlan Wiedemeyer said. "He'll want to know."

Lacey watched Wiedemeyer and Pickles skip away happily, hand in hand. This time she did laugh. *Those crazy kids. Exploding cupids in love!*

chapter 21

Lacey mentally shifted gears and picked up the phone to call the man who predicted to Brooke and Damon that he would soon be framed for the death of Cecily Ashton.

Hadley answered on the third ring and told Lacey he worked just off K Street, in Washington's legal and financial district. His office was only a few blocks away from *The Eye*. He preferred not to talk about his personal business on the phone, he said, and he refused to meet her at the newspaper offices. Everybody knows the government tracks journalists, he told Lacey. Hadley conceded that perhaps the government might not track every *fashion reporter*, but he still refused to be seen inside her newsroom.

Lacey pointed out there weren't enough G-Men in the country to track all the journalists in Washington, D.C. Personally, she could hardly imagine anything more dreary than listening to thousands of reporters' know-it-all conversations, and most reporters had too many opinions on nearly everything. *Except fashion.*

"And what about the voices," she asked, "won't they know where you are anyway? So what does it matter where we meet?"

"They don't need any extra help from me," Hadley said. "I like to keep them guessing. I try to baffle them. They can't read my thoughts, you know. Their transmission channel seems to be unidirectional. But of course, they can draw conclusions from what I do and say, and they have microphones and cameras *everywhere*."

Some reporters wondered how Lacey could keep a straight face when she talked with people like Hadley, but she was willing to listen to nearly anyone with a good story. And he wasn't the craziest person in Washington by a long shot. She recalled a man who used to ride the Metro wearing a contraption on his head made from a wooden box and a full-face motorcycle helmet, all stuck together with duct tape. He wore it strapped to his body with an elaborately belted duct-tape harness. She never learned what Boxhead Man's story was, but she wondered if he might be a friend of Martin Hadley.

She met Hadley at the statue in Farragut Square, across the street from *The Eye*, and then went for coffee. As they approached one particular park bench in the square, Lacey recognized the occupant as Quentin, a homeless man she knew. This was one of "his" benches. He put down his newspaper and grinned at Lacey. She waved back.

"Smithsonian! You lookin' good today. How you been? How's Mac's two little girls doin'?" Lacey said they were just fine and she slipped a few dollars into his cup. Hadley added a dollar of his own. He and Quentin exchanged a look.

"You say hello to Edgar for me now." Quentin pointed to his temple, and Hadley nodded. Quentin tipped his hat formally and resumed reading *The New York Times*. Lacey and Hadley crossed Seventeenth Street to the Firehook Bakery.

"The newspaper is out, but the bakery is okay?" Lacey asked, after they found a table with their lattes. "The voices don't reach inside bakeries?"

"Bakeries aren't too bad. Perhaps they don't want to torture the bakers," Hadley said. "Everybody's got to eat."

"Can't argue with that. And who's Edgar?"

They would get around to Edgar, Hadley promised her. It turned out Hadley was a lobbyist for a K Street law firm, but while he had a law degree, he said, he wasn't a lawyer. He considered himself a "citizen advocate." It gave him a fresh insight into the legislative process, he said. Lacey had her own suspicions about lobbyists. Hearing voices might explain some of them.

"What do you lobby about? Or for? Or against?"

"Oh, patent law, copyright, intellectual property, various other nebulous subjects," he said vaguely. "We have a lot of clients. This job gives you a real insight into how the government works, how laws really happen. Laws and sausage, you know that old saying? Two things you never want to watch being made? I get to watch."

Hadley removed his dark navy topcoat and draped it carefully over the back of the wooden chair, careful to avoid letting it touch the floor. He looked like any well-dressed Washington lobbyist. His dark gray pin-striped suit was well tailored, his pale blue shirt was crisp, and he wore an attractive and neatly knotted dark blue tie with regimental stripes. He noticed her analytical gaze and smiled sadly.

"Oh yes, I can pass quite well. Few outward signs of the inner—" He suddenly shook his head and tapped the side of it smartly with the heel of his hand.

"Headache?" Lacey reached into her purse. "I have some Advil."

"Not exactly. More like static. And it's just hard not to answer back sometimes when they taunt you."

"I thought you said they couldn't hear you."

"They can't read my thoughts. But there may be an implant of some kind in my brain. They seem to hear what I say, though it could just be the surveillance microphones they have all over this town too, which means they hear every word you say too." He lifted his eyebrows at her quizzically.

"Really." She leaned in close to his ear. "Well, navy and white will be big this spring! You heard it here first. It's a secret. Boy, I'd hate to see that get around too soon. Of course," she confided, "navy and white are always big for spring."

Hadley looked at her and then laughed, unexpectedly. "That's good, it'll drive them nuts. I know how it looks, talking to nobody. Sometimes I can't help talking back, but I put my cell phone up to my ear, so people just think I'm talking on the phone. Everyone looks crazy these days."

"Do you ever think you are crazy?" she asked him. "Not my opinion. Just a question."

"I used to. That's what they want me to think. That's what

they want you to think." He balled his fist and his breathing became labored for a moment. "Sorry. They want the world to think a lunatic killed Cecily Ashton. That way they can shut both of us up. But I'm not crazy."

"What do they think about the voices at your job?" Lacey asked, sipping her latte.

"Didn't exactly put it on my job application," Hadley said. "They might consider that worse than being arrested for murder. I've been questioned by the police, and as you know from Ms. Barton, Esquire, I rather expect to be arrested at any moment."

"Yeah, Brooke mentioned that," she said. "But a lot of people were questioned. I was questioned. That hardly means you're going to be arrested. Unless you actually killed Cecily Ashton."

"Let's just say I've got inside information."

"The voices?"

"Yes, the voices."

Hadley looked distracted for a moment. His attention seemed to focus inward and he shut his eyes. He rubbed his head hard and then opened his eyes again.

"Is something wrong?" Lacey glanced around the room to see if anybody was staring at them. People were concentrating on their newspapers and their coffee.

"Not really." He gave a brief shake of his head, as if to brush away an errant thought. "Those goofballs. It's Raj today," he sighed. "They subcontract some of the work out. To some call center in India. Outsourcing. Can you believe it!" Hadley laughed. Lacey didn't quite believe any of it.

"I can't understand a word Raj says sometimes, he has this thick singsong Indian accent," Hadley went on. "Or I'll catch every third word, just enough to drive you crazy, like a bad tech support call. Or a loud buzz, like electroshock therapy, to get my attention. But often it's just a babel of Indian voices. Sometimes it becomes background noise, like elevator Muzak. Could be worse. And Raj is really the least offensive of them. But why send those jobs to India? Senseless. False economy. No way to run a mind control project, if you ask me." He laughed again, but it sounded forced.

Lacey blew out the breath she'd been holding. She made a mental note to check out DeadFed dot com when she got back to the office. She actually loathed reading Damon Newhouse's paranoid conspiracy geek Web site, but she did try to monitor it sometimes when he was following her around. The site contained a bottomless well of bizarre information, misinformation, and paranoid fantasy. Searching on Raj, the outsourced mind-control voice from India, might prove entertaining.

"This may seem like an odd question," Lacey said. "But why are you telling me this? Aren't you afraid something will happen to your job if word gets out? In my newspaper, for example?"

"Sorry, Smithsonian, but you work for *The Eye Street Observer.* No one at my office would ever admit to reading it. If they did catch wind of it, I'd simply deny everything and blame it on you. Plausible deniability is the name of the game in this town. And yours is the newspaper of least respect."

"It's sweet of you to care." He wasn't saying anything she didn't know.

"Don't be offended, Ms. Smithsonian. I rather like your newspaper. I can't help it if people in Washington think it's a scandal sheet run by that vindictive, yet attractive, Claudia Darnell, who is simply out to get even with this whole town and pay back all the bastards who made her life miserable. I respect her for that. There are much worse reasons than payback to run a newspaper."

Another reporter, possibly one with some pride, or one from a bigger newspaper, might have stomped out. But Lacey wasn't that kind of reporter, she had too much curiosity, and the Firehook Bakery coffee was too good. For a reporter, insults were just the price and reward of curiosity. Hadley was a fascinating character, and besides, Lacey didn't disagree with him. There really were worse reasons to run a newspaper.

Hadley suddenly clenched his fists and pressed them against his stomach, his face contorted into a grimace.

"What's happening? You're in pain. Tell me, please. Can I help?"

"Nothing you can do. This assault really wasn't too bad. When they subcontract the work to India, the signal is weaker. I've been rolling on the floor with some walloping pain sometimes. You just want to blow your head off."

"Perhaps Raj is bad at his job," she suggested.

"We can only hope. Now Edgar, he's much worse. A sadist. And a sarcastic son of a bitch."

"Edgar is another voice?" Lacey stirred extra cream into her latte. Maybe that explained some of her homeless friend Quentin's problems. "How many voices are there?"

"Half a dozen or so. Edgar is the supervisor, then there's Raj and the Indian guys, and there's a woman at night named Alyssa. She's a part-timer. Those are the main voices, but there are others. I don't even know all their names yet, and it's been years. This thing doesn't come with caller ID."

"Do you ever think you might have made up the voices? Not deliberately, but—"

"Of course. I have tried my very best to convince myself of that. But I haven't. And by the way"—he paused to listen—"Edgar says you've talked with much crazier people than me."

"Good point." Lacey pulled out her notebook, but she wasn't sure whether she would actually write anything down. *Spy cameras everywhere!* "Please go on. Curiosity is my weakness."

Hadley stared at her. "Edgar says you might be the only one who can find out who killed Cecily Ashton."

"If they don't arrest you first. Did you kill her?" She held on to her hot coffee just in case he didn't like the question and she might have to throw it in self-defense.

"No, of course not. Besides, there are too many people ahead of her on my list." She spilled a little coffee on the table. "A joke! A poor one, I see. Sorry. Go on, ask your questions."

"How well did you know Cecily?"

"Well enough to know she was a selfish idiot who had the means and opportunity to help people but chose not to. I'm not sorry she's dead."

"You had a big fight?"

"That was orchestrated by Edgar. We needed her help, her name and resources could open doors for us. She threatened to sue us if word got out that she was a TI. I threw her out of the meeting and threatened to countersue. Edgar says you should follow your instincts, by the way. He means you, specifically, Lacey Smithsonian."

"Excuse me?" That was exactly the kind of ringing endorsement she needed to further her career. *Lacey Smithsonian: Number One Choice of the Voices in Your Head!* "I take it Edgar reads my 'Crimes of Fashion' column?"

Hadley stopped and listened to nothing Lacey could hear. "Edgar's got a whole dossier on you. He says you're hardheaded. It's a compliment, of sorts. He means you're impervious to them; they can't get inside your head."

"Good for me. I'm a blockhead." Probably too crowded in there. *My own thoughts tumbling around in there are plenty, thanks.* "You said there was another voice, a woman?"

"Alyssa. Part-time at night. She torments me sometimes, she can be wicked. Other times it's as if she's just reading from a script. She's a grad student somewhere, I think she believes this is some kind of research project for her psychology department. She doesn't know what she's doing. She's being used. Like me. At least she's getting course credit. But of course Alyssa, sweet Alyssa, is just a code name. She let that slip too. They're all code names, except perhaps for the ones in India. Why bother with code names when you can't understand them anyway?"

"Good question. Have you had any, um, professional help?"

"A shrink? Yes. Help? No." Hadley addressed her unasked questions as if he'd read her thoughts. Or perhaps Edgar was reading her dossier to him. "I do not have a split personality, Ms. Smithsonian. I do not at any time give up my awareness of my identity, or my surroundings, or the universe, or the year, or whoever the current occupant of the White House is. I am not schizophrenic, I am not manic-depressive or bipolar or borderline or whatever it is they're calling it this year. I'm not a madman, and I'm not sick. I am, however, tormented and depressed and damaged by this, and I know victims of this assault who have been driven to madness and suicide, or worse. Make of me what you will, Ms. Smithsonian."

"I haven't said I don't believe you, Hadley."

"It's hard to believe, Lacey. I accept that. At least you're listening to me. And if you can find out who killed Cecily Ashton and keep me out of the hands of the police and the courts and the prison system, where I would be even more completely at the mercy of the government's mind control wizards, more power to you."

"I make no promises about anything." Lacey took her last sip of coffee. It was much better than the newsroom's, but she wanted to get back to the normality of the newspaper. "Martin, what can you tell me about Cecily's missing fabric?"

"Ah, the fabric. I've never seen it. She said it might be capable of shielding the wearer from some of the uglier aspects of electromagnetic terror, which as you have seen sometimes causes terrible pain in various body parts, particularly the head and the sexual organs. Searing, debilitating pain. Obviously, such a fabric would be very valuable to those of us who are suffering from this terrorism. She said she had it, but she wouldn't share it. She wouldn't even show it to me. She was a selfish, callous, manipulative witch."

"She was working with some sort of chemist? I'd like to talk to him."

"I was never told the name, but there's someone I can call," he said. "Privately. If you'll excuse me."

Hadley pulled out his iPhone and went to the men's room. When he returned, he handed Lacey a neatly torn piece of notebook paper. It had a name and a phone number written on it.

She looked at her watch, hoping Mac hadn't noticed she was missing yet.

"Don't let me keep you," Hadley said. "I have to go too. Back to the scintillating world of patent law. Thanks for listening."

GOVERNMENT GOONS FRAME MIND CONTROL PATSY: FIX IS IN, TI SAYS. EXPECTS IMMINENT ARREST. It was the lead story on DeadFed dot com when Lacey reached her desk.

Damon Newhouse had been busy with his "eyewitness account" and "exclusive interview" with Martin Hadley, the TI or "targeted individual" at the center of a government mind-control conspiracy. The prose was lurid, if not quite purple, and all from Damon's unique bird's-eye, alternate-reality point of view. Lacey was relieved to see her name mentioned only once, along with others in the PI class.

Unfortunately, her name was also linked, and she clicked on it. It took her right to the Lacey Smithsonian *pages.* She was horrified. There were links to her stories in *The Eye.* That wasn't bad enough. Newhouse had a whole gallery of embarrassing photographs of her. Just how did he manage to find so many grimy photos taken at horrible angles? No doubt with a cell phone. She steamed silently. There was even a short gossipy item on how fashion reporter Smithsonian planned to take a course in private investigation in Falls Church. It was dated a week before the class started. *Good Lord, who might be reading all this?* She felt the blood leave her face.

Lacey dialed Brooke's number and gave her friend a piece of her mind.

"Damon probably didn't think it would bother you," Brooke said. "You're a reporter."

"Meaning I'm public property? He told the whole world where to find me! Why wouldn't that bother me?"

"Okay, okay. I'm sorry. Damon's sorry," Brooke said. "Or he will be. I'll have him take down the link."

"I want it off today."

"You're right, it was thoughtless of him. I'll see what I can do. Promise."

Lacey was only slightly mollified, but it would have to do. After that, she couldn't bring herself to check out Stella's blog.

Once her blood pressure had fallen to something approaching normal, Lacey pulled Martin Hadley's piece of notebook paper from her purse. The name was Simon Edison. She called the number and left a message. She was pleasantly surprised when he called back a few minutes later.

Edison was consulting on the upcoming Cecily Ashton exhibit at the Bentley Museum of American Fashion. He had been assisting Cecily personally, he said. "Cecily said I was a cross between a research scientist, a magician, and a feng shui artist," he chuckled. "In other words, she liked telling me what to do, and I tried to do it."

They agreed to meet in person. She preferred talking to her sources face to face. She had noted an appalling trend in Washington to kill off the face-to-face interview. Politicians, officials, and even the lowliest bureaucrats were starting to demand that any and all questions from journalists be sent via e-mail instead. Hours or days later they would e-mail back their bland written answers, carefully vetted through invisible layers of bureaucracy and attorneys and PR specialists. It eliminated nearly everything a reporter hoped to get in an interview. No wild card questions, no follow-ups, no slipups, no spontaneity, no surprises, no unexpected revelations, no asides, no nuances of body language or expression or tone of voice. The result was "news" that was preplanned, canned, controlled, colorless, flavorless, lifeless, and generally useless. Washington officialdom loved it. Lacey hated it.

For all its drawbacks, the fashion beat wasn't like that. It still offered Lacey the chance to talk to people in person. Simon Edison sounded much more approachable than the mad scientist she had been led to expect. He suggested they meet at the fashion museum.

"Cecily loved it there," he said. "It's as good a place as any to mourn her."

chapter 22

With its sleek open spaces, the Bentley Museum of American Fashion looked serene and inviting. The fabulous gowns on exhibit beckoned to her, but Lacey didn't have time to dawdle. She headed purposefully for an exhibit area still roped off from the public. The entrance was nearly blocked by a large sign announcing the Cecily Ashton Collection of Twentieth Century Haute Couture would open soon. And in big letters: MUSEUM STAFF ONLY—NOT OPEN TO THE PUBLIC. There was just enough room for Lacey to slip by.

Inside there were mannequins waiting for their clothes. Undressed, they looked like an artist's idea of fashion as conceptual art. Many of the mannequins wore delicate frameworks of thin wire. They would gracefully support the billowing folds of a ball gown or the flow of a flaring skirt, as if to freeze a moment in motion. Plexiglas pedestals were waiting to show off Cecily's one-of-a-kind accessories as if they were floating on air. The lighting was clean and subtle, pools of light playing over the circular platforms where Cecily's exquisite couture creations would shine in the spotlight one more time.

In the middle of the room, Simon Edison sat on a large wooden bench. He stood up as Lacey entered. He was a large man, but not physically imposing. Wiry strands of thinning brown hair made a shaggy halo around his head. His glasses clung to his nose at an angle. His expression struck Lacey as slightly goofy, but his smile was kind.

"You must be the glamorous fashion scribe, Lacey Smithsonian."

"I'm Lacey Smithsonian. I don't know how glamorous that is." She offered her hand. "Call me Lacey."

"Simon." He put out his hand in response and shook hers with gusto. He grinned nervously. "Nice to meet you. I read your article in Sunday's paper. I think you really captured our girl. My God, it's such a shame. I still can't believe it."

Our girl. It sounded rather intimate, possessive yet friendly. And they did have knowing Cecily in common, as if they belonged to the same club.

Simon was wearing a lumpy navy sport coat, a blue shirt, and a red tie with a small pattern that looked like stuffed green olives, but somehow he looked as if he might still be in the process of getting dressed. The tie was crooked and he'd missed one button over his stomach.

"Fashion's not really my thing, you know," he was saying, gesturing at the exhibit. *I never would have guessed,* Lacey thought. "So you're wondering what on earth Cecily saw in me, aren't you?"

"No, of course not," Lacey said. Cecily probably saw a kid brother, brilliant but a little goofy.

"Then you're very kind," he smiled, which made her feel guilty for her thoughts. His shirttail had come loose. He hastily tucked it back in, but the other side pulled out. Simon Edison's clothes seemed to have a life of their own, tucking themselves in and out, bunching up of their own volition.

Edison was not a social creature. Although he must have been in his late thirties, he seemed more like an overgrown kid, alternately eager and shy. He was the kind of man who collided with chairs, rather than merely sitting on them. He had a tendency to knock into things. Lacey feared for the mannequins.

"These thin wire superstructures were my idea." He touched one of the wire cages awaiting a gown over a mannequin's bare legs. "I wanted animatronics, in very subtle motion. The museum wouldn't go for it. So when they're dressed, the cages will give the impression of movement. Not too bad. Better than just letting a gown hang."

"I can see that," Lacey said. "They'll give every outfit some life." It hadn't struck her at first that they were like cages, but she saw it now. Each cage enclosed a mannequin.

"Exactly. Life, that's what Cecily and I wanted. So when the clothes are draped over them, they give an impression of life, of how they might drape and move and flow if Cecily were actually wearing them." He was silent for a moment, lost in his own thoughts. He carefully adjusted one of the structures.

Simon Edison met Cecily and her then-husband Philip Clark Ashton about five years ago at a cocktail party, he told Lacey, a fund-raising reception for a research foundation where he was working and where Philip Ashton was donating money. Cecily felt out of place amidst the scientists and politicians, and her husband was preoccupied with making some deal.

"We got along instantly," he said simply. "Go figure. We got to be sort of buddies."

"What did you talk about?"

"Lots of things. Everything." Simon seemed a little shy. Perhaps he was also uncertain how much he could trust a reporter. When Lacey asked him a direct question he had a habit of looking away and ducking his head.

"Tell me about the fabric you made for Cecily."

He nodded his large shaggy head and the halo of hair waved. "She wanted something to protect her against— against the pain. And I understand pain."

Simon didn't specify the source of his own pain. His shyness was written silently in every awkward piece of clothing he wore. He looked like someone who might be much more comfortable in a laboratory.

"Was this about the voices?"

"You know about that?" He looked surprised.

She nodded. "Do you believe she really heard voices inside her head?"

Simon took his glasses off and rubbed them clean with a handkerchief.

"Well, yes. I do believe it. Let me make it quite clear, though, I assume the voices were part of her mental illness, not a government conspiracy. I believe Cecily herself came to the same conclusion, that they were probably her own voices, even though she wanted to believe they were something else." His big shoulders slumped as he sighed deeply. "She never disassociated from reality. She was always aware, always functional, always bright and caring and— But it was awful for her to live with, whatever it was. It weighed on her."

"What did you make of it, Simon? The voices and the other people like Cecily?" Lacey needed to ground this story somewhere in reality, something she could make sense of. A scientist, she hoped, would be grounded in reality, facts, and logic. She took off her coat. She looked around and tried to imagine what the exhibit would look like when it was finally filled with Cecily's treasures, all in frozen motion.

"There are a lot of people like her. More than you'd imagine." Simon pushed his glasses up. He glanced at Lacey to see if she was laughing at him. She wasn't. "But it seems to me every generation, every era, has its own mysteries and unexplained phenomena. And we all have fears we can't escape from. Real fears get rolled up with mysteries into myth, fantasy, legend, even insanity. I suppose every culture has wrestled with their fears and mysteries, since we started drawing on walls in caves."

"Fear and mystery, reaching some sort of critical mass." Lacey thought of Damon and Brooke.

"There's always something scary in the woods, a mystery just out of reach. We use fairy tales, magic and leprechauns, witches and warlocks, to make sense of it, to manage our fears. '*Up the airy mountain, Down the rushy glen, We daren't go a-hunting, For fear of little men.*'" Simon removed his glasses again and looked away.

"But why manage fear? Why not try to overcome it, live without fear?"

He put his glasses back on and they promptly slid down his nose. "Maybe fear of the unknown has survival value. It keeps us out of the dark woods. If the dark woods are full of monsters, we stay close to the campfire and we live longer.

So we tell monster stories around the fire to scare the living daylights out of each other. Maybe in evolutionary terms we're safer if we're still a little scared of the dark."

"You've thought a lot about this stuff." Lacey imagined him out in the woods, a big Boy Scout in his rumpled uniform, telling ghost stories around the campfire. He nodded.

"I'm a scientist, I study patterns in phenomena. Elves, fairies, little men? Monsters, ghosts, alien abductions, mind control conspiracies? I wonder if they're all just part of the same phenomenon. That's the ultimate mind control, the way we subconsciously manipulate our own fears to control each other's behavior."

Fear didn't save Cecily, she mused. "What about Cecily's fears?" Lacey tried to steer the conversation back to her. She realized Simon Edison might talk all afternoon if she let him. "What did she hope the fabric would do?"

"Ah, yes, the fabric. Something to block out the pain. She said the pain came from the voices and it was controlled by them. They could strike anywhere at any time, she had headaches too, but they seemed particularly to attack the, um, female organs."

"Did she see doctors for the pain?"

"Oh yes. She was in perfect shape, physically. Nothing explained her symptoms. She asked for my help. At first, I thought perhaps if she *believed* a high-tech fabric of some kind could help, then maybe it really *would* help."

"Aha. So the fabric was just a placebo?"

"Well, at least that, I hoped, and maybe more. Sometimes placebos really work, you know. It's a kind of mind control, isn't it? Make your mind believe something works and your body follows?"

"Cecily never told me about the fabric."

"She wouldn't have," Simon said. "She didn't report it missing in the burglary either, as far as I know. It wasn't in the newspapers. Cecily didn't want anyone to think she was crazy. That was very important to her. But I wonder, if you're really crazy, do you care what people think? I'm not a psychologist, but I don't think she was crazy either. She just had this—crazy problem. She made it very clear she didn't want to be associated with the 'foil-wrapped fruit-cakes,' as she called them."

"Here's a question, Simon. If these people really are being attacked by some kind of electromagnetic rays being broadcast all over the globe through the atmosphere, why doesn't everyone feel them? Why don't I? Let's say evil agents of some shadowy government conspiracy really are targeting random people with these mysterious rays."

"Or nonrandom experimental subjects," he offered.

"Say *you're* a nonrandom experimental subject. Or *she* is." Lacey stood up and pointed at one of the mannequins. "A big fat mind-control ray heads straight for her at the speed of light. But just then, I walk in front of her." Lacey stood in front of the mannequin and spread her arms to protect her. "Wouldn't I get zapped by the ray? Wouldn't I hear the voices and feel the pain? So why isn't everyone in America complaining about this, and not just the 'foil-wrapped fruitcakes'?"

"Good question! Unless your test subjects have some sort of receiver implanted in them. But did the government secretly abduct and implant thousands of people? A bureaucratic nightmare. We're right back in *The X-Files*. Monster stories. So maybe some people are simply more sensitive to that particular radiation, whatever it is."

"Are you saying these people hear voices because they're just wired that way? They're like human radio receivers?"

"I wish I knew," he said. "Maybe someone could have done more for Cecily."

"But *you* tried to help her, didn't you?" Lacey said, steering him gently back to Cecily again. "You created the fabric for her."

"Yes, the fabric," he agreed. "An interesting challenge, protecting a human being from theoretical electromagnetic attacks. We've had radiation-proof garments for years, but they shield for particle radiation, not electromagnetic. Lead-lined suits for nuclear power plants, lead aprons for X-ray techs, things like that. Stiff, heavy, ugly stuff. The new radiationproof fabrics like Demron, a special polymer bonded to a synthetic, aren't much better. Nothing Cecily could wear to a cocktail party, that's for sure. Besides, you need a conductive metal to block electromagnetic radiation too, like microwaves, TV and radio, cell phone signals, the whole spectrum. And she told me the voices would stop sometimes in elevators. I went *aha!* You need something like a Faraday cage." Simon stood up and led her to one of the mannequins. It wore one of the delicate metal frameworks designed to support a long flowing skirt.

"A 'Faraday cage'?" Lacey said, following him. "I'm going to need the subtitled version of this, Simon." Lacey peered closely at the mannequin, and she noticed for the first time that its face was Cecily's face. All the mannequins wore Cecily's face. They wore several different stylized expressions, but they were all modeled on her.

"A Faraday cage is basically just an enclosure or shield of conductive metal. You use it to block electrical fields and electromagnetic radiation, either coming in or going out. Doesn't have to be solid metal, a metal mesh will do, and you can control which frequencies you block by the size of the mesh, like in the door of your microwave oven in the kitchen. Some elevators are partial cages, that's why your cell phone signal drops out. Your whole microwave oven is a good Faraday cage. An aluminum foil beanie is, let's say, a very primitive Faraday cage. But metal mesh is much better."

"Metal mesh?" Now she had the picture. At last they were back in *her* universe. "Designers have used fine metal mesh in haute couture for years. Gold, silver, bronze, aluminum. It can be draped so it flows over the body beautifully."

"Exactly. I found a way to bond a radiation-blocking polymer to a very fine metal mesh. Cecily funded the research. I added the conducting polymer to shield from ionizing radiation and UV protection. I developed the new polymer and the bonding technique, put it all together. I have a patent."

"Can you describe it for me, Simon? Simple picture, not a chemistry lesson."

"I thought the best sample was really quite beautiful." He closed his eyes and his hands moved as he talked, as if they were caressing the fabric. "It was a very soft gold mesh material, sheerer that anything I'd worked with before. Turned out really well. I had just enough to make something the size of a shawl. Gold is a terrific conductor, and the clear polymer backing layer gave it some body. It was less sheer than the mesh by itself, so it didn't make a woman look quite so, um, naked."

"And that was the sample that was stolen?"

"Yes, when she wasn't using it as sort of a shawl she kept it hidden in that vintage makeup case she loved so much. She said the sample really helped, and she liked the look and feel of it. She was amazed. I was too. We were getting close to creating something really special. But then . . ." Simon picked up his overcoat. He suddenly seemed anxious to leave.

Lacey touched his arm. "I realize Cecily's death probably stopped everything in its tracks, but—"

"You don't understand, Lacey." He backed away from her, almost colliding with a mannequin. "It was *before* she died. We had . . . sort of a falling out. I'm ashamed to admit we weren't really on speaking terms when she was killed."

"Over the fabric?"

"Not really. It was more than that." He ducked his head and looked at the floor. "I was in love with Cecily. Pretty pathetic, huh."

"I see." Cecily loved the wrong men. The wrong men loved Cecily. "Did you tell her?"

He nodded. "It went badly. She didn't want— I told her she didn't have to love me back, but . . ."

"Oh, dear." Lacey said it softly. Simon stopped talking. He pulled out his wrinkled handkerchief and wiped his eyes. "When did you tell her how you felt?"

"When I gave her the material. Just before Christmas. I was pretty proud of it, it was so beautiful, and I thought maybe that was a good time—"

Lacey could imagine the scene, poor gawky Simon Edison offering Cecily the fruits of his labor, the magical mystery fabric. Unfortunately, he also offered her his heart. Cecily might not have dealt with that very well. In her own way, Lacey suspected, she probably treasured his kid-brotherly friendship more than she did the men she used and dallied with. But had the thought of sweet awkward Simon as a lover embarrassed her? Offended her? Or worse, amused her? Had she laughed at him?

"Simon, I'm so sorry," Lacey said.

"I didn't expect her to fall in love with me, but I wanted her to understand that I would always be there for her. Who knows, maybe eventually . . ." A new note crept into Simon's voice, one of frustration or anger. "I understood her better than anyone, but she didn't want to see me anymore. She insisted on wasting herself on all those idiots. They weren't all handsome, they weren't smart, or even kind to her, and they weren't worthy of her. But she never looked at me that way."

Simon's voice cracked. Lacey didn't know how to comfort him. He took a deep breath. "Well, the fabric was a success with Cecily, even if I wasn't. She told me it seemed to block some of the attacks, the voices and the pain. She would tie it around her head, like a beautiful golden gypsy. She wanted a lot more, enough to line several outfits with it. But I refused to make any more of it for her. I was still furious with her."

"And then her house was burglarized. Simon, did you have anything to do with the burglary?"

His mouth dropped open in surprise. "No! I only found out about it when she called me. She was frantic. She begged me for more fabric. We fought on the phone, we ended up saying some terrible things. Words that can't be taken back." He closed his eyes to shut out the memory. "It was as if Cecily built me up and then broke me into pieces."

"What happened after that?"

"I locked up the formula, all the patent information, and my notes, and went to London for the holidays. I have a sister there."

"Did you ever see Cecily again?"

Simon was slow to answer. Too slow, Lacey thought. "No, I thought about it, I wanted to, but I didn't. Now she's dead. I can't forgive myself."

"Who killed Cecily?"

He sighed. "Could be Philip, could be anyone. Don't look at me like that! I could never hurt her, not like that." He shook his head emphatically. "Look at me, I'm a scientist. I live in a lab. Understand, if I were going to kill someone I'd need to study it like a chemistry problem, formulate hypotheses, develop a complex plan, and then probably abandon the whole idea in disgust. But I could never kill Cecily. And I'll spend my life wanting to apologize."

"You still could develop the fabric. There are people who would want it. If they thought it worked. People you could help." Simon turned away from her and struggled into his rumpled overcoat, yet another item of clothing that seemed set against him. He needed his own magic fabric, Lacey thought. She handed him her business card. "I'd like to write something about her efforts to develop the fabric, and yours. Call me. When you're ready."

"I don't know." He stared at the card and smiled sadly. "She'd like that. She wanted to leave something behind, besides all those closets full of clothes. She always wanted children, but Ashton wouldn't hear of it. The miscarriage was hard on her."

"When did that happen?" *New information!* Lacey tried not to register surprise. *A typical Washington source, dropping the bombshell on the way out the door.*

"She became pregnant a couple of years into their marriage," Simon said. "She was in heaven, but he said he'd never raise another child at his age. His first family didn't turn out so well."

"Funny, I didn't think I could hate that guy any more than I did, but what do you know? Now I do," Lacey said.

"It was an accident, riding a horse in one of their stupid fox hunts. She didn't want to ride, but Ashton made her. I've always wondered if maybe he spooked her horse on purpose. Whatever it was, it did the trick, she lost the baby."

"That's terrible." Lacey felt weighed down by the burdens of Cecily's life, losing a baby, losing her husband, losing her place in the world. Finally losing her life. "Do you think she'd want your miracle fabric to be lost forever too?"

"I'm not ready now. Maybe someday." Simon started for the door.

"Simon, before you go. The fabric. What is it called?"

He looked a little sheepish. "Well, the other samples just had lab numbers. But I've been calling it— Don't laugh. *Celestine*. It sounds, I don't know, heavenly. Celestial. And it reminds me of Cecily."

Lacey nodded thoughtfully, and Simon Edison hurried out, leaving her alone in the museum. She gave Cecily's mannequins one last long look and gathered her things. Maybe someday she would write about Cecily and Simon's magical mystery fabric. But not today.

On the cab ride back to *The Eye,* Lacey called Detective Jance, the Falls Church detective who grilled her the day the body was discovered. He seemed annoyed by having to talk to a reporter. That didn't surprise her. He was a busy cop with important things to do, and she was a fashion reporter asking irrelevant questions. She apparently didn't even make a convincing suspect anymore. He managed to work in a casual insult about her Sunday feature article on Cecily Ashton.

"I learned more about ladies' shoes and handbags and clothes and closets than I did about the deceased, for crying out loud," the detective said. "And all those 'accessories'! When I talk about 'accessories,' it's usually in relation to a crime."

Lacey refrained from pointing out that Cecily's accessories were very much "in relation to a crime." The Ashton woman had "more money than sense," Jance went on to opine. As for Lacey's article, it didn't shed any light on the murder, and that was that. Yes, the detective had also checked on her burglary. Nothing new there, no tips, no stolen goods recovered. Jance seemed to be in a rush to get her off the phone. *Is there a football game I'm interrupting?* she wondered.

"Do you have any viable suspects? Like, for starters, Bud

Hunt? Or Martin Hadley, Nigel Griffin, Philip Clark Ashton, or even Gregor Kepelov?"

"You are not a police reporter, Ms. Smithsonian." Jance laughed brusquely. "And even if you were, I don't believe I would be sharing that information with *The Eye Street Observer*, or any other newspaper, at this stage in this investigation."

Lacey ignored his tone. She assumed Trujillo had already gotten whatever he could from the closemouthed Detective Jance. She would get whatever Trujillo had.

"Can you at least tell me what kind of gun she was killed with?"

"A twenty-two. Only fifty million of those floating around. If we're done here, I'll get back to work. Thanks for calling." He hung up on her.

chapter 23

Lacey drove straight to Falls Church after work for the second session of her PI class. The sky was already inky black. She saw no sign of stars, nor of the "thunder snow" Marie the weather psychic had predicted. Lacey hadn't had time to change out of her red suit and heels, and she found herself wishing she'd gone home first to throw on her blue jeans. She'd have been more comfortable. And more prepared to run for her life, if the situation called for it.

The parking lot where Cecily Ashton's body had been found was lit by two dim streetlights. Lacey seemed to be the first to arrive. She locked up the little green BMW, mentally thanking Vic once again. She wished hers wasn't the only car there.

The trees stood sentinel around the parking lot in the dark, their shadows fluttering against the fence, giving her chills. She blamed it on the frigid January wind. Lacey saw a light go on in Bud Hunt's offices. She hurried down the steps, through the heavy back door of the building, and into the classroom.

To her dismay, Hunt wasn't there. Instead it was Gregor Kepelov, in his own inimitable style, black leather jacket, bright blue Hawaiian shirt, rumpled khaki slacks, and red and blue cowboy boots. The New Russia meets the American Dream. Kepelov turned around and smiled.

"Ah, Lacey Smithsonian! Looking good. You have a date after class perhaps? With Donovan, that tough guy of yours?"

"I wish." She decided not to mention Vic was out of town. "No date tonight. It's a school night, remember?"

"Don't worry. In that red suit I'm sure you get lucky. Donovan is not only big fish in Black Sea."

"You're all charm, Kepelov."

"I sense sarcasm, Smithsonian. Was invented in Russia, did you know?" He patted her cheerfully on the shoulder. "Path of true love never runs smooth. Always a detour. Shakespeare says so. Chekhov says so."

Kepelov, the KGB love guru. "Where's Hunt? Running late?"

"He asked me to run class tonight. I am a good teacher. I am available. What luck for you." Maybe Kepelov really did need the work. He seemed to be a bust at the Romanov treasure-hunting gig. "Don't look so disappointed, Lacey Smithsonian! Aha. So you checked my alibi with Falls Church's finest, yes? Too bad I cannot be your favorite suspect now. Maybe next time."

"You're always my favorite suspect, Kepelov." She looked at him, her eyebrow raised in a question mark. But if Kepelov had an alibi, what about Hunt? On Saturday Hunt had seemed a little too eager for the whole class to drop out. Was their instructor the first to go? "So, why isn't Hunt here?"

"No secret. Anyway he didn't say not to tell. He had people to see, places to go. He mentioned maybe the household staff of Cecily Ashton."

"So he wants to find out who killed her?" It must mean, Lacey thought, the police were all over Hunt, as Vic told her.

"Naturally he wants to find the killer. Or else the killer is busy covering his tracks. Always consider all possibilities."

"You think Hunt had something to do with her death?"

"Is a joke, Smithsonian. Where is your funny bone? You find funny bone in your very pretty red suit, and I go make coffee for us."

"Coffee would be good," she said. "Could you make some decaf?"

Kepelov shook his head sadly. "Smithsonian, what am I to do with you? Decaf is not real coffee! In Russia we drink real coffee. With vodka." He headed for the kitchen, still laughing.

According to the course outline, tonight's lesson would cover "Garbology, or the fine art of finding evidence in the trash." *Oh good,* Lacey thought, wrinkling her nose. Trash picking, a time-honored tactic of private detectives and *National Enquirer* reporters. Hunt definitely wanted to discourage them with the nasty business first.

Lacey sat down and looked through her notes on Cecily from talking to Martin Hadley and Simon Edison. She was deep in thought when someone came in and sat down next to her. The woman's hair was platinum blond and it seemed to have a life of its own, a frothy concoction of curls that bounced off the woman's shoulders. It was like cotton candy crossed with angel hair, and it drew the eye as if lit from within. Definitely not the sort of hair you often saw in the D.C. area, or even in Falls Church, Virginia. Perhaps a little further south. Lacey blinked.

"Willow? Is that you?" *It couldn't really be that shy little mouse, could it?*

"It's me." The woman smiled. "I took your advice. I went to see your Stella." Willow's face was still unadorned with makeup. It made her mop of white-blond hair look even stranger, like a visitor from another world, the Planet of the Peculiarly Pale People. Tonight she wore a gray sweater instead of a beige one. She patted her platinum coiffure. "Do you like it?"

Lacey nodded vaguely, wondering what to say. "It must have taken hours."

"Yeah, it seemed like all day, because she had to strip out my own color. If you want to know the truth, my scalp is a little tender," Willow said. "Stella was great, just like you said. She's so funny. And she's a wizard with hair color. She helped me pick."

"Yeah, that sounds like Stella." *That's not a color, it's the* absence *of color.*

"It's not too much of a change, is it?" Willow frowned.

Before Lacey could think of an answer, Edwina marched into the classroom. She stopped short when she saw

Willow's shockingly blond hair. It was a shade or two lighter
than Edwina's own color, but Willow's coiffure was fiercely
fluffy, while Edwina's style was long and sleek. The two
women couldn't have looked more different. Willow was
dressed in a shambles of a wrinkled colorless smock, while
Edwina looked smartly pulled together in a bright turquoise
cardigan over a crisp white blouse, black slacks, and a black
headband. Edwina's uniform look suited her self-image as
an upper middle-class suburban McLean, Virginia, matron
who had found her own style. Willow had found—*Stella*.

"Well, that's quite a change for you, Willow Raynor!"
Edwina announced. "My goodness, you need some makeup
to bring out your features. You look like a ghost!" Lacey was
grateful Edwina was the one to say it. Edwina examined
Willow with a practiced eye. "I mean, you've just got rabbit
eyes without a little makeup. Don't feel bad, we all need a
little color, don't we, Lacey? And so nice to see you, dear,
by the way, and my, but don't *you* look very polished tonight
in that lovely red suit of yours!"

"I came right from work," Lacey said.

"See what I mean, Willow? A little color never hurt
anyone."

Willow looked to Lacey for confirmation. "It's true, Willow, a little makeup would help finish your new look." *And
a new wardrobe,* Lacey added silently. *And what on earth
was Stella thinking with that hair?!*

"Good," Willow said, her head nodding like a bobble-
head doll. "Stella said she'd teach me how to put on some
makeup and buy some clothes."

"Stella?" Her stylist was really jumping right in on this
fashion victim, Lacey thought. Obviously Stella's work was
not done here. At this rate, Willow would be tattooed by
Wednesday and sporting a nose ring by Friday. Or worse,
she would be "Gidget Goes Surfing with the Jetsons," like
Stella's own new look. Lacey wasn't sure which would be
worse. "Stella's a doll, but don't let her get carried away,
okay? I love Stella, but I'm not kidding."

"Stella?" Edwina inquired.

"My stylist," Lacey filled in.

"She's in Dupont Circle, in D.C. It's a really cool area," Willow chirped, her face finally showing some animation. "She did my hair. She was so much fun."

"I have my hair done in McLean," Edwina sniffed. "Same stylist for years and years. She's very predictable, where it counts."

Other students showed up and took their seats, but several faces were missing tonight. Dropouts after all, Lacey thought. The murder Saturday apparently scared some of them away. Damon Newhouse finally arrived, grinned hello to Lacey, and stared at the fluffy-haired blond Willow. He started to introduce himself, thinking she was a new student. Finally Kepelov took his place at the front with a steaming mug of coffee.

"No Bud Hunt tonight. My friend is off being PI, instead of teaching PI. Fortunate for you, you have me! Tonight we are supposed to talk about what private investigators can do that the police cannot do. And that is? Nothing much." There was a smattering of laughter. Lacey stifled her inner critic. She readied her pen for pearls of wisdom.

"But! What private investigators have got," Kepelov continued, "if your clients have the money? Is *time*. Time is something police never have. So many crimes, so little time. Time lets you cover same ground more thoroughly, cover new ground, meet more people, follow more avenues of information, ask more questions. Ask questions police never bother to ask. Mostly because they have no time. You know what else you have got? You got people's trash. One subject of tonight's lesson. Garbology. Old Russian word. Meaning one man's trash is maybe your treasure. But don't get too comfortable, I maybe have surprise later."

Edwina groaned audibly. "Trash! The things I do to win a bet."

Kepelov smiled at her and continued. "You learn a lot about people from what they throw away. People are not so careful about what they throw away. Bills with credit card numbers, phone bills with every number they call, receipts of everything they like to buy, receipts from where they like to go to eat, postcards from where they like to go to cheat.

People think, I threw that away in the garbage! It is gone forever! No one will ever see *that* again! Not true. Private investigator—*you*—will see it."

"Garbology is the study of who you are, based on what
you discard?" Damon piped up.

"You don't mean to tell us that we are expected to go
pawing through people's garbage?" Edwina's eyes were
wide in shock.

"Exactly!" Kepelov's smile lit up like a Christmas tree.
"Garbology. Garbage plus *ology*. Some people call it 'urban
foraging.' If the Dumpster is very old, we call it archaeology.
Gives the garbage more class."

"That is disgusting," Edwina said.

"Is dirty business, but someone has to do it," Kepelov
shrugged. The guys in class were laughing. Lacey didn't
laugh. It sounded pretty distasteful to her too. "Remember
your rich client, the one with all that money? And you, poor
little private eye, with nothing but time? Time is money. If
you don't like trash, or money, what will you think about
peeing in a bottle on surveillance?" The guys roared.

Edwina clucked her tongue in disgust and turned back to
her notebook, but Lacey noticed she wasn't taking notes.
Edwina was doodling a picture, a cartoon of a garbage can
with a stick figure poking it with a stick while holding its
nose. She wasn't bad. Lacey was a note taker, a writer, not a
doodler. She didn't have whatever gene it was that made
someone draw pictures instead of writing words. Doodling
must be some kind of visual shorthand, she concluded, and
simply not one of her skills, but she admired Edwina's little
cartoon. It seemed to sum up tonight's class so far.

"I recommend always wear the heavy rubber gloves," Kepelov was saying, "and you keep N-95 respirator in your PI
kit, which of course you have in your car at all times. You
never know what's in somebody's garbage. Maybe coffee
grounds, maybe needles with AIDS, maybe vial of anthrax.
You never know who somebody really is—until you see
their garbage."

There's a pleasant thought. Lacey's stomach turned.

"And you never know who is after *you*," Kepelov continued. "Right now, someone could be following your life, your every move, going through your garbage, waiting to steal your identity. If you are spy like me, you have many identities. So many spies in Washington, you all have secret identity, yes? Perhaps you can spare one or two. But most people have only one identity. Guard it with your life."

Lacey thought about Stella, and all of the identities that her friend liked to try on. She wondered how long this blond phase of her stylist would last. *Until she turned all her new clients blonder than blond, into little blond clones of Stella?*

"Secrets are revealed in many ways. Hair, skin, mud, blood, cigarettes, receipts, used Kleenex, maybe even used condoms in trash," Kepelov said. "Bingo! Proof of identity, proof of infidelity. Also in dirty sheets. Sheets are like a diary you write on all night. I myself have purchased on several occasions wonderful used sheets from hotel maids. Excellent cheap source of DNA. Makes good evidence in divorce case."

"That is the single most disgusting thing I have ever heard!" Edwina threw her pen on the desk. The look on her face was priceless. "Picking up dirty condoms out of wastebaskets? Buying dirty sheets? Peeing in a bottle? This is not a profession for a well-bred woman!" The guys thought Edwina was as funny as Kepelov.

Kepelov stopped and pulled a jangling cell phone from his pocket, flipped it open, and put it to his ear. He smiled, spun around for some privacy, and said something Lacey couldn't hear. He listened and laughed briefly. The big Russian flipped the phone shut and clapped his hands.

"Enough of garbage. Tomorrow you paw through garbage with Bud Hunt. Time for surprise. Tonight, we do vehicle surveillance."

"But the vehicle surveillance isn't scheduled till Saturday," Damon piped up.

"I take liberty of rearranging your schedule. Don't thank me."

There was a murmur from the students and their spirits seemed to rise. Vehicle surveillance sounded a lot more exciting than picking through garbage.

The object of this exercise, Kepelov explained, was to follow the "subject car" and observe where the occupant or occupants went, who they met, and what they did, without either losing the car or being "made." He pulled out two-way radios from Hunt's desk and explained how to use them. They would work in teams, three "follow cars" to "surveil" one subject car, with a team of two or three students in each car. The follow cars would stay in touch by radio and take turns in the lead, so the subject car would see more than one vehicle in the rearview mirror. Each team would keep a log of the subject car's route and the team's observations, noting the time and location whenever someone left the subject car, entered a building, met other people, or did anything notable. The exercise might also include a foot surveillance, and he would give them further instructions and tips as they went along. He cautioned them above all to "act natural." No skulking, he said, and no "driving like drunken Russians."

"You have accident, you get speeding ticket, you lose your subject? You are pathetic excuse for PI. Don't forget coffee, you can pee in the empty cup." Predictably, the guys all laughed. Edwina, Willow, and Lacey groaned in unison.

The students grabbed their coats and scarves and some fresh coffee and stood in the cold parking lot, awaiting instructions. Kepelov would be in the subject car, a large gray Ford Crown Victoria. He strutted toward the parked cars, coffee mug in hand, and stopped at Lacey's car.

"Look at this! Beautiful old BMW. Vintage 1974, yes? Forest green. Nice little car."

"That's mine." Lacey patted the hood with pride. "Do you want me to be a driver?" She hoped so, she loved showing it off, and it was fast.

"Rare old green BMW? And so shiny? Absolutely not! That car would be made in a minute. You will be passenger."

Damon looked smug, but Kepelov ruled out his wheels as well. "Ah, Mr. Newhouse, not one to blend into the crowd, yes? This is your hippie van? This ancient Volkswagen bus, with CONSPIRACY CLEARINGHOUSE written on side? DIG THE TRUTH? Ha! More outrageous than Smithsonian's cute little car! Now, show me more cars, people. Who has sensible surveillance vehicle? No bright colors! Only gray, black, rust, primer, dirt. Dirt is good."

Kepelov selected three gray sedans belonging to Martin Hadley, Willow Raynor, and Edwina Plimpton. They would follow his own pavement-gray four-door Ford Crown Vic. He rubbed his hands together, pleased.

"My BMW is not dirty and it is not *gray*," Edwina protested. "It is *platinum*."

"Whatever. Hundred shades of gray. Yours is expensive gray." He surveyed the lineup of his dark gray subject car and the dark gray follow cars. "Now, this is very nice. Looks like line of lesser Soviet diplomats. Maybe for state funeral."

Lacey hoped she would be able to ride with Snake Goldstein, the least likely person to be interested in fashion or believe in alien abduction. But Kepelov selected the teams, and he apparently thought it would be funny to pair the socialite with the ponytailed, tattooed bounty hunter and one of the burly ex-cops. Edwina looked appalled as the guys climbed into her precious platinum BMW. Damon Newhouse and an ex-military guy were teamed with Martin Hadley in Hadley's slate gray Lincoln, a typical Washington lobbyist's car. Lacey's spirits sank as she drew Willow Raynor and the newly blond woman's rusty silver-gray ten-year-old Toyota Corolla, the one with the crunched right rear fender.

Why do I get the loser car? I always get the loser car! Lacey reluctantly opened the passenger side door and got in. At least she was placed in command of the two-way radio and the all-important log.

"Wow, I'm so glad we're paired up." Willow turned the ignition key, to the sound of grinding. Finally the Toyota wheezed to life. "I was afraid I'd have to go with Mr. Goldstein. He really scares me. That python tattoo and all."

"I think that's the whole point of the tattoo," Lacey said. "Part of the tough-guy image."

"Really, you think so?"

"I'm sure he's a nice guy, a nice tough guy." Lacey thought Snake looked like he might have good stories to tell, unlike Willow.

"I can't believe we're doing this. Cars and radios and

everything." Willow rubbed her face and took a deep breath, then blew it out. She adjusted her mirror and her seat belt. She looked up. She eased the car out of its space, hit the gas, and killed the engine right at Little Falls Street. "Oh, no! Everyone else is gone."

The radio crackled to life in Lacey's hands and made her jump.

"Smithsonian, where are you? Over."

chapter 24

Lacey peered at the two-way radio and hit a button, hoping it was the right one.

"Damon, is that you? We're still here in the lot. Um, over."

"Aha. I thought you were using a secret Smithsonian tailing technique, so secret even a master spy couldn't find you. Over."

"You can cool the sarcasm. Over."

"But I do it so well. Turn left out of the parking lot and left on Broad Street. Look for a subtle line of gray cars. Remember, we have to stay in contact. Over." Lacey set the radio down.

"I'm so sorry I messed up," Willow said.

"Don't worry, just drive," Lacey commanded. She realized a hint of irritation had slipped into her voice. "How are you doing? You okay?"

Willow looked both ways before cautiously turning onto the street. "I'm a bit freaked out about the whole thing Saturday, that woman in the car, you know. I can't get the picture of her out of my mind, her eyes, all that blood on the windshield."

"It's difficult, I know," Lacey agreed. Willow stopped at Broad Street and Lacey tried to catch a glimpse of the other cars. The radio in her lap crackled again and Damon's voice came through.

"Smithsonian, I still don't see you! Over!"

She pressed a button. "We're at Broad. We had some trouble with Willow's car."

"Silver Bimmer here." It sounded like Snake Goldstein's

voice. "I don't think the point is to lose you so soon. Over."
He clicked off.

"Oh, God, I'm gonna fail at this!" Willow's voice cracked.

"You're doing fine, Willow, just turn left," Lacey ordered
again. "So why did you decide to take this course?" She
couldn't imagine what Willow was doing here, she seemed
to be uniquely unsuited for the work. Even Edwina, with her
country club "win the bet at all costs" attitude, would make
a better private investigator.

"I needed a change, I guess," Willow squeaked. "That's
why I took the PI class, partly anyway, to get out of my rut."
Lacey nodded. "I know I'm too, you know, shy to be a private investigator. But Mr. Hunt said there's lots of work behind the scenes, online searching, information gathering,
that sort of thing. He didn't really mention following people
in cars, for heaven's sake!"

"And so here we are." *Lost at the gate.* "A little faster,
Willow?" Willow gave the little car some gas. It didn't seem
to help.

"I can be very detail-oriented when I put my mind to it.
And I've met some really interesting people, like you and
Edwina. And it seemed like it would be really fun, but the
very first morning—*that* had to happen." Willow's voice
broke. A tear rolled down her cheek. "That woman died.
And I'm not very strong when it comes to that."

"Look, Willow, nobody is good at that sort of thing."

"I saw her dead. All that blood on the window. I couldn't
look away." She wiped her eyes.

"You can't drive if you're crying," Lacey pointed out as
gently as possible. She pulled a tissue for Willow from a box
on the dashboard. "Please don't cry."

"Thanks. You seem so smart and capable, Lacey. You'll
make a great investigator."

Lacey saw a large gray sedan blocks ahead of them, probably Hadley's Lincoln. She felt immensely relieved.

"You give me too much credit. Really." *After all, I got
stuck with you.* "We don't have to talk about Cecily Ashton
if it upsets you. Look, I think I see the other cars. They're
turning right on Maple a couple of blocks up ahead."

"Okay." Willow nodded vigorously and timidly pressed down on the gas. "Do you think the police will want to talk to me again?"

"Hard to say. They let you go home Saturday. You didn't know her, did you?"

Willow changed lanes to the right and closed in on Edwina's platinum BMW. "Me? Know someone like Cecily Ashton?" Willow shook her head. "But you did, didn't you? I read it in the Sunday paper yesterday morning. I always read your stuff." Lacey didn't know whether she should be pleased or horrified. She was always a little disoriented to meet an actual reader. Suddenly everybody she met was reading *The Eye Street Observer*, Lacey reflected. She'd have to announce that at the next content quality meeting. She was more accustomed to people refusing to own up to reading the city's lowest-ranked newspaper, even if they secretly did. Of course most people didn't read newspapers at all anymore, except for the freebies handed out at the Metro stations. They got their news on TV and the Web. "You really read my work?"

"Your columns? Oh sure, I've learned so much about fashion from you."

"No kidding?" Lacey gazed at Willow's overly beige oversized overcoat. Like her former hair color, it was as colorless and lifeless as a dead mouse. *Now you're really depressing me.*

"Oh, yes, I didn't mention it before because I didn't want to be a pest. After all, you're like a celebrity."

She's never seen colors before, she learned her nonexistent fashion sense from me, she looks like an alien, and I'm a celebrity. What planet is this woman from? Help!

Willow suddenly braked the car to a screeching halt. A horn blared behind them. "The light was yellow!" She looked like she might cry again. Edwina's car turned right on the yellow light and disappeared. Lacey sighed and jotted a note in her log.

"What do you think happened to her, to Cecily Ashton?" Willow asked.

"I have no idea. Other than she got up Saturday morning,

got dressed, drove her Jaguar to Falls Church, Virginia, and was shot to death."

"You've written about these sorts of stories before. You get involved in them."

"That doesn't mean I'll be involved in this one, Willow." Lacey really didn't care to discuss her thoughts on the subject. "Why don't we talk about something else? You have me at a disadvantage, you've read my stories. Tell me about yourself. Nobody in D.C. is a native, so where are you from?"

If she could get Willow talking about herself, Lacey wouldn't have to talk, and she could concentrate on the task at hand. She jotted their street location on the log and thumbed the radio button that was supposed to buzz Edwina's car, but Snake didn't respond.

"I'm from all over. My folks were in the military, so we lived in a lot of places, but recently I'm from Pennsylvania. Philadelphia."

"What do you do when you're not in PI class?" *Or wrecking the surveillance exercise?*

"I work in an office now, secretarial temp stuff. So boring you don't want to know. But in Philly I used to work in one of those cute little art stores, you know the kind, they have art supplies and it's also kind of a gallery?"

Lacey looked at Willow, who was concentrating very hard on traffic. The light turned green. The battered gray Toyota lurched forward and made a right turn into a residential neighborhood. Lacey tightened her seat belt.

"Some of Cecily Ashton's vintage pieces were displayed in an art gallery in Philadelphia, last fall. Did you happen to see them?"

"Maybe. I'm trying to think." A large black limousine passed swiftly on the left. The driver flipped them an obscene gesture and shouted something inaudible. Only Lacey saw him. Willow was oblivious, trying to focus on the road ahead. "There are so many galleries in Philly."

"Lots of galleries here too, if you were looking for a change."

"The one where I worked was so small. It was a fun job, though." She sounded wistful.

"So why move here?" The question hit some sort of nerve. Lacey saw a tear sliding down Willow's cheek. She handed her another tissue from the box. The little Toyota apparently witnessed a lot of tears. "I'm sorry, that's not usually such a touchy question." Lacey tried to be sympathetic, but her patience was stretched thin. They were flubbing the class exercise; it would be Willow's fault, and Lacey would get blamed.

"It's not that." Willow wiped at her face and drove even slower. "It's . . . Something happened in Philly. My best friend was killed a few months ago."

"Killed?"

"She was murdered." Willow dropped her voice and Lacey had to lean in to hear her. "The police said it was random, a drive-by shooting, but I don't believe it. I told them what happened. They didn't pay any attention to me."

Lacey looked at the woman's anguished face. "You're not taking the class to try and get involved and solve the murder, are you?" That was one of the first things Hunt had warned them against.

She shook her head and took a deep breath. "No, I'm taking the class to try to learn how I can *disappear*. You understand?"

"You don't want someone to find you?" So that's why Willow's clothes made her fade into the woodwork, Lacey thought.

The radio crackled ominously. "Smithsonian, you taking a secret detour? Try to stay with us, you dig? Over."

"Car trouble again, Snake. Over."

"Tell her to put her foot on the gas pedal, not the brake. Over."

"I will! Really!" Willow yelled, and the vehicle lurched forward again.

"I thought Toyotas were reliable," Snake snarled. "Over." The radio crackled again and he was gone. Willow's lips trembled.

"I thought I could learn how to get away and disappear, so he can't find me."

"He? Who is he?"

"Eric, my ex-boyfriend. He killed my friend Nina. But no one believes me."

"Eric and Nina who?"

"Eric O'Neil. Nina Vickers," Willow whispered. She broke into sobs. Lacey wanted to stick her head out the window to clear it, but she fought the impulse. She had lost all sign of the follow cars, much less Kepelov. And Willow couldn't stop crying.

"You should pull over on Annandale Road, right there. We'll change drivers."

Willow nodded. "That would be good." Her hands were shaking as she pulled into a fast food restaurant's parking lot and stopped the car. They swapped seats and Lacey took the wheel. She showed Willow how to use the radio to call the other cars. Newhouse in Hadley's Lincoln responded first: They were several blocks away, heading southwest on Lee Highway. Lacey put the Toyota in gear, turned around, cut through a side street, and breathed a sigh of relief when she spotted one of the other follow cars. She passed Hadley's car and Edwina's to move in behind the gray Crown Vic.

The radio crackled again with Snake's pungent New York accent. "Smithsonian! Long time no see. Glad you could join us."

Willow fumbled hopelessly with the radio. Lacey grabbed it and pushed the button. "We changed drivers. Bite me. Over." She threw the radio on the dash. "It's a crazy world, Willow. What makes you think your boyfriend is the killer?"

"Because it was supposed to be me!" Willow took another deep breath, as if she needed it to push this story out. "Nina and I worked together at the gallery, that's how we met. We were meeting for dinner that night. Italian. Nina loved Italian. I couldn't get off work in time to get to the cleaners, but she got off earlier and said she'd pick up my things on her way to the restaurant." She dabbed at her eyes with the now-soaked tissue. "It was supposed to be me. I'm the one who was supposed to die."

"Why would he want to kill you?"

"I don't know, he was just—I think he was crazy. He was

doing weird things, threatening me and yelling. He didn't like it when I worked late, he thought I was fooling around on him. Nina was at the cleaners, so I think he thought she was me."

"But surely he would know you."

"It was dark. She was wearing my coat. It's my fault."

Willow's reaction didn't surprise Lacey. The death of someone close often inspired feelings of grinding guilt.

Crackly chatter came over the radio. "Hey! Greg, I mean our *subject*, just pulled ahead," Damon said. "He said not to speed, but he's sure as hell speeding. Over."

"Fall back, Gray Toyota! Silver Bimmer's takin' the lead," Snake responded. "Over."

Lacey saw Edwina's car change lanes and speed up, still far behind Kepelov. Lacey tried to keep pace in the old gray Toyota. She found herself stuck in traffic behind Hadley's Lincoln.

"Why are we speeding? Are we supposed to be doing this?" Willow seemed to suddenly become aware of the surveillance maneuver.

"Yes, we are," Lacey responded. "So tell me, did the police arrest anyone? Did they question your boyfriend?"

"No. The police didn't believe me. He had some kind of alibi anyway. People lie about alibis, don't they? The police said it was probably a gang drive-by shooting and Nina just got caught in the crossfire. They questioned some people, but no one was arrested."

Willow Raynor seemed an unlikely victim, but stalkers had their own reasons. Lacey realized she shouldn't make judgments based on Willow's plain looks, especially if she was trying her darnedest to disappear. "It was over, but he kept calling and showing up, waiting for me after work," Willow continued. "I moved here, and I thought he was still in Philly. But—" Her tears started again and her voice came out in a high squeak, her face was red and clenched. "When Cecily Ashton was shot right there while I was in class—" She gulped back a sob and looked at Lacey. "I wonder if maybe he knows where I am? Maybe he came here and killed her as a warning?"

"Warning for what?" The little mouse's logic eluded her. "Willow, that makes no sense. I hate to say this, but if he wanted to kill you, he would have killed *you*, not her."

"Maybe he mistook her for me?"

Lacey blinked in surprise. *Twice? Is he blind?* And could someone really mistake this mouse in a plain brown wrapper for the beautiful and obviously expensive Cecily Ashton in a Jaguar? *Impossible.* But after being close in one way or another to two murders, Willow might easily imagine someone was after her.

"If it makes you feel any better, I don't think so," Lacey said.

The radio wheezed with another announcement. "Attention everybody," Snake said. "Subject vehicle's trying to shake us. We were a block behind him and he just wailed on through a red light at Gallows Road, right near Merrifield Garden Center. We lost him. He coulda turned down a bunch of side streets, no way of tellin'. Over."

"Why not stay on Lee Highway," Lacey said. "If he gets back on, we might catch him. Over." There were two slow cars between her and the silver BMW. She crossed Gallows Road, but she lost track of Hadley's car. She couldn't find it in her mirrors; perhaps he had turned off Lee Highway. "Gray Lincoln, what's your location? Over."

"Taking a shortcut. Over," Damon replied.

"Shortcut to where, Damon, the moon? Over."

"Eyes left, Smithsonian. Over." Damon and his team were cruising down the access road that stopped at the Merrifield Post Office. Lacey had no idea where they thought they were going. Was Hadley being guided by voices in his head? On the plus side, there was no traffic over there to slow them down. Lacey kept her sights on the silver BMW on Lee Highway. She thought Edwina and Snake somehow had a smaller chance of being beamed up to the mother ship.

Willow seemed to be paying no attention to the exercise. "Eric seemed nice at first. Cute. He was tall and blond and he had a nice smile, his teeth were a little crooked. We went out for a few months. Eric seemed really crazy about me, maybe a little too much, a little too soon. Suffocating, you know what I mean? He wanted to know where I was every minute. He didn't like me talking to Nina, but she was my best friend."

"Did he hit you?"

"Not at first." Willow was drawing little concentric circles on the logbook. "After a while, he started telling me how awful I was, how I was ugly, how I was lucky to have him and I would never find anyone else."

An abuser's tactics, Lacey thought. "You split up with him?"

"Oh yes. I made it clear it was over. He was so angry it scared me, he bruised me pretty bad, so I moved away. He e-mailed me a lot, but it slowed down and then stopped a couple of weeks ago. I hoped he lost interest, or maybe got a new girlfriend. But now I'm not so sure."

"Did you tell the local police about this guy?" Lacey changed lanes and caught up to Edwina in the lead position. But Kepelov had vanished into thin air.

"What good would that do?" Willow sat up straight and opened her eyes wide. "Give them someone to look for after I'm dead? Like Nina? I need a private investigator, like Mr. Hunt. Maybe I can talk to him tomorrow night. I'm changing how I look so Eric won't find me. Like my hair."

"Your hair?" Lacey gave her a sidelong glance. *Oh yeah, no one will notice* that *hair*. "You do look different," Lacey conceded. "You really think the killer in the parking lot could be your Eric?"

"It sounds crazy, doesn't it?"

"Yes." A couple of cars passed them and tucked into her lane, putting distance between the gray Toyota and the lead car. Lacey thumbed the radio. "Gray Toyota calling anyone. Any sign of subject vehicle? Over."

"No!" Snake sounded flustered. "Greg scrammed out of here at top speed. Where's the Lincoln? Over, damn it."

Damon's voice crackled in faintly. "We're conducting a reconnaissance through a group of warehouses. We saw a big gray vehicle turn in here. Over."

"Was it our subject?" Lacey asked. "Over."

"Unknown. Um, anybody get the gray Ford's tag number? Over."

"His rear tag light is out, but we got a partial," Snake put in. "Virginia JKL something. Over."

"Copy that," Damon replied. "You sure it wasn't JFK something?"

What a bunch of ace spies we are! Lacey gradually closed the gap between Willow's old Toyota and the silver Bimmer. The three follow cars drove up and down the side streets off Lee Highway in Vienna for another ten minutes, looking for an invisible gray Crown Vic with a tag number no one could quite remember, or had written down. Willow seemed lost in her thoughts.

"I just can't stop wondering about her, dead in her car. I'm wondering what's going to happen next," she said.

"Cecily Ashton had her own problems, Willow," Lacey said. "There are other suspects."

"I guess, but do you really think Cecily's death might have nothing to do with me?" Willow sighed deeply. "That would be great! I mean, for me. Not for someone else." She leaned back against the headrest and smiled. "You see, there's this new guy. I kind of fell for him while I was breaking up with Eric. We—Well, it's been kind of a secret."

"You have a new boyfriend?" Lacey hoped she didn't sound too astonished.

Willow didn't want to divulge his name just yet, she said, she didn't want to jinx it. She proceeded to describe a dreamy combination of Sir Galahad, Hugh Grant, and George Clooney. *Let Willow have her fantasy Prince Charming*, Lacey thought. She suspected this very troubled woman was the kind who always had some imaginary soap opera going on, in her head if not in her real life.

Just as Lacey was back on Lee Highway and taking the lead position ahead of the silver BMW, another voice came crackling over the two-way radio.

"Where are you, my lost little chicks?" It was Kepelov, his voice dripping with sarcasm. "Your subject is back at school. Class is in session. School bell is ringing! Come to grandma, little red riding hoods! Big Bad Wolf. Over."

*   *   *

Kepelov was waiting for them when they returned. He was leaning against a car, not the Crown Victoria in which he'd led them a merry chase, but a dark older model car. It was an ancient purple Gremlin, which struck Lacey as exceedingly odd. Hadley pulled his Lincoln in last and parked next to Edwina's silver BMW. No one wanted to park too close to Willow's shabby Toyota. Kepelov waited for all of them to park and assemble around him under the dim streetlight. Their surveillance leader and master spy crossed his arms. His mustache bristled. His cold blue eyes seemed to be enjoying this.

"You ran a red light, buddy." Snake was the first to speak. "You were speedin' like a demon. And you said we had to be good. What's the deal?"

Kepelov shrugged. "Funny what people will do when they know they are being followed, isn't it? You learn to do what's necessary. Takes time."

"So we screwed up?" Damon looked distressed.

"Yes, Mr. Newhouse." Kepelov lifted himself up off the hood of the Gremlin. "You will have another chance to impress me. Lucky I am no longer KGB, you would all be sent to driving school. In Siberia. Lucky I am such a nice guy. My little Hansels and Gretels lost in the woods, we will talk about how not to hug the bumper, how to swap positions and stay in contact, how not to lose your cool and your subject, and how not to freeze in parking lot before exercise begins."

"Wait a minute," Lacey asked. "What happened to your gray Crown Vic?"

"I have so much spare time out there all alone, I go car shopping. Nice wheels, eh?" Kepelov looked at his watch. "Take a break! Meet me back in classroom in twenty minutes. We talk about how to do surveillance like pros."

The students were silent. They looked embarrassed. Willow burst into tears.

"I think that went well," Lacey said as she headed toward the back door. "I need coffee."

In the office's little kitchen, Lacey poured herself another cup of Kepelov's decaf with plenty of cream and sugar and

popped it in the microwave. She was wondering what to tell
Vic when he asked how class went tonight when something
outside the window caught her attention. It was Kepelov
again, but with a woman. They were kissing and laughing,
oblivious to the cold and dark. Lacey found this tableau very
interesting. The last woman Kepelov had been involved
with—that she knew of—had shot him and left him for dead
in Paris. Lacey understood that reaction to Kepelov. She had
wanted to do the same thing on more than one occasion, including just now.

Kepelov was one tough ex-Soviet spy. He survived that
shooting and it apparently hadn't diminished his love of the
ladies, either. Despite his cool blue eyes, his bushy mustache, his nearly bald round head, and his bad jokes, they
seemed to love him too. Who was this latest femme fatale?
Lacey couldn't see much through the kitchen window, it was
too bright inside, too dark outside. The microwave dinged.
Lacey grabbed her coffee cup and took it with her.

She opened the back door and caught a cold blast of
wind. It carried the sweet aroma of cool night air and wood
smoke. Also the malodorous reek of cigarette smoke. Snake
Goldstein was grabbing a furtive nicotine fix. He nodded to
her impassively and turned his back into the wind. Lacey
stepped around the corner of the building.

Kepelov was wrapped in the generous arms of a volup-
tuous laughing female figure, her long thick dark curls
spilling over her red velvet coat. In the cold streetlight glare,
Lacey saw what looked like a purple skirt and purple suede
high-heeled boots. The woman's laugh was deep and
throaty, and Lacey recognized it.

It couldn't be! Here? With this guy?

"Marie? Marie Largesse?" Lacey said. "Is that really you?"

chapter 25

Kepelov's zaftig lady in red velvet spun around at the sound of Lacey's voice.

"Why, it's Lacey Smithsonian! Goodness gracious, girl, it's been simply ages!" Marie wrapped her up in a great big hug and nearly tipped the coffee out of Lacey's hand. "It must be a whole month since I saw y'all last!"

Marie Largesse was the owner and resident psychic of The Little Shop of Horus in Old Town Alexandria, a little storefront with a distinctive New Orleans flavor near the river. She sold candles and crystals and New Age books and consultations with the resident psychic. Despite Marie's spotty record as a seer, Lacey always enjoyed visiting her. Marie had a big heart to match her generous figure, and chatting with her was like a lazy trip back to the Big Easy.

"Lacey Smithsonian," Kepelov said archly, "you are skipping ahead in the workbook? Spying on the master spy?"

"I was spying on the spy who led us on a wild goose chase," Lacey admitted. "Marie, I had no idea I'd find *you* here with the wild goose himself."

"Well, here I am, honey!" Marie's laugh was deep and comforting. "I'm no apparition. Flesh and bone. More flesh than bone, y'all."

"But what are you doing here? And with—" Lacey looked from one to the other. "Him?"

"Greg? My big Russian doll baby? If y'all'd come around more often, Lacey, you'd know these things." Marie winked broadly. "I owe him all to you, you know. So thank you kindly, honey."

"Me?" Lacey was horrified. "You can't blame this guy on me!"

Marie and Kepelov both burst out laughing. "Last fall," Marie explained, "after your little adventure down Nawlins way? Well, I just had to read all about it in *The Times-Picayune*, my hometown paper. My cousin Louisa down in the Quarter sent me all y'all's juicy clippings. And I read all your stories in your own little paper, *The Eye*, of course. The whole adventure was just humming with psychic vibrations! I took one look at that picture of Gregor Kepelov. He was standing behind you and I *knew*. Something about those blue eyes of his, don't you think?" Kepelov smiled and wiggled his mustache and opened his eyes wide for Lacey's benefit. "I felt like I'd been seeing those beautiful eyes in my dreams for years."

Lacey was glad she didn't see Kepelov's blue eyes in her dreams. He was more like a nightmare for her. She still hadn't forgiven him for being on the other side of that adventure that so captured Marie's imagination.

"Is funny." Kepelov gave Marie a hug. "Life, you know?"

"Pretty funny, all right. I'm really happy for you, Marie." Lacey smiled brightly for Marie to see, but she felt downhearted and confused. She didn't want the credit or the blame for bringing Kepelov into Marie's life. Lacey wasn't psychic, but she saw disaster ahead. "I'm freezing, I better go inside. We are still finishing the class, right, Kepelov, after our big surveillance flop?"

"Here, Smithsonian." Kepelov pulled a flask from his leather jacket. "Little shot of vodka. Warm you up."

"No thanks. Not on a school night."

"Smart woman. Never touch the stuff myself." Kepelov winked at Marie.

"Before you go, sugar, I just have to tell you one thing." Marie took Lacey's hands in hers and pulled her aside. "I'm getting some kind of funny vibration here. Sort of a tapping vibration, you know? Something tapping on my shoulder?"

Marie Largesse once told Lacey she often felt her "psychic vibrations" tap-tap-tapping gently on her shoulder to get her attention. That's why she had the mystical symbol of the Eye of Horus tattooed on each shoulder blade, to help her watch for the more subtle vibrations. Lacey privately suspected a pinched nerve, or an overactive imagination. She remembered vividly the time she dragged Marie to a crime scene, hoping desperately for some psychic clue. Marie took one look, closed her eyes, and fainted dead away, her "psychic circuits" overloaded. Lacey hadn't asked her again.

"Marie, my darling all-seeing eye," Kepelov teased, "you would tell me if you are sensing diamonds, maybe, or rubies? Or pearls, perhaps, large natural pearls from the bottom of the sea? Lacey Smithsonian here, she is like a dousing rod to find water, only Smithsonian finds diamonds. Or maybe pearls this time."

"Sorry, Kepelov, I only find dead things," Lacey cracked. "The Romanov diamonds were a bonus."

Marie focused on a spot in the dark just beyond Lacey's head. "No, I don't see jewels or pearls, only a box. Some sort of funny box."

"A jewelry box? What kind of—"

"A box of secrets." Marie suddenly flinched and grabbed her head, massaging her temples as she squeezed her eyes tight shut. Her purple painted nails gleamed under the streetlights. "It's not over! The hunting season isn't over till the prey is captured! There's a deceiver in the woods!" She opened her eyes.

A deceiver? Take your pick, Lacey thought. Kepelov, a professional liar, a man of many identities? Griffin, a professional—whatever he was? Bud Hunt? Martin Hadley? Philip Clark Ashton? Simon Edison? Someone else in the PI class? Willow Raynor, Edwina Plimpton, or even poor dead Cecily herself?

"This is where it happened, isn't it?" Marie gazed up at Kepelov. Rimmed in purple kohl, her eyes looked huge and dark. She pointed to the far corner of the parking lot, shadowy and empty in the night. "Over there. That's where it happened. But the hunting isn't finished."

"Not to worry, darling," Kepelov said. "Gregor will take care of you. Nothing will hurt you. Go home and stay warm and I will be there soon." He put his arms around Marie and walked her to the ancient purple Gremlin, waiting in a pool of pale streetlight.

"Oh my God, Marie. Is that *your* Gremlin?" Lacey's breath was a puff of white vapor in the chilly air. Marie laughed and her curls danced. She seemed quite herself again.

"Don't you love it, Lacey? I just bought it. Needs a little work, but when I saw that purple paint, honey, I just *knew.*"

Just like Kepelov, Lacey thought. *A fixer-upper for Marie to remodel.*

"But a Gremlin? I didn't know any of those were still on the road."

"Might be the last one," Marie said. "Greg doesn't like it much. I had a little car trouble tonight and he rode to my rescue, the sweet thing. Damn, honey, is it gonna snow any second tonight or what?"

"Look at this thing, Smithsonian! Purple! A rolling target, a grape on wheels," Kepelov complained, his mustache bristling. "And slow too, worse than Yugo. Maybe I soup it up with extra horses. Big American V-8, eh? Vroom vroom."

"I'm as fine as a day in June now, Gregor, I didn't mean to scare y'all. I wasn't trying to tune into that terrible death, believe me. But I knew that's what it must have been, when that whirlwind started inside my head, and I was hearing— I don't know, darlin', all I can tell you is, whatever it is, it ain't finished."

"What did you mean about 'hunting season'?" Lacey asked.

"Hunting season? I said that? No idea. Come see me at the shop, you hear now?"

Lacey read the bumper sticker on the back of Marie's new old purple Gremlin: HAVE YOU HUGGED YOUR PSYCHIC TODAY? The driver's door creaked loudly as she opened it. Kepelov kissed Marie good-bye, warned her to lock her doors, and said he would see her after class.

Another mysterious couple, Lacey mused. Marie apparently felt no psychic warnings about being with this ex-KGB spy. Did that mean Kepelov wasn't really a bad guy? Was he just a bad spy? Or was Marie just a bad psychic? Lacey and Kepelov watched Marie's comical purple car pull away from the curb and disappear into the night.

"Come inside, Smithsonian. Cold night. Time for class, part two. What we learn from failed surveillance. How not to let your subject make a fool of you." Kepelov turned toward Bud Hunt's classroom building. Lacey fell in beside him.

"Speaking of fools, Kepelov, Marie is a friend of mine, you know. I care about her. I don't want anyone making a fool out of her. You hear me?"

"She is my friend too," Kepelov laughed. "Very special friend. And she is no fool. Have no worries, Smithsonian. Love is funny, no?"

"And this is love?"

"Always so serious you are! I am the teacher here, but you are, what, guidance counselor?" He stopped and turned to look at her under a streetlight. "Are my intentions honorable, you wonder? Marie Largesse has never betrayed me. Or shot me. I have never betrayed her. Or shot her. And such a bountiful woman. An abundance of beauty. You see it too, I can tell. Yes, perhaps it is love. No fooling."

"Love can turn sour," Lacey said.

"Yes, like the very blond Willow and her boyfriend Eric-something."

"She told you about him?"

"Heard it on the radio. Yours, Smithsonian. Did I not show you how to turn radio *off*?"

"Damn you, Kepelov!" He laughed loudly. "And I am not getting in a car with her again, I don't care how many times we do that damned surveillance exercise over."

"Not your fault. Instructor gets the special spy radio. I listen in to all the follow cars, not just you. The stuffy Plimpton woman and the Snake, that was also worth listening to. But you and the strange woman, Willow? That was most interesting."

"What do you think of her?"

He shrugged his big shoulders and dropped his voice. "She is thin and very nervous. She needs a better car. And a better life. Perhaps she is not so suited for surveillance work."

"You got that right. So who do you think killed Cecily Ashton?"

Kepelov stroked his mustache. "I like easy answers. They are so often right. A woman is murdered? Look for her man. Her ex-husband hated her? He can buy whatever he wants? He can pay to cover his tracks? He is the easy answer. But then this Ashton woman, she lived a messy life. There may be many other interested parties."

"Like your friend Nigel Griffin?"

"Ah! Nigel is always popular with the ladies," he said. "Up to a point."

"What about you?"

"Me? Ha! Cecily Ashton was way too skinny for me. Look at her. All skin and bones, and problems. Look at Marie. Who wins? My Marie, hands down."

"What about Bud Hunt?"

"Another messy life." They reached the back of the building and Kepelov stepped lightly down the stairs. "Interesting thing, Smithsonian. A mystery is like a Russian doll. You know Russian dolls, yes? We call them *matryoshka* doll. Open up the doll. Inside is another doll. Open up that doll. Inside is yet another, and another and another, until you find the final tiny doll, no bigger than the tip of your little finger, a simple piece of painted wood. One tiny little mystery inside so many other mysteries."

Kepelov pulled the door open and held it for Lacey.

"Which doll are we on with Cecily Ashton?" Lacey asked. "A big one or a little one?"

"Many dolls to go, I fear."

chapter 26

On Tuesday, a big bouquet of pale pink roses, white lilies, irises, and daisies awaited Lacey at the main desk in the lobby. They were a burst of spring on a winter's day.

"My, my. Who sent you these beauties?" LaToya Crawford demanded as Lacey signed for the flowers. An attractive African-American city reporter and one of Lacey's favorite people at *The Eye*, LaToya loved collecting information on anyone and everyone. She was in a blaze of yellow today, from her shoes to her dress to her matching overcoat. "I don't get any flowers! Why doesn't anyone ever send me flowers? So who was it?"

"It's a mystery." Lacey gathered up the immense bouquet in her arms. "I haven't had a chance to read the little card yet. I may not read it for *hours*."

LaToya snorted. Her perfectly manicured hand reached out and grabbed the card attached to the arrangement. "Well, girlfriend, I suggest we find out. Right now!"

Lacey snatched the card back from LaToya's crimson-tipped fingers. "A little privacy, please?" She swept up her burst of spring and proceeded to the elevator, followed closely by LaToya.

"All right, you want your privacy. I respect that," LaToya said, smirking. *As if,* Lacey thought. "But I'm a journalist, baby. I ask questions because I want to *know* things, you know. Just between us girls, who the heck is sending you flowers? That handsome fella you been seein', or some other handsome fella, if you know what I'm sayin'?"

Their elevator arrived and LaToya pushed the button for their floor.

"I don't know," Lacey said innocently. "Could be any handsome fella, probably. There are so *many*." LaToya snorted. Lacey buried her face in the bouquet and inhaled the sweet scent of the blush-colored roses until the doors opened again. She raced LaToya to her desk, set down the vase, and ripped open the card.

"Well?" the city reporter demanded. "Is it who I think it is?"

"They are from a certain Victor Donovan. You may vaguely recall the name."

"Oh, *that* handsome man! The one you brought to the Christmas party? He's a fine specimen as I recall, extra fine. You let me know if you ever break up with him."

"You bet. Don't hold your breath."

"What does the note say?"

"We're awfully nosy today." Lacey smiled at her.

"Reporter here." LaToya pointed to herself.

Lacey read the note again. *Darling, please wait to pick up the permit paperwork. Home soon. Love, Vic.* He meant the concealed carry permit, of course. How romantic. Was he afraid she'd go off on a shooting spree without him?

LaToya was still trying to read over her shoulder. "Well? What's it say?"

"It says, 'Love, Vic.' "

"Ah, that's so sweet. I wish I had me a sweet man who'd send me flowers for everyone in the whole damn office to see. With a mushy little love note. Hold my calls, girls, I'll be working on that." LaToya flounced away to do a story on her city beat, or as she said, "something about the silly mayor."

Wait on the gun permit? Lacey glanced at the card again and sniffed the flowers. *Like I've got time right now to pick up the paperwork.* She understood Vic Donovan was the kind of guy who demonstrated his love and concern for her comfort and safety in practical items, like providing the BMW, and wanting to work on the self-defense thing to-gether. Like a guy. He had offered her a gun in the past. He seemed a little more cautious now, maybe because she'd been in so many scrapes. The flowers were definitely a nice touch. He was learning. She especially appreciated that they were sent to the newsroom, as LaToya had pointed out, for everyone in the whole darn office to see.

She picked up the morning newspaper that was left on her desk. Lacey's update on Cecily's couture collection at the Fashion Museum was featured on the inside of the front section. It was in a box, near the other Cecily Ashton stories.

Tony Trujillo's piece quoted a police spokesman as saying the Arlington detectives, who were helping the Falls Church Police Department, were still running down leads in the Ashton murder. Which probably meant they were out of good leads and they were running the bad ones. Having been a cop, Vic had told her often enough how cops thought. There's typically an "obvious person of interest" or two in any murder, he said. If the obvious suspects have solid alibis, it's back to square one, and after forty-eight hours the odds against closing a case grow longer every hour. Forty-eight hours had passed.

Another Trujillo brief said Philip Clark Ashton was offering a $100,000 reward for any information on the murder of his ex-wife. Just pocket change for him, but good public relations? *Priceless.*

She searched the article for any hint of skepticism. There was none. Tony had written it straight. Lacey wondered how she would have written the story. COPS CLUELESS! EX REMORSELESS! ODDS—HOPELESS?

You're a fashion reporter, for crying out loud! It wasn't her job to solve the murder, she lectured herself. Mac just wanted a follow-up story with some fashion angle, any fashion angle. He wasn't asking her to bring in the killer. He was always telling her *not* to try to bring in the killer. Lacey could write her little follow-up story and reassure herself that poor Cecily hadn't gone looking for her the day she died. She could take her beautiful bouquet and go home. And be stuck on the fashion beat forever.

If this isn't the kind of story I was longing for when I signed up for that wacky PI school, she thought bitterly, *an awful story, but a story that practically fell into my lap—then what the hell am I looking for?*

Where to begin? Lacey decided to listen to her Cecily Ashton interview tape again. Maybe she'd missed something subtle, something that might resonate differently now that she was dead. Maybe Lacey had forgotten something that sounded irrelevant at the time, like any mention of Simon Edison's exotic fabric or Edison himself.

Lacey didn't own a high-tech digital recorder, the kind other reporters were beginning to use. Her tape recorder was pure analog, an obsolete last-generation cassette recorder. It was noisy but serviceable. She popped in the tape and pressed the button and cringed. The tape was full of the usual hisses and pops and clicks. Lacey had never gotten used to the sound of her own voice on tape. Her voice sounded low and breathy and intimate, not crisp and impersonal and businesslike. Hearing the dead woman's well modulated and pleasant voice felt odd too. Cecily might have been the hostess of her own TV show, giving a tour of her fabulous home for the cameras.

"This is the largest closet, which was designed around my morning routine. The Aubusson carpet is antique, the crystal chandeliers are by Swarovski . . . "

We should all have such closets, Lacey thought. Her own morning routine depended so much on having an outfit ready and set out to wear the night before. If she neglected this vital step, she would spend precious minutes tearing apart her tiny closet and trying on and rejecting outfits and running late and generally driving herself nuts. Today, she wore the outfit she had selected the previous evening, a snowy white blouse with flared sleeves gathered tightly at the wrist, a vintage black wool vest fitted snugly at the waist, a green and blue plaid skirt, and medium-heeled black patent leather Mary Janes. Lacey thought it looked businesslike and scholarly, and it was comfortable enough to wear all day and to PI class that evening.

Unfortunately, Lacey's headphones didn't give her any privacy. Wearing them didn't stop people from trying to talk to her and ask her about the flowers or inquire about her follow-up story or a dozen other distractions. Her fellow journalists paid no attention to her frantic hand signals telling them to go away, she was listening to something important. Among these oblivious souls was the senior police reporter.

Tony Trujillo was nosing around Felicity's desk across from hers, looking for crumbs of whatever the butcher-and-bakery beat might offer today. It was nine-thirty in the morning, time for a police reporter's breakfast. He was wearing blue jeans and a blue turtleneck with a Brooks Brothers blazer. Lacey looked at his feet. Today's cowboy boots were black snakeskin with scuffed toes.

"Aha, cherry Danish! Score! Felicity comes through!" He picked up a slice of pastry oozing with a white glaze of frosting. "Whatcha' doing, Smithsonian?" Scrounging for food and reading over other reporters' shoulders were two of his favorite things.

Lacey gave him her Go-Away Look, but he sat down on the edge of her desk anyway. She removed the headphones and switched off the recorder. "What?"

"You're not working, are you?" He turned on the hundred-watt smile. She frowned.

"No, I never work. I'm a fashion reporter. I just—"

"You just what?"

He waited. Lacey almost said, *I just solve murders*, but that would smack of hubris. Saying that would guarantee she would never solve another murder. And at the moment she was not, in fact, solving a murder. She was hunting for a clue, perhaps a chance comment or nuance that would send her in a new direction.

"I'm just trying to find a quiet Zen-like moment. If you see one, it's mine. I keep losing it."

"Good luck with that. But you may like what I've found. I know everything the cops know about Cecily Ashton's murder. Every last thing. I know when she died she had in her fancy purse a copy of that weird little drawing you just wrote about, for what it's worth. I even know the caliber of the murder weapon." He seemed very proud of himself.

"Could it have been a twenty-two?" She looked for her

coffee cup. Cecily had a copy of the drawing with her? *Why?*

"Curses, Lois Lane, what fiend leaked that information? You're not the police reporter. They're not supposed to tell you cool police-reporter stuff like that!"

She smiled. "I have my ways."

He folded his arms and scowled. "What kind of ways?"

"I annoyed Detective Jance. He had to say something to get me off the phone."

"Annoying people: Your secret weapon. What else aren't you telling me?"

"Why, Tony Trujillo, I always tell you everything." She batted her eyelashes. "Honest. The whole truth, and"—Lacey crossed her fingers—"nothing but the truth."

"Hey, aren't we a team?"

"Only when you want to steal my story," Lacey said, replacing her headphones on her ears. "We're a team like you and that stolen pastry are a team."

"Share, Lacey," he corrected. "Not steal. I want us to *share* the story."

"I'm working on a fashion story. About fabric. A total snooze. Wanna share that?"

Tony narrowed his eyes. "Likely story." He lifted another gooey pastry from Felicity's desk, and he and his snakeskin boots made their escape. "I'll be back."

The taped interview offered nothing new—until Cecily's cell phone rang on the tape and interrupted their conversation. She had excused herself to take the call in the room next door, a room full of shoes, Lacey remembered. Her muffled voice could still be heard faintly in the background. Lacey had let the tape run on, recording a brief conversation with Hansen, whose voice was loud and clear.

"Do you believe this place?" He was referring to the labyrinth of closets. "I feel like I'm in some kind of crazy department store in *The Twilight Zone*. Behind the scenes, where it's just racks of clothes going on forever."

Lacey heard herself agreeing with him. "I know. It would be like living all alone in a Neiman-Marcus store or something." There was a rustling noise. Hansen was moving around the room, looking at the clothes.

"Some of these dresses still have tags on them, did you notice?" Hansen's voice was incredulous. "Who needs this many clothes anyway? It's weirding me out, man, like she's some creepy department store mannequin come to life, with a whole store full of clothes to wear? And then she freezes *us* into mannequins, right, and she makes us replace her in the window display, so no one figures out she's escaped, and then—"

"You've been watching too much science fiction, Hansen."

"Yeah, I think you're right, man. But really, Smithsonian, this place isn't natural. The woman must have a thousand pairs of shoes in there. Are you sure she's human? Does she have more than two feet?"

It was another world to Hansen. The photographer's entire wardrobe consisted, as near as Lacey could tell, of about five pairs of blue jeans and khakis, a few long-sleeved shirts, a few T-shirts, and a handful of ratty sweaters. He wore the same fluffy overstuffed down ski parka whenever it was cold. He wore one worn navy sport coat, if absolutely necessary, for formal occasions. He had one tie. It was probably wadded up in his camera bag for emergencies. His fashion accessories consisted of half a dozen press badges for access to various government buildings, including one for Congress and one for the White House. Hansen was not exactly a fashion plate, but the long tall shaggy blond photographer never seemed to notice or care. If anything, it seemed to make him more attractive to women. He was no shallow metrosexual fashion plate. If you loved Hansen, it wasn't for his wardrobe, it was for the inner Hansen.

"I tell you, Lacey, if Cecily Ashton starts to freeze back into a department store dummy, I am out of here." Both of them laughed at this. It overloaded the mike and made a horrible racket on the tape. Lacey had to pause the tape and rub her ears.

"But don't you think Cecily is pretty?" The tape continued with Lacey's question.

"Yeah, she's a babe, but she's plastic-looking. All that

work she's had done? A mannequin. I like my ladies a little more natural, you know? I like women who can move their faces."

There was a commotion in the background on the tape, and Hansen and Lacey shut up. Cecily's voice rose to an audible level through the wall.

"I don't know what you're talking about! Who is this? What about him? What about Philadelphia?"

Lacey wrote down what Cecily said, but it didn't enlighten her in any way. Who is *he*? And what *about* Philadelphia? Cecily soon returned to the room, apologized for the interruption, and continued the interview. She seemed somewhat more distracted than before. She repeated herself a couple of times, as if her thoughts were elsewhere. And Lacey now remembered that Cecily had once more picked up the 1942 photograph of Rita Hayworth and turned it over and over again in her hands, gazing at the pencil drawing on the back. Was the caller who upset Cecily her ex-husband, Philip Ashton, the man who had given her the photo?

Lacey stopped the tape and rang Hansen's desk, half expecting him to be out on assignment. She was surprised when he picked up his phone.

"Yo, Lacey, what's up?"

"I'm just listening to that interview with Cecily Ashton again."

"Yeah, I was wondering when you'd start doing your thing on that."

"My thing? What thing?"

"You know, the old 'Smithsonian's going to get to the bottom of this case if it's the last thing she ever does' kind of thing."

"Hansen, I do not do that." She tapped her pen on the desk.

"Sure you don't," he snorted. "So what can I do you for?"

"I wanted to know—and I'm not necessarily doing that *thing*, I'm just curious. Do you remember anything about that day at Cecily's house that struck you as odd?"

"Jeez, Lacey, everything struck me as odd! I don't remember anything that didn't strike me odd. First we go to the faux French château like beggars at the freaking castle gate, we meet the amazing plastic Barbie doll princess who lives all alone in this place the size of a hotel, well, all alone with her *servants*. And her *clothes*. And then we spend an hour or two, or ten maybe, wandering around lost in her closets, her crazy multiple freaking interconnecting closets, like a carnival funhouse full of clothes, if you call that fun. And, if I didn't know any better, I'd say she was coming on to me."

"She *was* coming on to you, Hansen, and that was the strangest thing of all, dude. She totally dug your wardrobe." Hansen laughed on the other end of the line. "But anything particularly strange, other than all of that?"

"I don't know." Hansen fell silent. "You sure she really died? Like, she wasn't an android or something? I mean, did you really see blood?" His words brought back to Lacey the image of the delicate tracery of blood sprayed on the inside of the car window.

"I saw blood. Trust me." Lacey shivered as a sudden chill coursed down her spine. "You remember when she got a phone call?"

"Phone call? I guess. Seemed to freak her out a little."

"Did that old photograph of Rita Hayworth mean anything to you?"

"The one the burglar left behind? Not really. But if you're gonna break in, why not take that too? Weird." There was a loud noise on his end of the phone, as if Hansen had sprung up from his chair. "Oh crap, I'm late! I gotta go to the Hill. Later, Lacey."

Mac strolled past her desk, one hand holding a cup of coffee, the other balancing a piece of Felicity's popular cherry Danish. A copy of today's *Eye Street Observer* was tucked under his arm.

"Smithsonian, come talk with me." Mac gestured to follow him to his office.

At this rate, she'd never finish listening to the tape, let alone write a story. Lacey entered Mac's palace of newsprint, papers perched precariously on every surface. She noticed a wood-framed picture on the credenza behind him. It was one of those department store specials, a package deal, a few eight-by-tens and sheets of wallet-sized pictures of the entire family in several poses. The package deal price didn't really matter. The content was priceless.

It was a bright color photograph of Mac's recently expanded family. It didn't seem possible to Lacey, but Mac had obviously agreed to sit for a photo session with Kim, Jasmine, and Lily Rose. They were all grinning like mad. Almost thirteen-year-old Jasmine wore a blue turtleneck sweater and her little sister, ten-year-old Lily Rose, was in a matching pink one. Their lustrous black curls were carefully arranged over their shoulders. Almond-shaped eyes and dusky skin glowed in the photograph. There was no trace of the sad wariness Lacey had seen in the children's eyes when she first met them.

Lacey sat down in one of two chairs, after removing a stack of file folders from the seat. She sighed.

"It's not that bad," he said.

"I'm just weary. What's up, Mac?"

He pressed his fingers together. His eyebrows leaned in toward each other. Lacey knew that look. It was his Wise Leader of the Newsroom Tribe look, his I Have Been to the Mountaintop look. *Lord,* she thought, *he probably wants me to do some sort of special report on top of all my regular work.* She could hardly wait. *What is it this time?*

"I was pondering what you were doing on a Saturday morning. At an office building in Falls Church. Where Cecily Ashton's body was found."

There was no reason for Mac to know about her personal business, not on weekends. Weekends were hers. *Damn it, why did Cecily Ashton have to die while I was there? Why did she have to die at all?* Lacey said nothing.

"Across the street from the Falls Church Police Department, come to find out," he continued. "Do you really want to be a private investigator?"

"Who told you that?" She sat up in her chair, indignant.

Mac managed to looked both smug and concerned at the same time. "Trujillo made some calls."

"He's such a jerk. He is such a No Girls Allowed in Our

Boys' Club kind of—boy." Lacey shifted in her seat and narrowed her eyes.

"All true. So?"

"So maybe I want to learn something new. So maybe I'm interested in improving my investigative skills. Maybe I want to find a way to get onto a new beat, something worthwhile, something hard news, something not fashion-related. So sue me."

"You don't like the fashion beat?" He looked nonplussed, like it was a brand-new thought. Like she hadn't mentioned it a hundred times or more.

"Mac! I've been telling you that since the day after Mariah died! Or maybe it was two days after she died, I'm not exactly sure, not knowing the exact time of her death. Because she died at her desk! And not a living soul even noticed she was dead! Because she was the damn fashion reporter! I don't want to die at my keyboard, Mac."

"More drama. You should be the drama critic." Her editor rolled his eyes. "Give it up, Smithsonian. You're a star. The fashion beat is your Milky Way. You've made it what it is."

"What would that be? A joke?" Lacey needed some coffee. She noticed that Mac's coffee cup was full. He stabbed at his cherry Danish, popping a piece into his mouth. Lacey briefly wondered what would happen if the food editor ever wanted a new beat too. Nothing, obviously. Mac would never give up the cakes and pies and endless goodies Felicity Pickles baked as research for her column. They were both stuck.

"Your 'Crimes of Fashion' and 'Fashion Bites' columns are among the most widely read features in *The Eye Street Observer.* Did you know that?"

"My columns are not just about fashion. Nobody reads my stuff for the fashion. This is the city fashion forgot, remember, Mac? And I'm turning into the fashion reporter time forgot, just like Mariah."

"No, they're not just about fashion. Your columns are about that kooky sensibility you bring to it, the way you decode it, like it's some sort of secret code and you're the fashion spy, the secret agent of style. It's a little scary, Lacey. I live in fear you might decide to decode me someday. Dissect everything I wear. I mean in print, not just in your head, where you're probably doing it right now."

Not exactly a challenge, she thought. Anybody could decode Mac's style, or lack of style. It didn't take a genius code-breaker to read the message in his mismatched clothing. To his credit, Douglas MacArthur Jones wasn't like the beige and gray bureaucrats who floated colorlessly through the D.C. streets. From his tattered brown corduroy jackets to his motley assortment of clashing plaid shirts and garish striped ties and neon slacks, his wardrobe was living in the past. It declared that he was a down-home, man-of-the-people, sixties-intellectual kind of guy, a truth-and-justice-seeking man of the Fourth Estate. A journalist! And possibly as blind as a bat, dressing by sonar.

"Face it, Lacey, you care that people in Washington dress badly, because you think it speaks badly of them in some way. Or maybe it speaks badly of all of us, or badly of America, I don't know. I don't get it, but you do, and you care, and I think that's great, whether *they* care or not. And some of them really do care, because *you* care. You couldn't write the stories you write if you didn't have passion. And that's without any of the dangerous stuff, all that stuff I'm always telling you not to do, and you end up doing it anyway."

"It's not enough, Mac. I'm burned out. I want a chance at another kind of story. There's more to life than this year's accessories and last year's shoes and next year's—"

"Of course there is, especially when the accessories come wrapped up in a murder story. You get those 'other kind' of stories. Flirting with danger is not your job, you just invite it, and so far you've gotten away with it. Why would you want to give up a beat like yours? It's got everything!" She tried to object, but he plowed on like a steamroller. "A certain number of our reporters envy you that whole 'murder magnet' thing. They have so-called hard news beats where nothing ever happens, some of them. Some fossilized government agency *almost* makes a decision and then decides not to, and that's their big headline for the month. You really want a beat like that? They're jealous of you, damn jealous."

She fixed him with an icy glare. "What an honor."

"You have a gift, Smithsonian. Deal with it." He picked up a pen to mark up a story, signaling the end of this fatherly chat. "By the way, how are you coming with the Cecily Ashton follow-up?"

"I'm working on it. You might not want to get too close, Mac. You know, that 'murder magnet' thing."

Lacey stood up on her high heels and stomped out of his office.

If I'm never going to get off the fashion beat, why not just do whatever I want?

chapter 27

The flowers on her desk brought back Lacey's smile. They reminded her of Vic, so his plan was working. She put all the rest of it out of her mind, the fashion beat and deciding what she wanted to be when she grew up. All of it but Cecily Ashton.

The nonexistent state of her elusive follow-up on Cecily depressed her, as did the apparent state of the police investigation into Cecily's death. The cops weren't talking. All Trujillo seemed to have was the caliber of the gun, and Lacey had that too. The obvious suspects had alibis, like Bud Hunt, or money, like Philip Clark Ashton. Then there was Simon Edison, who was in love with Cecily and had been furious with her for humiliating him. She realized she didn't know what his alibi was. She picked up the phone and called him.

"Oh, Lacey, I'd have to know the exact time of death to know exactly what I was doing right then," Simon mused. "And the paper said they haven't determined that yet. Once they do I can check my daybook and get back to you." *Scientists,* she thought. *Ask a simple question, like did you kill somebody, and they go all technical on you.*

"Okay, what were you doing that day, in general terms, not second by second?"

"I suppose I wasn't too far away," Simon said. "I live in Falls Church and I visit the Farmers' Market every weekend. Organic vegetables, you know, they have the greatest— Oh my God! She might have been there looking for me! You don't suppose she meant to meet me there? My poor sweet Cecily." His voice broke.

"Did the police talk to you, Simon?"

"No, why do you ask? Do you think they will? I'm sure if they have an exact time I can tell them exactly what I was doing—"

Lacey promised to get back to him. Simon Edison had a knack for disorienting her. She thought of the other possibilities, the nonobvious suspects, like Hadley and Griffin, who were busy throwing themselves in front of Lacey, expecting to be arrested at any moment. Willow Raynor expected to be shot at any moment, and Edwina Plimpton was stocking up on cocktail party chatter.

Philip Clark Ashton was Lacey's favorite candidate in the murder sweepstakes, but favorites could be wrong. No doubt the not-so-grieving ex-husband was capable of ordering his ex-wife's murder as casually as he might order a drink at the bar. And a hired professional killer would probably be long gone and difficult to track. Lacey had no idea how to crack Ashton's wall of money and lawyers. She was certain he wouldn't willingly speak to her again, after that meeting in Claudia's office went so well. If she went after Ashton, she couldn't do it alone.

But maybe it wasn't Ashton after all. He certainly had the money and the power to have someone killed, but why bother? Hadn't he solved all his Cecily problems with the divorce decree? Did he still have some lingering secret she might have exposed? Or would this be one of those cases where the cops finally get a DNA match and the murderer was a wild card, completely out of the blue? The killer would turn out to be, say, the garbage man, for example, not one of the many known suspects, likely or unlikely?

Willow Raynor's story bothered Lacey too. Was there really a shadowy assassin out there tormenting that very shy retiring woman? Killing other women around her by accident? Or at random, so when he finally murdered her no one would see a connection? That was part of the tangled story of the infamous "D.C. Snipers" a few years earlier, where the real target among all the random shootings seemed to be an ex-wife.

Lacey searched the Web for anything about Nina Vickers, the woman Willow claimed was killed instead of her. There wasn't much, just a link to a newspaper story on her unsolved murder. There was even less on Willow herself. But Lacey did find out the name of the art store and gallery where she'd worked, Up and Downtown Arts, which had several locations in Philadelphia. She made a call and she discovered that Willow Raynor hadn't been entirely frank with her. Willow worked at a smaller location, but the larger gallery had been the one to feature Cecily Ashton's small exhibit of her vintage accessories. Willow had helped out, her friend Nina too. That probably warranted some follow-up. *Why did Willow lie?*

Willow said she was in hiding from an abusive exboyfriend and she wanted to learn how to disappear. So perhaps she was reluctant to be quite candid because of the man who had frightened her so much. It might be hard to understand how someone could be so meek, so trapped, so hopeless, unless you had experienced it. Willow had been desperate enough to leave her home just to get away from him, and to change her looks. And yet she hadn't changed her name. Yet. Maybe that was part of what Willow hoped to learn in PI school, how to assume a new identity and drop out of sight.

At their first class session, Hunt said some of his typical female PI students seemed to be "dames with a personal problem." Lacey wondered what his take on Willow might be—one more thing to ask Hunt about, she realized, like whether he'd killed Cecily. She tried Hunt's PI office and his cell phone number from the class contact sheet. No answers, only voice mail.

If this Eric O'Neil was as unstable as Willow claimed, she was in real danger. But how could Willow's abusive boyfriend have anything to do with Cecily Ashton? It made Lacey's head hurt.

She spent an hour on the phone finding someone from the Philadelphia Police Department to talk to about Nina Vickers. The case had no new leads, she was told by one of the detectives who worked the case. He seemed to barely recall the murder. The slug that killed Nina was never recovered. There was no other evidence, no reliable witnesses, no viable suspects, no arrests. She asked about Eric O'Neil, but was told there was "no paper" on him. He'd been questioned; that was all. They had nothing.

Lacey remembered she had a secret weapon. If anyone in D.C. knew more about Willow Raynor than what little she or Bud Hunt did, it would be the woman responsible for Willow's new blond hair: *Stella*. Stella loved to talk, and people loved to talk to Stella. A little shampoo and head massage under Stella's knowing fingers and her clients eagerly spilled their deep dark secrets. Lacey was now glad she had sent Willow to see her. Willow had already talked to the Stella Broadcasting Corporation.

Lacey didn't need an excuse to visit her friend at the salon, but if she paid for a service, she'd feel better about pumping her for information. She looked at her hands. Her nails were a mess. *Perfect!*

She walked the eight blocks from her office on Eye Street, across Farragut Square and upper Connecticut Avenue, to the Stylettos salon at Dupont Circle. The walk gave her a chance to clear her head. And window shop. Filene's Basement always had something amusing to look at. Lacey would get a manicure and pick Stella's brain over her lunch hour and grab something to eat on the way back. As a bonus, she could avoid discussing the matter with Mac.

Stella was busy layering a client's hair when Lacey strolled through the door. The stylist wore her new blond bob, and a bright yellow miniskirt under her black Stylettos smock. She tottered on improbably pointy high heels, yellow with black polka dots. They looked incredibly painful. Lacey couldn't wait until those nasty pointy-toed stilettos went out of style again. Only people like Aladdin should wear pointy-toed shoes, Lacey firmly believed, and maybe Ali Baba and his Forty Thieves. *Put those shoes on a magic carpet and send them to Never Never Land!*

"Lacey! Hang on, be right with ya!" Stella danced over as soon as she finished with her client. Lacey held up her nails and sighed dramatically. "Oh my God, Lace, you are so right. Nail emergency! I don't know how you can face the world with those disgraceful digits. But we'll fix you right up. Sit, sit, sit. Tell me everything."

"I have something for you too. That article you wanted on"— Lacey reached in her bag and pulled out Stella's copy of Brooke's secret document; what was the code name Brooke told her to use?—"Pretty Cute Curls."

"Say what?" Stella looked blank as she took the envelope.

"The PCC," Lacey said with a broad wink. "You know. Pretty in *pink*? It's from our mutual friend, Blond Ammunition?"

"Oh! The Code! Lace, I've been waiting for this!" Stella squealed happily and flipped through the leatherette folder, like the one Brooke made for Lacey. "Gee, that's so great. Blondie said you'd be getting it to me. She didn't trust e-mail. Wow, so many pages! I've got some homework to do. Back in a sec, I'll go stash this in my locker."

Stella skipped to the back of the salon and returned with her assessment of Lacey's look for the day.

"Ya know, Lacey, that outfit of yours? Totally Our Miss Brooks. Black Mary Jane heels? Please! Well, it just totally cries out for a French twist. You soak those claws, I'll do the twist." Stella set her up with a manicurist and slid behind her with hair pins and a wide tooth comb. Lacey felt her hair being pulled, professionally but not delicately.

"Ow! What happened to that light touch I tell everyone you have?"

"Stop fussing. You had a snarl." Stella whacked her lightly on the head with the comb. "I'm not even charging you. It's a freebie on account of I'm in a good mood."

When Stella handed Lacey the mirror her hair was in an elegant twist with long bangs swept to the side. "Very nice, Stel, even though you bruised my scalp."

"Beauty knows no pain, Lacey, doncha know that?"

Lacey's hands were massaged gently by Stella's shy new manicurist, who said not a word. Just as well; Stella wanted to talk. She slipped off her Stylettos smock, and Lacey noticed Nigel Griffin's golden key was still dangling in the

V-neck of Stella's tight yellow angora sweater. Stella fingered it fondly. She wanted to talk about Nigel.

"Lacey, you really gotta give Nigel a chance here. My hope is you'll come to like him by the time we're walking down the aisle."

"Stella, he hasn't asked you to marry him yet, has he?" Lacey's heart sank.

"Not yet, but he's going to. A girl can tell these things."

Everyone seemed to be coupling up these days. *All these odd couples,* Lacey thought. Brooke and Damon were certifiably loony together. Wiedemeyer and Felicity too, and Felicity polished her ring every five minutes for the entire newsroom to see. Marie and Kepelov seemed all too improbably cozy, and now Stella was talking about tripping down the aisle with the very inappropriate Nigel? It could give a single woman a complex, especially with her Vic out of town. Not that Lacey was so eager to get married just yet, and she had a history of fleeing commitment.

"You really shouldn't get your hopes up, Stella," Lacey began to say. "He's such a—" *Man slut? No, better not say that.* "You know. Such a flirt."

"Don't worry about a thing, Lace." She twirled the key. "It's written in the stars, as they say. Marie told me. We had a consultation this morning."

"Marie told you? Unreliable source. She's discombobulated by love too."

"So she knows what it feels like. You just don't know, Lacey." Stella spread her left hand and slipped a silver ring off her right index finger onto her wedding ring finger. Her baby pink fingernails were perfectly manicured. She sighed. "I wonder what my wedding ring will look like? Nigel has such good taste in jewels and all. Maybe platinum, with an emerald cut diamond? Maybe he'll surprise me."

Lacey cocked an eyebrow, as her hands were busy being manicured. "A smart woman would probably want to help pick out the ring herself, or at least the setting."

"Yeah, but with Nigel being in the jewelry biz, or the jewel retrieving biz, I'm sure he'd pick out something fabulous. But I get you, Lacey. Something so important, a girl wants a little quality control." Stella played with the ring on her finger. "Something you're going to wear every day for the rest of your life? Ought to be pretty special."

"Anything particular in mind?"

"Oh, I dunno. Haven't really thought about it, you know, been so busy."

"Liar!" Lacey grinned at her. "You've probably looked at every ring in town."

Stella grinned back. "Well, maybe every other ring! Nothing so big that I couldn't hold my hand up, but not so small that people would feel sorry for me either, or have to like *squint* to see the stone. And it has to be a diamond! I'm traditional that way. I'm a new wave old-fashioned girl. Diamonds are a girl's best you-know-what."

The manicurist put another coat of color on Lacey's nails, then a top coat, and she was nearly done. She switched on the miniature fans to dry Lacey's nails and went on her lunch break. Stella took her chair and settled in on the other side of the table.

"You want something appropriately gaudy, is that it?" Lacey asked.

"Absolutely." Stella's eyes sparkled like diamonds. "Appropriately gaudy and, you know, tasteful too."

"Of course. Tastefully gaudy."

"And you know our wedding could be quite an event. An international soiree. Maybe even a double wedding."

"What? A double? With who?" *Not with me!* Stella couldn't be referring to her and Vic, could she?

"You never know, romance is in the air. Me and Nigel? Marie and Gregor?" Lacey exhaled in relief. "Ha! You didn't think I meant *you*, did ya? You and Vic, the late bloomers of love? You two were on the Stubby Special Ed Bus To Love for so long I was beginning to think you'd never get there. Lord only knows when *you'll* take the plunge. When it comes to men, Lacey, you got the coldest feet I know. I just hope you don't need a walker to get down the aisle. You'll trip on your train. How am I going to deal with that as your matron of honor?"

"Okay, I get it." *Stella, my matron of honor?* "But before

you did your blond Surfin' Sandra Dee thing, I never heard you talk about getting married." Lacey had never wanted to start planning her wedding far in advance of the proposal, as many women do. But she realized if she didn't plan it, Stella might plan it for her. *Eloping might be nice.*

"Before I met Nigel, I was completely not interested in wedded bliss. I was like totally playing the field. But *now*—"

Let's change the subject! Please! "Stella, I meant to ask you. I sent a woman named Willow Raynor to see you."

"Oh, yeah," Stella said. "I've been meaning to thank you for that. She spent a ton of money here. And she's a pretty decent tipper too."

"You made her really blond, Stella. I didn't expect that."

"Don't go thinking it was my idea, Lacey. I didn't really want to take her so blond, not all of a sudden anyway. It can be a shock to your system, Suddenly Blond Brain Death Syndrome or something. But she insisted, and it wasn't that hard. She had way virgin hair, even if it was really dull, like dead varmint color. It had never even been bleached or permed! Can you imagine? Was she living under a rock?"

"So you were thrilled to get your hands on all that virgin hair," Lacey said.

"So sue me. She wanted it. It's like one step beyond my own color, it's called 'pillowcase white.' It's like platinum blond, it's the very same color Marilyn Monroe used. Very few people can pull that off. It was a professional challenge. And I am nothing if not up for a challenge. Besides, she said she wanted to look totally different on account of she's hiding out from some old boyfriend of hers, she tell ya about him?"

Stella's attention was caught by her own reflection in one of the salon's mirrors. She leaned forward and wiped an imaginary speck of dirt from beneath her elaborately made-up eyes and their dramatic eyeliner wings. She cocked her head and fluffed her golden-blond tresses with her fingernails.

"She's on the run from that evil abusive Eric guy; she told me all about it. If a woman is in that kind of trouble, I am the first person who's going to help her out. And you wanted to help her out too, Lacey, or you wouldn't have sent her to me."

"I figured if anyone could work some color magic on the colorless Willow Raynor, it was you."

"A compliment! For once! From the famous Lacey Smithsonian! Lemme write this down so I can put it in my blog!" Stella beamed and gave Lacey a quick hug. Lacey would have hugged her back, but Stella grabbed her hands and stuck them back under the nail dryers. "Don't ruin those nails! You know how you are, you are always knocking them into something before they're dry and scratching the polish and making me redo it."

"My flaws have been duly noted," Lacey said. She made a face and kept her hands still. Stella sat down again, and the mirror behind her reflected the 'pillowcase-white' blonde herself, just leaving one of the private rooms devoted to more personal services like waxing and massage. "And there she is! What's Willow doing here?"

"Oh, didn't I tell you? She's here for her expert makeup lesson. She's been back there with Michelle, getting the works. Who needs it more, right?"

"That was quick. She looked pretty pale last night at PI class."

"Yeah, she said you recommended a shot of color." Stella waved at the woman. "Hey Willow! Look who's here?"

The transformed Willow looked striking. Lacey stared in surprise. Michelle's makeup session had enhanced and brought out her small, pale features. A bit of lavender shadow emphasized the color of her eyes. Lacey noticed for the first time that they were a violet blue. Her mascaraed lashes contrasted dramatically with the fluffy white-blond hair. She looked rather like a starlet, from the neck up. Below the neck, however, she was still the same woman drowning in an oversized sweater and shabby khakis.

"Hi Lacey! It's the new me, do you like it?" She seemed anxious for approval. "Now all I need is a new wardrobe too."

"I told her to start with something simple," Stella explained. "Classic. Like Audrey Hepburn."

"The famous little black dress?" Lacey ventured doubtfully. Willow's look was about as far from Audrey Hepburn as you could get.

"You're reading my mind." Stella twirled the golden key.

"That's such a pretty necklace, Stella."

Willow reached out as if to touch it, and Stella quickly covered the key with her hand.

"Don't touch! Something special my Nigel gave me."

"Sorry." Willow pulled her hand back reluctantly. "Nigel is your new boyfriend, right?"

"He's the one!" Stella gave Willow a big grin. "And it's okay, Willow, great taste is universal, right?"

"I was just thinking I need something special to really perk up my wardrobe," she said, gazing into the mirror. "Some new jewelry to go with the hair and makeup? I don't think he'll know me, do you? I hardly know me."

Lacey broke in. "Eric, you mean? Can you tell me more about this Eric O'Neil? Like what he does for a living?"

Willow shut her eyes. "Let's please forget about Eric, okay?"

"If he has nothing to do with Cecily Ashton and he's not menacing you anymore, yes, we can forget him. But—"

"He's a manager for some computer company." Willow hesitated. "I don't know exactly what he does. Software, hardware? Something. Okay?" She sighed resignedly. "I'm sorry. Talking about him makes me jumpy." Willow sat down in the chair and put her face in her hands. "No one believes me. See, Eric is really charming, he just has everyone in the palm of his hand. But it's like he's two different people, it's scary. He's a smooth liar. People believe everything he says." She looked up meekly.

He worked in computers in Philly. Maybe Lacey could find the guy herself. "And that gallery you were telling me about—Up and Downtown Arts—it has a second gallery, doesn't it? The one that displayed Cecily's collection?" Willow stared at the floor and fidgeted like a small child caught in a lie. "Look, I know you said you didn't know Cecily Ashton," Lacey said, "but I called the gallery and they said all the staff at both galleries helped out with the Ashton show. They said you were there."

"Yes." Willow's eyes filled with tears, but she fought them from falling and smearing her fresh makeup. "I did see the exhibit, it was so beautiful, all those exquisite things. I met her once, at the opening, and she was very nice. Eric was at the opening and we had a terrible fight. I never expected to see her here in D.C. But then she died! Right there at the PI school and I totally freaked out! I immediately thought of Nina and how she died and I thought of Eric. Now I can't get the picture of Cecily out of my mind."

"You poor thing." Stella sat in the chair next to Willow and gave her a hug. "You knew that Cecily woman that got killed in the parking lot? Wait a minute, you told me this Eric creep killed your friend Nina instead of you—you think he followed you here? And you think he killed Cecily too? Holy cow!" She looked out the window in alarm, as if Eric O'Neil might be out there.

Willow nodded furiously. "It's like he was leaving a message for me. He knows where I am. It's like he's just getting closer and closer."

Lacey stared at her, unmoved. "You might have told me that last night." Stella loved a sob story, every hair salon is full of them, but Lacey was suspicious. It wasn't that hard to tell the truth, was it? She hated the way people like Willow would leak a story bit by bit, telling petty lies about the embarrassing parts and making a reporter spend days dragging vital pieces of the puzzle out of them. When called on it, the source would invariably say, *I didn't think you wanted to know THAT! It's not like that's IMPORTANT, is it?* Lacey knew her face betrayed her irritation, she could see it herself in the salon mirrors.

"I'm so sorry, Lacey." Willow raised tearful eyes to Lacey. "I didn't mean to lie about Cecily. I didn't really know her. It was one of those work things. But I didn't want to talk about her because it all feels like I'm being followed."

"Give her a break, Lacey," Stella cut in, smacking her lightly on the arm. "You of all people should know how murder affects people. It makes you totally crazy. And Willow here is so sensitive."

Willow raised her head, her eyes swimming. "Please forgive me, Lacey. It's just that I'm so freaked out and I'm trying to be brave, but I'm not really good at it." A tear trickled down her cheek, leaving a black mascara trail.

She would have to learn about waterproof makeup, Lacey thought. Whatever the real truth was, Willow was pretty interested in pinning a murder or two on her former boyfriend. Did she really believe he killed both women, or did she hate him so much she was willing to implicate him? Was Willow really so unstrung by recent events that she was afraid to tell the truth, or did she just see a way to punish a jerk who'd hurt her?

"Hey, don't cry, Willow, you'll smudge your makeup! No crying in my salon," Stella ordered. She hated crying because she was so likely to join in. "It's bad for business. People will think you got a bad haircut or something."

"I wouldn't want people to think that." Willow swallowed a sob.

"And look at yourself, Willow." Stella gently turned her around to look in the mirror. "You're a completely different woman from the drab little gerbil who walked in here a couple of days ago."

"I'm not completely different yet," Willow said. "Not on the inside."

"On the outside," Stella reassured her. "The inside? You're gonna be fine." Stella smoothed her hair soothingly. Willow wiped her eyes and tried to smile.

The front door chime rang as someone entered the salon. Willow jumped nervously at the sound and dropped her purse. She bent down to retrieve it.

"Well, well, well, what have we here?" Lacey spun around at the sound of that particularly irritating British accent. "Could it be the Murder of the Month Club? Solved the mystery for us all yet, Smithsonian?"

If it wasn't Nigel Griffin, always the biggest smarty-pants in the room.

chapter 28

"You have the most irritating way of saying hello, Griffin."

"Did I forget to say hello? Hallo, Smithsonian! There, I said it," Nigel Griffin said. Stella scampered to the door and flung herself at Griffin's neck for a kiss. "Hallo, love. What news, Smithsonian?"

"Cecily Ashton is still dead," Lacey said acidly. "You heard it here first. Killer unknown, forecast cloudy, one-hundred percent chance of scattered confusion."

He looked down his nose at her. "Heaven only knows where you get your reputation as a sleuth, Smithsonian. Fashion clues indeed."

"Nigel, baby! Be nice to my friends."

Griffin kissed Stella and gently fingered the key she wore around her neck, touching her neckline lovingly. Lacey looked away before her eyes started rolling, but she noticed Willow staring at this picture with a kind of awe. Lacey hoped this new blonde was immune to Griffin's peculiar charms. *I can't be the only one.*

"Are we on for lunch, or are you terribly busy with all these *customers*?"

"Lacey was just here for a manicure. You should have seen those talons of hers. Disgraceful!"

"Brilliant, Stella, my sweet," Nigel interrupted, "but Smithsonian has work to do. You needn't aid and abet her in the dereliction of her duties."

Stella stroked his cheek and purred. "Nigel, you have to let Lacey do her own thing and sometimes that means a beauty boost. Like her nails might be soaking, but she's always thinking deep thoughts."

"Very well," Nigel said, indulging her, "but the clock is ticking." He glared at Lacey. "Despite what your crazy friend with the 'voices' says, Falls Church's finest are not very interested in him."

"They're still looking at you? They don't like your alibi?"

"They don't like it one bit. Driving to Richmond alone leaves something to be desired as an alibi. Like a witness. Let's say I'm on their top ten most popular suspects list, but this is not the kind of popularity I crave."

"Because of your affair with Cecily?" she prodded.

"I didn't sleep with the late Mrs. Ashton! Will you just get off that, Smithsonian? Besides, when I met Cecily I was seeing someone else at the time."

Lacey gave him a sharp look. "Do tell."

"It was before I met my lovely Stella here, which actually—and oddly—I have you to thank for. And those romantic autumn nights in old New Orleans—"

"And this other woman who wasn't Cecily?"

Griffin looked uncharacteristically somber. "It was short. It ended badly."

Why am I not surprised? she thought. *Does anything* not *end badly with this guy?*

Stella turned her wide and overly made-up eyes to Lacey. "Lacey, please! Nigel's reputation is at stake! As a man and a jewel retriever. Not to mention his freedom, and that would totally frost my sheets, if you know what I mean."

"Enough said." Lacey put up her hands in surrender. "I've got the picture and it's making me queasy."

"Sorry to break in," Willow said softly to Stella. "I have to get going."

"Oh Willow, I want you to meet Nigel, my boyfriend," Stella gushed, pulling the paler blonde over to meet him. "He's the one who gave me the key! To his heart, you know. Nigel, Willow Raynor. I have worked miracles here." She indicated Willow's hair.

"Charmed." Griffin shook Willow's hand and Lacey thought he held it a little too long. Nigel smiled the bad boy smile that melted so many too-susceptible hearts. "Have we met?"

"Um, no." Willow managed a small smile and smoothed a hand through her hair.

"You wouldn't know her, Nigel honey. Doesn't she look great now? She looked totally different two days ago. Mousiest hair you ever saw. No offense, Willow."

"None taken. I guess it was a little dull." Willow looked mortally embarrassed. She edged toward the door.

"Nice color." Nigel squeezed Stella's shoulder. "I would never have believed she wasn't a real blonde."

"She is now," Stella cracked. "Real blonde, just not a born blonde."

Willow picked up her khaki canvas bag. "I'm going shopping. All the places you recommended, too."

"Remember, no beige," Stella cautioned. "Lacey's Law. No beige and no boring."

"I remember." Willow waved. She seemed to be carrying herself a little more confidently since her makeover. *Never underestimate the power of a good makeover,* Lacey reminded herself.

Stella grabbed her purse too. "Me and Nigel are off to lunch. Want to join us, Lacey?"

Nigel flinched. Lacey couldn't help smiling. It would almost be worth it just to annoy Stella's boyfriend, she thought. *But not quite.* It would annoy her even more.

"No thanks, I'm off to think those deep thoughts I'm so famous for." She waltzed out the door, hearing it chime behind her.

Back in the newsroom, Lacey ran searches on the Web, called the Philadelphia police again, and finally put together enough information to find an Eric O'Neil. He worked for a computer repair company called Cyber Rescue Squad on Chestnut Street in Philadelphia, but she couldn't get past their voice-mail hell. Apparently her call was very important to them, but all available technicians were busy assisting other customers, and the first available Cyber Rescue Specialist would be with her shortly. Business seemed to be booming.

She finally drilled through the voice menus to Eric O'Neil's mailbox and left a message for him to call her back. She said she was writing a story about Nina Vickers. She assumed mentioning an unsolved murder for which he might have been a suspect would get his attention. It wasn't a complete lie, she thought. She didn't know what she was writing about yet, so a Nina Vickers story was a remote possibility. Lacey didn't mention Willow Raynor or Cecily Ashton.

Now what? Lacey hated this part of the journalist's job, racing to make a call based on some hot new lead and then waiting and waiting for a call back. In the meantime, something at the salon bothered her, something about the ornate little jeweled skeleton key Stella wore around her neck, the bauble that Willow had reached for and Nigel had fondled. It was an unusual key and it looked like real gold, not just an antique brass key someone had polished. The fluted edges, the precious stones stayed with her. The key reminded her of something. It tickled her brain. It drove her crazy.

She dug out from her files the picture of Cecily's vintage Rita Hayworth makeup case that had run with her feature article. The ornamental brass plate around the key hole had fluted edges and a pattern set in what looked like the same precious stones. The ornate head of Stella's key looked like a match.

Had Nigel given Stella the key to the Louis Vuitton makeup case? Or a key very much like it? Just how had he gotten his hands on such a thing? Lacey's eyes went very wide. *Did Nigel steal the case and give Stella the key?*

"That weasel!" She yelled out loud. Felicity looked over at her.

"Weasel? I don't have any recipes for weasel."

"Sorry, talking to myself. Working on a story. You know."

"Me too. I'm so confused." Felicity returned her gaze to her own screen. Lacy looked over and saw a Web page filled with elaborate wedding cakes.

Poor Stella. She thought she was going to get a wedding cake out of Nigel. And a ring. Surely Nigel knew where that key really came from, and Lacey suspected it wasn't from some little antique shop somewhere. What kind of game was he playing? There was only one thing for Lacey to do. *Talk to the weasel. Ewwww!* She took a deep breath and called Stella at the salon. They must be back from lunch by now.

"Hi Stella, listen, I need to talk to Nigel."

"Oh you missed him, he just left. He's driving to Richmond again. Is it important?"

Good question. Telling Stella anything about this was too dangerous. She would certainly jump to the wrong conclusion, and Lacey didn't even know what the right conclusion was. She wasn't about to tell Stella about the key, not without the full story. If Nigel was responsible for the burglary in some way, or even just fencing the stolen goods, Lacey might need backup herself.

"Not really. I just wanted to ask him, ah, if he's heard anything new. Or if anything from the burglary has, you know, turned up?"

"Far as I know, zip. You wanna call him on the road? Call his cell, Lace. He told me not to give out this number, but for you it's totally okay, 'cause you're gonna prove he's innocent, right? So did you check out my blog yet?"

Right. The blog. "Yeah, that's some blog. Stellariffic. Gotta go, Stel." Lacey called Griffin's secret number. She got his voice mail and left a message telling him to call her back. She knew he wouldn't.

Lacey Smithsonian's

FASHION BITES

Shopping Safari: Hunting for the Elusive Little Black Dress

All you really need is one great Little Black Dress.

You've heard that one before, haven't you? The perfect LBD will take you *anywhere*. That's another fine fashion fib, a style stumper, a clothing conundrum.

The LBD is a thing of myth, the stuff of urban legend. The perfect little black dress is one you can wear anywhere and everywhere, to dinner, to a cocktail party, for a visit with your grandparents, for a company reception, for a first date with a new guy, for a Big Date with your serious boyfriend, for a wedding. Even to a funeral, in a pinch, if you camouflage it with a black sweater and a pin and a pair of sensible pumps and a tear in your eye. Do you really own one of those perfect dresses? Utterly reliable, never fails, always appropriate? Me neither.

The Classic Little Black Dress worked for Audrey Hepburn, so why isn't it working for you and me? Because let me tell you, the real authentic little black dress that works for any occasion is rarer than a Baghdad snow.

The sad fact is that there is a huge difference between a perfect little black dress designed by Hubert de Givenchy, who designed the iconic dress Audrey Hepburn wore in *Breakfast at Tiffany's*, and that very imperfect little black dress hanging on the rack in the bargain basement, designed by absolutely *no one*. Which of those two dresses is the dress you and I are more likely to actually buy? Exactly. Hang that thing back on the rack right this minute!

What's the problem? It could be that you are not built like a broomstick. Or Audrey Hepburn. It might be that most little black dresses are simply dresses that are *black*. They are not necessarily dresses that are black and are well made and will flatter *you*. Every year the stores are full of garments advertised as *the* little black dress. And you've fallen for them, haven't you? You've fallen for their false promises of sophistication and glamour, not to mention their magical thinning properties.

Remember, the magic isn't in the *blackness* of the dress, it's in the *dress*.

Check out the dresses in your own closet, the dresses you have called, with more hope than truth, your "perfect little black dresses." Ask yourself, are they really perfect? That one, the one with the cap sleeves that cut across your arm in the wrong place and make you look like Popeye? Or the one with the wildly asymmetrical hemline that looks like it was sewn by a drunken seamstress aboard a storm-tossed tramp steamer? The third contender has that bizarre ruffle at the bottom, or the tie in the back suitable for a second grader, or the bad seams that make you look like an overstuffed sausage about to split its casing. Or, worst of all, the one with the enormous bow in the back, creating a striking *bustle* effect: For the woman with everything, that bow gives you a little more of it where you need it the least.

The reality is: It's a challenge to find that little black dress. And the question is: Are you up for the challenge? This isn't a sprint, it's a marathon. It separates the women from the girls. Keep in mind these tips.

- Avoid catalogs. The perfect LBD is not hiding in the pages of a catalog, where you can't get a good look at the material or the seams, or see that the model is wearing a sample size dress that's been clipped in the back with clothespins to make the thing look like it fits her and has some shape. Chances are you'll be sprinting to the post office to ship it back. When they ask if the package contains anything hazardous, what are you going to say? *Yes, this dress is hazardous to my figure and my self-esteem!*

- The first rule of hunting and gathering the right little black dress is *commitment*. Commitment to trying on as many black dresses as it takes until you find the one that fits, whether that means two dresses or twenty dresses. You're looking for the dress that has classic lines, a skirt that is flattering and does not "spring out" in the bottom, straps that stay up, and seams that do not pucker or split. You want a dress that flatters your shape, but is not too tight. You want it to make you look like you, only *better*.

- The second rule is: Pace yourself and reward yourself, or you'll burn out and settle for second best. Rewarding yourself is important after a tough day in the glare of unattractive fluorescent department store lights searching for the mythical perfect dress. Whether it's a cup of coffee, a cappuccino, a copy of your favorite author's latest book, or a slick magazine, you deserve a treat.

- The third rule: When you find it, *buy it!* If you happen to find the perfect little black dress for you, drop everything and go in for the kill, even if you're shopping for towels or a bathing suit. You think you've spotted it in the wild, now you know where to find it, and you'll return when you've lost those five pounds or have the cash or your hair is looking better? The legendary and elusive perfect LBD will be gone.

Finally, remember, Constant Shopper, you may have failed today, but you lived to hunt another day. The perfect Little Black Dress is out there, right around the corner, lurking on that next rack. Happy hunting!

chapter 29

"When your pretext becomes your identity twenty-four-seven, you've gone undercover," Bud Hunt was saying. "Some people go there for months. Years. Deep cover requires a different skill set and a whole separate mind-set. You've got to have a talent for that kind of work. You either got it or you don't."

Hunt had reappeared from his own undercover mission, whatever it was, and he was holding forth during the Tuesday evening lecture.

"When you are undercover, you no longer skulk in the shadows. When you have a plausible pretext for being whoever and wherever you are, it is imperative to act like you belong there. When you go undercover, you become so familiar to the subject of your investigations that he or she doesn't think twice about you. You're just the guy in the corner pouring drinks, the friend of a friend shooting the bull, the woman balancing the books."

Kepelov was nowhere to be seen. *Skulking in the shadows,* Lacey presumed. Hunt failed to mention his absence at the previous class, or Kepelov's commandeering the surveillance exercise. If Hunt learned anything from Ashton's staff, he wasn't sharing it. Lacey had called Cecily's housekeeper herself, but the woman wasn't talking, because, she said, the police had told her not to.

"Not even reporters?" Lacey had asked her. "Not even reporters who were also friends of Cecily?"

"Especially not reporters who were Mrs. Ashton's

friends," the woman replied. "No one. Not even that nice Mr. Edison." So Simon *was* trying to find out something too.

Hunt, on the other hand, might be on closer terms with the staff, having been on closer terms with the mistress of the house. If she were a real D.C. insider, Cecily's housekeeper would have danced around a bit to see what Lacey might offer her, and then talked "on background." But she was just a working woman worried about her job.

Maybe Vic could find out what Hunt knew. Lacey planned to talk with Vic later that evening. She added her question to her long mental list of things to say. It began with, "I'm crazy about you, when the hell are you coming home?"

"Okay, now you're undercover. How do you get close to your subject?" Hunt regained her attention. "You become part of your subject's world. If he bowls, you bowl. If she golfs, you golf. If he sails a boat, you rent the slip next to him. The boat slip thing, by the way, is a perfect way to keep track of somebody's comings and goings, not to mention the comings and goings of your subject's known associates."

Willow strolled in late in the middle of his comments and stopped the class dead. Her white-blond hair piled high on her head, she wore sky-high heels, full big-evening makeup, and a close-fitting cherry red dress. It didn't reveal much skin, but it revealed that there really was a trim female body under all those frumpy sweaters she had been hiding in. *Stella strikes again—and hits a home run.*

Edwina Plimpton stared at her. Snake the bounty hunter offered to buy her a drink after class. There was a low wolf whistle from somewhere in the back of the room. Willow ducked her head shyly and sat down next to Lacey.

"All right, people, quit gawking at the pretty lady," Hunt demanded. "Are we gonna get through this class tonight or what? Nice dress, by the way."

Under her breath, Lacey asked, "What does your new boyfriend think?"

"He flipped for it." Willow's face glowed.

"As I was saying," Hunt said, "you have to join their club. Whatever it takes."

"Joining the yacht club sounds expensive," Damon New-house said.

"Depends on the case. Maybe you're the guy who swabs the deck. Depends on how deep you need to get, how much your client's willing to pony up."

"What kind of cases are we talking about?" Damon asked. "Your client here isn't necessarily the guy next door, right?"

"Your client might very well be a city or state government agency with deep pockets, chasing around the world for an embezzler living high on the hog. You may be working with local cops, or maybe a local bounty hunter to conduct the takedown."

"Yo." Snake put two fists in the air. "That's where I come in."

"It takes a certain kind of person who can sustain an identity undercover," Hunt continued. "Tough to stay focused. Easy to get sucked into your own cover, especially if you're around drugs and money. For example. But if you're tough enough, quick enough, creative enough, you might be in line for some interesting work. Money can be good."

"Have you ever gone undercover?" Lacey already knew he had been under Cecily's covers.

Hunt nodded thoughtfully. "Not really my thing. It can wear you out. When you're undercover, it's a whole different ball game. You're not invisible, you gotta have your pretext down cold, make no mistakes, play the part twenty-four-seven. You might wind up your sleazeball subject's new best buddy. Home might be months away. That's tough on a marriage. Anybody here married? Want to get divorced? Working undercover's a good way to do that."

Lacey wondered whether Edwina or Snake or Willow was savvy enough to go undercover. Was she?

"Sounds like fun." Edwina sounded like she was making another wager with her bridge club girlfriends. "I'll take the yacht club assignment, I already know that club."

Edwina's tinkling laugh was interrupted by the sound of heavy footsteps pounding down the outside stairs and through the office doors. Hunt stepped out into the reception area, but a uniformed officer pushed right past him into the classroom. Another waited at the classroom door. The lead cop paused for a long moment. The classroom chatter stopped.

"Falls Church Police. We're looking for Martin Hadley."

All eyes were on Hadley. He looked tired. His face was drawn. He seemed resigned, and perhaps a bit relieved, now that the moment he'd predicted was at hand.

"I'm Martin Hadley."

"If you'll come with us, sir," the first cop said. "We just need to ask you a few questions."

Hadley stood and gathered his overcoat and class notes methodically, as if he were a senator humoring an impatient aide. Damon Newhouse jumped up beside him, ready to assist in his lonely struggle.

"Solidarity, dude."

"Not you, sir." The cop blocked Newhouse. "Mr. Hadley's the one we want."

Damon remained standing. He seemed at a loss. Hadley looked over at Lacey for a moment and smiled sadly, as if to say, *I told you so.*

Lacey left her seat and followed them to the reception area. The cops were waiting while Hadley put on his overcoat. Snake passed Hadley his card and said he knew a good bail bondsman.

"Hadley, don't sweat it, man, he'll have you sprung in no time."

The lead cop cleared his throat and held the door open.

"Edgar says I should never doubt him," Hadley said to Lacey. "The son of a bitch."

"You're not under arrest," Lacey reminded him.

"Not yet." He sighed deeply and walked through the door, one cop before him, one behind. The door slammed behind them.

Bud Hunt never quite regained order in the classroom. He seemed flustered by the intrusion, but perhaps also relieved that it was Hadley the cops wanted, not him. Snake started a betting pool on whether Hadley was, in fact, Cecily's killer, and how much his bail would be. Everyone suddenly had an opinion on the murder, it seemed. It was possible, some thought, that Hadley could have left the first session during the break, just long enough to, quote, "pop the lady in the Jaguar."

Edwina sniffed that Martin Hadley didn't look like a killer, even if he was "stark raving loony tunes." Damon Newhouse countered that they were all "tools of the power structure" and this obviously was a "dirty low-down setup." Hunt seemed content to let people talk it out. He looked pleased to be off the hook for the moment.

"Willow, are you all right?" Lacey asked.

"I'm confused! It was Mr. Hadley who killed Cecily Ashton? So it couldn't have been Eric?" Willow's colorful new face looked a little shell-shocked and Lacey hoped she wouldn't cry again. "Is that what the police think?"

"I don't know. Hadley seems to be a suspect, but just one of many. Bud Hunt is another. And Nigel Griffin, Stella's boyfriend that you met today. And her ex-husband, Philip Clark Ashton. Probably others too. Eric will just have to get in line. But you know, maybe we should try to find out more about your Eric anyway."

"Please, Lacey, I don't want to think about Eric anymore, I don't want to talk about him anymore. It scares me. I told you how people just fall under his spell." Willow took a deep breath and lifted her head. "It's wonderful that you've helped me out, you'll never know how grateful I am. But now I look so different and the police have arrested someone else, so maybe Eric doesn't matter anymore."

Lacey wondered what Willow's real story was. Was she more afraid of the police talking to Eric, or of not talking to him?

"I need a drink," Edwina announced loudly, "and I don't mean coffee."

The class session was in a shambles, and anyway it was time for a break. Hunt proposed adjourning to Ireland's Four Provinces, the Irish pub on Broad Street a few blocks away, and this proposal was met with popular approval. Most of the PI students straggled down the street to the pub, except for Willow, who told Lacey she was going home. She was exhausted from all that shopping. Besides, she said, her new guy was staying over that night, to protect her. Lacey gave her a wink and wished her luck.

The Four Provinces was warm and inviting, the staff was friendly, and the Guinness was perfect. There was no band playing live that night, but lilting Irish music filled the air. Lacey ordered a Virgin Mary. She had no desire to get drunk with her fellow PI students, but she wanted to listen in on the scuttlebutt. It was better than second-guessing what they might have said and missing all the action.

Snake and Edwina, who had unexpectedly bonded during the abortive surveillance exercise, placed bets on whether Hadley would actually be arrested, and if he would lawyer up. Edwina thought Hadley was in big trouble. Snake Goldstein disagreed.

"Come on, Winnie, he's a K Street big shot of some kind. Those guys never do serious time," Snake said. "Sometimes they jump bail, but they're pretty easy to catch. They make me laugh."

"I thought you liked Martin," Edwina said.

"I do," he answered. "He's all right, for a nutball. I'm just sayin', you know?"

Damon pointed out to Lacey two big men in black suits sitting at the bar, quietly nursing clear drinks. "It's an Irish bar! And they're drinking club sodas! They couldn't stick out more if they tried. It's a lousy covert surveillance."

Lacey peered at them. "Please. Lawyers heading for night court."

"Ha. Men in Black." Damon kept an eye on them. "Listening to what we say about Hadley." He reached into his backpack and pulled out a mini radio frequency scanner. Lacey recognized it. Brooke had used it, or one just like it, to check their hotel room in Paris for concealed listening devices. Damon scanned the table and stared at the little screen, frowning. *No bugs.* He pocketed the scanner and shrugged.

Edwina was drinking too much too fast, and soon her husband had to come and collect her from the bar. "She's not usually like this," Mr. Plimpton apologized, as he struggled to bundle her up into her sensible black wool coat. "Really, she never has more than one at the country club." He put some bills on the table to cover her drinks.

"Thass right!" Edwina had lost her headband and her blond hair flopped in her face. She kept swatting it away with one hand. "I never drink more than one on a school night 'cept once in a great while like when people die and people get arrested and people get hauled out of class by the cops 'cause you know it makes it kind of hard to concentrate on your *schoolwork*."

"I don't know what's gotten into her since she started taking this class," her embarrassed spouse said.

"I know what's gotten into her," Snake chuckled. "Three double martinis! Ain't that right, Winnie?"

Edwina suddenly giggled. "I wanna change my bet. I bet it was *you*, Snakey Wakey!"

"Come on, Edwina," her husband said. "Let's get you home to bed."

"We're going to bed! Oh goody, take me to bed baby." She threw her arms around her husband's neck. "Hey big fella. Let's go look at the stars, honey, you think the stars are out? Maybe we'll see the Big Dicker!"

The rest of the would-be PIs burst out laughing, even Lacey and Damon. Even the waitstaff, who had probably seen many patrons much drunker. Edwina Plimpton sagged into Mr. Plimpton's arms as he dragged her through the door.

"What do you know," Snake said. "Never thought that dame would loosen up. I like her better this way. She's kind of cute. She grows on you."

Eventually, the conversation returned to the hapless Hadley. By the end of the evening, by a jury of his slightly inebriated peers, Martin Hadley had been arrested, tried, and convicted. He had jumped bail to Bali, been bagged by Snakey Wakey the bounty hunter, and been beamed up to the mother ship, which flew him back to the government mind-control laboratories on his home planet.

They all agreed: *Life is just one great big conspiracy.*

chapter 30

Martin Hadley, as it turned out, was not arrested. Brooke called Lacey's cell phone the next morning while Lacey was entertaining herself at the newsroom with Damon's latest DeadFed story.

"Apparently, the Falls Church detectives just wanted to grill Hadley about Damon's story about him on Conspiracy Clearinghouse." Brooke said. "It seems they don't have enough for an arrest. They were unamused that Damon had exposed their murder investigation game plan. They had no idea Damon was sitting right there in your class, or I think they'd have grabbed him too. They said something about Damon and Hadley muddying their investigation. As if it could be any muddier. Damon will not be cowed. He has every right to publish Hadley's story."

Lacey read DeadFed dot com's lead story for Wednesday on her computer screen. COPS ROUST AND BULLY MIND CONTROL VIC; FIRST AMENDMENT, FREE SPEECH AT STAKE. It was turning into Damon's own soap opera. *As the Conspiracy Turns.*

"So Hadley's voices are just wrong? The Edgar voice told him he'd be arrested and framed for the murder. Or is Hadley just delusional?"

"Or the voices are playing with him for their own twisted reasons," Brooke said.

"Maybe Hadley really did kill her," Lacey said, trying the idea on for size again. "Just walked right up to her Jaguar and pulled the trigger. He's odd and intense and he hated

Cecily. But he's smart, making everyone think he's simply crazy. People who hear voices are crazy, right? So it's an insanity defense: 'The voices made me do it.' He gets off, goes to a mental ward, makes a miraculous recovery, gets out."

Brooke laughed. "And you think Damon's version is crazy."

Lacey turned away from the screen. She'd worn brown wool slacks and a matching sweater that morning, so she felt at ease to prop her feet casually on the window ledge and watch sunshine pour over the neighboring office buildings. She played with the ends of her multicolored scarf as they talked.

The smell of warm baked goods permeated the space as Felicity waltzed through with today's offering, some sort of almond cake with a lemon filling and glaze and topped with whipped cream frosting. It was hard to pay attention with that aroma filling the air. Lacey gave in and took a sample. *A little piece of paradise.*

"We have more important things to do right now, Brooke."

"More important than Hadley? More important than freedom of the press?"

"It's Stella. She's still under Griffin's spell. Like the song says, she's got it bad, and that ain't good."

"A Pink Code Talker in need of an intervention? You're right. Perhaps we should sponsor another girls' night out with guns. Ladies Night at the range."

"I was thinking more along the lines of deprogramming her," Lacey said. "We take her away for a weekend, some lazy beach town, find her some real bad boys, the kind she likes. Tattoos, piercings, motorcycles. Black leather, blue hair, maybe a Mohawk." She thought of Snake Goldstein; now *he* was Stella bait. "I never thought I'd miss her old weird boyfriends. Whatever happened to that Bobby Blue-Eyes she was so hot for?"

"You got me, I don't keep track."

Lacey's desk phone rang, interrupting their plans to free Stella from the tentacles of the toxic Nigel. She signed off with Brooke. The call was from Philip Clark Ashton.

After their last meeting, she dreaded whatever he might

have to say to her. She was surprised he hadn't had a lawyer make this call. His raspy voice was so harsh Lacey had to hold the receiver away from her ear.

"Mr. Ashton. So nice to hear from you again."

"Well, be that as it may, Ms. Smithsonian, you've probably just saved me a lot of grief. This is my personal thank-you call."

"Really. How thoughtful of me. How did I do that?" She kicked her feet off the windowsill and sat up straight.

"Didn't think you'd be doing me any favors, did you?" He sounded smug even over the phone. "You might have gotten me off the suspect list. Did you realize that?" He had the nerve to chuckle. Lacey said nothing. Ashton continued. "Because it's always the husband, isn't it, Ms. Smithsonian? Always the husband who pays and pays. Always the villain." He chuckled again. "Oh yes, the police have been pressing me, politely of course, but enough to be monotonous. Why, I believe even *you* probably think I did it. But that would be ridiculous. There are so many other civilized ways to deal with one's problems. That's what lawyers are for."

That's how he viewed his ex-wife. Cecily was just one of Ashton's problems, Lacey thought, and buying people off or intimidating them is certainly more civilized than killing them. And in the end, he could certainly make their life a living hell.

"No doubt. What exactly are we talking about?"

"I reread that story you wrote about Cecily. One little thing nagged at me."

"And that was?" *Not a complaint about a fact error, not now,* she prayed. *Please.*

"The photograph of Rita Hayworth. I bought that picture from a rare photograph dealer when Cecily and I were first married, a little something to go with the Rita Hayworth makeup case and those lovely pearls. I bought the picture frame in Spain. I wanted it all to be perfect, for my perfect jewel, my new wife. That's what I thought back then. Anyway, I checked the paperwork." He paused and Lacey heard papers rustling.

"The paperwork?" This was clearly a man who liked

making people wait for him. Lacey drummed her fingers on her desk.

"The guarantee of authenticity from the dealer. There's a detailed description of it. For insurance purposes. According to my papers, there was no little doodle, as you called it, on the back of the Rita picture. It would have been noted. If there were such a thing it might have been drawn by Rita Hayworth herself, which would have made it even more valuable. Another thing, the photograph had never been out of the frame after I bought it. Until the burglary."

"The doodle is new, then," Lacey answered like a good student.

"Yes," he chortled. "The doodle is new. I do believe our thief signed his work."

Lacey thought the thief might have left fingerprints, but she never thought he might also have left the drawing.

"Wait, you think you see a connection between the burglary and her murder?"

"Give the lady a cigar," Ashton said.

"What connection could there be?" Lacey asked.

"A message, perhaps? Don't you see, the drawing was a warning for Cecily. 'A bird in a cage,' you wrote that yourself. Did you know her middle name was Robin? And why leave the photograph? The thief could just as easily have taken it with the frame. Someone wanted to put our rare bird in a cage," Ashton said. "That might be why she was acting so bizarrely, worse than usual. And believe me, I would know." He coughed suddenly. To hide a sob? Lacey wondered. "She knew what this drawing meant, but she didn't tell anyone. If she had asked for my help, I would have protected her."

Brave words after the fact. Lacey wasn't quite convinced by the billionaire's logic, but he had a point. Of course he might also have arranged the burglary and left the cryptic message on the photograph himself. But then it struck her. Could the "cage" in the drawing be what Simon Edison had talked about, a "Faraday cage"? Did Simon plan to put Cecily in a cage somehow? What did that mean? And why did she have a copy with her when she died, as Trujillo mentioned? To confront Simon at the Falls Church Farmers' Market? Or to show it to Bud Hunt and plead for his help?

"Do you have any suspects in mind?"

"My dear Miss Smithsonian, we should let the police accomplish something on their own, don't you think? They should start with her lovers, she had so many. That'll keep them busy."

"Are you including Nigel Griffin?"

"No comment."

"Do you believe he had anything to do with the burglary?" Lacey prompted.

Ashton paused for a moment. "No comment. If you're working through a list of her male admirers, this could take all day."

"What about Simon Edison?"

Ashton snorted. "Please, that dreamer? He adored Cecily. Besides, they weren't lovers. I always knew who they all were, she could never keep a secret."

Until she was dead. He sounded pleased with himself. Philip Clark Ashton wins another game on the chessboard of life and gets to rub a humble reporter's nose in it.

"Mr. Ashton, you make such a good argument about the Rita photograph. Would you mind faxing me a copy of it? And the back side, with the drawing? I know I already described it in my story, but would you mind? And the dealer's paperwork too?"

"You really are a reporter," he laughed. His laugh was even raspier than his speaking voice. "I'll deny that I provided them to you."

"I'll deny that I got them from you. I'll just say the photograph and documents 'were obtained' by *The Eye Street Observer.* What do you say?"

Ashton laughed again. He was enjoying himself this morning. "Sure. I'll have my secretary fax all of it to you."

"Thank you. It'll make a good story. And Mr. Ashton, I was also wondering about Cecily's funeral arrangements." Lacey wanted to pay her respects.

"There will be no funeral. I'm having her cremated. As soon as they release the body."

"You'll be having a memorial service then?"

"There's no reason. It would turn into a media circus. Cecily didn't believe in anything in particular. She had no family to speak of. Let people remember her as they please."

"Very well then. I'll wait for the fax. And I'll give your regards to Claudia."

Ashton paused and Lacey thought she heard a sigh on his end of the line.

"And to answer your earlier question, Ms. Smithsonian. Yes. I did love Cecily." He hung up the phone. And yet he would have no funeral for her.

Lacey sat back at her desk and shook her head to clear it. It didn't work, it just made her head hurt. She didn't know what to make of Philip Clark Ashton now. While she waited for his faxes to come through, she made another call to Cyber Rescue Squad. She'd had no response from O'Neil. This time, however, she reached a live human on the phone, the receptionist.

"Eric isn't here this week," the woman said. "He wouldn't even be checking his voice mail. He's gone hunting."

Hunting?! Marie's cryptic words about "hunting season not being over" echoed in her ears. Willow had called him a "hunter" too. She'd half chalked up Eric O'Neil's very existence to Willow's overactive imagination. Lacey hoped he wasn't hunting for anyone she knew.

The receptionist was still chatting away. Eric was a "real outdoorsy kind of guy," the "nicest boy, and everyone loved him, just loved him." *Just as Willow said.* He'd called in to say he was having a very good hunting trip. The receptionist said he was due to call in again, and she'd relay the message.

Lacey spent the next half hour checking the newsroom fax machine every five minutes until all of Ashton's images were transmitted. She studied the photo of Rita Hayworth and the odd little drawing on the back. Her offhand description of it was "a bird in a cage," but now it suggested something else to her. She consulted a dictionary and the Internet. Lacey started her story with this headline:

ASHTON MURDER LINKED TO "BIRD IN CAGE"

The unsolved murder of Cecily Robin Ashton may be
linked by a mysterious drawing of a so-called "bird in a
cage" to an earlier burglary at her home, *The Eye Street
Observer* has learned . . . .

She wrote the story about Philip Clark Ashton's new information on the Rita Hayworth photograph as straight as
she possibly could. It didn't need any spin. She left out her
Internet research and Trujillo's tantalizing tidbit about Cecily having a copy of the drawing with her when she died. It
wasn't confirmed, and she had no idea what it meant. The
paper might have been in her purse for days.

Lacey stared at the lines on her computer screen, lost in
thought. Finally she sensed the presence of another person
behind her. She turned around and felt her face light up before her eyes had even met his. Then she saw his green eyes,
grass green and welcoming, and his wicked grin.

"Vic Donovan! Oh my God. Thank heaven you're here."
She was instantly on her feet and in his arms for a kiss. She
broke away just long enough to look around for newsroom
gossips. Then she kissed him again, seriously this time.

"Can't live without me, can you?" he said when they
came up for air.

She hugged him hard, then held him at arm's length to
feast her eyes on him. "I didn't expect to see you till this
weekend."

Vic's jeans were faded and fit him well and his black
sweater hugged his muscles. He was wearing the brown
leather jacket she'd given him for Christmas. It wasn't exactly a fair trade; after all, he'd given her a car, her wonderful little restored BMW. But it was the nicest thing she could
afford and he wore it well.

"I was hoping you'd turn around and notice me," he said
in a slight drawl. "And I was hoping I wouldn't have to wait
all day." Lacey didn't ask how he'd slipped past the security
desk downstairs. He always managed to do that.

"You could distract a woman from her work."

"I was counting on that," Vic said. "I'm here to take you to lunch, lady. Can you tear yourself away from all this?"

It was noon and she hadn't even noticed. She quickly reread her story, with Vic reading over her shoulder, then sent it to her editor. Mac could make of it what he would.

"Hey, I didn't get to the end, and what the heck is going on now?" He spun her around, his eyes dark with concern. "How involved are you?"

"You're so cute." She grinned back at him. She slipped Ashton's faxes into her purse and grabbed her coat. "Let's go, cowboy. You buyin'?"

"You better be hungry. I came a long way."

"Oh, yeah, I'm hungry." *I'm a starving woman and you are my candy bar.*

Vic examined the small image on the faxed copy from Philip Ashton. He held it up to the light at their table in the dim restaurant. "The creature in the cage? A bird?"

"I don't know what to think. Her middle name was Robin, but I don't think that looks like a robin, do you? Look closer. See? It sort of has the head of an eagle and the body of a lion. See the tail?"

Vic leaned back and sipped his iced tea. He took his time examining the drawing. "You think it's a *griffin* in a cage?" He raised his eyebrow. His black sweater showed off his strong shoulders. *Yum.* Lacey was in danger of losing her train of thought. "A griffin as in *Nigel* Griffin?" he prompted.

She shrugged. "He's the only griffin I know."

Vic drummed his fingers on the table. "Nigel didn't draw it. First off, he can't draw. He can barely write. I went to prep school with him, I should know. Second, he may be an idiot, but he's not dumb enough to sit down and sketch something during a burglary and leave it behind. And third, it strikes me as more likely someone wants to *implicate* our bad boy Griffin in that burglary. Assuming what Ashton said is true. Though it's an odd way to try to do it."

"But it probably wasn't Cecily who drew it, was it? She told me she didn't," Lacey said. "And if she drew it, why would she have a copy in her purse to show someone? Then there's the little matter of Stella's key."

"Stella's key? That is another chapter I seem to have missed while I was on the opposite coast."

Lacey filled him in on the key that appeared to match the Louis Vuitton makeup case, the little skeleton key that now hung on a chain around Stella's neck.

"This is all highly entertaining, Lacey, but not as entertaining as running away with you this afternoon and taking the phone off the hook."

"People will talk." She slid over closer to him in the booth.

"Not to us. We won't answer the phone. We'll give 'em something to talk about though."

"But first we have to go to the horse's mouth," Lacey said. "Or should I say the griffin's mouth?"

"Yup." Vic squeezed her hand. "And we're going to pull his teeth."

After lunch, they parted at the restaurant with a kiss and a plan and a promise to meet later. Lacey took a detour to St. Matthew's Cathedral on Rhode Island Avenue, a place she often visited for quiet and meditation. Today, surrounded by the marble and mosaics of the church, she lit candles for Cecily Ashton, because it was only right to say a prayer for the dead.

Someone had to do it, and the man Cecily loved would not.

chapter 31

Lacey tried Nigel Griffin's cell phone repeatedly and finally made contact. Of course he hadn't returned her calls on the road, he said, he was on business. However, now that he had returned from Richmond, he agreed to meet her at an up-scale martini bar and restaurant on Sixteenth Street. Just the sort of place a snob like Griffin would appreciate, with its mix of cool neon and sleek industrial metal and exposed pipes in the ceiling. Lacey found the décor far too cold, she would take rococo any day of the week.

She arrived first and was seated in the restaurant loft area above the bar. She helped herself to the fresh bread and olive spread and ordered a lemonade. From her perch overlooking the front door, Lacey saw Nigel stroll in casually from the slushy sidewalk, looking like the eternal prep school boy. He flirted with the hostess for a moment, then took the stairs with a jaunty bounce.

"What news, Smithsonian? Or should I say, *felicitations*, darling Lacey! You look simply smashing! How are the folks, how are the little ones, hugs and kisses to all, peace on earth and to all a good night! How's that?"

"You're a laugh a minute, Nigel."

He took the seat opposite her. "Stella says I should be nicer to you, so I am. Now the niceties are out of the way, what news?" She gave him The Look, the one she had perfected for people like him. "As charming as I am, I'm sure you're not interested in my company."

"Oh but I am! Don't worry, there is a reason you're here."

Lacey's attention was diverted by the welcome vision of Vic bounding up the stairs. He slid in next to Lacey and kissed her before eyeing Griffin.

"Donovan," Griffin said.

"Griffin," Vic said.

"Aha, an ambush." Griffin did not look amused. "Shall I simply start bleeding now? It would save us both a lot of huffing and puffing."

"No huffing and puffing. More of a tête-à-tête," Lacey said.

"Right. First the ground rules. No hitting." Nigel looked worried. He had met the blunt end of Vic's fists before.

"No hitting before *cocktails.* This is a classy establishment." Vic smiled like someone who made his own ground rules. "Don't worry, when it comes to huffing and puffing, we'll take it outside."

"We have questions," Lacey said.

"For the last time, I did not sleep with Cecily Ashton."

"You're anticipating," she said. "We don't care about that now."

"There are several matters to discuss," Vic said. "Ladies first."

"The key you gave Stella," Lacey said. "Tell me about it."

The waitress arrived and took their orders. Vic ordered a Sam Adams brew and Nigel asked for a glass of Merlot. He told the waitress it would nicely match the color of his blood, after it was shed by his friends. She was charmed. Griffin hadn't answered Lacey's question.

"Nigel. The key matches the Louis Vuitton makeup case. The one stolen from Cecily." Lacey waited for him to deny it. He didn't.

"It would seem so, but we'll never really know, will we, now that the bloody box is missing."

"Where did you steal the key?" Vic asked. "With the makeup case? When you stole it in the burglary?"

"Get off it, Donovan. I'm hardly a cat burglar. Cecily was very likely her own burglar. She hid the case and the jewels and reported them stolen. Case closed."

"But you stole the key."

"I stole nothing. I *obtained* the key from the dealer in New York City who sold cranky old Ashton the damned Rita Hayworth case in the first place. I was sniffing up leads after the burglary. As one does. I touched base with the dear fellow to see if he'd heard loose talk in the trade. You'd be surprised how often jewel thieves try to fence the loot back to the dealer who last sold it legitimately. Sometimes it even works."

"He had the key?" Lacey scoffed. "Convenient."

"Said it had been misplaced in his shop. He'd sold the case to Ashton without the key. It latches, but does not lock. The dealer meant to call when the key turned up much later, but he told me Philip Clark Ashton wasn't the kind of customer you wanted to deal with more often than absolutely necessary. Also he didn't want to confess to being careless with his priceless merchandise. So he'd kept the pretty little key. He only showed it to me as a curiosity, one professional to another in the trade. All that remained of the legendary Louis Vuitton–Rita Hayworth case. So sad."

"So what did you pay for it?" Vic asked. "And did you keep the receipt? You might need it."

"If you must know, I sort of persuaded him to just give it to me."

Vic laughed. "You pocketed the key? You weasel!"

"You say *weasel* like it's a bad thing. No, I simply pointed out that it might look, ah, *suspicious* for him to have even so much as an innocently misplaced key connected to such a notoriously stolen one-of-a-kind item. People might think he had more than just a key, I said, if that got out, and it would. He saw my point. So he entrusted it to me, because I represent Cecily Ashton's insurer. I promised to take good care of it."

"Sure you would," Vic snorted. "In the Nigel Griffin Retirement Fund."

"After all our good times in prep school, Donovan, you wound me. And I mean that literally. No, I was going to present it to Cecily, as a humble token of my recovery efforts on her behalf. It is of such simple gestures that a gentleman's reputation is born."

Their drinks came and the waitress took their order for appetizers.

"The upshot, Nigel, before we're old and gray." Vic lifted his beer.

"Ah yes." Nigel took up his wineglass, swirled the liquid, sniffed, and deigned to sip it. He pronounced the Merlot drinkable. "Well, I hesitated. Cecily was acting very strange. I was afraid she would see it as a romantic offering, a come-on. She was making enough of those to me herself, and I wanted no part of it. It felt like I was being set up. She was a little too crazy, even for my tastes. And then Stella happened, et cetera. Give the cute little key to one crazy out-of-control millionairess who couldn't care less? Or to adorable Stella, who would jump up and down and get excited and demonstrate her heartfelt gratitude? The woman with the key to my heart? A clear choice."

Lacey didn't care who legally owned the silly key. She knew one thing. Stella would be heartbroken if she had to give it up, and Lacey wasn't going to play the villain in this piece. "What else can you tell me about the burglary?"

"Nothing. What has this got to do with Cecily Ashton's murder?"

"Humor us, Nigel." Lacey gestured with her glass. "One thing leads to another. What if the burglary and the murder are connected?"

Griffin leaned back and crossed his arms. "I'm convinced Cecily had something to do with the burglary. It was an inside job. Too neat, too clean, too selective."

"Maybe," Vic said. He leaned in closer. "But she's not the only one who had access. Tell me, Nigel, who else wants to set you up? And who would be able to do it?"

"I don't know what you mean. Set me up *how* exactly?"

"Do you know a Simon Edison?" Lacey asked.

"Who?" Nigel squinted. "In connection with Cecily? Can't say I do."

Their waitress came back with a hot cheese dip and pita chips. "Fresh and hot! Hope you like it. Let me know if you need anything." She smiled for an extra second or two at Griffin before she left.

Lacey and Vic shared a look. Lacey pulled the faxes out of her purse. She spread out the fax of the little drawing on the back of the photograph.

"Now what?" Nigel leaned over and peered at the picture.

"What does it look like to you, Nigel?

"I have no idea. A bird?" The lightbulb turned on. "Is this the famous doodle you described in your closet article?"

"A bird? Or could it be a griffin?" Vic kept his voice low. "A griffin in a cage?"

"Oh that's ridiculous." Nigel picked it up and examined it more closely. "Huh. It is sort of a griffin. Takes one to know one, eh? Not terribly accomplished though, is it? What are you getting at here?"

"Philip Ashton swears this drawing was not on the photo when he bought it," Lacey said. "He swears the photo was never out of the frame until the break-in."

"So our burglar is an artist? A bad artist? Well, it's Cecily, of course. She did the burglary, so she had plenty of time to doodle."

"But what if it wasn't Cecily?" Vic fingered the drawing. "She was surprised to see it when Lacey showed it to her, and she was taking it to show someone when she was killed. This wasn't your typical burglar either. Seems to me someone might have planted this to implicate you in the crime, Nigel. In a subtle way. As if someone, maybe a disgruntled accomplice, was saying, 'Put the griffin in the cage.'"

Griffin threw up his hands. "Oh good God. That's absolutely the most demented thing I've ever heard." He scooped cheese dip onto a pita chip and shoved it in his mouth. He followed it with a swig of Merlot. "If this is some kind of stunt—"

"It's not a stunt. Philip Ashton called me today," Lacey said. "He thinks it's enough to get him off the most popular suspects list. It might be enough to put you on it."

"This whole thing is preposterous! I had no accomplice, because I didn't burglarize the bloody house." Griffin scooped up more dip and spilled it. "For pity's sake, I wouldn't have stopped at the Vuitton case and a few trinkets.

I'll tell you one thing, if I ever *were* going to do such a burglary, I would never—"

"Go on," Vic said, "I love talking shop with jewel thieves."

"An adolescent mistake, Donovan. The record has been
expunged."

"Except from the golden memories of we lucky few who
knew you way back when."

"Oh whatever. I would never share a haul like that with
any accomplice, past or present. You may call me a weasel,
Donovan, but I am not a stupid weasel."

"Hi, guys!" Stella's voice preceded her blond bob up the
stairway. "Having fun? You ought to be! You started without
me." Vic and Lacey exchanged another look. *Of course*
Nigel had asked Stella to join them.

"What's up? What's new? Lacey? Vic? Nigel?" Stella
pulled up a chair next to Griffin. "Vic! You're back!" She
jumped up and hugged Vic. "Thank goodness! Lacey has
been draggin' her ass like a little lost puppy without you. So
fill me in! Nigel honey?"

"Don't know where to begin, love." He looked morose.
"We're just chatting about mythological beasts. Griffins.
Weasels. That sort of thing. Why don't you order up a
drink?"

"I wish I could order up the one we're inventing," Stella
said. She waved to the waitress and asked for a Pink Lady,
"because it sounds pretty." She turned to Lacey as she shed
her pink coat, revealing today's outfit. It was tight, it was
pink, it was Stella. "Nigel and me, we're creating this winter drink for D.C. A mixed drink with a name that says it all
about Washington in the winter. Then we'll invent one for
the summer too. Guess what we're calling it!"

Lacey groaned. Stella always had some new party game
to play. "How about a Frozen Filibuster? Or a White House
on the Rocks?"

"Not bad, Lace, not bad. But we got you beat. It's the
Washington Wintry Mix."

"In honor of the beastly winter weather you have here,"
Nigel roused himself to say gloomily. "What your weather-
men always call it so cheerily on the telly: 'We're expecting

the usual wintry mix!' So if you have to slog through it, Stel and I think you should at least be able to get drunk on it."

"We haven't perfected it yet," Stella went on excitedly, "but a Wintry Mix has to be really frozen and *slushy* for all the slushy streets here, with lots of vodka because vodka's from cold countries, right? And it'll have that blue liquor in it to give it that blue winter light. Like right now! Wow, look outside the window! So pretty. And we're thinking coconut sprinkles on top to make the ice and snow, and maybe an ice-blue maraschino cherry frozen in an ice cube, and then we serve it in—" She stopped and looked from face to somber face. "Whoa. Did I miss something? What's up, guys? Okay, never mind, I'll just listen." She helped herself to Griffin's appetizer.

"Nigel," Lacey said, "when you were in Philadelphia, working on that little exhibit Cecily had there, did you meet a Nina Vickers?" Lacey didn't know quite why she asked that. *One thing leads to another.*

Vic gave her a look, his Why-Am-I-Always-One-Chapter-Behind look. She realized she hadn't gotten around to telling him about the unsolved Philadelphia murder that couldn't possibly be connected to Cecily's unsolved murder, unless Willow was right about her ex-boyfriend. Griffin's wine-glass stopped in midair.

"Who's Nina Vickers?" Stella's eyes were large and questioning. "Did you know her, Nigel?"

"Before I met you, Stel." He nodded slowly. "A girl I met in Philadelphia last year. She worked at the gallery that displayed the Ashton exhibit."

"And how well did you know her?"

"We, um, dated. A couple of times. Not very long." Nigel seemed to run out of words. Stella turned to Lacey for an explanation.

"She was murdered, Stella, in a drive-by shooting of some kind."

"Oh my God." Stella made the leap. "Willow's friend?"

"This is all insane!" Griffin said. "I don't know what kind of story you're spinning, but I barely knew her. Nina was a nice girl. It was a casual date or two, maybe a couple of parties, it wasn't any kind of big romantic *thing*. I was out of the country, in Paris in fact, playing ring-around-the-rosy with *you*, Smithsonian, when she was—when her unfortunate death occurred. I didn't even hear about it till much later. None of this makes any sense."

"I am totally confused," Stella said. "What does this woman have to do with anything?"

Lacey didn't know that either. But having sown fear and confusion, her work there was done. It was time to go to her PI class. She reluctantly gathered her purse and coat and kissed Vic a lingering good-bye. She hugged a worried Stella and gave Nigel the Look. On her way downstairs she heard the fear and confusion resume.

"Bloody hell, Donovan! Two murders and a burglary, and I had nothing to do with any of them! Swear to God! Why in the world would someone try to implicate me?"

"I don't know, Nigel," Vic said as he tilted his beer, "but I'd say the 'wintry mix' is about to come down on you hard."

chapter 32

"What's on the agenda tonight?" Once again, Lacey was the first student through the door, right behind their instructor, Bud Hunt. She was starting to get used to the dark, windy parking lot, though the rustling of the dead leaves could still make her jump.

"You mean on the lesson plan?" Hunt sighed heavily. "Or whatever the hell wacky sideshow is gonna happen tonight to put us even further behind in this course?"

"The lesson plan. I could use a break from the wacky sideshow myself."

"You're way early, Smithsonian. There's doughnuts. I'm making coffee. You want some?"

She stood in the doorway of the kitchen and watched Hunt meticulously measure coffee into the coffeemaker.

"Hadley wasn't arrested after all," she said.

"So I heard. I'm just surprised they didn't slap him with a charge of impeding the investigation. I don't know what the PI field is coming to. I mean, my God, the man hears voices. I used to get regular guys in this class. Now I get wackos who pick up transmissions from the Great Unknown or something." Hunt looked beat. The circles under his eyes had deepened. "I hear there's some new information too, a possible connection between the burglary and the murder?"

Lacey hesitated. She realized she was talking to one of the suspects. "I guess my story hit the Web."

"The TV news too. Pretty tenuous though, I'd say, unless you got something they didn't mention."

"It's a news story. People tell me things, I write it down." Lacey shrugged. "And speaking of people telling me things, I was wondering if I could ask you something."

He gave her a long look and then nodded. "I guess Donovan must have told you about Cecily and me. Must have surprised you. Surprised everyone. Surprised me too."

"He said it wasn't much of a secret."

"'Fraid not. Secrets always leak out. Let that be a lesson. Our lesson plan for this evening," Hunt said with a rueful smile. "Hard not to fall for someone like her, who has season tickets to *everything,* and in the owner's box too. God, that was sweet." He rubbed his face. "And she was beautiful. She was something. Not worth the cost, though."

"Did you find out anything from the housekeeper or the staff?"

"About the murder? Nothing. I did find out Cecily had no trouble warming her bed, before or after me. I already knew that. And that stupid burglary? Supposedly someone 'forgot' to reset the alarm system that night. Bull. The system is automatic, you have to override it to turn it off. Everyone's lying about that idiotic little burglary. Doesn't make any sense."

The enticing aroma of fresh coffee filled the room. Lacey peeked in the Krispy Kreme doughnut box. He'd picked up a dozen assorted. They looked delicious. *You want great doughnuts,* she thought, *send an ex-cop.*

"Help yourself." He gestured toward the box.

She took a glazed, chocolate-iced piece of paradise. "Do you think Cecily set up the burglary herself?"

"Why? To blame it on her ex?" Hunt wore a grim smile. "Couldn't happen to a nicer son of a bitch."

"Maybe. Or maybe for the attention? For some guy?"

"She got plenty of attention, believe me. Besides, what she really wanted no one could give her."

"What could she possibly want that she couldn't buy?"

"Love. Security. Family. Most of all, she wanted a baby. But she couldn't. She tried."

"I heard she had a miscarriage years ago."

"She couldn't have kids after that." Hunt rinsed out cups

and set them in the drainer. "People are wrong about Cecily, about all the things she had. Like all those clothes. You saw all that, right? She loved them, but she didn't live or die by them."

"Maybe she did."

He rinsed his hands and wiped them with a towel. "Well, you got a point."

"Martin Hadley thinks she was trying to see him the day she died, but he doesn't know why. Do you think maybe she drove out here to see you, instead?"

"The thought has crossed my mind. She knew I was avoiding her calls. But she never made it to the door, and we'll never know why."

"Do you have an idea?"

"After the break-in, she called me for help. I hadn't seen her in months. I'd worked on the divorce settlement for her, chasing down Ashton's assets. That's where she and I, you know, got together. But that was a while ago. I made it clear I couldn't look into the burglary for her. Because I didn't want to get involved again. And because— Well, just because."

"Did you ever meet someone named Nigel Griffin?"

Hunt shook his head. "Should I?"

"Her insurance investigator, or one of them. He's sort of a recovery specialist. He thinks she staged the burglary to get his attention, because she wanted him in her bed and he turned her down."

"God." Hunt laughed. "Everyone's an egomaniac, you ever notice that?"

"Bud, I hear the cops have been pressing you pretty hard."

"Oh hell, they know I didn't kill her. They do think I'm holding something back, like I know more than I'm telling. Believe me, I know *nothing*. But I do know about obstruction of justice in a murder case. I was a cop, for crying out loud. They're just grasping at straws. They got nothing better, so I get the treatment." He grunted and turned his attention to the coffee dripping into the carafe. "That's off the record."

"Got it."

He poured two cups of coffee. Lacey added cream and sugar and they walked back into the classroom. They stood by the desk at the front, sipping their hot coffee.

"Almost class time. You know what I think?" Hunt grumbled, surveying his empty kingdom. "This class is cursed."

There was a loud explosion, followed immediately by a second. The classroom windows shattered and glass shards sprayed across the room like daggers. Hunt instinctively threw himself across Lacey to protect her, but she'd already hit the floor, covered with hot coffee, doughnuts, and jagged glass. Then there was silence. They lay still for a moment.

"Damn it! What the hell was that?" Hunt sat up, staring at the mess covering the floor. "What the hell do you want from me? I'm just trying to make a living here!"

Lacey sat up and looked around. Her pulse was pounding like a jackhammer, but she was unhurt. She brushed glass fragments carefully from her sweater, and picked some out of her skin, fighting the urge to cry. "I am never wearing this sweater again."

"You okay?" Hunt gave her his hand and helped her stand up. "Watch the broken glass. Shotgun, probably. Could have killed us easy if they wanted to." Hunt's voice sounded calm, but his hands were shaking. "Sending me a message, I guess, but what the hell? Freaking illiterates! You can't spell with a shotgun!"

The wind whistled through the empty window frames. Lacey didn't want to look out the shattered windows into the cold night, afraid she might see a gun pointed right at her. But she forced herself to look. There was no one there.

Hunt unholstered his phone to make the inevitable 911 call. "The guys at the station are gonna hate me. Did I mention this class is cursed?"

Heavy boots pounded down the stairs and Snake Goldstein burst through the door, his pistol drawn and ready. He looked around and whistled.

"Man, what in the name of holy crap went down here?! You got bad guys spraying shot at you? Brother Hunt, you got enemies or what?"

"Excuse me. I have to—" Lacey ran to the ladies' room. She made it there just in time to throw up.

When Lacey got home it was late. Her eyes burned, her muscles ached, and she was tired to the bone. A folded piece of paper was peeking out from underneath her apartment door. Her keys in her hand, she bent down to pull it out by one corner. It wasn't the usual flyer for the local Chinese restaurant, or another plea from the landlord to keep the lobby doors closed. It was a message, scrawled in block letters with a thick black marker.

SMITHSONIAN: TONIGHT WAS JUST A FRIENDLY WARNING!
STOP ASKING QUESTIONS. DON'T LOOK FOR TROUBLE.
YOU MIGHT BE THE NEXT DEAD DUCK. A FRIEND.

A friend? A friend who blew out the classroom windows, with her and Hunt inside? Obviously this "friend" did not understand reporters. Backing off wasn't an option. Lacey wasn't close to figuring things out yet; she'd barely started pulling the threads together to find a pattern. *I haven't even begun to look for trouble!*

Lacey let herself in and locked the door behind her. She considered her options. She could share this information with Detective Jance. He would thank her and counsel her to do exactly what the note suggested: Back off. Leave it to the pros, lady.

Were tonight's events prompted by her news story about the drawing on Cecily's photograph? It must have touched a nerve for her "friend," a friend with a shotgun and the willingness to use it. And whoever wrote the note knew where she lived and where she went to class.

She slid the note into a big manila envelope so as not to smudge the fingerprints she knew would not be there. She decided not to call the cops yet. Her thoughts were too chaotic to make sense of them for a puzzled cop. The shotgun blasts had shattered her nerves like glass. This message seemed to be what Kepelov had said: Another Russian doll. There was only one person she wanted to talk to, but she

didn't expect to see Vic again tonight. She'd called him several times from Falls Church and left him messages about
the shotgun attack, but he hadn't called back. She knew he
sometimes had to work all night on some case or another,
sometimes in secure government locations where cell
phones were not allowed. And he needed some sleep, after
flying in from the West Coast. Or maybe he was still out
carousing with Nigel and Stella?

Lacey felt on the verge of tears. She'd been holding it in
all night, ever since the windows had exploded and she
found herself on the floor covered with glass. She was heading for the bedroom when the phone rang.

"Lacey, where are you? Are you safe? Are you all right?"
It was Vic. "I was in that damn courthouse, they make you
leave your cell phone with Security, and I just now—"

"Oh, Vic. It's okay. I'm all right. I'm home."

"You're really all right? Not a scratch?"

"Not a scratch." Maybe some cuts and bruises, but no
scratches. "But persons unknown have left me a note. Under
my door. Here at home."

"A note? What kind of note?"

"The threatening kind. Vic, honey, I don't know what to
do—"

"I'll be right over. Don't let anyone in. Except me."

"You're late," Mac said when Lacey waltzed into the
newsroom at ten o'clock Thursday morning.

"Rough night." She was glad she'd chosen one of Aunt
Mimi's fabulous outfits. The perfect vintage outfit helped remind her how tough a woman can be. It gave Lacey the
strength she needed to deal with cranky bosses and grumpy
police detectives. Today's selection was from a 1939 pattern,
a simple black crepe dress with an emerald green satin
wraparound sash and a matching emerald and black bolero
jacket. Shades of Rita Hayworth herself. No one since about
1939 had made anything like it, and Vic had found it irre-
sistibly alluring that morning. But these days, Lacey realized, Vic would find a burlap feed sack alluring as long as
Lacey was in it. Preferably not in it for long.

He arrived last night with guns and ammunition. Vic had missed her and worried about her and he had proven it to her satisfaction. Lacey smiled at the memory.

"I know I'm late for class, teach, but I have a note." She handed her editor a copy of the warning message.

"A note?" Mac grumbled as he took it. "What kind of note?"

"Fan mail. My fans love me. The original is with the Falls Church police."

Mac read the threatening message, his eyebrows bouncing indignantly. She filled him in on the shotgun blasts at PI class in Falls Church the night before. Lacey translated the brows' message: Incredulous, followed by angry. "What did the police say?"

"That I should take its advice," Lacey said. "Maybe *they* sent it."

"You think it's from the shooter? The one last night?"

"Oh sure it is, don't you think? Sorry the letter writer wasn't more specific, but you know how people are today. I blame e-mail. I'm just glad he didn't text me. I never would have figured that out."

Mac growled and the eyebrows danced again. "Lacey, we joke about your peculiar ability to land in the middle of these situations, and the Smithsonian bravado is duly noted, but it is officially time to ease off this story."

"Not you too? What kind of journalist does that?"

"The live kind."

Lacey turned and headed for her desk. "Maybe later. First I have to call the usual suspects, so they can deny all knowledge of the note."

Mac followed her. "I got news for you, Lacey. I'm not running any more of your stories on Cecily Ashton until this shooter is caught." Lacey opened her mouth to protest, but he continued. "Besides, you're meeting Kim and the girls for lunch and their hair appointment tomorrow, and they're looking forward to it. Don't get yourself shot and disappoint my girls!"

"You know I wouldn't miss that." Lacey herself had introduced Mac's foster daughters to the pleasures of having their hair professionally cut and styled. This appointment with Miss Stella was a big deal for them. "How come they're out of school anyway?"

"Some kind of teacher planning day."

"Don't worry, the worst that can happen is Stella will dye their hair blue. No wait, blue and pink."

Mac stared at her, slack-jawed. "I expect you to ride shotgun on that," he said, oblivious to his choice of words.

"No blue and pink hair for Jasmine and Lily Rose. I'll *try* to remember." Lacey flounced out the door before he could say anything else. In the light of day, she felt fine. One night with Vic and she could even say the word *shotgun* without cringing.

Easy calls first, she thought. Her list began with Simon Edison, who said he had read Lacey's story about the drawing. Of course he had nothing to do with the shooting or the note, he said.

"Then let me ask you this, Simon. When I saw that little drawing of what might be a bird in a cage, I thought about your Faraday cage."

"Oh, like the drawing is a rebus? That's pretty clever, isn't it? I'm not sure I would have thought of that." There was a long pause. "Do you suppose someone is trying to say something about the fabric? Like Cecily was a bird in a gilded Faraday cage or something?" She wondered if Simon Edison was playing with her. "I don't know, but you should be very careful, Ms. Smithsonian! I wouldn't want you to end up like my Cecily."

That sounded a little threatening too. "Simon, did you write that note last night?"

"Of course not! There is no way I would place a nasty note under your door. I don't even know where you live. I mean I wouldn't *anyway,* Lacey. You know what I mean."

She wasn't sure what he meant. Was he cagier than he looked? She called Willow next, the home number from the class contact sheet; no answer. She did catch Edwina, who said she was so flustered by everything that happened in class she was off to the range with her girlfriends to shoot skeet.

"It relaxes me," she said. "Better than bridge."

"Did you happen to slip a note under my door last night?" Lacey asked.

"Why on earth would I do that?" Edwina said she had to go, her shooting party had arrived.

Hadley also denied any knowledge of the note. He was late to class last night because of snarled traffic on the George Washington Parkway, he said, and when he saw the police cars in the parking lot he turned right around and went home. He assumed they were there for him. He waited all night for the inevitable knock on the door, which never came. Lacey inquired about the voices. Hadley said Edgar seemed to be on leave. Raj was in charge, and Hadley couldn't understand half of what he was saying. And he assured her the voices never left threatening notes or any physical evidence at all.

"Of course, Edgar and the others often order me to do very strange things. Part of the torment is resisting their bizarre commands. But I would never actually harm someone! I don't know if that goes for everyone like me." He offered the local mind-control group's help in protecting her. Lacey thanked him.

But is tinfoil bulletproof? She didn't let herself laugh until she hung up the phone.

"Hey, newshound. You all in one piece?" Trujillo stopped to smell the bundt cake on Felicity's desk. It was a luscious cinnamon chocolate concoction, dripping with caramel frosting. Lacey used her mighty willpower to ignore it, but Trujillo, the notorious food and story poacher, cut himself a large slice.

"I seem to be all in one piece, thanks."

"What can you tell me about the shoot-out at the PI corral?"

"Nothing much. Boom boom. No casualties. Except the windows."

"Mac's deciding whether we want to play it up big or not." He dug into his cake. "The perp may just be after the attention."

"In that case, maybe the perp's a politician running for president."

"At any rate, you're off the story."

"Go away, you smug pencil pusher." Lacey waved him away and he took the hint. But the cinnamon chocolate caramel cake finally got to her. She sliced off a tiny sliver just as Felicity bustled back to her desk. Eating it would be bad for Lacey's waistline, but it made the food editor smile.

"Lacey, Harlan and I have been talking about the wedding," Felicity said. *As if they talked about anything else these days.* "Well. Gosh. We would really like you to be one of my bridesmaids. Would you?"

A parade of the most dreadful bridesmaids' gowns imaginable suddenly flooded Lacey's imagination. Being sprayed by broken glass was bad enough. Wearing a dress devised by Felicity Pickles for her Big Day was unthinkable.

Lacey was glad for once her mouth was full.

chapter 33

"Are you Lacey Smithsonian?"

Lacey looked up at the man in the blue jeans and green-brown camouflage jacket standing between her desk and Felicity's. He didn't look like someone who would be looking for her. Probably in his late twenties, he was boyish and nice looking, with sandy hair and a smattering of freckles over his nose and cheeks.

"Yes," she said. "That would be me."

"I'm Eric O'Neil." He extended his hand and grinned. Lacey hesitated and then took his hand. He had a firm grip. "Call me Eric. You called my office yesterday?"

Her hand hit her coffee cup and it shattered on the floor. She picked up the pieces.

O'Neil? Willow's murderous stalker, that Eric O'Neil? Lacey took a breath and tried to stay calm. *What the hell is he doing here? Can just anybody wander past the security desk in the lobby?* Her next thought was that this guy was much too attractive for Willow, but of course that was just prejudice based on looks. Obsession was blind, and she was still thinking of the old Willow.

"Your office is in Philly, right? Cyber Rescue Squad? I never expected to see you here in D.C." Her heart was beating way too fast.

"Right on my way home." He tilted his head a little when he smiled, an oddly endearing gesture for a potential killer. "Heading back home from North Carolina. Hunting trip."

"What kind of hunting?" Her heart was still pounding. Lacey thought her voice sounded a little squeaky. She hoped it sounded more confident to Eric O'Neil.

"Quail, grouse, pheasant," Eric said. "Just birds this trip. They're on ice in my truck. Season's almost over." He unzipped his camo hunting jacket, revealing a well-worn olive drab sweater. It looked like military surplus.

"Ducks?" Lacey's mouth felt a little dry. *Am I the "next dead duck"?*

"Not this trip. You look a little flushed, Ms. Smithsonian, are you all right?"

"I'm good." Lacey cleared her throat. She took a sip from her water bottle. "Call me Lacey. Have a seat. Please."

Eric grabbed the office's floating chair, the Death Chair, in which the former fashion editor had died. Decorated with a skull and crossbones, it was a sturdy oak arm chair with casters. No one in the newsroom wanted it anymore, but it was too indestructible to get rid of. He sat down.

"I checked my messages and there you were. I never heard of your newspaper, but you said you were writing something about Nina, so I wanted to—" He stopped.

Her breath caught in her throat. "Yes, Eric?"

"Well, I'd do anything to help find who killed Nina. Her death was such a shame."

"How well did you know her?"

"We dated for awhile. She was a sweet girl." Eric looked Lacey straight in the eye. He seemed utterly normal. Charming, just as Willow had said. *Perhaps he's a charming sociopath,* she thought.

"You dated?" Willow hadn't mentioned that little factoid.

"It was pretty casual. She was like a butterfly, you know? She never landed anywhere for very long. But don't get me wrong, Nina was very cool. I liked her a lot."

"I heard she was dating someone else too," Lacey said. "English guy?"

"Yeah, English guy. Griffith? Or something Griffith. Griffin? Nigel something?"

Nigel Griffin strikes again. "Jealous of him?"

"Me? Of him?" Eric made a face. "Why would I? Nah. I

think I only met the guy once, at a party someplace. Nina and I weren't going out anymore by then anyway."

Trujillo had sidled up to Felicity's desk again. *Prowling for more cake, or more juicy crumbs of my story?* Lacey wondered.

"Still hungry, Tony?"

"Must have missed lunch. Hey, man, you don't look like a fashion story," he said to Eric. "Unless Smithsonian here is suddenly into camo."

"Fashion story? The last thing I'd be," Eric said. "I'm just here about Nina."

"Nina?" Trujillo looked puzzled. Lacey hadn't filled him in. Now wasn't the time.

"Tony's one of our police reporters," Lacey said. "He knows everything the police know. I'm sure he's got important work to do." She gave Trujillo a gentle shove in the direction of his desk. "I'm glad you came by, Eric, I've got some questions."

"Can we sit outside? Some air would be good." Eric looked around at the bustling newsroom. "Looking at this many computers, I feel like I'm back on the job! Like I should be running diagnostics or something. And I'm still on vacation. Anyhow, I'd like to get a look at Washington, besides the Beltway."

Eric wasn't giving off stalker vibes, but then she wasn't the target of his supposed obsession. Lacey was also pretty sure he couldn't have smuggled a gun into the newsroom. Since an assault before Christmas on one of *The Eye*'s editorial writers, metal detectors had been installed at the street entrances to the lobby.

"Well, I'm expecting a call," she hedged. She tried to think of the safest place to take him. What could be safer than the highly secure area around the White House, only a few blocks away? "I could use a walk, Eric. We're close to the White House. We'll go over that way."

Time to leave the prying eyes, and safety, of the newsroom. Lacey saved her files and grabbed her mouton coat. The sunshine was bright, but the temperature was falling. She and Eric walked in measured steps out the door to Eye

Street, then toward Sixteenth Street and south past the lovely Hay-Adams Hotel.

"You said you were bird hunting, Eric. What kind of gun do you use for that?"

"Shotgun, of course." He seemed surprised at the question, as if everyone knew that. "Oh you mean what gauge! Sorry. I'm a twelve gauge man. Remington pump. Hey, you want to see my birds? Had a good trip. Prettiest little things you ever saw. The quail especially."

Yeah, and pretty dead too. But not dead ducks! Am I being sent another message? "Um, no thanks. Do you have a handgun too?"

"Used to. I had an old Smith & Wesson twenty-two-caliber revolver of my dad's. Got stolen. Too bad, it was a nice little gun. Had some others too. You ever do any shooting, Lacey?"

"Once in a while," she said.

Eric stopped short in the middle of Lafayette Park. "Whoa! Would you look at that! The White House! I gotta take a picture!" He pulled out his cell phone and snapped some photos. "This is great, Lacey, thanks. I go right past D.C. on I-95 a lot, but I never get to stop."

Lacey watched a group of tourists taking pictures of each other. "I heard Nina was killed in a drive-by shooting last fall."

"It was terrible." His face changed. He looked sad and thoughtful. He put his cell phone away. "It's an awful crazy world. I'm wondering, why are you interested in her now? The police never arrested anyone. Is there some kind of new lead or something?"

"Some people think her death might be connected to a shooting in Northern Virginia last Saturday." Eric looked surprised, but he said nothing. "Did anyone hate Nina enough to kill her?"

"No way! I don't think so. Like I said, she was a good person. Everyone loved Nina. The cops said it was a random shooting, like maybe a gang thing, and she got caught in the crossfire."

"Then let's talk about your former girlfriend."

Eric shrugged. "Okay. Which one?"

"Willow. Willow Raynor."

His mouth fell open. "Willow? Are you kidding me? She has *never* been my girlfriend. Not ever. Whoa. Where did you get that? No way, Willow's a total nutcake." Eric seemed embarrassed. He wiped his hands on his jacket as if to clean them. "Willow Raynor! Give me a break. Hey, is this a setup? Some kind of weird joke? You filming this for YouTube?"

Lacey felt disoriented again. It was becoming a familiar feeling. Every time this story shifted it knocked her off balance. She didn't like it one bit.

"Willow Raynor was never your girlfriend?"

"I don't know where you got that idea. No way. Not ever."

"But you do know her. How?"

Eric groaned. "Blind date. About a year ago. Not my idea, believe me. Buddy of mine was dating Nina. She has a shy friend, he says, somebody she works with, could we double up? Nice girl, he says, he'll fix me up. It was a total pimp-your-friend moment."

"Could you explain, please?" Lacey buttoned up her coat against the frigid air.

"Our big date was like this: Dave comes into the restaurant with Nina, and she is smokin' hot. Long dark hair, big eyes, great smile, killer body. How bad could her friend be, right? So I'm feeling pretty hopeful. Then Willow gets there late. You should have seen her! She was colorless, like a zombie or something. Wearing some kind of terrible sack thing. She had dirty hair and pasty skin. Blank look on her face. Too shy to even talk. I wasn't sure she *could* talk. Almost like she was paralyzed. Then she clings to me like Saran Wrap. I keep looking for the hidden camera, you know? Like a reality show: *Amazing but True Horrible Dates!* I couldn't wait for it to be over. Nina felt really sorry for Willow, I think. She kept trying to get something going for her, but it never worked out. Anyway, that's where I met Nina too. Dave moved on, Nina and I went out for a few months, had some good times, then we both moved on."

"What about Willow?" Lacey asked. "Did you ever see her again?"

"Not if I could help it. She hung around Nina a lot, she'd show up at the bar or at parties, and Nina was so nice, she didn't want to tell her zombie friend to get lost. Nina was running out of patience with her though, Willow could be an awful pest. We talked about how she could drop 'the Zombie' without hurting her feelings. Then after Nina died, Willow was all over me. She called me all the time, she followed me around, waited for me in my truck, she really wanted us to get together, but I always put her off. I mean, dude, zombie girl! Yuck."

Eric fell silent. Lacey watched him admiring the White House like an awestruck little kid. He wanted to go look at the statue of Andrew Jackson on his horse. He said he loved Andy Jackson. Lacey led him to a park bench with a view of the statue. And a view of the security guards on the White House grounds.

"Let's sit here. Do you mind?"

"No, this is great, Lacey." He sat down next to her. "Wow, the White House looks exactly like it does in pictures. I can't get over that. This is so awesome!"

"What did Willow talk about? Do you remember anything in particular?"

"Oh, man, Willow. What a zero." Eric concentrated. "No. She never really said much. She just sat there on our one and only date and stared at me goggle-eyed all night. How is this going to help with your story on Nina?"

"I don't know. Sometimes I have to ask a lot of questions." Lacey folded her arms. She was cold, despite the sunshine and her warm coat. The light was golden, the shadows deepened, and the wind kicked a newspaper with her latest story about Cecily across the park past Andrew Jackson. "Do you know where Willow is now?"

"Don't know, don't care, don't want to know." He squinted up into the sunshine. "Whoa! Wouldja look at that! Sun dogs! Why are we talking about Willow anyway and not Nina? I mean, I want to help, but how—"

Sun dogs? Damn! Why don't Marie's predictions come with subtitles?

Lacey stood up and turned to face Eric, blocking the sun. "You haven't been stalking her? Or me? With a shotgun? Or sending threatening messages?"

Eric looked up at Lacey. "You're kidding me again, right? I mean, you really are kidding. This is like something you have to ask everyone who knew Nina, right?"

Ask the question and then shut up and listen, she told herself. She took a breath.

"Willow says you shot Nina. But it was a mistake. You really meant to shoot her. So you've been stalking her. And now me. Is that true?" The words sounded ridiculous to Lacey the moment she said them, but she shut up and listened and watched his hazel eyes blink. He shook his head.

"That's so bonkers, I don't even know what to say. No! Not me. Me shoot Nina? And stalk people? No." He held her gaze and didn't look away, but his eyes clouded over with anger. "Oh man, that is so insane. What is she thinking? She told the cops back home I shot Nina. Lucky they figured out I was okay, I wasn't even around when it happened. Now she's saying this weird crap about me? I gotta say I wish it had been her instead of Nina. Willow needs help, she is certifiable. What do you know about her anyway? Where is she? No, don't tell me, I don't want to know. This is freaking me out." He stood up and took a step toward Lacey. She stepped back. He seemed baffled, not threatening. "God. I gotta get back on the road. I better throw some more ice on my birds too."

"Did the police ever talk with you about Nina?"

"Once. They talked to all her friends. I couldn't help much, I didn't know anything. I was working overtime that day." He shook his head and looked at her, puzzled. "You know, it's funny how death freezes everything. Makes you remember the littlest things?" He closed his eyes. "I remember everything I did that day. I worked late at Cyber Rescue and there was a baseball game on that night. My buddies came over and we had a good time. I didn't hear about Nina till the next day, but I remember seeing the news, hearing her name and feeling sick, just sick to my stomach. Why did it have to be Nina? Life is freaky, huh?"

"Yeah, it is. Eric, one more question. Did you know Cecily Ashton?"

"That crazy billionaire's wife? Oh yeah, I hang with lots of billionaires," he cracked. "When I'm fixing their computers. No, I'm not the fox hunting kind of guy she'd probably hang with. Just me and my birds." He zipped up his camo hunting jacket. They started walking back toward *The Eye.* Eric stopped suddenly and turned to her.

"Oh no! That's too much! Did I shoot this Cecily Ashton too? Is that what you want to know? Is that what Willow is telling people?"

"Did you?"

"No! I've never shot anybody! Only ducks! Quail! Pheasants! What the hell is this all about? It's like she's trying to drive me out of my mind. She is one sick little girl."

"I don't know yet. If you think of anything that might help, call me." Lacey handed him her card. "Can I call you if I have more questions?"

"Yeah, I guess, any time. Find out who killed Nina. But please try and leave that maniac Willow out of it. She scares me to death."

"I'll see what I can do."

"Let me know what happens, okay?" He pulled a business card out of his wallet. "My cell is on there. You know, Nina's family would really like to know why she died."

Who was the liar, Lacey wondered, Eric O'Neil or Willow Raynor? She wasn't sure she should believe either one of them. But Eric had good eyes, she thought, for what it was worth. He didn't look away from a hard question. And there was that one gesture he made when she mentioned Willow, wiping his hands on his jacket, like he was trying to wipe her away.

Lacey watched him swing himself up into his big black Dodge Ramcharger. Inside the truck somewhere there were shotguns and ammunition and dead birds on ice. Eric looked at her and waved. She stood and watched until he was out of sight; then she wrote down his Pennsylvania license plate number. She took one last look at the sun dogs fading in the January sky.

chapter 34

"You still need the shoe leather," Bud Hunt was lecturing his PI students. Lacey's attention had wandered to the drizzly evening outside the classroom windows. They'd already been replaced with nice clean new glass. Lacey realized just how dirty the old windows were.

"With all our new high-tech gadgetry in the last few years," Hunt said, "maybe you think you can be a private eye by remote control now. You can, to some extent, but not a good one. Computer databases and global positioning systems and so forth make finding people and information a lot easier, but some poor slob still needs to analyze the data and make the decisions. Despite all the technology, this is still a very personal business. It takes eyes and ears and a brain. Gut instincts. And shoe leather on the sidewalk."

"But you can't do the job without technology now," Damon protested, tapping something into his laptop. "I mean, there's so much data on the Web. And everyone is under surveillance now, right?"

Hunt sat on his desk and folded his arms. He looked tired. "Sometimes technology can help you a lot. Take vehicle surveillance. And forget that little follow-the-leader exercise with my buddy Greg the other night. He's a joker. We'll do that over the right way this weekend." A few of the PI students laughed ruefully. "With the awful traffic in this area, you can't count on being able to tail anybody visually anymore. You just try to cowboy down 66 or I-95 hot on someone's tail while you're stuck in traffic. See where that gets you. A GPS unit and a vehicle tracking device on your subject could be your best friend."

"That's legal?" Lacey asked.

Hunt shrugged. "It's not illegal. Yet. In Virginia anyway. You can get a tracking device with an antenna about the size of a hair. You brush casually against someone's bumper, it just happens to attach. Keep in mind, you can't do that in D.C. It is illegal in the District of Columbia to 'alter' someone else's car. You can't even adjust somebody's side view mirrors. That law was an attempt to deal with their massive vandalism problem. Like vandals in the District care about the law. Like they even know about the law." There was another smattering of chuckles. "But *you* need to know the law, so you'll know what you can get away with. And so you can pass the test and get your Virginia PI registrations."

"And if every sixth person in D.C. is a spy," Lacey said, "how do you conduct surveillance on spies who are spying on you?"

"Spies don't care about city ordinances either," Damon noted.

Hunt picked up his coffee mug and took a long slurp. "I don't care how much new technology you got, when you get right down to it, sometimes you need old-fashioned skills and guts and dogged determination." Hunt thumped himself on the solar plexus. "You don't need all the gizmos and gadgets. You need grit, guts, and gumshoes."

Oh, good quote, Lacey thought. *Grit, guts, and gumshoes!* She wrote that down in her notebook and circled it.

"Sometimes you have to turn off the TV, the Internet, and all those noises in your head." He looked at Hadley. "You hear me? It's the voice inside *you*, the one that's got nothing to do with the government. That's the voice you gotta listen to. You got a mind? You got your own mind control."

"What's your gut telling you about the dead lady in the parking lot, chief?" Snake asked. "And that craziness last night. 'Cause my money's always on the ex."

Hunt shook his head. "Nine times out of ten you're right. But if Philip Clark Ashton had her killed, he'd have come up with a lot smarter way to do it. He's a bastard, but he's no

dummy. He could arrange a nice, quiet, convincing little suicide. You got a rich woman, unstable, history of mental
problems? She overdoses on something, the medical examiner might even call it accidental death. She takes her pills,
has a drink or two or three, 'forgets' she took her pills, takes
some more. A sad little death, but eminently explicable, as
they say. If it was Ashton, that's the way it would have happened." Bud Hunt's voice trembled a little. "And believe me,
the bastard is capable of anything. But he wouldn't have left
such a mess in public."

Lacey agreed that Philip Ashton would avoid any nega-
tive publicity. He didn't need the embarrassment of the
lovely Cecily gunned down in her Jaguar, or the memory of
the blood spray on the windshield, or the police photos that
might someday find their way to a tabloid reporter. If indeed
Philip once loved Cecily, as he had told Lacey he did, a gunshot would not be the way he would do away with her.
Would it?

The class was even smaller tonight. As they were taking
their seats Hunt announced they had some more dropouts
after the previous evening's shoot-out at the PI corral. Willow had called in with 'the sniffles,' Hunt said with a hint of
sarcasm, but she said she'd be back. To Lacey's surprise, Edwina Plimpton was there, none the worse for her recent martini binge and being stopped at the police tape last night.
Tonight she wore khaki slacks, a black sweater, and a white
shirt, straight out of Talbots. Lacey gave her credit for tenac-
ity. Once the woman sank her teeth into a style—or a
class—she didn't let go. At the break, Edwina sought out
Lacey to share her theory about Cecily.

"Obviously it's an inside job! It's someone in the household staff," Edwina insisted. "First they staged that silly burglary. After all, someone knew the security codes. Cecily
caught on. That's why she came here to see Bud Hunt, to
have him investigate for her. But they got to her first. I'll bet
the staff have already cleaned out that poor woman's fabulous closets. Had to be the servants. Who else would know
her comings and goings so intimately?"

"You have a point," Lacey said.

"The very same thing happened to me," Edwina confessed.

"Really?" *You were shot dead in your Jaguar?* Lacey suppressed a smile.

"Well, not exactly the same thing." Edwina inspected her perfect nails. "I had a housekeeper once, her name was Mirta. Good, thorough, pleasant. Best housekeeper I ever had. But little things began to disappear. Not valuable things at first, just some costume jewelry here and there. I thought I'd simply misplaced them, but it got to the point where I thought I was losing my mind. Then I lost a necklace my husband had given me for our tenth anniversary. I always kept it in a velvet jewelry box. It was just a single ruby on a gold chain, but it carried great sentimental value for me." She rubbed her throat unconsciously.

"What happened? How did you figure out the house-keeper took it?"

"I caught Mirta wearing it! Can you imagine? She thought I was so rich she could steal my things right under my nose and I wouldn't notice. I confronted her and she broke down. She told me how sorry she was. How it was so beautiful, she couldn't help herself. And you know, maybe if it hadn't been that particular necklace, I would have just fired her. But I pressed charges, I had to. She disappeared after they fingerprinted her. Never even showed up in court." Edwina sighed. "I don't have a full-time housekeeper any-more, just a cleaning service once a week. Bonded, insured, the whole nine yards."

"She simply wore the necklace? Around the house?" Lacey found that part interesting. "She didn't sell it for the money?"

Edwina shook her head and rubbed an imagined spot from her diamond ring. "I never realized how much some-one could resent you for the things you have. And we are not rich! Not *that* rich, anyway. But Mirta thought we were. I suppose she resented it. She thought she was getting away with it, laughing at me. The last straw was wearing my own necklace in front of me in my own house. That's when I re-alized how much she must have hated me." Edwina had unsuspected grit, Lacey reflected. "So you see, if it wasn't Cecily's ex-husband, it must have been the staff."

"The entire staff en masse," Lacey asked, "or just one of them?"

"Probably just one. If they were all in on it, they'd be squabbling over her clothes by now. Someone would have squealed on the others. I'll tell Bud Hunt. The police should be looking for one of the servants. They probably haven't thought of that." Edwina stalked off to bend Hunt's ear.

Lacey took her cell phone into the hall to call Willow. Was she really sick, terrified by the shooting last night, or just avoiding Lacey's calls? *Or had Eric O'Neil bagged another bird?*

Willow did not answer; her machine picked up. Lacey couldn't quite think of what to say. She didn't leave a message.

Chapter 35

"Hey, Lacey, you there? Listen, I got a perm control situation here."

It was Stella's urgent voice on Lacey's voice mail. She'd missed the call during Mac's Friday morning staff meeting. "Listen, my five o'clock from yesterday had a bad reaction to the perm rods and now she's totally got, um, curly pink hair and it's making her very unhappy, and me too, and she says I gotta fix the pink right now! Did I mention it's pink? So, here's the deal; I gotta cancel your eleven o'clock today and take care of this perm-rod situation, 'cause, uh, with the pink hair and all she won't come to the salon, so I'm in my car and—"

What on earth is Stella babbling about? Pink hair? Lacey was quite certain Stella had never accidentally given a client pink hair in her entire career. On purpose, yes, but never by accident. And of course she was chatting away on her cell phone while driving, which is illegal in the District.

Stella's voice rushed on at top speed. "I can't possibly do Wednesday, not Wednesday, you got that? So how about Valentine's Day, and bring Blondie with you, make it a party. I know it's far away. Valentine's Day, remember? Now, be careful with your permanent! Some people say a cold water rinse is the thing, but the key is that you have to watch out for hard water, 'cause with hard water there's this major sudsing problem in the rinse. The rods fall out so suds are key. Watch for hard water."

Her voice became muffled. Stella was talking to someone

else too, but Lacey couldn't make it out. "One more thing, if you want that permanent, Girl Friday, do it right now, pronto, do not wait twenty-four hours like they used to tell you. Shampoo right away to set the activator in motion or your hair will fall out! Fall right out! Lace, are you getting this? Damn, I gotta go—"

"That's total nonsense," Lacey said aloud, but no one paid any attention to her. Everyone around her in the newsroom was checking out the Friday weekend section, or surfing the Web, or picking out a wedding cake, or deep in the middle of their own personal soap operas. She heard more muffled voices and traffic noises and then Stella's message cut off.

An uneasy feeling spread from the base of Lacey's spine and traveled rapidly upward. She pressed redial. It rang Stella's cell phone number. No answer. She listened to the message again and typed it out.

Was she babbling the Pink Collar Code that Stella and Brooke had concocted over margaritas? Was she just testing Lacey to see if she'd learned it? Maybe Lacey should have actually *read* the code? It was no time for a pop quiz on the silly code, but a test was what Lacey hoped it was. She was due to meet Stella and Kim and the girls at Stella's salon at noon to go to lunch.

Lacey dialed the salon. The receptionist didn't answer the phone and the voice mail didn't pick up. She checked the number and dialed again. No answer. Stella sometimes opened the salon all alone and let the others come in later. Lacey told herself this was some silly game Stella was playing, but the feeling that something was desperately wrong won out. If Stella were playing, there would have been giggles. Lacey found Brooke at her law firm between meetings.

"Stella left me a message in the Code. I *think* it's in the Code. Or else she's just playing some screwy mind game."

"The Code?" Brooke was instantly at full attention. "The Pink Collar Code?"

"It involved somebody's pink hair. She didn't sound panicky, she just sounded—I don't know. Intense. Hurried. She said pink hair a couple of times."

"Extra pink is good. We decided we'd have to say *pink* more than once in the message to mark it as code, remember, and not just about something that's really just, um, pink." Brooke sounded excited. "Stella has definitely invoked the Code."

"She's talking about perms and rods and rinsing and Valentine's Day, not Wednesday, and I don't know what she's talking about. Help me out here, I don't have the Code with me."

"Lacey, you didn't memorize the Code? Jeez. I am so disappointed in you."

"Sue me. I'll take a makeup exam later." Lacey checked her watch. It was a quarter to ten. "I think there's something really wrong, Brooke. She's talking about a perm. I don't have an appointment today, and I don't want a perm, I'd never get a perm. You know the Code, don't you?"

"I *created* the Code. Mostly." Brooke sounded huffy, as if Lacey had accused her of not doing her homework. "I need to hear the message."

"I typed it up. But here, just call my voice mail and listen to Stella. I'll hold." She gave Brooke the numbers. There was a long pause. Finally Lacey had to say something. "Brooke, are you there? What do you think?"

"I'm not sure. She's mixing things up." Brooke was alarmed. "She's gone way off script."

Lacey reached for her coat and purse. "I'm grabbing a taxi to Stylettos. I'm supposed to meet her for lunch anyway."

"I'll get my car and meet you there."

"Your car?"

"You never know when you'll need two tons of horsepower and steel."

No one knew where Stella was. Stylettos' assistant manager Michelle was at the front counter fielding calls and resetting appointments. She told Lacey Stella hadn't opened the salon as planned, which was unusual, though not unheard of. There had been the occasional hangover. Michelle had simply opened it up when she got there and assumed

Stella was running late. Michelle gave Lacey a big wink, as if they both knew why Stella might have a hard time getting out of bed in the morning these days, with her new boyfriend and all. But still, Michelle thought it was a little odd, because Stella's two youngest fans were already there. She waved at Jasmine and Lily Rose, who were heading to the shampoo bowls.

The girls spotted Lacey. They squealed and waved at her in their mirrors, and she waved back. Kim, Mac's petite wife, came rushing up. She looked confused.

"What's up, Lacey, you're early. Where's Stella?"

"I don't know, she may be in some kind of jam."

The front door chimes sounded as Brooke sailed through the door of the salon. "I'm in a no-parking zone. What did you find out?"

"Stella never showed up," Lacey said. "No one's heard from her."

"Give me the message. You said you typed it."

Brooke sat in a salon chair to read it and compare it with her master copy of the Pink Collar Code. Ten-year-old Lily Rose bolted out of her chair and hurled herself at Lacey. Big sister Jasmine was close on her heels, but she stopped short of a big hug. Twelve-year-olds who are totally *almost* thirteen do not hug. She gave Lacey her biggest smile. *Then* she hugged her.

"Guess what, Lacey!" Lily Rose shouted. Jasmine shushed her and she shifted her voice to a loud stage whisper. "Me and Jasmine are gonna be 'dopted by Mac and Kim! And after we're 'dopted we'll all be a family and no one can take us away ever!"

"Adopted!" Lacey had hoped that might be in the works, but Mac hadn't tipped his hand. "That's wonderful, Lily Rose." Lacey leaned down and whispered, "But you have to keep Mac in line, okay?"

The girls' giggles were infectious. "We already do that," Lily Rose said.

Kim smiled at Lacey. She turned to her youngest foster daughter. "What did I tell you, Lily Rose?"

The little girl's eyes opened wide. She clasped her hands

over her mouth. In an even louder whisper she added, "It's a secret!"

Jasmine burst out laughing. "Lily Rose can't keep secrets."

"Can too!" the smaller girl insisted.

"Lacey's a reporter and now it's going to be in all the papers," Jasmine teased.

"No, it isn't!" the younger girl insisted.

"It's spectacular, and I promise not to tell." Lacey said. "Not until you tell me I can."

Brooke jumped out of her chair, Code in hand, and broke up the family circle. "Lacey, we have to get going. Right now."

"You can't go, Lacey," Jasmine said accusingly, "we're supposed to go have lunch after our hair appointment! You promised!"

"No time for lunch," Brooke said. "Lacey and I are on a rescue mission."

The only way to deal with the kids was complete honesty, Lacey knew, no matter what other people said, and she didn't take breaking a promise lightly. Even lunch.

"Come here, girls." She sat down and put her arms around them. "I have to tell you something. Stella isn't here and we don't know why."

"Did something bad happen?" Jasmine asked.

"We don't know. But yes, it could be something bad. Now, Brooke and I," she indicated the gray-suited attorney, "we have to go try and find her. We have to find her right away."

"Is she going to die?" Lily Rose looked very serious. Even at ten, she already knew that death was something that could happen to people you loved.

"Not if we find her in time."

"We'll go with you and help," she insisted. Jasmine looked up at Kim, who put her hand on the girl's shoulder.

Lacey couldn't help but smile. Both girls were ready to go with her anywhere and throw snowballs at the Devil if necessary. "You stay with your mom. She'll take you to lunch. I'll come along next time."

"We helped you before," Jasmine protested. Lacey remembered the night she had to tell them their mother was dead. The night their mother's killer chased them in the storm. The night they threw snowballs at a murderer and stayed with Lacey as she fought for her life. The night they met Mac and Kim and their lives changed forever.

Lacey gave the girls a hug and stood up. "Yes, you did, and I couldn't have made it without you. But today, you need to stay with Kim and keep her company. She needs you too. Brooke will be my backup."

Jasmine stared at Brooke and sighed. "If you say so. But she looks like a lawyer."

"I am a lawyer," Brooke said. "But I'm a good lawyer. Really."

"We know all about lawyers." Jasmine scowled.

Lily Rose imitated her big sister's scowl. "Yeah, we know about them."

"I hope I never get you two on a jury," Brooke said.

Kim gently put a hand on each girl's shoulder and gave Lacey an encouraging smile. "Go on, Lacey, we'll be fine. We'll take a rain check."

"What's a rain check?" Lily Rose asked.

"Be careful," Kim said.

"Be extra careful." Jasmine gave her a stern look.

Lily Rose was not to be outdone. She grabbed Lacey's hand and implored, "Be extra, extra careful! 'Cause we love Miss Stella."

Lacey promised. Brooke was already out the front door, leading the way to her car in its no-parking space. Brooke wasn't quite running, but Lacey had to run to catch up.

"Where are we going?" Lacey asked.

"Valentine's Day," Brooke said.

chapter 36

"I don't understand half of it." Brooke slid behind the wheel of her sleek pavement gray Acura and keyed the ignition. She flipped quickly through her copy of the Pink Collar Code again while Lacey slid into the passenger seat beside her. "That message of Stella's is all garbled. She says 'pink' over and over, so she has clearly invoked the Code, but it almost starts to make sense and then it doesn't. What is Stella thinking, getting way off the Code like that?"

"She's improvising. Exactly what you'd do if someone were kidnapping you." Lacey slammed the door and buckled her shoulder harness.

"Who said she could improvise?" Brooke threw the Code on Lacey's lap and put the Acura in gear. The front tires squealed.

"This is Stella Lake, stylist extraordinaire. Woman of a thousand styles, all with extra Stellarifficness. Improvisation is her middle name. And of course she expects me to understand it all. With my EFP," Lacey complained. "She gives me too much credit. Damn it, Stella! Where the hell are you? Why did you have to use the Code?"

"You're right. We really should have discussed our personal communication styles and how we all process and disseminate information differently." Brooke peeled rubber into Connecticut Avenue's lunch hour traffic, whipped around Q Street onto Nineteenth Street, and headed for Dupont Circle. "I assumed we would do that after our next girls' night out at the range."

"You're kidding me, right?" Lacey glanced at Brooke, who was spinning the steering wheel like a Formula One driver. The Circle was full, as usual, and Brooke was changing lanes aggressively. Lacey closed her eyes.

"All I'm saying is that if we'd been up to speed on this thing in advance—"

"Give her a break! She's scared. Someone is holding her captive, maybe at gunpoint. She had to use the Code, or something like the Code."

"If only she'd actually learned the Code! And why would they let her call you?"

"Stella must have said I had an appointment, and if she wasn't at the salon when I arrived—"

"You'd get suspicious and start asking questions."

"So she was able to make a call to me, half in Code and half just winging it. She's in trouble."

"She'd better be in serious trouble, or I'll kill her." Brooke screeched to a stop for a red light at Massachusetts Avenue.

"We're not fighting, are we, Brooke? Because we don't have time to have a fight. Do we?" Lacey's heart was beating furiously and her mouth had an unpleasant metallic taste. She hoped she wouldn't be sick again. Brooke would frown on Lacey throwing up in her immaculate Acura.

"Of course we're not fighting, we are merely discussing the issues in a forthright and direct manner. Like we always do."

"Good, because I think I should read Stella's message again before we fight."

"It's in my folder, with the Code."

Lacey read it twice. What was Stella trying to say? *Valentine's Day* was Code for Virginia. Brooke obviously got that part, she was heading that direction. *Not Wednesday* definitely meant not in Washington. *Permanent* or *perm* meant something to do with death or murder. *Perm rods* meant a gun was involved, but whose gun? Their Pink Collar Code could have been a bit more precise, Lacey thought. Besides, the way Brooke had written it, Lacey couldn't even read it without falling asleep. Apparently Stella couldn't either. But *cold water rinse, emollients, suds*? Those weren't in the Code. Nor was *set the activator in motion!*

"Okay, let's think about this," Lacey said. "What do emollients do in water? They make it sudsy, like shampoo. Suds. Why cold water? Suds are—suds. Soap bubbles. Foam? Running water makes foam, right, like suds?"

"But what's that supposed to mean? There's nothing in the Code about *suds*. It doesn't mean anything." Brooke looked up through her smoked glass sunroof and yelped. Large fluffy chunks of white were hitting the car. "Oh, no, just what we need! Snow! Damn it, why today? It's only January!"

The city had seen a little snow before Christmas, but in Washington the first major snowfall often held off until well into January. As a true Washingtonian, Brooke was instinctively prepared to deal with lobbyists and politicians and scandals and conspiracy theories and mind-control victims, but she could not deal with snow.

"Deep breath, Brooke. It's okay. I'm from Colorado. This is nothing. You want me to drive? Just tell me where we're going."

"I'm fine, you just navigate. And think! We need a target smaller than the state of Virginia!" Brooke was accelerating west on P Street, crossing the bridge over Rock Creek, heading into Georgetown.

Lacey's hands were freezing, but she thought asking Brooke for a little more heat might be a distraction. She reached into her jacket pocket for her gloves and pulled out a piece of paper with them. She unfolded it. It was her faxed copy of the cryptic little drawing on the back of Cecily's photograph of Rita Hayworth, the one she and Vic had showed Nigel and Stella. The drawing Cecily had with her when she died. Even Nigel agreed it looked like some sort of a griffin, the mythological beast that was half eagle, half lion. But why was it in a cage? Lacey looked up as the Acura sped past a stand of bare weeping willows overhanging Rock Creek.

"Damn! I'll never understand art! It's not a cage. It's a *willow* tree." She stared at the doodled drawing's shaky lines. "It's Willow. Willow has Stella."

"Who's Willow?"

"I told you about Willow, didn't I?"

"No. You never tell me anything. Start talking." Brooke glanced at Lacey's paper.

"Watch the road, please." The car bounced over a Washington pothole. Lacey smoothed the fax paper. "The drawing on the back of the photograph? First of all, it's not a stupid bird in a cage, or a robin in a Faraday cage, it's a griffin. And it's not in a cage." She held it up. "It's a weeping willow tree caging a griffin."

Brooke abruptly slammed on the brakes and turned into a driveway on P Street. She put the car in park.

"What did you stop for?" Lacey asked.

"I know what a safety nerd you are. Now let me see that." She examined the drawing closely in the flat winter light. Snowflakes were sticking to the windshield. Brooke looked up, her expression full of admiration. "Oh, Lacey, this is good. Very good! I'm so proud of you. It is a willow tree. Now what does that mean?"

"The important question is, where did Willow take her? We don't have a code for this, so Stella had to make it up. Hair falling out? Cold water rinse? Suds. Hard water. Cold dangerous water? Maybe whitewater, or a waterfall? And *set the activator in motion* just means 'Help! Hurry! Get moving!' Are you with me?" Brooke nodded and backed out of the driveway. Lacey closed her eyes and held her breath. She tried to listen to her EFP, the extra-*something*-ary perception Stella was always telling her she had. "Okay. I have it. Across the Key Bridge, take the GW Parkway north to Great Falls on the Virginia side of the Potomac."

"Got it. Tell me why in a minute, too busy to chat now." Brooke punched the accelerator and Lacey held on. The gray Acura sped west on P Street, past the grand town houses of Georgetown to Wisconsin Avenue and then down to M Street and west again. Lacey was always amazed how fast and efficiently her friend could drive through the convoluted streetscape of Washington, and Brooke knew every escape route home across the Potomac. Now if only it would stop snowing.

Brooke found an elusive hole in M Street traffic. She slipped the Acura through a yellow light onto the Key Bridge heading for Rosslyn. They were out of the District. They would be on the Virginia side of the river in less than a minute.

"Talk to me, Lacey."

"I'm thinking."

"Good. Stop thinking quietly and start thinking out loud. Why Great Falls?"

"Because it was the site of Stella and Nigel's famous outdoor assignation. Remember? You went *ewwww*? Cold dangerous water and the Falls. It's a hunch."

Brooke whistled. "Parkway to Chain Bridge to Old Georgetown Pike, right? Now tell me how we came to this awesome conclusion."

"First I have to call Vic." Lacey pulled out her cell phone.

"As long as I get to listen." On the Virginia side of the Potomac River Brooke turned onto the George Washington Parkway and headed north.

"Hey, sweetheart," Vic answered. "Have you seen—"

"I'm in hot pursuit. With Brooke."

"Hot pursuit of what? Lacey, slow down. It's snowing out there."

"Brooke is driving. We're good, but Stella is missing. Can you round up Nigel and meet us at Great Falls?"

"Great Falls?" His voice took on a darker tone. "This is no day for Great Falls. What's going on?"

"This is going to sound like a crazy story."

"Darling, I'd be pretty damn disappointed if it didn't. Hold on," he said to someone else. She heard another male voice in the background.

"It's Willow. I told you about Willow, didn't I? Everything points to Willow. Well, not everything, but enough. She killed Nina Vickers, she killed Cecily Ashton, and now she's got Stella. I want you to bring Nigel there so we can swap him for Stella."

"Hold on a minute, Lacey," Vic said. "Do *what* with Nigel?"

"Swap Nigel?" Brooke glanced uneasily at Lacey. "This is our big plan?"

Brooke was passing traffic uphill as they climbed the Parkway overlooking the Potomac. The trees were frosted with a white icing of snow, an alluring but dangerous scene. Lacey waved at her to watch the road.

To Vic she said, "We swap Nigel for Stella. Remember the drawing? It's not a cage holding that griffin, it's a willow! Like a weeping willow? For some reason Willow wants Griffin. God knows why. I say let's give him to her. In exchange for Stella."

"I'd like to say you've made this all perfectly clear. But"—Vic paused—"they're at Great Falls?"

"I'm pretty sure. You should know I don't have a lick of proof for any of this."

"All right. Nice snowy day for a walk in the park with my girl. And a killer. At least you're not leaving me out of the loop this time."

"Can you find Nigel?"

"Yup. Got him right here. He just ran into my office with this wild tale about Stella disappearing. He's frantic. We were just wondering where to start looking, but you already have this great plan. This *is* a great plan, isn't it?"

"Nigel's really worried about her?"

"Are you worried, Nigel?" Vic yelled away from the phone. Lacey heard Griffin yell something back to Vic, something like *". . . out of my bloody mind!"* Vic's voice was calm: "We're swapping you for Stella, Nigel. You're the fall guy. How do you like that?" She heard Griffin's voice rise an octave. "He's worried now," Vic said back to Lacey.

"Should we call the police, Vic? Tell them it's a kidnapping?"

"Are you sure it is? Tough call to make without proof," Vic said. "When someone goes missing the cops generally wait twenty-four hours, unless you have a witness to an abduction or a ransom note. We'll call when we get there and see what's going on."

"I adore you, Vic."

"You can prove it later. Keep your phone ready, I'll call you down the road. Keep in contact, don't do anything crazy, and don't take any risks."

"I wouldn't dream of it," she promised. They hung up. The way Brooke was speeding, Lacey wondered if they'd soon have a police escort without calling the cops.

"I'm listening, Lacey," Brooke said. "What's this got to do with Willow? I remember her, she's the mousy one being stalked by some wacko, right?"

"That was her story. And I swallowed it. Hook, line, and sinker." Lacey was still sorting out the picture in her head.

"How'd she find you? How does it involve Stella?"

"I'll start at the beginning. Keep in mind I'm making this up as I go along. In the beginning there was a plain little Willow who had a beautiful friend named Nina."

"The one who was killed in Philly?"

"Yeah. Last year sometime, Willow falls for a guy named Eric, but she creeps him out. He dates her friend Nina instead, so now a jealous Willow hates Eric and Nina. Then Nigel Griffin goes to Philly for Cecily's insurers, to run the security at an art gallery exhibiting Cecily's pretty things. Willow denied knowing Cecily, but in fact she worked on the exhibit at the gallery. So did Nina. Willow now sets her sights on our charming Nigel. Go figure, but some women love him. Willow is invisible to Nigel, who hooks up with beautiful Nina. Now Nina's taken two men away from her."

"Am I going to need a spreadsheet to follow this?"

"I hope not," Lacey said, "but if anyone could spreadsheet this, you could."

"So Willow killed Nina?"

"It's a theory. Yet Willow finds killing Nina doesn't get her either of the men she wants. Willow is obsessed with Nigel, but now there's another obstacle: Rich divorcée Cecily wants him too. And Nigel leaves Philly to chase the Romanov corset, and you and me and Kepelov, in France. He meets Stella in New Orleans, with me. Willow searches the Web for news of Nigel and finds his name in my stories in *The Eye*. How to get close to Nigel? Maybe by getting close to *me*. She signs up for the same PI class. She acts timid as a mouse, but she's turned a corner somehow and now she'll do anything to get whatever guy she locks in on. She can't afford a PI, so she'll become her own investigator."

"But how did she know you'd be in the PI class?"

"How, I wonder?" Lacey lifted one eyebrow as high as it would go. "Could it be Damon and his accursed Web site, where everything I do or think or plan to do is plastered all over his little gossip column? Courtesy of his number one spy girl, Brooke Barton, Esquire?"

"I plead the First Amendment, but point taken. Profuse apologies. Please continue."

"Willow needs to know everything about Nigel to get his attention. Being herself doesn't work. But she's a quick learner. She knows what Nigel likes now. He likes pretty flashy women, women who stand out in a crowd. Dark-haired Nina, brassy blondes. Nothing against blondes, Brooke. I'm the fashion reporter in her PI class, so she asks me what to do with her mousy hair and looks, and unknowingly I send her right to Stella. Bingo."

"And Stella does the rest," Brooke said. "She can't stop talking about Nigel, so Stella becomes target number three. But you can't blame yourself."

Lacey paused for a moment and closed her eyes. She was glad Brooke was driving, even if she was afraid to peek over at the speedometer.

"Willow knew something else about Nigel," Lacey continued. "He's drawn to rare and expensive luxury items. Like that Louis Vuitton makeup case of Cecily's that was on exhibit in Philly. If Willow could manage to get her hands on it, maybe she could arouse Nigel's interest after all." Lacey sighed. "It's a theory. Is this making any sense at all?"

"You know me, Lacey, the more out-there your theory is, the better I like it. But you're not saying Willow pulled off that weird little burglary, are you? How'd she do that?" The Acura skidded on a slick spot in the road. The Parkway hadn't been sanded yet, and the snow was starting to stick on the overpasses. Brooke smoothly eased off the gas and corrected their course.

"I don't know. It strikes me that Willow decided to become friends with Cecily too. She worked on the exhibit, so maybe the gallery sent her to D.C. with Cecily's collection to put it away again. Willow pays attention, learns the layout, the staff, the security codes, maybe she bribes someone, who knows? Or maybe she just hid in a closet till the house was empty. The place is huge, plenty of hiding places, with security cameras at the entrances, but not in all the rooms."

"Still, no one was suspicious?"

"People ignore Willow," Lacey said. "Before the makeover, anyway. She can be so meek and colorless that she melts into the background. Men never gave her a second glance. No one did, except for poor Nina. She's one of those people you try not to see."

"I know the type. You see them at a cocktail party and avoid them like the plague. Later when they mention it, you say, 'Oh I'm so sorry, I never *saw* you!'"

"She comes across as so pathetic you feel guilty for disliking her."

"I never feel guilty about that," Brooke said. "Pathetic is pathetic." Brooke turned off the Parkway at Chain Bridge Road. It was snowing a little harder now. "I turn on Georgetown Pike? First right past the CIA?"

"Don't you dare give this to Damon till after my story runs. Promise me, Brooke."

"But Lacey—"

"Swear on the Code."

"Oh, all right, I swear on the Code. Is there more?"

Lacey smiled triumphantly, even though she knew it wouldn't keep Damon off the story. "Willow steals the Rita Hayworth-Louis Vuitton makeup case and scoops up the pearl necklace and the jeweled picture frame. For some reason she can't resist a little taunt that only she understands. The sketch on the back of the photo. Her idea of a private joke, or perhaps a message to Cecily: The willow has the griffin in her grasp. Or *nyah nyah, I win.*"

"But why did she decide to kill Cecily? She did kill her, right?"

"I think so. She must have seen Cecily as her rival for Nigel, but I don't think Willow planned to kill her. Not until Cecily figured it out."

"What?! Cecily never even saw that drawing till you pointed it out to her!"

"Cecily drove out to Falls Church on her last day with a copy of the drawing in her purse. Trujillo told me the cops found it in her effects. She didn't know I was there, so she must have planned to show it to Bud Hunt, to convince him to help her with the burglary investigation." Lacey was certain she must have some of the details wrong, but the more she explained it to Brooke, the more sure she was of the big picture.

"Willow was late to class that first day, but of course no one paid any attention to her. She saw Cecily's Jaguar pull into the lot. Willow has a gun, possibly Eric O'Neil's stolen twenty-two revolver. She and Cecily may have had words, I have no idea, but it ends with Willow shooting her in the head and walking away. She had time to hide the gun, wash her hands, and slip into class. The entire class was her alibi."

"She won the lottery with that." Brooke said, dodging a sand truck which had finally arrived to impede their progress. "Idiot luck."

"She got lucky the first time, when she killed Nina," Lacey said. "I guess she figured she could get away with it again. And she did."

"But what a screwy plan!" Brooke was incredulous. "I can't believe no one saw her. Or heard the gunshot."

"She didn't plan that part. Vic says gunshots on the street are routinely ignored."

"Right, that's why the District is putting microphones on rooftops to listen for gunfire," Brooke interrupted. "Go on."

"Willow's the original invisible woman, which is why I thought she'd make a good PI. I think it made her crazy. Irrational. But methodical. Willow also recognized Stella's key from Nigel. She knows it fits the Louis Vuitton makeup case, because she has the case."

Willow had even begged Stella to let her touch the key, and the gesture had seemed so touching and pathetic. It made Lacey sick now to think she had been the link that led a killer to her friend.

"What? Stella has the key to that thing?" Brooke slowed to pass another sand truck where Chain Bridge Road met Dolley Madison Boulevard in McLean. She gave Lacey a long look. "You never told me that."

"I've been busy." She sighed deeply. Suddenly a staccato burst of static cut across the soft classical music from WETA on the radio.

"Did you hear that?" Brooke said. "My radio does that every time I go past the CIA! Right here on Chain Bridge, or on the Parkway on the other side. That *dit dada dit dada dit dit dit* and so on, like a telegraph key? I swear it must be the CIA spy frequency jammers. Did that sound like Morse Code to you? They're probably saying, *WE control the vertical! WE control the horizontal!*"

"You've been reading too much DeadFed, Brooke. And listening to Martin Hadley. It's probably just their lunch-break whistle or something."

"We're skipping lunch today. Listen, I don't really want to ask this, Lacey, but why not just—*dispose* of Stella? Why bother taking her somewhere?"

"Oh, that's the weird part."

"*All* the parts of this are the weird parts."

"Willow wants to know how to capture Nigel's heart. Apparently Stella already has, so Willow wants to become Stella. Only more so. Stella dyed her hair blond to please Nigel. So Willow goes blonder. Stella was rocking her wacky take on Swinging Sixties couture, so Willow goes all the way back to Marilyn Monroe. Stella and Nigel had a passionate escapade at Great Falls, so maybe Willow needs to see that and raise it. But to do that she needs to learn all about how to be a better, blonder, sexier Stella for Nigel. She needs to suck the last drop of Stella-ness out of our friend. Stella's already given her the big makeover, now all she needs to do is talk. And heaven knows, Stella is always willing to talk."

"Like you said, Lacey, it's a theory. The only theory we've got. It's crazy. I like it." Brooke turned right on Old Georgetown Pike and headed toward Great Falls. "My God, it's snowing baseballs out here. How much snow are we supposed to get today?"

Lacey fought back tears. She hoped desperately they were speeding off in the right direction, not just plunging foolishly off into the snowy woods on a wild Willow chase.

She prayed that Stella was right now somewhere at Great Falls, eagerly babbling to Willow everything she possibly could tell her about anything she could possibly think of, spinning it out and playing for time until her friends could get there. *And do what exactly? Make a deal with a crazy woman?*

"Brooke, I don't want to think about what happens when Willow gets everything she wants from Stella, and Stella runs out of things to tell her! What happens when they stop talking?"

"Don't worry, Lacey. Stella never stops talking."

chapter 37

The road to Great Falls National Park lay deceptively peaceful beneath a thin blanket of fresh snow. Lacey's cell phone rang and made her jump. She didn't recognize the number.

"Lacey, Marie Largesse here. I'm worried about Stella. I haven't been able to find her. Y'all seen her today?"

"I'm looking for her right now, with Brooke."

"That's good. Always fight evil in numbers. You know, the reason I called, I keep seeing and hearing that thunder snow I told Stella about."

"It is snowing." The storm was heavier here above the Falls, and the Acura's windshield wipers were having trouble keeping up with it.

"No sugar, that's not it. The sound is *like* thunder, but it's really gunfire, I think, and Stella is— Oh, hang on, I'm a little dizzy! And Stella—"

"And Stella what, Marie? Marie! Are you there?"

"Now what?" Brooke hunched over the steering wheel and squinted through the snow. She turned into the park entrance and drove on through the gate. It was off season, and a snow day. There was no one at the little entrance booth to take their fee.

"It's Marie, but she—"

Another voice came on the line. "Smithsonian, is that you?"

"Kepelov? What happened? You're with Marie?"

"She fainted," Kepelov answered. "I think it is not a good sign."

"Oh, hell. We're screwed."

"What?" Brooke said.

"Marie fainted." Lacey fought a feeling of nausea. "It's a bad sign."

"Lacey Smithsonian, where are you right now?" Kepelov demanded.

"At Great Falls Park, looking for Stella. We just drove in the gate. I think she's been kidnapped by Willow Raynor. Long story."

"Ah. The little mouse. I never trust her. Too quiet. Never look you in the eye."

"Now you tell me."

"We are coming there. We will find you." Kepelov hung up.

"Hey," Brooke said, "what kind of reporter are you? Give me the news."

"Kepelov said he and Marie are coming. And I don't know if that's a good thing or a bad thing."

"If he's on our side for a change, I'll take him," Brooke said. "But good luck getting here in this storm, Kepelov."

Lacey's phone rang again. Mac's number popped up. She thought about letting it go to voice mail, but she picked up. "Yes, Mac."

"Where are you? Kim tells me the girls are worried about you and your pal Stella." He sounded exasperated.

"Hard to explain."

"You're a wordsmith. Start talking."

Lacey gave Mac the briefest possible version, promising an update soon. Mac was noncommittal about her story, but Lacey thought her own theory of why Willow would kidnap Stella sounded a little less improbable every time she told it. Mac laid down the law: He would run no stories about this till the shooter was caught.

Brooke swung the Acura into the nearly empty parking lot by the Great Falls Park visitors' center. The pavement was still wet and dark, but snow was already starting to cover a few Park Service vehicles. They hadn't moved for a while. There was only one other car: Stella's bright red Mini Cooper with an American flag painted on the roof. Lacey felt relieved and vindicated. So far her hunch, and her reading of the Code, was working.

Brooke parked next to the Mini. It was locked and empty. There was no one around. The park was silent and deserted in the snow. The visitors' center, the Potomac River, and Great Falls itself lay just down the trail through the trees. There were faint footprints in the fresh snow on the trail, two sets of prints partially filled in by fresh snow, one in boots, the other wearing high heels. *Only Stella would be wearing stilettos with a snowstorm on the way,* Lacey thought.

"I hate to sound like you, Brooke," Lacey said, "but I think we have to formulate a plan."

"Don't worry, I have a plan. I have a gun in the trunk."

"A gun? You keep a gun in the car?"

"Chill, Lacey, I'm heading to the range tonight with Damon. I *was*, anyway. All bets are off now. But I only brought the three fifty-seven. It'll have to do."

Brooke opened the trunk of the gray Acura. She unlocked her padded gun case and calmly loaded the shiny stainless Smith & Wesson revolver. Lacey felt her heart pounding.

"I don't want to use a gun, Brooke! I just want to keep her talking till Vic and Nigel get here. Maybe we can solve this without—"

"Talk all you want. I'm loading the gun. Now what? Wait for Vic?"

"No, we have to find Stella." Lacey pulled out her phone and called Vic. "We're here at Great Falls. Where are you?"

"We're on the road. It's a mess out here. There was a pileup in the snow on the damn Parkway, you must have missed it. The Jeep is good, but there are cars sliding all over the road. Where are you exactly? Is anybody else there? Nigel says he and Stella have been up there before. Do you see anything?"

"We're right by Stella's car in the lot. I see two sets of footprints in the snow."

"You spotted her yet?"

"No, but only Stella would wear those death-defying heels out in this weather."

"Okay, I'm calling the big dogs in. I'm just afraid the police will be busy working all the roads, who knows what they can spare for this." Vic said something to Nigel, then returned to Lacey. "We'll be there in five, maybe ten minutes. Wait for us."

The footprints on the trail were beginning to fade beneath the new fallen snow. It was getting colder and Lacey could just imagine Stella out there in the blowing snow, wearing practically nothing, as usual, and in those sky-high heels she loved so much. And Willow, pointing a gun at her head.

"That's too long, Vic! I can't leave Stella out there with that woman!"

"You don't know what you're getting into here. Lacey, I'm serious. Please wait for me. Five minutes!"

Lacey took a deep breath. "No, Vic."

"What? Lacey—"

"I can't wait for you. Please come quickly before *my* footprints disappear." She clicked off the phone. He rang back instantly. She let it ring. She turned to Brooke and brushed a little snow from her friend's hair.

"Let's go find Stella," Lacey said. Brooke nodded and picked up the gun.

The footprints led them through the passageway between the two small buildings of the visitors' center, and the park opened up before them. Below the bluffs on their left they could hear the roaring of the Great Falls of the Potomac. The river tumbled over massive boulders into whitewater before funneling into the narrow Mather Gorge. The main trail led south past a picnic area to hiking trails down the river. Smaller trails forked off to the bluffs and cliffs. Lacey and Brooke stopped where a short side trail led off to a wide cliffside observation deck commanding a dramatic view of the falls.

"Didn't Stella mention the roar of the falls?" Brooke asked. "When she was here doing the deed with Nigel?"

Over the rushing water a clap of thunder split the air like a gunshot. They both jumped. Lightning illuminated the low gray clouds. Thunder, not gunfire.

Lacey was grateful she'd worn tall leather boots and her wool slacks. She fastened her coat and snugged down her faux fur hat.

"Perfect," Brooke muttered, pulling on her stocking cap.

"Now we have thunder *and* snow. Yay, Marie. Which trail? Any ideas?"

Where are you, Stella? Lacey tried to remember exactly where Stella said she and Nigel had enjoyed their Great Falls sexcapade. One of the overlooks above the river? The highest one? That would fit Stella's flair for exhibitionism.

"This way." Lacey pointed to the next trail. Through the bare trees they caught a glimpse of a tiny walled overlook at the highest crest of the bluff above the Potomac. The trail twisted around trees and climbed over wet boulders and exposed bedrock, slippery with snow. As they came around one boulder, Lacey caught sight of two blondes standing at the edge, beside a jagged wall of rough native stone and masonry surmounted by a waist-high wooden railing. Below them, the waters roiled and rumbled over stone as they had for eons. The thunder cracked again.

Wrapped in a silver parka, Willow looked like an otherworldly creature, a snow witch or an ice goddess. Her startling white-blond hair was dusted with blowing snow, and the only color in her face was on her lips, a smear of blood-red lipstick. She was pointing a gun at Stella, who was wobbling on her high heels, shivering in her baby blue jacket and tight blue slacks.

"We have to get closer." Lacey led Brooke off the trail and over the rocks, slipping behind one boulder after another. As they came around the last boulder, another flash of lightning lit the snow. They heard yelling, but the words were muffled by the storm. Willow poked her hostage with the gun and made her turn to face the Falls. Lacey saw Stella peer down over the side of the bluff into the black water below.

Lacey and Brooke moved closer to the overlook, crouching low, until they were within fifty feet of the women. If there was some way to distract Willow, Stella might be able to make a break for it. Lacey eyed fallen branches she could throw to get her attention. But the choice was made for her: A branch laden with heavy wet snow cracked above their head and fell at Lacey's feet, blowing her cover.

Stella spun around and saw Lacey and her eyes went

wide. "Oh my God, Lacey, I knew you'd come and get me, but where's the posse?"

Willow turned to face them. Around her neck, she wore a fortune in Cecily's pearls—the pearls that had once belonged to Rita Hayworth.

"What are you doing here?" she screamed. "Go away!"

Lacey stepped behind a nearby tree, Brooke right behind her. "Put the gun down, Willow. Don't do anything stupid."

"I'm not stupid! Don't you know that by now? Don't tell me what to do! I know what I want and I'm going to have it."

"You're right, you do. You wanted Cecily's antique makeup case and her pearls, and you took them, didn't you?"

"She didn't need them. She had so many other beautiful things. Cecily had too many things. I'm just redistributing the wealth."

"I think you're really smart, Willow." Lacey was willing to bet Willow craved a little recognition for all her accomplishments.

Willow smiled. "It was pretty easy."

"You really fooled me. All of us."

"Not too hard. I just followed Mr. Hunt's rules. I joined your girls' club to learn more about Nigel."

Stella couldn't contain herself any longer. "Lacey, she wants my Nigel."

"Shut up, bitch," Willow screamed at Stella. She grabbed Stella's throat with one hand and pointed her gun at Lacey, a large flat black automatic pistol. Lacey couldn't identify it, but it certainly wasn't Eric O'Neil's old .22 revolver, the gun she expected Willow to have.

"Where did you get that gun?" Lacey asked. She was aware of movement behind her. Brooke was getting impatient behind her tree.

"I don't know," Willow said. "Somebody reported it stolen."

"Like Eric did, when you stole his gun to shoot Nina? And Cecily too, right?"

"I had to get rid of that one," Willow said.

"You must have really hated Nina," Lacey said.

"No!" Willow waved the gun for emphasis. "I never hated her. Nina was my friend, but she got in the way. No one ever looked at me when she was around. That's the way it was. But not anymore."

"I know you want Nigel, but you don't have to hurt Stella to get him now."

Willow's hollow laugh carried over the falling water and the wind. It was the first time Lacey had heard her laugh. "And why is that?"

"Because Nigel's coming here," Lacey said. "He'll be here any minute. Nigel is who you really want, isn't it? You take him, we'll take Stella, and nobody will get hurt." She took a step forward.

"Nigel isn't all I want. Don't come any closer." Willow held the gun in her right hand, and from her left dangled a key on a gold chain. Stella's key.

"You have everything you need, Willow. You're a whole new woman now. You have what Nigel wants. You have the key. And now you'll have Nigel too." Lacey took another step.

The woman laughed again. "It's mine now, not hers. Nigel belongs to me."

"That's right. Everything's all right now."

"Lacey, what are you doing?" Stella blurted out. "You can't let her take Nigel—"

"Shut up!" Willow commanded with a wave of the gun. To Lacey she said, "I have to kill her so he'll never have to think about her again. It's only logical."

"You're wrong about that, Willow," Lacey said. "If you kill Stella, he'll always remember her. He'll never stop thinking about her. But if you let her go, he'll forget all about her, and he'll focus on you. That's what you want."

"She's right," Brooke broke in from her tree next to Lacey, her gun held out of sight at her side. "He'll forget her. But if you kill her, he'll dream about her. For the rest of his life."

"Hey, what do you mean he'll forget about me?" Stella complained.

Willow tightened her chokehold on Stella and swung the gun at Brooke. "Who is that?"

"I'm a friend," Brooke said.

"You're not my friend. You go away," Willow commanded. "Both of you. Before I kill you both."

The next lightning strike was so close it must have hit the river. The thunder was deafening. Stella grabbed for the gun, but Willow smashed her across the face with it. Stella staggered back against the wall. Willow spun around toward Lacey and Brooke and fired. Lacey saw the flash from the muzzle, but the sound of the gun was lost in another crack of thunder. Brooke pushed backward into Lacey and they both hit the cold wet ground.

Lacey shoved Brooke bodily into the mud and snow behind a boulder and dived in after her. "Brooke! Are you all right?" She could hear Willow laughing over the roar of the Falls.

"Yes! I'm okay, but that bitch is totally out of her mind. Come on, let's go get her." Brooke crouched and brushed wet leaves and snow from her stainless steel revolver. "We'll make her wish she was never born." Lacey pushed her back down to the ground with a plop. Brooke looked up at her in surprise.

"No. Just me. This is my battle, Brooke. I need your gun."

"Wait a minute! You're the one who didn't want to use the gun—"

"It has to be me," Lacey said. "I'm the one who sent Willow to Stella, I'm the one who has to fix it. I need the gun. Now!" Another bullet flew over their heads and ricocheted off the rocks behind them. They ducked again. "If anything happens to Stella, I'll never forgive myself. So don't even think about adding to my psychic burden by getting in the way of a bullet here!"

Brooke stared at her. "But Lacey—"

"Please, just stay here and wait for Vic. I can't wait any longer."

Brooke reluctantly handed over the .357. "I'll be right behind you."

In her peripheral vision, Lacey caught sight of a dark line coming her way, a line of men: Vic in a knitted cap, bareheaded Nigel, and Kepelov in some sort of big Russian fur hat. But they were very far away up the trail in the snow.

More bullets screamed over Lacey's head through the tree branches and falling snow. She crouched down and slipped out from behind the rocks and trees to get a clear line of sight at Willow. She heard Stella screaming. Lacey reached the uneven open ground at the overlook to see Willow and Stella struggling by the wall. Stella fell hard on her bottom, high heels in the air. Willow lunged for her, but Stella grabbed for the gun and tripped her. Willow went down, the gun went flying, and Stella raked Willow's face with her candy-pink talons. She drew blood.

Then a voice came out of the storm. It carried an English accent, but somehow he sounded like any frightened man shouting for the woman he loved.

"Stella! Stella!" It was Nigel's voice, followed by Nigel himself, slipping and falling in the snow, a hundred yards or more up the twisting trail. Lacey caught a glimpse of Vic, just ahead of him.

"Nigel!" Stella screamed back. "I'm here, Nigel!" She clambered to her feet and leaned back against the railing to catch her breath. She shielded her eyes to peer through the snow for Nigel. Willow was on her knees pawing through the wet leaves. She found the gun at Stella's feet and sat up and looked at it.

"Stella, look out!" Lacey screamed. She ran toward them carrying Brooke's gun. Willow fired wildly at her. Lacey ducked and slid in the snow and nearly fell down. Stella reached down for Willow's gun, but Willow grabbed Stella's legs and lifted her up over the railing and pushed. Stella disappeared over the wall. Her cries died away into the roar of the river.

"No!" Lacey screamed.

"You're next." Willow laughed and waved her gun at the place where Stella disappeared. "I have to kill you too. You have to go over the wall."

You don't shoot to kill. You just shoot to stop. Vic's words came back to Lacey. With tears running down her face, she swung the revolver into her shooting stance with both hands and steadied her grip.

"What? You're going to shoot me?" Willow taunted her.

"I don't think so. You're just a silly pretty girl, a weakling. You don't know how to do this. I do." Her laughter carried on the wind between thunderclaps. She pointed the black pistol at Lacey.

Lacey aligned her gunsights on the center of Willow's torso, just as if she were aiming at a silhouette target at the range. She held her breath and squeezed the trigger. The sharp crack of the .357 was lost in the thunder.

Willow fell.

chapter 38

Blood turned the snow to red slush beneath Willow's body. Lightning flashed again, farther away this time. The thunder rumbled down the river and headed for Washington. The snow was falling harder now, but the wind was dying down.

Willow's gun had flown from her hand when she fell. She groaned and tried to roll over, clawing with both hands for the gun in the snow. Brooke sprinted to her and kicked Willow's gun far away from her searching hands. The woman on the ground screamed in pain, her white blond hair streaked with mud and leaves. Brooke stood guard over her.

"I'll kill you, you filthy hags!" Willow screeched. "I'll kill you! I'll kill you both!"

"No, you won't," Brooke said. "You're lucky to be alive."

Lacey sprang to the railing and peered over the rock wall where Stella had disappeared. "Oh, God. Stella." Tears blurred her vision. Vic was suddenly there beside her, his arms wrapped around her.

"You did good, darling. I saw it all. I'm so damn relieved you're alive."

"I don't know, Vic. . . ." Lacey looked past his shoulder to see Stella lying among the rocks below the bluff, wedged between the boulders among a tangle of tree branches and leaves. She was moving. She was alive.

Griffin ran up to the wall puffing furiously and vaulted right over it, crying, "Stella!" He grabbed at the railing with one arm and searched for a foothold on the other side. He didn't find one and he fell, scrambling, sliding, and banging down the rocks. Lacey watched him and flinched with each thump. He finally fell the last dozen feet to the tangled branches, not far from Stella. He crawled to her and brushed blood and damp hair from her forehead.

"Stella my love, are you all right?"

"I am freezing my damn ass off, Nigel baby, and I think there's something wrong with my ankle. It's like totally broken. Will you please get me the hell out of here, and by the way I love you!"

Oh yeah, that's our Stella. She'll be all right. I hope.

Nigel's clipped voice came up from below. "I say up there! How about a hand? Or a rope?"

"Wait till the rescuers get here, Griffin!" Lacey hollered down to them over the roar of the water. "Don't move her! Just put your jacket over her and keep her warm, I'm calling nine-one-one right now!"

"They're already on their way." Vic folded her into his arms. "I called the Park Police. They're sending a helicopter. You did exactly the right thing."

Lacey felt weak. Vic's arms suddenly were the only things holding her up. "Can they take us out of here?" She sobbed into his shoulder and let him take Brooke's gun from her hand.

"No rescue choppers for you, darling, you're coming home with me. I'm your rescue team."

Willow hissed at them from the red slush where she lay under Brooke's watch. "You tried to kill me! You'll go to prison! This is all your fault! How did you even know where we were? How'd that hairdresser hag warn you?"

Lacey crouched down and spoke low so only Willow could hear. "We have a secret code. Stella told me over the phone, right under your nose. If you were really part of our girls' club, you would have known that. But you'll never be a member of our club, Willow. You're the one going to prison. You'll be invisible again."

Vic squatted beside Willow to look her over. The gunshot wound was in her abdomen and she was bleeding heavily. He took Willow's right hand and pressed it firmly against her wound. She grimaced in pain.

Kepelov trudged up to the observation platform and grinned at them. He kissed Lacey on both cheeks and said he would help with Willow. Lacey suspected that aside from his questionable humanitarian instincts, Kepelov just wanted a closer look at the priceless pearls around Willow's throat. He knelt down in the snow beside her and took over applying pressure on her wound to stop the bleeding. Willow spat at him like a snake.

"Is this a nice way to behave when people are saving your worthless life?" Kepelov pressed a bit harder on the wound and she turned her face away. "You remind me of Snow Queen. Heart of ice."

"I think she'll live. That was a pretty good shot, Lacey," Vic said. "You been practicing without me? What did I say about waiting for me?" He held her tight and whispered something gently into her hair.

"I couldn't wait any longer," Lacey said. "I ran out of time."

Marie Largesse brought up the rear, bright against the white landscape in a splash of red and purple, her long black curls dotted with snow. She carried a stack of colorful blankets in her arms. She walked right up to the railing with them and dropped a couple of them over the edge to Stella and Nigel.

"I had the worst feeling," she explained to Lacey. "Cold to my bone. A vision of Stella in the icy river." She wrapped Lacey's shoulders in a blanket and hugged her.

Brooke stood over Willow, furiously keying away on her BlackBerry to Damon Newhouse. With his free hand, Kepelov took a flask from his jacket and offered it to Lacey.

"Hard day, Lacey Smithsonian? Have a drink. Warm you up."

"You could say it's been a hard day." She took a sip of his vodka and coughed, but he was right, it warmed her immediately.

"We shall talk at length about this someday."

"Over barbecue at your ranch in Texas?" Vic said.

"Excellent idea," the old spy agreed. "By a roaring fire." He turned his attention back to Willow and her gunshot wound (and her pearls), while Marie crouched beside him with her hand on his shoulder. She covered Willow with another blanket, and Willow stopped struggling.

The tableau suddenly struck Lacey as a scene from a fairy tale. Something that might be hand-painted on a set of Kepelov's nested Russian dolls. The fallen snow witch, the big blond Russian spy, and the Gypsy woman kneeling in the drifting snow beside the river.

chapter 39

"Tell me about the Pink Collar Code." Vic nuzzled Lacey's ear.

"You'll have to subpoena me, copper," Lacey said. The Code had become a little game between them. She nuzzled him back. She couldn't resist him in a tuxedo. She couldn't resist him in anything, she decided. Lacey wore a lipstick red crepe cocktail dress that had been her Aunt Mimi's. She felt it suited the occasion quite as well as his tuxedo. "And I'll never talk, not even under oath. I know *nothing*."

"That's not what Stella says."

"Stella's got a big mouth, or haven't you heard? Ask her yourself. Stella will tell you *everything*. Except the Code."

While the Park Service rescue team was loading her into the helicopter at Great Falls, Stella kept babbling about "the Code," how Lacey and Brooke and the Code had saved her life, how they were now "the Sisterhood of the Pink Collar Code." Lacey chalked it up to stress, and relief, and the painkillers the paramedics gave Stella for her broken ankle and the bumps and bruises from her fall into the rocks. And to Stella's flair for the dramatic.

Vic and the other guys had heard plenty about the Code since then from Stella, but not the Code itself. The Code was too important to reveal to mere men, Stella said. "And like, what if we need to use it again? It's totally top secret! The Sisterhood can't have just everyone knowing our business!"

Lacey wasn't about to break the Sisterhood of the Code, not even for Vic. And she certainly wasn't about to hand over Brooke's top-secret document, the one she and Stella never quite got around to reading. Vic would find it all way too hilarious. Something he and the guys would chortle about at the next meeting of the No-Girls-Allowed Boys' Club. He and Nigel Griffin even tried to puzzle it out together from Stella's cryptic message to Lacey. They didn't get very far. They got about as far as "curly pink hair."

Nigel seemed different now, after that day at Great Falls. He suffered a wealth of scrapes and lacerations himself, but no broken bones. He and Vic were not quite as antagonistic. Not exactly old friends either, no matter how much Nigel tried to play on their prep school ties, but not quite enemies anymore.

"Come on." Vic was at his seductive best in a tux. "You can trust me. Besides, I'll bribe you. I'll buy you dinner after this thing is over. I'll even go dancing with you. That's a serious bribe, darling."

Laughing, Lacey broke from his embrace to admire another display in the Cecily Ashton exhibit at the Fashion Museum. It was the opening night reception and there were champagne and music and beautiful things, and she wanted to see *everything*.

She ran into Mac and Kim, resplendent in their evening attire, though Mac kept tugging at the collar of his starched tuxedo shirt. Mac had astonished Lacey at the newsroom the day before with the announcement that he wouldn't dream of missing the exhibit. "After all the trouble that woman caused," he grumbled. "Almost lost me a reporter. I'm not about to miss seeing that stuff!"

Mac and Kim took her aside at the reception. Mac had a gleam in his eye. "Kelly Kavanaugh's been sniffing around your beat, you know," he said.

"Kavanaugh of the cops beat? Khakis and sneakers, more freckles than sense?" Lacey was taken aback. "She's interested in the fashion beat? What for?"

"She says she thinks it might be interesting, all those weird crime stories you work. Says maybe she could bring something new to the fashion beat."

Lacey knew Mac was baiting her, but she bit anyway.

"Well, what she brought wouldn't be any fashion sense! Kelly Kavanaugh wouldn't know extra-fashionary perception if it bit her in the—" She caught Kim's amused expression. "Kavanaugh couldn't write her way out of a Wal-Mart shopping bag."

Mac lifted one woolly eyebrow. "She gives me column inches on deadline, what more could an editor ask for? And if you took her on as a junior, it would take some of the load off you. I'd still need a fashion column from you, say half the time. The other half, you could tackle some other kind of stories, whatever you want to tackle. Write your own beat. After this story? You get a free pass. Within reason, of course."

Is this really Mac? Are we really having this conversation? "Give me a break, Mac. Trying to run half a brand-new beat while I train a junior fashion reporter, one without a stylish bone in her body? In what universe? Ask me again Monday morning. I'll have a list of demands. We'll talk." Mac just laughed.

She found Vic again and led him to the one thing she most wanted to see. It was Cecily's Rita Hayworth makeup case by Louis Vuitton, safe within its Plexiglas enclosure, illuminated like the rare treasure it was. The fine tooled red leather and brass fittings gleamed beneath the spotlights. The case was propped open and tilted forward, so the mirrored panels could reveal all of its many velvet-lined drawers and hidden compartments. Rita Hayworth's priceless pearls spilled out from their red velvet-lined secret drawer and hung free in the light like a frozen waterfall. Beside the case lay its small jeweled skeleton key on its own pool of red velvet, reunited at last.

Lacey turned at the sound of crutches tapping on the polished wooden floor.

"Stella, look at you! You're mobile! And indomitable!" Stella wore a very sleek little black dress, cut just a little too low and a little too tight to be perfectly classic. Thinking herself, no doubt, Audrey Hepburn, but with boobs. On crutches, with a cast.

"Damn straight I'm indomitable, whatever that is."

Stella's cast was hot pink and covered with rhinestones. "Mobile? Not so much."

"The rhinestones are a nice touch. Very sparkly."

"Totally! I did it myself. I've spent so much time on my ass with this cast, I had to do something. And you don't think I'm gonna miss my chance to see this fancy-schmancy Louis Vuitton makeup case, do you? I overpaid my dues for this thing."

Stella swung herself right up to the Plexiglas enclosure on her crutches. She stared quizzically at the case and shook her head, which was now a mass of tousled cupid curls in a lovely mahogany brown. The blond "Gidget Gone Wild" look was long gone.

"I like your hair." Lacey gave her a quick hug and ruffled her curls.

"Yeah, well, the blond thing wasn't working for me, you know what I mean? You're born to be a blonde or you're not, Lacey, and I am *so* not a blonde." Stella's smile was almost impish. She tilted her head at the Rita Hayworth case. "I don't know, Lace, I thought this thing would be lots bigger somehow. Like a whole freakin' steamer trunk or something, you know? We nearly died over that thing."

"Sorry you couldn't keep the key."

Stella had been happy in the end to part with the key, much to Lacey's surprise. "Are you kidding me? That key is totally cursed, like the Hope freakin' Diamond." The beautiful golden key had caused her and Nigel quite enough trouble, and she wasn't about to wear it ever again.

"Totally okay. I got something lots better in trade." She lifted her left hand off her crutch and wiggled her fingers.

"Oh, my God, Stel, a diamond? A *big* diamond!"

"And you know, he picked it out *himself.*" Stella started laughing. "Can you believe it? It's humongous! One point seven-five carats. I counted 'em personally."

Lacey heard the sound of laughter behind them. More of their party had arrived. Marie Largesse and Gregor Kepelov, hand in improbable hand, and Nigel Griffin, in a tux and hobbling along on crutches with considerably less grace than Stella. He had twisted an ankle and torn a knee tumbling down the rocks at Great Falls.

It was still a minor mystery to Lacey just who had managed to retrieve the case for the Ashton estate before the police got around to searching Willow's apartment. It might easily have ended up in a police evidence locker, never to be seen again. Lacey thought it was much more beautiful right where it was, where people could marvel at this relic of legendary Hollywood glamour. Perhaps Griffin was a better stolen jewel retriever than Lacey had given him credit for. He, unlike Stella, wasn't talking. And Lacey suspected Kepelov, Griffin's now-and-again partner, was a key player in the retrieval of the lost goods.

Brooke and Damon hadn't arrived yet, but they were on their way. The plan was to see Cecily's memorial exhibit and be seen at the reception and then go to dinner. It had been Stella's idea originally, but everyone wanted to go. "It's a celebration, get it? We're celebrating being alive," Stella had said. "And it's an order!"

They could always leave early, Vic promised Lacey, if she really couldn't stand this motley company. But she knew she would tough it out, for the sake of her last guest, Cecily's friend Simon Edison, who finally appeared in the exhibit hall, a little dazed by the glittering crowd. His rented tuxedo looked like it was trying to climb right off his back. He spied Lacey and marched straight up to her at the display case as if they were the only ones in the room.

"I want you to see something," he said. He grinned and led her to an exhibit in a far corner, one of the mannequins wearing Cecily's beautiful face. She was gowned in a simple vintage halter top dress in ivory. Over her outstretched hands was draped a length of shimmering gold material, a metallic mesh shawl. "What do you think?"

Lacey looked at Simon and then back at the shawl. "They recovered the fabric? The Celestine fabric?"

"Yes, it's the Celestine. It's for our girl."

Lacey kissed him on the cheek. He blushed. "Let me introduce you to the others." She handed him off to Stella, who happily latched on to him and chattered away like a magpie. Simon wouldn't have to say another word all night.

"Alone at last." Vic swept her away to a dimly lit corner with a glass of champagne.

"I can't believe Nigel gave her the ring," Lacey told him, thunderstruck. "He must really love her. Is that even possible? I mean Stella's pretty lovable, but Nigel?"

"Danger makes the heart grow fonder, darling. Haven't you learned that yet?" He leaned toward her, his green eyes alight with amusement. And something else. "Reminds you of what's really precious to you. Shows you what it would feel like to lose it. Makes you willing to make a commitment to keep it."

"Like hurling yourself over a cliff?"

"Like that. And that's what I'm talking about. Hurling myself over a cliff."

Lacey's breath caught in her throat. "Is that what it feels like?" *Are we really talking about what I think we're talking about?*

"Sometimes. A little. Sometimes it's like climbing a mountain. Or flying high above the clouds. But it's quite a ride, either way."

"Don't worry, cowboy, I'll catch you if you fall." She held his tuxedo lapels and pulled him closer.

"You promise? I'm already falling."

"Promise." Lacey felt her eyes filling up. "Whether we're falling or flying."

"I'll never let you fall. I promise. You're dangerous, Smithsonian, and danger makes the heart—"

"Love longer." She sealed the deal with a kiss.

By the time they finally left the reception, the champagne was all gone and the crowd had thinned out. The party was winding down. As Lacey took Vic's arm to leave, she looked back into the hall, nearly empty now but for the beautiful things Cecily had loved, floating in their pools of light.

Lacey hadn't seen Philip Clark Ashton there that evening. She had never expected to see him again. But there he was. An elderly man sitting alone on a bench, staring at the lovely mannequins that still wore his wife's face.

A **Crime of Fashion** Mystery

by Ellen Byerrum

Designer Knockoff

When fashion columnist Lacey Smithsonian
learns that a new fashion museum will soon grace
decidedly unfashionable D.C., it's more than a good
story—it's a chance to show off her vintage Hugh
Bentley suit. And when the designer, himself, notices her
at the opening, Lacey gets the scoop on his past—which
includes a long-unsolved mystery about a missing
employee. When a Washington intern disappears, Lacey
gets suspicious and sets out to unravel the murderous
details in a fabric of lies, greed,
and (gasp!) very bad taste.

Also in the **Crime of Fashion** series:

Killer Hair
Hostile Makeover
Raiders of the Lost Corset
Grave Apparel

**Available wherever books are sold or at
penguin.com**

ELAINE VIETS

Josie Marcus, Mystery Shopper

High Heels Are Murder

Every job has its pluses and minuses. Josie Marcus gets to
shoe-shop ... but she also must deal with men like Mel
Poulaine, who's *too* interested in handling women's feet.
Soon Josie's been hired by Mel's boss to mystery-shop the
store, but one step leads to another and Josie finds herself
in St. Louis's seedy underbelly. Caught up in a web of
crime, Josie hopes against hope that she won't end up
murdered in Manolos.

Accessory to Murder

Someone has killed Halley Hardwicke, the hot young
designer of thousand-dollar Italian silk scarves, in the mall
parking lot—and police have their eye on Jake, the
husband of Josie's best friend Alyce. The couple lived near
the wrap maven, but it seems Halley and Jake were a little
too neighborly. So Josie decides to do what she does best
to help out her friend—go undercover and see if she can
find some clues. Because this time, there's a lot more at
stake than a scarf, even if it's to die for...

**Available wherever books are sold or
at penguin.com**

The Bestselling
Blackbird Sisters Mystery Series
by
Nancy Martin

Don't miss a single adventure of the Blackbird sisters, a trio of Philadelphia-born, hot-blooded bluebloods with a flair for fashion—and for solving crimes.

Also Available:

How to Murder a Millionaire
Dead Girls Don't Wear Diamonds
Some Like It Lethal
Cross Your Heart and Hope to Die
Have Your Cake and Kill Him Too
A Crazy Little Thing Called Death
Murder Melts in Your Mouth

**Available wherever books are sold or at
penguin.com**

Penguin Group (USA) Online

What will you be reading tomorrow?

Tom Clancy, Patricia Cornwell, W.E.B. Griffin,
Nora Roberts, William Gibson, Robin Cook,
Brian Jacques, Catherine Coulter, Stephen King,
Dean Koontz, Ken Follett, Clive Cussler,
Eric Jerome Dickey, John Sandford,
Terry McMillan, Sue Monk Kidd, Amy Tan,
John Berendt...

You'll find them all at
penguin.com

Read excerpts and newsletters,
find tour schedules and reading group guides,
and enter contests.

Subscribe to Penguin Group (USA) newsletters
and get an exclusive inside look
at exciting new titles and the authors you love
long before everyone else does.

PENGUIN GROUP (USA)
us.penguingroup.com